THE TALISMAN TRILOGY
Book Three

The
SHADOW
KING

KELLIE BELLAMY TAYER

ISBN: 0615874193
ISBN-13: 978-0615874197
Vagabond Press
Shaker Heights, OH

Cover design & format by MotherSpider.com
Illustrated by Jennifer FitzGerald

DEDICATION

For Jessica Quittenton

Acknowledgements

Special thanks to the readers of The Talisman Trilogy. I hope you have enjoyed Laura's, Andrew's and Miguel's journey as much I have. Thanks to my family and friends for supporting my efforts as a writer and for the words of encouragement along the way. And, finally, a note about doors. They say when one door closes, another one opens, but it's easy to get trapped between those two doors if the closing of one and the opening of the other are not simultaneous. No one ever really talks about the dark space between those two doors, but there's always a way through even if we can't immediately see the path. Thank you elduck123 for opening the door.

The
SHADOW
KING

TABLE OF CONTENTS

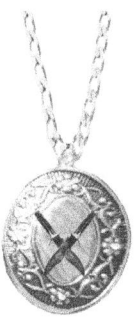

Prologue

Laura

"We dance round in a ring and suppose, but the secret sits in the middle and knows."

Robert Frost

I've never liked secrets—keeping them, telling them, not knowing them. Keeping information from the knowledge of others means that someone is in the dark. A psychic once told me that being in the dark isn't always a bad place to be and I had agreed with her—except when it comes to secrets. Once revealed they have the power to hurt...to crush the spirit...and, in some cases, the power to kill. When I embarked upon my new life—my second new life in less than a year, I had no idea that new truths would be unearthed, that secrets long kept would be revealed, and in so doing, history would be changed. I'd always thought that the past was unalterable, but I was wrong. Once upon a time King George the First fathered a son with a woman he believed to be a gypsy. But that gypsy turned out to be a princess. And now, more than three hundred years later, King George's descendent revealed his twenty-year secret: He also had fathered a secret son with a princess. Two royal dynasties permanently intertwined, yet forever changed all because of a secret.

Chapter One

BETRAYED

ANDREW

"Are you alright, sir?" asked Peter. He was staring at me from the rearview mirror.

"No. Take me to the London apartment, please," I barked the words as a command. I knew I sounded rude but I didn't care about that now. My mind was swirling with dark thoughts, accusations, questions. In the space of twenty-four hours, the life I had known had ceased to exist. I had no idea now who I could trust—who I could count on. My father's life was hanging by a thread and in his drugged out state of semi-consciousness he was spouting nonsensical ramblings. My mother was a complete emotional mess—distraught over my father's heart attack and totally clueless of the events of the last couple of days. My brother...well, I didn't know what to think about Tristan. He had completely lost his mind—his paralysis had clearly spread to his brain. And then there was the matter of my wife. Laura was gone—taken from me by the damned gypsies--kidnapped from the house in the dead of night against her will. I choked out a bitter laugh at the thought. I could spend all day trying to convince myself that Laura was a victim of the gypsies, but deep in my heart I knew better. I hated admitting it to myself, but I knew she had left of her own accord. She had betrayed me. She had never loved me and now she had run off with...*him*. As we drove through the London streets, I puzzled over Laura. Why had she married me in the first place if it was the damned gypsy thief she'd wanted? Oh, Tristan had spouted some nonsense about Father blackmailing her into it, but I didn't believe it. It was preposterous to think that my father had that much power over someone. And what could possibly be his motive in orchestrating such a contemptible crime? I closed my eyes and leaned my head back against the seat, blocking out Peter's concerned look in the mirror. The vendetta...decree...curse... call it whatever...didn't make sense. I forced myself to consider my father's state of mind. Why would he go to such elaborate lengths to fulfill that damned decree? And what was Laura's part in it? I rubbed my head, feeling pressure building inside my brain. Miguel Dos Santos--just saying his name inside my mind made my head feel like it would explode. I hated him. He had taken everything from me—my wife...my children... and now...even my own father? I'd heard the words my father had said. He wanted me to kill my brother...not Tristan...but... that thieving gypsy. Dos Santos was *not* my brother. Father was clearly under the influence of some mighty strong medication to say such a thing. I had to discount his rambling as drugged-out nonsense. My mind churned in confusion as Peter pulled up in front of the apartment building.

"Thanks, Peter. That'll be all tonight." I didn't hear his response as I jumped out of the car and hurried inside. Once in the apartment, I walked listlessly from room to room, not sure what to do. I was filled with anxiety and had the demeanor of a snake, coiled and ready to spring. In the kitchen I took a beer from the refrigerator and popped off the bottle cap. I drank it fast, not stopping to catch a breath between gulps. It felt good going down and I knew that it would feel even better in a few minutes when the alcohol found its way to my brain. Though it was never openly discussed in my family, I was keenly aware that my father had a drinking problem. I knew that he drank to fill an empty space...a space I had always assumed was caused by an unfulfilled life. I had heard my father say many times over the years how wrong it was that the House of Windsor had inherited the throne—that it should have been the House of Hanover living in Buckingham Palace. My father wanted to be king of the land. He wanted power, access and fame, but these things had eluded him. His ego had suffered over the years, standing in the shadow of Queen Elizabeth and it had left him bitter and thirsty to yield power he didn't have. My mother and brother and I had felt the wrath of his bitterness and we had suffered for it. Sometimes I hated my father and I often resented my mother for not standing up to him. And now it seemed that my father had been keeping secrets. It would be easy to believe that it was just the drugs talking, but my sixth sense told me that Father had been living a lie his whole life—or at least *my* whole life.

I tossed the bottle into the trash and opened another. I drank this one slower, reminding myself that I needed to keep my wits about me. Getting drunk wouldn't help me figure out what to do—it would only turn me into my father and I didn't want that. Now I replayed fragments of the words in my head that he'd muttered as I'd run out of his hospital room: *I need you to do something for me. I've had so many chances to do this myself, but I was afraid ...I should have been the King of England. I was planning to take over the throne but I realize now I was just trying to compensate for being a bad father and a bad husband to your mother—the very worst kind. I wanted to prove myself worthy of great things but I failed you...I know how it feels to love someone you shouldn't love—and can't have. I wasn't always this way. I loved someone once and it was wrong. It was a long time ago and I can't forget her...you know that King George the First lost his son to the gypsies...you know that...I had so many chances to finish this but I balked each time. But you are brave, Andrew. You must finish what King George the First started...I need you to finish this—to fulfill the vendetta. You must kill your brother. My son must die. You must kill my son...Miguel Dos Santos...and bring my grandchildren home.*

So Father had once loved someone he couldn't have. That was a feeling I could understand. But I had been a good husband to Laura. So we were young and hadn't been married that long...

so what? My feelings for her were real. I would've given her the world. I loved her—still loved her. And she was carrying my children. They were mine. If she thought she could run away and keep my children from me and raise them among gypsies like some modern-day Princess Gabriela, then she had another thing coming. I knew I had the law on my side. I knew she didn't stand a chance against me in the British legal system for I not only had the law of the land on my side, I also had the laws of the monarchy on my side as well.

I finished my beer then went to my room and sat down on the edge of the bed. I needed to think. I needed answers. I felt one of Laura's famous headaches coming on--just thinking her name made my head pound. I felt myself slipping into a state of despair and I knew that I would not be able to function if I let myself fall into a pity party. My father had secrets that I needed to be privy to and my brother had turned against the family and aligned himself with gypsies. My pregnant wife had left me and now I knew she had never loved me to begin with. I had been played for the biggest fool on the planet. Those damned gypsies were probably having the biggest laugh of their lives at my expense. I felt anger boiling up again, coursing through my veins, threatening to erupt. I jumped up from the bed and began to pace the room. My breathing changed—I heard every breath I took as it billowed up from my lungs and puffed out through my mouth. I felt my face redden as my blood pressure rose and my heart raced. I grabbed the lamp on my nightstand and threw it across the room, reveling in the sound of the shattering glass and the sight of the colored fragments showering down the wall. In one swift motion I upended the mattress, flipping it on its side as the pillows, blankets and sheets pooled on the floor. The mattress hit the wall and sent a picture crashing to the floor. With a sweeping of my hand I leveled the dresser—sending cologne, pictures, a clock, books and papers tumbling to the floor. When I had exhausted myself from my raging stampede, I surveyed the mess and felt a small pang of guilt at the knowledge that someone would have to clean up this mess. I went back out to the kitchen and stood there for a moment, looking around. I considered trashing this room, too, but thought better of it. I had already done enough damage. I grabbed one more beer from the refrigerator and forced myself to drink it slowly. Finally I was beginning to feel a numbness setting in and I realized why my father drank--because it felt good. It made problems more bearable. And I had a huge problem to solve. There was something I needed to know. If I could get the answer to this one question, I was sure it would explain everything else that had gone wrong in my life these past few days. I needed to know the answer to the million dollar question. *Who in the hell is Miguel Dos Santos?*

"Your father will recover, but he will have to make some serious changes in his lifestyle if he wants to live a long, healthy life," said the doctor. He was talking to my brother and me in my father's hospital room. My mother was here, too, but she seemed to have zoned off. She was staring off into space, her face troubled. She was tired and extremely unhappy. I knew she was just as worried about me as she was about my father, but when she brought up the subject of Laura, I changed it immediately. I did not want to talk about Laura right now. I needed for my father to feel well enough to answer my many questions. The doctor finished talking with my parents and left us alone. Tristan had been strangely quiet during our visit with Father and I sensed he wanted to avoid me at all costs. I had not been alone with him since my father had spoken to me about fulfilling the decree but Tristan couldn't avoid me forever. I needed to know how much he knew about Dos Santos and what his intentions were toward the gypsy female he had apparently fallen for.

Mother finally snapped out of her reverie and stood up. "I'm going to have Peter take me home. I'm tired and I want to get home and try to get to bed early tonight." She walked over to Father's bedside and leaned down, kissing his forehead. "I'll see you tomorrow, Ernst. Please do as the doctor says and don't get upset about anything. This mess with Laura will get straightened out. I love you." She nodded to me and Tristan and left the room. My father had remained quiet throughout the doctor's exam and Mother's departure. But now that it was just the three of us, he pressed a button on the side rail and adjusted the bed so he could sit up.

"We need to talk, boys," he said. "Tristan…?" He said Tristan's name as a question. "I want you to hear my side of this…"

"I don't want to hear it," said Tristan, cutting him off. "I'm only here to make sure you're OK and now that the doctor has said as much, I'm leaving." He started to wheel himself toward the door.

"Stop, Tristan," I said louder than I had intended. "I'll come with you. I want to talk to you." Tristan stopped on the threshold and looked back over his shoulder, waiting. I turned back to Father. "You and I need to talk as well but I'll come back later. I don't know what the hell is going on around here—I feel like I'm learning things in bits and pieces. I feel like a fool and you're partly responsible, but right now I need to talk to my brother." I didn't approach my father's bedside. I didn't want to touch him. I already felt myself pulling away from him emotionally and the physical distancing was a natural reaction to his deceit and my ignorance of the situation in which I now found myself.

"Come back when you're ready to talk, son. Remember that everything I did, I did out of love for you and your brother." He turned his face away toward the wall. I followed Tristan out of the room. We went to the elevator and while we waited for it, I called for someone to pick us up at the front entrance. Once in the car with Kevin at the wheel, Tristan turned to me, his eyes clearly troubled.

"Andrew…," he said, hesitating. "How are you?"

It was a funny question considering the circumstances and I didn't rush to answer it. I gave instructions to Kevin to take us to the apartment before responding.

"Not good. All I know for sure is, one morning I was happily married, or so I thought, with twins on the way, and the next my wife has run off with a gypsy and my father is fighting for his life in intensive care…not to mention my brother has lost his mind completely."

"Not completely," said Tristan. "Let's stop for food and take dinner home and talk about this. I understand that you're in the dark. I want to tell you what I know and then we'll figure out what to do from there. Nothing has to be decided tonight."

We rode in silence through the gathering darkness. I had Kevin stop at a Chinese take-out place and get us some food. He dropped us off at the apartment and we went upstairs. I got plates and silverware and beers and joined Tristan at the table. I let him start the conversation.

He told me that Father had blackmailed Laura into marrying me and having a baby to save the line of descendancy of the House of Hanover. He said that Father was convinced the gypsy curse had come true when he was paralyzed and that I was the only hope of carrying on the line. He told me that Father had arranged the car accident that had injured Laura's brother and that he had attempted to have a bomb planted in Laura's mother's car. He said that Father had been tormenting Laura the whole time she had been my wife—with threats to kill Miguel Dos Santos. At the mention of his name, I spat out rice onto my plate and shook my head in disgust. "Don't say that name in my presence. I hate him and his family for what they've done."

"But, Andrew…what have they done? Exactly what have they done? *Nothing*, that's what. They saved Laura. They have exposed Father for the desperate, half of a man he is. I'm more man in this damned wheelchair than he is with two good legs for all the pain he's caused Laura and the Dos Santos family." Tristan's voice rose as he continued. "I understand you're jealous. I get that. But this isn't anyone's fault but Father's. And when you've had time to process all of this, you'll understand. Father has been hiding deeds, jewelry, money and who knows what else from the Portuguese royal family for years. He was perpetuating the injustice his descendants began hundreds of years ago. Instead of doing the right thing and giving back to them what was rightfully theirs, he chose greed, violence and blackmail."

He stopped to take a breath and I jumped in. "So you're just taking their word for everything? For all of this madness? You don't even want to hear Father out? You would so easily believe that our father is capable of these outrageous acts of violence? And you love that gyspy girl? Really, Tristan? You're a traitor—

you're no better than they are." I pushed back from the table and dumped the contents of my unfinished dinner into the trash. I had half a mind to throw the leftovers across the room just for the thrill of it.

"I know you're saying this out of hurt, Andrew. I'm sorry about Laura. I know you loved her...still love her. But you're going to have to accept the fact that she loves Miguel and..."

"*Do not say his name in my presence!*" I shouted, interrupting him. "I hate that bastard. He has taken my wife and my children away from me. And as far as I am concerned, the decree is back on...or vendetta or whatever you want to call the damned thing. I'm going to get them back!" I paced back and forth in the kitchen, adrenaline fueling my movements.

"They're not your children," Tristan said quietly. "You're going to have to accept that."

"Dammit! Don't say that. You don't know that. I saw those damned text messages between her and that gypsy thief. I know she thinks he's the father but I *know* I am. Time will prove it. You'll see. Just because you can't have children doesn't mean I can't. I never believed that damned gypsy curse that our royal line would end. The proof is inside of Laura now. You wait!" I was done with this conversation and I wanted Tristan to leave so I could be alone. I had the urge to break something and I didn't particularly want it to be him. I walked over and opened the door. "You should go. Take the leftovers. I don't want them."

Tristan left the food on the table and wheeled himself to the door. He stopped in front of me and looked up at me. I saw pain in his eyes and I felt a stirring in my heart that I quickly stamped out. "Tell me you're not in love with that girl...what's her name?" I said, staring into his eyes.

He blinked and looked away for a moment, then turned his gaze back to me. "I love Catarina, yes, and there's something you should know, Andrew..." He stopped and stared at me, his face unreadable.

I didn't want to hear what he was going to say. I never should have mentioned her in the first place. I knew that whatever he said would probably send me over the edge. And I was right.

"I'm going to Portugal to be with her. I cannot live under

Father's roof after what he did to Laura and the Dos Santos family. I feel badly for Mother but she prefers to stay in her bubble of bewilderment and I'm sure Father will want to keep her there. My heart aches for you but you have to make your own choices and decisions. If you're smart, you will have your marriage annulled, let Laura get on with her life and forget the damned decree and get on with yours." He pushed himself out into the hallway and stopped to look back at me.

I stared at him dumbstruck. My brother was leaving the family for what? Gypsies? He was turning his back on his legacy just like that? I was appalled. "I thought blood was thicker than water, but I guess not…" I said. "You're a disappointment, Tristan. How can you do this to our family?"

"I don't have a choice. Blood may be thicker than water in a literal sense, Andrew, but not in a moral sense. Father doesn't deserve my love and loyalty and after what he's done to you, he doesn't deserve yours either. You should aim higher, little brother. I hope when some time has passed and your world begins to right itself again, you'll see that I was right. I love you, Andrew. It kills me to see you so broken…even more broken than I am. Please, think long and hard before you do anything crazy. Goodbye." He turned his chair around and wheeled himself down the hall and I slammed the door shut behind him.

I knew there was some truth to his words—somewhere in there he was trying to help me. But my hurt and sense of betrayal went too deep and were too fresh for me to accept his words of comfort. Right now I was angry. Angry at my father and my mother and my brother and my wife. But most of all I was angry at the gypsy thief. All the talk of decrees and vendettas aside, he had stolen Laura from me and in so doing, he had taken my children. What kind of a man would I be if I didn't fight for my family? Tristan might have decided to turn his back on his family but I would be damned if I would turn my back on mine. I would go to Portugal and I would get them back. And I would make Dos Santos suffer the way I was suffering now. I did not know why my father had referred to the gypsy as my brother, and I was quite sure Tristan was in the dark about that, too—he would have said something if he'd known and I had been too afraid to ask—but I supposed I would have to get to the bottom of Father's medicated mutterings eventually.

I went back into the kitchen and threw away the leftover Chinese food and dropped the dirty dishes into the sink. I heard a plate break as it hit the stainless steel and I felt a sick sense of satisfaction at the sound. I popped open another beer and sat down in the darkness of the living room to drink...to brood... and to plan my next move. It would take a lot more than a pep talk from my older brother to talk me out of fighting for what was rightfully mine--a lot more.

Chapter Two

CALLING HOME

MIGUEL

I studied Laura carefully, watching for signs of distress. We were in the kitchen of our country house on the outskirts of Sintra, sitting on the sofa that faced the fireplace at the far end of the room. Behind us, Catarina was fixing lemonade and sandwiches. Laura was psyching herself up to call her family in Rhode Island. She was anxious for them to know that she had left Andrew but was unsure how much to tell them. She figured they would want to jump on the first plane to Portugal if they knew everything that had transpired these past months, but she wanted to get used to her new home before facing them. My mother was sitting in a wing chair next to her, holding her hands and providing guidance. I could already see that having Laura here was affecting my mother positively. My mother, Sofia, who was in mourning for my father, still wore traditional black from head to toe as a reminder of the freshness of her grief even though it had been more than a year since his passing.

I had introduced my mother to Laura only a few hours ago and already they had bonded tightly. It was as if Laura were meant to be here...in this house...in this family...in this life...

with me. I turned my head toward the window and stared out through the trees as I thought about how Laura had come into my life. In the greatest of all ironies, I had Andrew Easton to thank for bringing Laura to me. When he had 'arranged' for Laura to find the gold talisman some fifteen months ago, he had unwittingly and irrevocably connected her to me and my family for life. I owed him a debt of gratitude but, of course, he would never know that. I seriously doubted Andrew Easton and I would ever have cause to carry on a civil conversation in this lifetime. We hadn't had one yet and it didn't seem likely now. I turned back to my mother and Laura and took Laura's hand. She turned to me, smiling, and leaned back against me. I held her to me and reveled in the feel of her in my arms. It had been a long time coming.

"Are you ready to call your parents? Do you know what you're going to say?" I asked her. "If you want, I'll talk to them." I hated the thought of her having to rehash any of this mess, even the less evil parts, to her parents. They would have questions and I knew Laura wasn't ready to answer them.

"No, thank you. They don't even know you, Miguel. They might think you've kidnapped me and you're placing a ransom call," she chuckled. "I have to do this myself. Can I call them in the bedroom? I think I need to be alone for this." She didn't sound convincing and I wished she would let me handle it. But I knew she was right. I had never met her family—it was something I regretted but hoped to rectify soon. My mother wished her luck and Catarina gave her a thumbs up sign as I led her upstairs to my bedroom where she would have privacy. I handed her the phone with her home number already dialed, just waiting for her to hit the connect button, but first I took her in my arms and held her tightly against me.

"You're very brave, you know that?" I said. I kissed her lips softly and felt her stomach brushing up against me. I smiled against her cheek and dropped my hand down to her belly. "What are you going to tell them about the babies? Will you tell them they're mine?" I wanted her to say yes but I had to understand if she decided that would be too much information too soon for her parents to handle.

She looked down and I immediately sensed that I had made her feel badly about the situation. It couldn't be easy telling your parents that you were pregnant with twins but your husband wasn't the father. I hated thinking of Easton as her husband. It made my blood boil. The sooner we had the marriage annulled the sooner I could marry her. Until she became my wife I would not feel a true sense of security. I tilted her face up so I could look into her eyes. They were troubled and I felt a pang of guilt.

"Never mind. There's time for that later. The main thing is that they know you and Andrew have separated and you're here in Portugal with…friends…trying to figure out how to proceed next. Be sure to give them the number here to the house." I pulled out a piece of paper from my pocket where I had written our address and phone number for her to tell her parents. I knew she missed her family and once she had placed this phone call, I was sure she would feel better about things in general.

"Miguel?" She pressed herself into my chest, as close as her belly would allow and grasped my arms firmly. "Is my family safe?"

I twisted my arms around so that I was holding hers now, my face only inches away from her beautiful one. "I promise you that your family is safe. I have a security team watching them around the clock. I wouldn't tell your family that though. But you can be sure they are safe—so are Lily and Gretchen. Just because you're here with me—safe and sound—doesn't mean there is no danger. Until we know what that damned duke has planned and what Andrew intends to do, no one is truly safe. Please don't worry about your family, *minha querida*. I will protect them…OK?"

She sighed, nodded and held up the phone. "Thank you… for everything. I love you."

I kissed her and held her to me once more before stepping out of the room to let her make her call in private. Once in the hall I considered eavesdropping but thought better of it and went downstairs to wait.

My family and I took these few minutes to speak in Portuguese to each other. My Uncle Antonio had already filled Mama in on what had gone down at the Easton estate but I knew she had questions for me. I figured she would launch into her questioning now but I saw that she had become quiet and somewhat melancholy.

"What is it, Mama?" I asked. I noticed then that her black hair had more gray than usual and there was a tiredness around her eyes. Though my mother was only forty-five years old, she seemed twenty years older than that now. I felt bad for her and wished there was something I could do to make her happy. I thought of the twins and I knew that in a few months she would have plenty to do to keep herself busy and content.

"It's nothing, darling. I'm so happy you brought Laura here. She is lovely and I can see how much she loves you and how much you love her. You and your brothers and sister have gone to great lengths to free her from..." Her voice trailed off. She stood then and walked into the kitchen and began to fix herself a plate of food.

I joined her at the counter, waiting to see if she would finish her sentence. She remained silent as she placed a sandwich and some salad on a tray along with a glass of lemonade. "I'm going to take this up to my room. I'm hungry and a little tired so after I eat I'm going to lie down for a while. Please tell Laura I will see her at dinner." Suddenly she set the tray down and rushed to me, throwing her arms around me and holding me in a tight embrace.

I put my arms around her and laid my head on top of hers. "Mama? Is something wrong?"

"Miguel...I just want you to know that no matter what happens or what has already happened in the past...that I love you more than life. You and Cat and the boys are everything to me. I miss your father so much. He was taken away from us far too soon. He should be here now. He would be so excited about Laura and the babies." She patted my back and dropped her arms, tilting her gaze up to mine. "A parent will do anything for their child...even if it turns out to be the wrong thing in the end. Remember that. You'll be a father soon and you'll know. You'll be amazed at the lengths you will go to protect your children. You've already experienced that with saving Laura and the babies and they aren't even born yet. Now I'm going to eat and have a rest and I will see you at dinner tonight. I love you."

"I love you, too, Mama." I watched her walk away and I wondered if she had been trying to tell me something. Her voice had sounded unusual…as if there was some sort of underlying message she was trying to get across. I shrugged and poured myself a glass of lemonade. Catarina had heard the exchange between us and I sensed she had picked up on Mama's tone, too. She cocked an eyebrow at me and shrugged then joined me in the living room to wait for Laura to finish her call.

"Have you heard from Tristan?" I asked.

"Yes. We talked this morning," Catarina set her lemonade on the coffee table and folded her arms across her chest. She had a faraway look in her eyes. "He's going to come here for a visit. But Miguel…our house isn't exactly equipped for a wheelchair. And he never travels alone. Will we be able to accommodate his…needs?"

"I'm sure we can figure something out. That should be the least of your worries. What did he say about…his father?"

"He's improving. They're going to move him out of intensive care soon into a regular room as long as he doesn't have any setbacks," said Catarina. She saw the look on my face and forced a grin. "I'm sure you'd like to give him a few setbacks. Wouldn't we all?"

I bit back a retort. What I would like to do to the Duke of Easton was something I would keep to myself. I would never feel resolution until he was punished for his actions but this wasn't a good time to go into that. I heard a noise in the hall and a moment later Laura joined us. Catarina jumped up and gave her a hug and told her she'd bring her some food. Laura sat down beside me and I pulled her into my embrace. I could see that she had been crying. Her face was red and her eyes were puffy. I had a feeling Laura had been doing a lot of crying these last few months. I could only imagine what hell she had gone through with the duke and his evil squad of punks watching her every move. The torment they had put her through…the bullying and the threats…I felt myself getting worked up and I knew I had to keep it together.

"How did it go?" I asked. I noticed she was shaking and I

tightened my arms around her, again noting her thinness in spite of her growing stomach. I could feel the bones of her arms and I saw that her cheek bones were prominent, her skin pale. I looked away over her head to some point on the wall. Just thinking about what had been done to her was causing a violent internal shift in my demeanor and I didn't want her to see it. I took a deep breath as she told me about her conversation with her parents.

"My mom was very upset and of course she wanted to come here now—today—but I talked her out of it. I do want to see her and my dad and my brother, but not like this..." She waved her arm over herself and frowned. "I look terrible and my mom already thinks I'm anorexic...imagine being a pregnant anorexic." She turned to me then and tears fell down her cheeks. "Miguel... I'm a terrible mother...I've put these babies through hell...I can't believe they've survived this long...I just wish I..."

I placed my fingers over her lips and stopped her. "You're going to be an amazing mother, Laura. You've kept them alive in situations that would have made most people just give up. Don't sell yourself short. You're one of the bravest people I've ever known." I kissed her and ran my hands through her long blonde hair, noticing its silkiness. I wiped away her tears and kissed her again. "So, what did you tell your parents exactly...about why you're here in Portugal?"

"I told them that I had married too young and Andrew and I weren't getting along. I told them I was very unhappy and stressed out and that I had come to stay with my best friend Catarina who I'd met at school. Kind of a little white lie I know, but it was easier than telling the truth. I told them I would be fine here and that I would see a doctor and that everything would be OK. I didn't tell them about you...it didn't seem like a good idea. I hope you're not mad..." Her voice trailed off. Catarina came in then with a plate of food and Laura picked up the sandwich and began to pick at the crust.

"I am not mad--of course not. Why would I be? You gave your parents just the right amount of information. This should buy us some time until we get things figured out. But right now, I want you to eat and then we can take a walk around the grounds. I want to show you the vineyard. Or...you can take a nap if you're tired."

"I want to do both actually," she grinned. "But only if you'll take a nap with me." She gave me a wicked grin and I couldn't help but laugh. Catarina shook her head at us and stifled a laugh, then disappeared to give us privacy.

"Whatever you want…this is your home now. I want you to know that everything I have is yours. But right now…eat!" I picked up the sandwich and put it to her mouth. She took it from me and ate and I felt myself begin to relax. It would take me a while to reconcile the duke's treatment of her, if I would ever be able to, but the important thing was that she was here now and she was safe. I forced thoughts of the Eastons from my mind and concentrated on Laura. In spite of her ordeal and the toll it had taken on her, she seemed in good spirits. She was beautiful and I was amazed at my good fortune at having her in my life. All because of the talisman. It had brought her to me. I looked at her neck and saw the chain there against her gaunt collarbone. "Glad to see you're still wearing your necklace."

"It's my good luck charm, for sure," she said, draining the last of her lemonade. She wiped her mouth with a napkin and pushed the plate away. "That was really good. I was hungrier than I thought," she smiled.

"Come here," I reached for her hand and she settled into me. My thoughts and emotions were suddenly swirling and I had the sudden urge to be alone with her. "Why don't we take that nap first and then a walk later…what do you say?" She tilted her face up to mine and kissed me.

"Sounds good to me," she whispered. We got up and carried the dirty dishes to the sink and then went upstairs to my room. I closed the door and locked it and Laura pulled me close, wrapping her arms around me. "I can't tell you how many nights I dreamed of being here in Portugal with you. I mean, I've never been here before but I knew this was where I wanted to be… with you."

"Oh, *minha querida*, I know the feeling. I've had the same dream. I wish I'd done things differently so we could have avoided all the pain and suffering you went through. I blame myself for what happened to you. I will make it up to you, I promise."

"You've got to be kidding…" She gently pushed away from me and walked over to the bed and lay down on it. "I wouldn't be here if it weren't for you. There is only one person to blame and we both know who that is." She held her hand out to me.

I crossed the room and joined her on the bed, tucking her into my shoulder. I stroked her belly under her shirt and felt the tautness of the skin. She was almost six months along now—getting so close to the end. It was early December and these babies would be here before we knew it. It occurred to me that we should think about preparing a nursery. I didn't know much about that stuff or babies in general, but Mama would help. It would make her happy and bring her out of her shell of mourning to have babies to care for.

"Let's not talk about that. I have a question for you…it's one of those questions designed to boost my ego. You ready for it?" I grinned against her hair and she turned her face up to mine.

"Let's hear it," she said smiling.

I kissed her forehead. "When did you know you loved me?"

She sighed and clasped my hand in hers. "That's easy."

"Oh?"

"It was at Brenton Point…my birthday…you saved Andrew…and me…for the millionth time…and then the next day I showed up unexpectedly at your house…remember?"

"Oh, I remember alright," I said, thinking back to last December. Seeing her at my front door that day was like a dream that I'd never wanted to end.

"Everything seemed hopeless and my life was a mess, but being with you…somehow…I felt like it would be OK. I never feel safer than when I'm with you." She pushed herself up closer to me and kissed me. I reveled in her taste and touch.

I leaned back and studied her face—so beautiful and delicate. "You know, it's almost your birthday again. Hard to believe it's been a year already. Any thought as to how you'd like to celebrate your big nineteen?"

She appeared to ponder my question for a moment. "Yes. I know what I want."

"Anything. Your wish is my command," I grinned at her.

"First, you have to answer the same question. When did you know you loved me?"

I lay back against the pillow and closed my eyes for a second. I already knew the answer but I liked making her wait. I felt her shift beside me, her hand sliding up my chest. I opened my eyes and covered her hand with mine and answered her question. "I can't remember a time when I didn't."

A tear slipped from her eye and snaked its way down her cheek. I wiped it away and let my fingers filter through her long blonde hair. She leaned down, shifting her stomach a bit so she could lean in closer to me. "I love you. Miguel. And, even though it isn't my birthday yet I'd like my gift now." She kissed me and I heard myself groan. I knew I couldn't deny her anything and the gift she wanted now seemed more like a gift for me than for her.

"I love you, too, *minha querida*. Happy early birthday. I'm all yours." I moved over her and kissed her. I promised myself I would make this gift last but it didn't happen that way. She was too beautiful and I was too eager to make her happy. Afterward she fell asleep and I watched her for a while. I kept my hand on her stomach and occasionally one or both of the babies would move, pressing against my hand. I loved the feel of it but I also felt the weight of the responsibility their presence would bring into my life—had already brought into my life. I was amazed at how strong the parental instinct was—how strong the feeling of needing to protect my children from harm was, just as my mother had said. I could feel it now even though the babies were a few months away from birth. As I watched Laura sleep, I thought about Andrew and his father. I knew they would put up a fight for these children. They wouldn't give up. We would have to be ready to do battle. I would die before I ever let an Easton get his hands on my children or Laura. I reached down and grabbed the extra blanket at the bottom of the bed and pulled it up over us and draped my arm over her. I realized at that moment that the first thing we needed to do was get her out of that marriage. She sighed in her sleep and I tightened my grip over her and closed my eyes. I couldn't sleep but I didn't want to be anywhere else right now than here with Laura.

The Shadow King

Chapter Three

RESENTMENT

LAURA

"It's so beautiful here," I said to Miguel as we walked through the vineyard. I imagined these vines hanging heavy with fat grapes and my mouth watered at the thought of eating one fresh off the vine. "What kind of wine do you make?"

Miguel ran his fingers along the tangled vines as we walked. "Mostly whites, but we started making dessert wines a couple of years ago. This was my father's passion. He was crazy about wine."

I heard melancholy in his voice—it always made him sad to talk about his father. I grabbed his hand as we continued to walk along the straight rows. I had so much to learn about Miguel and his family and their history. He was still very much a mystery to me, albeit a beautiful one. I thought back to yesterday and meeting his mother for the first time. I was struck at her beauty and youth, but I sensed that her husband's premature death had probably aged her considerably. She had welcomed me with open arms and already I thought of her as a friend. She had asked me many questions at dinner about my family and my life in America. She had not asked me any questions, however, about my recent ordeal and for that I was thankful. I suspected Miguel had told her not to bring it up. This morning at breakfast she'd seemed happier and I suspected it was because of all the baby talk at the breakfast table. Catarina had asked me if I had picked out any names and, even though I knew the answer—had always known my children's names—I said that Miguel and I hadn't really had a chance to discuss the topic yet. Miguel had met my gaze over his orange juice glass and raised an eyebrow but hadn't said anything.

We walked in silence for a few minutes with only the sounds of twigs and leaves crunching underfoot and the occasional chirp of a bird in the trees. It was a glorious day—huge white popcorn clouds floated by and the sun was warm on my skin. There was something in the air here—a crispness and a freshness unlike any I had ever smelled and the clarity of the sunlight filtering through the vines was mesmerizing. The vineyard was situated to the right of the house and a forested area stretched behind and off to the left of the house. It all looked surreal—almost manufactured. I felt like I was on a movie set—not that I had ever been on one—and I felt a thrill being here. I wondered if it would be hard to learn the Portuguese language. Thinking of language reminded me of something I'd been wanting to ask Miguel.

"Did you ever finish school? As I recall you said you'd left America rather abruptly and returned here after I moved to England." I glanced up at Miguel's profile as we walked. We were nearing the end of the row of vines and he tugged on my hand, turning us back toward the house. He chuckled softly and glanced at me out of the corner of his eye.

"I was never really a student at Portsmouth High School, Laura. I was only pretending to be one. I'd already graduated from school in Lisbon. I only enrolled there to be close to my brothers and to keep an eye on Easton. If I had known that Tristan was going to go to the small college on the island, I would have enrolled there to watch him. But he enrolled at the last minute and it was too late for me to get in, so I joined my brothers in high school instead. That turned out to be divine providence, as they say, considering how things turned out. And once you 'found' the talisman I needed to be there to watch over you. Though I didn't know you, I knew instantly that you were going to become the most important person in my life. I have Andrew Easton to thank for that."

Hearing Andrew's name made my heart thud. I didn't want Miguel to know how much I worried about Andrew. I knew it shouldn't matter what Andrew thought of me, but it did. I couldn't help but wonder what he was going through—what he was feeling—how much he knew about what his father had done. Then I thought of Tristan and felt a surge of excitement. Catarina had mentioned that Tristan was coming here for a visit. I could hardly believe I would be seeing him again so soon. I had feared he would hate me for everything that had happened though I realized he had no reason to blame me. I directed my thoughts back to Miguel. "You were already finished with school? Wow. So, if all of this madness hadn't happened, what would you be doing with your life now?" There were so many layers to Miguel, all waiting to be peeled back. I couldn't wait to know every facet of him.

"Well…first of all…I'm fairly certain my father would still be alive. My mother would be happy and my brothers would have a father." I heard a tinge of bitterness creeping into his voice and I felt a pang of guilt for asking the question. "I had planned to go to college and study business and then more than likely I would have taken over the family business—wine-making and cork exporting. I may still do those things—we'll see." His voice trailed off and he stared out into the distance.

I stopped walking and pulled him toward me. The sadness on his face and in his voice was killing me and I needed to make it go away. I wrapped my arms around him and kissed him, hoping I could turn his mood around. He put his arms around me, too, and held me tightly and rubbed his hand down my back. We stood that way for a couple of minutes and then he released me and asked me the same question. "What about you? What had you planned to do after school—if you weren't here with me now? University?"

"I wasn't exactly sure but I was thinking about taking classes at the community college where my brother goes. I was thinking about writing or going into publishing. I hate to admit it but I'm not very ambitious. I spent most of my childhood with my nose buried in books so that's where my interest has always been focused." We were getting closer to the house now and I took in its massive size. It was a two-story pale yellow house with a red tiled roof. There was a circular drive in the front of it and I noticed a couple of cars out front that hadn't been there earlier. I wondered who was here and if Miguel had been expecting anyone.

We approached the front steps and Miguel stopped me, taking my arm and turning me to him. "Laura, the lawyer is here. He's an old family friend and has taken care of my family's legal needs for years. I had Uncle Antonio call him about coming out to talk to us in regard to getting your marriage annulled. I'm assuming you're as anxious to get that matter taken care of as I am?"

I felt a rush of nerves as I smiled at him. "Maybe more so," I said. We went inside then and Miguel introduced me to Alberto Ruiz who was chatting with Sofia and Antonio in the kitchen. We spent the next hour discussing my marriage and how it came to be—the false pretenses, the blackmail, the deceit. I hated reliving it, but I knew this was the only way if I wanted my freedom.

"The problem here," said the lawyer, "is that Andrew was also deceived. He did not commit fraud and is also a victim in this case. If you had married the duke under these circumstances, this would be open and shut. But Andrew married you for love—I'm assuming—and had no idea of his father's deeds. Since it's Andrew you're divorcing and not the duke, this might not be as easy as we would like. That being said, I have no doubt that there is enough evidence to support your request, so you will be granted an annulment, but it might not happen instantly."

I nodded. "I just want it over—as fast as possible. Can I be free before my babies are born? They're due in April." I held Miguel's hand under the table and he squeezed my fingers gently.

"I'm sure we can resolve this matter before then. I will file the necessary paperwork with both the court and the church. Are you Catholic?"

"Yes, I am."

"Good. That will make it easier for you with the church. Andrew is Church of England, as are most royals, so the religious aspect of an annulment shouldn't affect him. I will file in London court—my firm has offices there—and hopefully this will be over quickly."

We talked a few minutes more and then the lawyer left. Antonio and Sofia walked him out and Miguel and I stayed at the kitchen table. I could feel Miguel looking at me but I kept my eyes averted. I felt a sense of embarrassment at being in this ridiculous situation and I felt badly for dragging Miguel and his family through this nightmare. I hoped it wouldn't cost too much to pay for the lawyer's services. I had no idea how much it cost to get unmarried.

"What is it, sweetheart?" Miguel asked. He got up from his seat and moved around to stand behind my chair. I felt his fingers comb through my hair and caress my back and I sighed, trying to fight back a sob. I pushed my coffee cup away and laid my head down on the table, using my folded arms as a pillow. "Everything will be OK, Laura. Don't worry. I promise you this will be over soon."

I lifted my head up and stared at the wall, shaking my head slowly back and forth. "I'm so sorry for all of this. I don't how much it costs to pay for this annulment but I will pay you back, I promise. I still have some money in my savings account. I promise I will…"

"Sh…sh…," whispered Miguel. He leaned over me, planting his hands on either side of me on the table and leaned his head down by my ear. "Is that what has you upset? The cost?"

I nodded and wiped my tears with a napkin. "I can't believe I married him. What was I thinking? Surely there was another way out…"

Miguel came around beside me and reached for my hands. I stood up and nestled into his arms, allowing myself to feel secure and loved.

"You did what you thought was the right thing to do. Never question yourself or have regrets. And you certainly don't need to worry about how much it costs to pay for a lawyer. I can assure you, Laura, we can afford it. The only thing you need to concern yourself with is right here." He turned me around and pressed his hand against my stomach and rubbed it back and forth. "This is your only priority…OK?"

I smiled weakly and nodded. He clasped his hands in my hair and pulled me to him, kissing me tenderly. I kissed him back, pushing my tongue against his mouth. Miguel stirred things up inside of me—passion and longing and need—and sometimes the feelings were overwhelming. His tongue found mine and I heard myself groan against him. I felt an insatiable desire and I knew I would have to rein myself in or Miguel would think I was some sort of maniac. I heard him laugh through our kiss and I stopped and leaned back, staring at him. "What's so funny?" I asked.

"You," he grinned. "I think I might have a little wildcat on my hands." He tucked my hair behind my ears and kissed my forehead.

"Is that a bad thing?" I whispered, laying my head against his chest.

He wrapped his arms tightly around me and rocked us from side to side in a swaying motion. "Oh, no, Laura…that's a very good thing…but right now…I think we've got company."

Mateo and Tomas arrived just then looking for food. I loved Miguel's brothers. They were so sweet and funny and so…big. They dwarfed the room and everything in it. Catarina came in after them with a woman I had not seen before.

"Laura, this is Juana. She works for us. She is a fierce cook. She's going to make us some *bacalhau*. It's a delicious dish of codfish and potatoes and other vegetables in a tomato sauce. You're going to love it," said Catarina.

I shook Juana's hand and said hello. She responded in Portuguese and, of course, I didn't understand a word she said. I turned to Miguel. "I think I'm going to need some language lessons if I want to be able to talk to your family and friends."

"That can be arranged, *minha querida*. All in due time," Miguel said, taking my hand and following Catarina outside to the front porch where we sat down on cushion-covered wrought iron chairs. I noticed that Catarina was excited about something.

"I talked to Tristan a little while ago. He has final exams next week and as soon as he's completed them, he's coming down here for the holidays. I already cleared it with Mama." She turned to Miguel. "I probably should have talked it over with you first, but I can't wait to see him. I can't believe how much I miss him."

"It's fine," said Miguel. "I always liked Tristan. It's the rest of his family I can do without."

I heard the familiar tone of contempt in his voice and I had to look away from him. I understood his feelings on the Easton family completely, but I still felt something for Andrew. Not romantic love...but friendship and a strange sense of loyalty because I knew he would never have wanted any of this to happen. And I knew I risked a fight but I had to ask.

"Did Tristan say anything about Andrew?" I asked quietly. Before Catarina could answer, a loud banging sound erupted as Miguel jumped up from his seat and kicked his chair hard, sending it smacking into the wall of the house. It clanged and fell to the porch floor. The back of the chair left a mark on the wall as well as a large dent.

"*Dammit*, Laura!" he barked, stomping down the porch steps. He stopped and looked over his shoulder at me, his face stony. "I hate it when you talk about him. Why do you care about him? *Dammit*!"

I felt a sudden rush of anger boiling inside of me. I was getting tired of Miguel blaming Andrew for things his father had done. It wasn't fair. "Andrew didn't do this to me, Miguel. His father did. I have a right to ask about him...to care about his well-being. Just because I care what happens to him doesn't mean I love you any less." I felt my blood pressure rising as heat rushed into my cheeks.

"I hate Andrew Easton. I hate everything about him." He paced back and forth in front of the porch, his hands balled into fists at his sides. "I hate him for what he did to you."

I jumped up from the chair and ran down the steps toward him. "What did he do to me? It was his father...not him. You know this."

He grabbed me by the shoulders and looked into my eyes. His own dark ones were filled with some intense emotion. "He took something from us—from me and you—that we will never get back. Something that wasn't his to take. I try not to let it bother me but I can't help it, Laura. Chalk it up to the Latin blood that flows through my veins but every time I think about you…and him…that way…it makes me want to hurt him."

I gasped and stepped back from him, his words cutting through me like a blade, sinking into my heart. I always knew this would come back to haunt me. I knew it. I hated myself for losing my virginity to Andrew Easton but it could not be undone. Miguel had never said anything before about it and I had thought…hoped…he had made peace with it…but I was wrong. It had been eating away at him all this time…probably even all the times he and I had made love. It had been there all along waiting to strike. I felt tears burning behind my eyes as I backed away from him and ran up the porch steps. Catarina stood and reached her hand out to me but I brushed past her and ran up the stairs to our bedroom. I shut the door and threw myself on the bed and sobbed into the pillow. *Why now?* I asked myself. *Why is he bringing this up now?* This was one wrong that could never be made right and I would have to live with it for the rest of my life. But that would be hard to do if Miguel couldn't…or wouldn't…let it go. I tried to control my sobbing. I felt my body shaking as I gasped for breath. I suddenly felt dirty and used and that made me cry all over again. I burrowed my face deeper into the pillow and tried to stifle the sound of my crying. I heard the door open and I felt Miguel's presence next to the bed. I kept my face in the pillow and clutched it to me tightly as if it were a life preserver. I refused to look at him. I felt his hand on my hip and a massive wave of déjà vu washed over me—it made me thankful for my metaphorical life preserver.

"Laura…listen to me. I'm sorry. I shouldn't have said what I said out there. It was wrong and it wasn't your fault. None of this is your fault. And if I'm being honest with myself, it isn't Andrew's fault either." He removed his hand from my hip and I heard him walk around to the other side of the bed. He climbed onto the bed and pressed himself against my back. He put his arm over my side and brushed the hair off of my cheek. I felt him tug at the pillow covering my face and I let him pull it out of my hands. "Turn over and look at me. I need to see your eyes," he said quietly.

I hesitated. I wasn't sure I could look at him. I had felt so much shame over what had transpired between me and Andrew physically and I had already tried to forgive myself for it. But now it was all dredged up again and I would have to go through the process of forgiving myself all over again—if I even could this time. And then something occurred to me—something so awful I could barely allow myself to think the words. I felt sick to my stomach at the revelation opening itself up to me. I turned to Miguel and sat up, pushing my back up against the headboard. It took some doing considering the size of my stomach. He sat up, too, and I was sure he saw something in my eyes—something that made him catch his breath.

"I know what this is about, Miguel. I know what you're thinking." I started to get up from the bed to put some distance between us but he grabbed my arm and wouldn't let me up.

"What? What am I thinking?" he asked quietly. His eyes were dark and I sensed the emotions churning inside of him.

"You think they're his, don't you? You aren't sure, are you? You think Felipe and Gabriela are Easton babies…not Dos Santos babies. Go ahead and say it." More tears fell down my cheeks but I didn't care anymore. It wasn't like shedding tears was a new thing with me. It seemed I had an endless supply of the damned things. I tried again to pull my arm out of his grasp but he held on tightly.

"I know who their father is, Laura. I've always known. Maybe you're the one with the doubts." He tried to pull me closer to him but I jerked my arm away and got up. I went to the other side of the room, to put some space between us. My mind raced—trying to keep up with the beats of my heart which threatened to burst right out of my body. I wrapped my arms across my stomach and looked down at it—bulging out so big and obvious. And I felt the shame and the doubt and the fear all over again. I had been so sure all this time…but now…Miguel had planted the seed of doubt in my brain and now I felt what I truly was. I was no better than a whore. I hated that word but it fit me. I was a whore. I opened my mouth to speak...to cry... and a cracked sob came out as I slid down the wall to the floor. Miguel was up and across the room in a flash. He sank to the floor at my feet and took my hands—now icy cold—into his big, warm ones.

"Laura...I'm sorry. They're mine...I know it. You know it..." his voice tapered off as I shook my head vehemently back and forth. I pulled my hands out of his and covered my face in shame.

"No...no...," I cried. How could I reconcile this awful feeling of being a cheap, immoral....whore...as if there were any other kind. My shoulders shook as I tried to get a grip on my emotions.

"What is it, sweetheart?" he asked me—his voice barely more than a whisper.

I took a gulp of air and spoke through my hands. "I feel dirty...disgusting. You must think I'm a..." I couldn't bring myself to say the word out loud. I didn't want to audibly validate this awful revelation.

"Stop...do not say it," he said, sounding angry. He pulled my hands away from my face and scooted over next to me against the wall and took me in his arms. "Don't you dare say it. These feelings I have are not about you, Laura. You are still as pure and perfect as you've ever been. Do not think that ever again. This is something I have to make peace with. I told you before that I would not hold against you anything you had to do to stay safe and keep the peace. I meant it then and I mean it now. This is not about you. It's about me and my macho...egotistical...brain." He hesitated between his words and I felt the passion in them.

I wanted to say something but my mind was rattled. I knew I was being hard on myself but I couldn't help it. I couldn't seem to get past it. Suddenly I felt a heated sensation rush over my chest and I gasped out loud and grabbed at my throat.

"What is it?" Miguel cried. "Laura?"

I looked at him first, then down at my chest. The talisman, which had become like my second skin lately, was suddenly hot against my breasts. I saw it glowing through my blouse. I grabbed the chain and pulled it out where we could see it. It was hot in my hand and I dropped it quickly. Miguel picked it up. The crossed swords were there just as they always were.

"Turn it over," I whispered to him.

Slowly he turned the talisman over in his hand. We looked at it together. Engraved around the coat of arms were four initials, one sitting in the North position, one in the East position, one in the South position and one in the West position:

$$
\begin{array}{c}
\textbf{M} \\
\textbf{F} \quad \textbf{G} \\
\textbf{L}
\end{array}
$$

Miguel closed his hand over the disk and squeezed, then tilted my chin to meet his gaze. "If there was ever a doubt in your mind, let it go now, Laura. The talisman is never wrong. It knows the truth. You know the truth and I know the truth. These children are Dos Santos children. They could never be anything else. No matter what anyone else says or believes…they are yours and mine—only. Do you understand?"

I nodded, wiped my tears and pressed myself into him, finally believing it.

Chapter Four

CONFESSION

ANDREW

I stood outside my father's hospital room waiting for the doctor to finish his exam. My mother was with him—I could hear their voices through the glass wall but I couldn't make out the words. Mother had been here most of the day and she had asked me to come and spend time with Father this evening. She'd said he wanted to talk to me. He'd wanted Tristan to come, too, but Tristan had refused. My brother couldn't forgive and forget and I wasn't sure I could either...but before I made that decision I needed to know what to forgive and forget. As much as I hated the thought of hearing what my father had done, I knew I had to find out so I could decide how to proceed with my life. I still wasn't convinced that Tristan's story about Father's blackmail scheme was the truth, but I could at least hear Father's side before passing judgment. Mother caught sight of me waiting in the hall and stood and kissed Father good-bye. Out in the hall, she hugged me and asked where Tristan was.

"I don't know. Probably at school. He has finals this week."

"What about you, darling? When are your tests?" she asked.

I helped her into her coat as I answered.

"I took them already. I told the dean I had a family emergency and he arranged for me to take them early. I'm finished with school until January."

"That's good, darling. I'll see you for dinner then?" she asked as she headed toward the elevator.

"No, not tonight. I have plans." I waved to her as the elevator doors closed between us. The only plans I had for tonight involved a twelve-pack but she didn't need to know that. I turned to my father's door and hesitated before entering. I had a feeling that I was going to regret coming to see him today. I swallowed a lump of anxiety and went inside.

"Andrew...I didn't think you'd come...thank you," said Father. "Where's your brother?"

"Studying. How are you feeling today, Father?" I asked. The question didn't sound sincere even to my own ears. I did care how he felt but I was having trouble showing it today.

"I feel pretty well all things considered. I might even get to go home in a day or two. I've been up moving around and it feels good to be back on two feet. I'll get better faster once I'm out of this place."

"Has Queen Lizzie been in to see you?" I asked. I knew it was disrespectful to call her that, but for some reason, I just couldn't help myself.

"No, of course not, but Camilla and Charles stopped in last night. It was nice of them to come by." He pointed to a chair by his bedside. "Why don't you have a seat so we can talk. I have some things I need to say to you and I'm sure you have questions for me."

I closed my eyes in a slow blink. *Here it comes*, I thought. I sat down in the chair and crossed my legs and waited.

Father adjusted his bed and sipped from his water glass. He picked up the pitcher and held it up to me in question. I shook my head and watched as he refilled his glass. I wanted something much stronger than water and I bet my father did, too. I wondered how much the heart attack would affect his drinking.

"Andrew...," he said, sighing. "I want to explain what happened with Laura. I will admit to you that I treated her badly and

I am sorry for that…but…I did it for you."

I put my hand up to stop him. I was already annoyed and he'd only spoken two sentences. "You treated her badly? Really, Father? Tristan told me you forced her to marry me. Why would you do that? How is that a good thing for me?" I wanted to yell at him and curse him out but that would have taken more effort than I was prepared to give. I watched emotions play across his face and I had the sense that wheels were turning inside his head. I hoped he wasn't planning to lie to me because I would have enough trouble believing the truth as it was. My instincts were working overtime. I was fairly sure I would be able to see through his lies. It made me tired just thinking about it.

He leaned forward and adjusted the blanket over his legs. "I've had time to think about it, Andrew, and I know I acted out of fear. Tristan had just been paralyzed and I feared you were going to get your heart broken and I thought maybe I could save you since it was too late for him. And I've lived in fear of that damned gypsy curse for years. It's been hanging over my head since I first learned about it because I knew it was due to come to pass during my lifetime and…my sons.' And I admit I was afraid. I've made mistakes, I know I have." He stopped finally and leaned back against the pillows. He seemed winded and I noticed for the first time that his blond hair was now mostly gray. He looked old for a man in his early fifties. I uncrossed my legs and leaned forward in my chair, resting my elbows on my knees. I looked down at the floor and wondered what the point of all of this was.

"What did you do to Laura? How did you make her do this?" I asked the question in a monotone. I felt like my personality was splitting in two. I wanted to run at him and rage and rail against him but my legs were filled with lead. Even my head felt too heavy for my shoulders. I had been drinking a lot of beer lately and now I thought maybe I should lay off of it.

Father cleared his throat and shifted in the bed. "I threatened to cause problems for her family."

I looked up then. His answer wasn't sitting well with me. It sounded…hollow. "Is that all?" I asked.

He turned his head slowly toward me. "I also threatened…

the gypsy."

Just the mention of him made my blood boil. I felt the lead in my legs turning to hot liquid. I sat up straight in the chair and looked at him. "Why would threatening Dos Santos bother her enough that she would marry me against her will just to save him? She hardly knew him then."

"She knew him better than you realized. I'd had her followed and I had an occasion to go through her cell phone." I started to speak but he raised his hand to stop me. "Before you get upset at the invasion of her privacy…you should know that I did it out of love for you. I was afraid she was going to hurt you and I wanted to prevent it."

"So you forced her to marry me because that was the better option?" I felt empty. "Damn you, Father. You're a son of a bitch, do you know that?" I got up and began to pace around the room. I was desperate to leave but I knew I couldn't until I'd heard the whole sordid mess.

"I'm sorry, son. In retrospect, it was wrong. But at the time…" His voice trailed off. I went back to my seat and we sat in silence for a few moments. I tried to gather my thoughts.

"Did you have anything to do with Nick's car accident?"

He didn't answer so I chose to take his silence as a yes. I shook my head in disgust. It seemed there was nothing beneath him. I felt sick.

A long silence stretched between us. I leaned against the back of the chair and stared at the ceiling. My father had just admitted to blackmail and though he hadn't answered my question about Nicholas, I had to assume he was also guilty of attempted murder. This was madness. It seemed the madness of King George had been passed on to the Duke of Easton. Thinking of King George reminded me of something I had been blocking from my memory--the night of Father's heart attack—the things he'd said in his drugged state--words that had made no sense. I had been suppressing the memory but now I needed to face it. "Father..." I hesitated. I questioned my judgment in wanting to know the answers to these impossible questions.

"Yes, son?" His voice was a whisper now. He was growing tired and so was I.

"You said some things the other day…maybe you don't remember…you were on a lot of medication…it didn't make sense…do you know what I'm talking about?" I held my breath as I waited for his response. I'd almost convinced myself it had been merely drug-induced rambling and there was nothing to dread.

Father passed a hand through his matted hair. I saw something cross over his face—as if he were shutting down…or… contemplating whether to tell me the truth or lie his way out of it. My stomach clenched and my mouth watered. I would kill for a drink right now.

"I know what you're talking about," he said. "I had decided that I wouldn't talk about it unless you brought it up. Part of me hoped you would forget."

"What is it? What was all that nonsense about killing my brother? Not Tristan but…" I absolutely could not say his name again.

Father remained silent for a minute. He studied his water pitcher as if waiting for it to give him a sign. Finally he shifted uncomfortably in his bed, grimacing as he adjusted himself so that he was turned toward me. His face was impassive…giving nothing away. I swallowed visibly. Dread filled my body. I watched his face as he seemed to be gathering courage. It must be hard for him to talk without being influenced by brandy or bourbon. "Andrew…" Suddenly the monitor attached to his chest began to beep. I stood up and went to his side.

"Are you alright?" I was so not in the mood to save his life again. I wasn't sure I could do it a second time.

"Yes, I'm OK. I just need to focus and get the words out. Andrew…I've been keeping something from you…and Tristan… and your mother…for twenty years. I don't know how to say it…"

I stepped back from his bedside and inched toward the door. I felt a repeat of the other night coming on when I had run from this room trying to block his words from my mind. I knew I should leave now before he pulled me into his secrets…before he told me something I would be forced to live with for all eternity.

"When I was about Tristan's age—give or take a few years—I met a woman who—without sounding like a damned romance novel—beguiled me. I was married to your mother already and Tristan was a toddler at the time. I had gone on some official business for the queen in Europe and…I…met a woman named Sofia. She was beautiful and I was stupid." He stopped to take a sip of water.

My stomach ached and I wanted to stop him but I knew he had to tell this damned story and for whatever reason, it was apparently my destiny to hear it. I waited for him to continue.

"I took one look at her and I knew…I had to have her… even if it was for only one day or one week or forever…I had to have her. We met at a special dinner where she had been seated next to me. She was there alone. She wasn't married at the time. She was young and very beautiful. I had a momentary lapse of judgment and I refused to leave her side that whole night. Even if your mother and Queen Elizabeth, along with the entire royal guard had walked in and dragged me away from her I would have slipped right through their restraints to get to Sofia. It was fate. After the dinner she told me she had to leave. I begged her to see me the next day for lunch. She finally agreed. I admit I lost my mind a bit that day." He stopped for a breath and took another drink of water.

I shifted uncomfortably in my seat. Dark thoughts swirled in my head but they had no form…no substance. I asked Father a question though I felt I knew the answer already. "Where did this take place?"

Father glanced at me quickly then turned his head away. "Lisbon."

I closed my eyes…my hands automatically formed into fists at my sides. I wanted to tear the chair I was sitting in to pieces and the rest of the room, too.

"She met me for lunch the next day and afterward we walked all over Lisbon. I tried to get to know her but she didn't tell me much about herself. All I knew was that she was engaged to be married, that she worked for the family business though she never told me what that business was. She never even told me her last name. Thinking back on that day, I guess I did most of the talking. Anyway, we went to my hotel and I invited her to my room. I thought she would say no. Up to that point, she hadn't made anything easy. I'd had to work hard for the meal, for the walk afterward, for her company and the conversation. She put me through the ringer though I'm sure she was unaware of her effect on me. Long story short...I finally wore her down and she spent most of the night with me. To this day, that night has haunted me. It has played over and over in a loop in my head. She left the next day before dawn and I figured I would never see her again." He stopped there, exhaling deeply and laid his head back on the pillow.

I had not made a sound throughout this story though I was screaming inside my head. I needed to get up and get the hell out of here. I knew what was coming and I knew once the words were spoken I would erupt into rage. I unclenched my fists and grabbed the arms of the chair and held on tightly. This roller coaster was about to go down, come loose from its tracks and take me down with it and there was nothing I could do to stop it. Father carried on.

"That woman was Princess Sofia of the House of Braganza—the Portuguese royal family. Of course, I didn't know that at the time. To me she was just this beautiful, mysterious, dark creature who had cast a spell on me. When we had walked that day all over the streets of Lisbon, gypsies had come up to her and had talked to her and had touched her. I didn't speak Portuguese so I had no idea what they were saying or why they flocked to her. Lisbon has a huge gypsy community. Many of them lived in white tents on the hills outside of the city proper. She was always polite to them and when I asked her what that was about, she just passed it off as gypsies admiring her dress. I had sensed there was more to it than that, but I never bothered to find out. Maybe if I had..." He refilled his cup and sipped some more.

I maintained my silence because I didn't trust myself to speak. I was in the throes of car accident syndrome when you know you shouldn't look...when you know better than to make someone else's pain your problem but you stop to look anyway. I should have left the room. At this point in the story, it wasn't too late to get out before the blood of the accident was spilled—

the blood of the accident that was my Father's confession. But I didn't move.

"A few weeks after I had returned to London, I read in the paper that Princess Sofia—my Sofia--had married a lesser blue blood by the name of Alfonso Dos Santos. About eight months later she gave birth to a son—Miguel Dos Santos. They call that a honeymoon baby but I had my doubts. At that point in time your mother was less than a month away from having you. I was going a little crazy so I went to Portugal to see Sofia. I needed to know the truth. She met me at a café and I didn't waste time getting to the point. I had two questions for her that day. Why had she not told me she was royal and who was the father of her son."

"I don't think I want to hear anymore," I finally spoke. My head was seriously pounding and now my mouth had gone dry. I needed a drink.

"Hear me out, son. I need to get this weight off my chest. She told me she had not mentioned her royal status because she felt it wasn't relevant to the situation—to us--considering the government of Portugal no longer recognized royalty in the traditional sense. The Portuguese royal family lives in the shadows as civilians. I'd disagreed with her on that but it was a moot point. And she told me in all honesty that she hoped her husband was Miguel's father. She *hoped*. I asked to see a picture of the baby. She showed me his photo, taken a few days after his birth. It was like looking at Tristan. I pulled his photo from my wallet and placed the two pictures side by side on the table. They were virtually identical. I will never forget her reaction to seeing the pictures together. She took my hand and asked me to keep quiet—to keep it a secret. I remember seeing unshed tears in her eyes. I was completely in love with her but I knew we couldn't be together. She told me she loved her husband and he had no reason to believe he wasn't Miguel's father and could we just keep it that way. Because I loved her, I agreed. And I had another baby on the way anyway, and just so you know…I loved your mother and I didn't want to hurt her. I still love her. She doesn't know the truth—it would kill her. She's a good woman but she deserves better. And Tristan doesn't know either. This needs to stay between you and me."

I never knew bile tasted so bitter. I felt myself shaking with a violent rage I could barely contain. I had to remind myself that I was in a public place with sick people everywhere and I absolutely could not lose it here …not now. I stood up and moved to my father's bedside. He looked into my eyes and I saw fear and something else in his. Regret? Guilt? Embarrassment? I wasn't sure. I needed to speak but I didn't trust myself. I wasn't even sure I knew what to say. I was trying to process his confession…his secret…but only one thought was able to break through the tangled mess of words in my head and form into something I could decipher. But it was too preposterous to believe. It couldn't be true.

"Say something, Andrew. Call me a disgusting son of a bitch or a monster or a deadbeat. Call me whatever noun you think applies but please say something." He seemed to draw himself up under his blanket as if he expected me to hit him. And, oh, how I wanted to. I gripped the rail of his bed and watched my knuckles turn as white as the sheet that covered him. I hated him in this moment more than I had ever hated anyone…except…

"You make me sick," I heard my words come out on a sob. I felt the prick of tears behind my eyes. I fought them—I didn't want to cry in front of my father. I didn't want to be weak like him.

He coughed and turned away. I heard his monitors speed up. I was afraid a nurse would come in to see what was causing the change in his heart rate. I wanted to rip out his IV and strangle him with the tubing. I wanted to hurt him the way he had hurt me. I was completely unprepared for the tidal wave of violence and pain that engulfed me. This room was suddenly too small and there wasn't enough oxygen to breathe. I felt a stifling oppression and I knew I had to get out. I slowly began to back away toward the door, willing myself not to break anything or yell out the profanities that rang in my head like a carillon.

"I'm sorry, son. But the past is the past. It can't be changed. But we can move forward. We can put this curse behind us."

"You said you wanted me to kill your son. Do you still want that?" I had to ask, and though his answer really didn't matter to me, it surprised me nonetheless.

His gripped the bed railing tightly as he answered. "It's like our history is stuck on repeat, playing the same damned song over and over. First Princess Gabriela and King George, then me and Princess Sofia, and now you and Laura. Over and over it keeps repeating and we need to stop it." His voice was tiring and I noticed his gray pallor. "They say things happen in threes, son. Gabriela lost her true love—some damned soldier in the Portuguese army. Sofia lost hers when Alfonso died and Laura is next. And you know why, son? Because King George lost *his* love and I lost mine and now you've lost yours. I want retribution for the king...and for you. Miguel Dos Santos is trouble. He will always be the bane of your existence if you don't eliminate him. Someone needs to pay for three hundred years of missed opportunities and it may as well be the people who started it all—the Portuguese royal family. We could have joined kingdoms and been the most powerful royal rulers in the world. Kill him, son. Fulfill King George's decree and bring my grandchildren home to Great Britain where they belong. It's your destiny."

My stomach heaved and I grabbed my chair and lifted it off the floor. Though it was heavy it felt like a feather in my hands. My father cowered as I brought my arm back. But I didn't throw it. With trembling hands I placed it gently back onto the floor. I resisted the urge to kick it through the glass wall into the hallway. I was no longer able to stop the damned tears that had been burning behind my eyes. I felt them falling down my face and that made me madder still.

"I hate you, Father. And I hate him. It will be my pleasure to end his life. But I will not bring your grandchildren into your home. You don't deserve them. Laura is still my wife and I intend to make sure she stays my wife. Those are my children, not his, and *I will not rest until I have them back.* King George was a coward and so are you, but I'm not. I'm not afraid to go after what's rightfully mine. Good-bye, Father. Thank you for ruining my life." I kicked the chair and shoved the door open hard, spraining my damned wrist in the process. I heard my father calling my name as I ran to the stair well. I didn't have the patience to wait for the elevator. I ran down flight after flight after flight of stairs and sprinted through the lobby and out into the darkness. I didn't bother calling my security for a ride. I hailed a cab and went back to my apartment.

I paced around the rooms, touching things at random. I wanted to throw things but I resisted the urge in favor of just touching the objects instead. I drank beer after beer and lined the empty bottles in a straight line along the kitchen counter. Eventually I ran out of beer. In the living room I slumped onto the couch and sat in the darkness trying to think and not think at the same time. My life had gone to hell just like that. I needed to get out of this oppressive apartment but I wasn't in any condition to even walk. I stretched out on the couch and closed my eyes. I had never felt such a sense of emptiness and worthlessness in my life. My mind drifted to Laura. I wanted to punish her for loving him. Why wasn't I good enough? I had so much more to give her than he did. Why couldn't she love me? Why? The more I thought about her, the madder I got until the rage threatened to overwhelm me. I couldn't comprehend the fact that Miguel Dos Santos was...my...*brother*. My mind was incapable of processing that bit of information. Just thinking it made me want to vomit. How could she choose a gypsy over a prince? Nothing made sense except the knowledge that I loved her and I wanted her in my life. So I would go to Portugal and get her back--plain and simple--I would just go and claim what was mine. I was well within my rights. I would show her why I was better for her than he was. I would end this once and for all. I would be damned if history would repeat itself on my watch. I would not give up without a fight. But I would need help. I couldn't do this alone. I reached inside my pants pocket and pulled out my cell phone. I pushed a button, the numbers glowing in the darkness. I dialed a number and waited.

The Shadow King

Chapter Five

TO THE PALACE

MIGUEL

"Carmen? When did you get here?" I had just entered the kitchen to get orange juice for Laura and found Juana's daughter at the sink. I spoke to her in Portuguese.

"Miguel! You're back!" She dropped the dishcloth she'd been holding into the sink and threw her arms around me. "I thought you were still off somewhere overseas."

"We've been back a few days. What have you been up to? Are you finished with school?" I gently extricated myself from her arms and went to the cupboard to get two glasses.

"I'm finished until the middle of January. I'm here to visit my mother. She doesn't even know I'm back yet. I didn't expect to see you." She watched me pour two glasses of orange juice and place four pieces of bread in the toaster oven. "Hungry?" she asked, grinning. She moved closer to me and I felt my guard go up.

"It's not all for me." I turned my back to her as I watched the bread heating in the oven. I was about to tread on delicate territory and I had to be careful. It was strange to see her here in my kitchen. The last time we had seen each other had been the day before I had left for Rhode Island last year. I had ended my relationship with her then and it had not gone well. Today she seemed normal and didn't appear to be holding a grudge. Maybe she had moved on with her life. As far as I knew she didn't know anything about Laura or why I'd really been in England—or even the United States for that matter. I'd told her I was having a study abroad experience and she had been satisfied with that. But now she was here, unexpectedly, and I had a bad feeling.

"I've missed you," she said softly. "Did you miss me, too?" She moved next to me and touched my arm. I froze, wanting to shake off her hand, but not wanting to hurt her feelings.

The toaster oven dinged and I opened the door and reached for the toast. "Dammit!" I yelled, dropping the toast on the counter. I looked at the blistered spots on my fingers and cursed again under my breath.

"What did you expect…sticking your hand in a hot oven," she said. She came over and picked up the toast and put it on a plate. "What do you want on it? Your usual? Butter and strawberry jam?" She took a knife from the silverware drawer and reached for the butter.

"I'll do that," I said, a little more harshly than I had intended. I took the knife from her and moved everything further away, to the other end of the counter.

"Whoa. No need to bite my head off," she said, hurt. "I guess that's a no then…?"

I didn't answer. I didn't know what to say to her or how to bring up the subject of Laura. As it turned out, I didn't have to worry about it—the subject came up all on its own when Laura walked into the kitchen.

"What's taking so long?" she said, smiling. "Your children are hungry." She had her hands on her stomach and she looked beautiful. She saw Carmen and a look of surprise crossed her face. I glanced from her to Carmen and back again. I held up a glass of juice.

"Sorry. It's just now ready," I said. I could feel Carmen's eyes shifting back and forth between me and Laura. Her eyes traveled to Laura's stomach and she gasped.

Laura's face drained of color. She dropped her hands from

her stomach and stepped back toward the door. "Sorry…I didn't mean to interrupt…" she said quietly.

I rushed toward her and handed her the glass. She took it from me and I saw confusion on her face. "Laura…this is Carmen, Juana's daughter." I turned to face Carmen, willing her not to say or do anything we would both regret. "Carmen…this is Laura, my fiancée."

Carmen opened her mouth but didn't speak. Her face reddened and I could see that she was becoming agitated but trying not to show it. She composed herself and nodded at Laura, who stepped forward, saying hello and extending her hand in greeting. Carmen looked down at Laura's outstretched hand and for one interminable second I thought she was not going to accept it. I glared at her, silently daring her to do the right thing. She tentatively held out her hand and shook Laura's for a moment and then dropped it quickly as if she had been burned. She turned to me in confusion, her eyes welling with tears. And then she said a few choice words to me in Portuguese in a deathly quiet, barely controlled voice and stormed out the back door.

I felt the tension rolling off of Laura in waves. She had no idea what she had just walked into and I hated having to tell her. This was a small complication we did not need in our lives considering the big ones still looming in the future.

"I think the toast is cold," I said. "I'll make more." I went back to the toaster oven to start over.

"No, this is fine," said Laura. "Miguel…? What just happened?" she asked softly. "Is…was…Carmen…your…?" Her voice trailed off. I heard something in her tone—something bordering on suspicion tinged with jealousy.

I spread jam on the toast and put the plates on the table. "Come and sit down, sweetheart. Would you like something to go with the toast? Eggs? Ham?"

"No, the toast is plenty." She sat down and sipped from her juice glass…and waited.

I joined her at the table and pushed my plate away. My appetite had just taken a nosedive. "Carmen is a friend…we grew up together…more or less," I said, knowing full well this answer wouldn't be enough to appease her curiosity.

"What did she say to you...just now...before she left so abruptly?"

I didn't answer right away. I didn't want to lie knowing the truth would cause too much trouble. But this was Laura and I didn't want any secrets between us so I translated—roughly—Carmen's parting words. "She was shocked that I called you my fiancée...and that you're...pregnant. Then she called me a few nasty names and told me she hated me. That was pretty much it." I drained my orange juice and refilled my glass, more to keep myself busy than out of thirst.

"When you say 'grew up together,' what exactly do you mean by that? Was she your girlfriend?" By the sound of her voice I could tell she already knew the answer.

"Yes," I replied. "We went out for a while...but it ended a long time ago—before I went to Rhode Island. It was more of a teenage romance, I guess you could say."

"You're still a teenager, Miguel, so it couldn't have been that long ago. And from what I just witnessed, she isn't over you." She pushed her toast around on the plate and played with her juice glass, turning it round and round on the table.

I got up and went to stand behind her, taking the glass from her hand and sliding it down the table out of her reach. I wrapped my arms around her and held her close against me. Her hair smelled like lemons and felt like silk against my jaw. "I've known Carmen most of my life. She and her family are what people call gypsies. My father hired her parents to work for us years ago and Carmen and her brother, Carlos, came along to work with them every day. Her father worked in the vineyard and was our handyman—he died a few years ago--and her mother cooks for us and supervises the cleaning staff. Carmen and Carlos and I played together as children and worked together in the vineyard. My parents are paying for their education. They come from a very poor family and my parents were able to give them a nice life. And yes, we dated for a couple of years, but, Laura...it's over. I ended it before I went to America. And then I met you. I love you and only you. You never have to doubt that, OK?"

She turned in her chair and pulled me into her arms. I felt

her lips graze my neck and I closed my eyes for a moment, enjoying the feel of her mouth against my stubble. As much as I thought I had loved Carmen at the time, it didn't compare to the way I loved Laura. I took her face in my hands and kissed her and searched her eyes to make sure she knew she had nothing to worry about. She put her arms around my neck and sighed.

"I'm sure you had a life before me…even though I've not had time to give it much thought, but then again, I've been a little preoccupied lately," she said, frowning up at me. "But I want to know everything about you—*everything*—and if that includes ex-girlfriends, then so be it."

"Girlfriend—singular--only one. And we have a whole lifetime to get to know each other. Now I'm going to make you a proper breakfast—eggs and bacon and hot toast. No arguments." I prepared our meal and when we finished eating I put the dishes in the sink and then grabbed the car keys hanging on a hook by the door. "I want to take you for a ride and show you some of my country. Sound good to you?"

"Sounds amazing. I just need the ladies' room and I'll be ready. And, thanks for breakfast. You're a pretty good cook, Miguel." She gave me a kiss and disappeared down the hall.

I walked out onto the porch to wait for her. The weather was nice—puffy, white clouds, sunshine and a cool breeze--a perfect day to show off Sintra to Laura. I wanted to show her my family's other homes—the ones we would have been living in today if we were not a royal family in the shadows. I wasn't sure why it was so important to me to show Laura where my family came from—to show her my legacy—but I think Felipe and Gabriela had a lot to do with my sudden desire to embrace my lineage. Truthfully, I preferred living in the civilian world and I was quite sure all the pomp and pageantry of royal life would annoy the hell out of me, but I was proud of my family's history and I wanted Laura to be proud as well. Every year in the months leading up to the national elections there was always a movement to put a referendum on the ballot that would reinstate the monarchy and every year it was tabled. There were many citizens of Portugal who wanted a reigning royal family, but there were just as many who felt that there was no place in modern-day Portugal for the romantic notions that inspired kings and queens and princes and princesses. I used to side with the latter, but now that I had two children coming into the world I was feeling an internal shift on the subject. I heard the door shut behind me and turned to find Laura coming down the steps. She had changed into a blue dress and I saw the chain of the talisman glinting in the sunlight around her neck. She was wearing her hair down around her shoulders and she looked like a princess. As soon as the thought crossed my mind my mood turned dark as I realized that in a manner of speaking she was one already—she was a member of a royal family—the wrong one. I shook off the thought and reached for her hand.

"You're gorgeous. That color suits you," I said, thinking that, in fact, every color suited her. We walked around the side of the house to the garage. "This is my car," I said, pointing to the yellow Fiat.

"Wow…nice," Laura said. "Kinda puts my Jeep to shame."

"I like your Jeep. I wouldn't mind having one someday." I opened the passenger door and helped her inside. Now that I was thinking about it, a Fiat might not be the best car for a pregnant woman. It took her a moment to shift herself comfortably in the seat.

I drove down the long driveway. Sunlight filtered through the dry branches of the plane trees which would form a natural canopy over the driveway in the spring and summer. I glanced at Laura. She was taking in the scenery as it unfolded. "There are so many places I want to take you, but today I thought I would show you one of the royal palaces. And there is a little restaurant where we can eat later that is a favorite of mine. It's called the Post Office because it used to be a post office. It still looks like one inside but instead of stamps you get steak."

Laura laughed at my sad little joke. "It sounds great. I haven't had steak in a long time. I tried to be a vegetarian once. That lasted about a day and then I had a cheeseburger. Best one I ever had, too." She put her window down and I watched as her hair swirled about her face. I reached over and tucked some of it behind her ear. I loved seeing her like this—light-hearted and carefree. It had probably been a long time since she'd felt this way. I wished there was a way I could make this state of being last for her. We drove along the highway and headed into Sintra proper. I pointed out places of interest along the way, including where I went to primary school before I became a student at the American School in Lisbon and the sports academy where I played football, or soccer, as Laura called it, all through my childhood.

"What's that?" Laura asked. She was pointing at the *Palacio da Pena*, situated high up in the Sintra mountain range. "It looks like something out of a fairy tale."

I shifted into first gear and we started the steep ascent up toward the palace. The road twisted this way and that in switchbacks as we climbed. "That's one of the royal palaces—it was used mostly as a summer palace for the Portuguese royal family back in the day. I thought you might like to see it up close."

Laura looked at me, a puzzled expression on her face. "Portuguese royal family…as in…your family, right?"

"Yes, one and the same," I said, giving her a half-smile. I didn't want her to think I was showing off, but I wanted her to see where my family came from and where, if a majority of the public ever got its way, we would be living again one day. I doubted it would ever happen in my lifetime, but the possibility existed that one day my family would return to a seated royal status. We rounded the last corner and arrived at the parking area for the general public. I by-passed the lot and drove up to a gate nearer the palace's right portico. I approached the guard station and a uniformed security officer stepped from the guard post and stopped my entry.

I rolled down my window and reached across Laura to open the glove compartment. The guard leaned into the window and looked us over.

"I'm sorry, sir, this is not an entry point for visitors. You'll have to turn around."

I handed him a document and my driver's license and waited for him to examine it. And just as I knew he would, he handed it back to me and smiled—even bowing slightly. "My apologies, sir. You may enter and park next to the building. I'll put an electronic parking permit on your car and it will be removed when you're ready to leave. Enjoy your visit."

I thanked him and pulled the car over, parking next to a security vehicle. I got out and came around to Laura's side and helped her out. She stood next to the car and looked up at the clock tower. I watched her take in the beauty of the palace. It always inspired awe in people the first time they saw it. I still felt it every time I came here. It never got old.

"Miguel...," she whispered. "This is...wow...a fairy tale come to life. It's absolutely magnificent." She took my hand and we walked to the side door where the security guard who had let us into the parking lot was waiting to unlock the door. He handed us each a magnetic card on a chain and instructed us to wear them at all times while we were inside the palace.

We entered the palace and walked down a long hallway, passing several closed doors, many of which were administrative offices. We climbed some stairs and eventually came to the cloister. I waited for Laura's reaction to its striking colors.

"Oh, my god," she breathed, taking it all in. She gazed up at the sky above. "What happens when it rains?" she asked.

"Someone presses a button and a ceiling magically appears," I said, trying to suppress a smile. I pulled her into my arms then, unable to resist her innocence. I pressed her against me and kissed her until she pushed back from me, gasping for air. Then I laughed. I loved seeing the palace through her eyes— it reminded me of the first time I came here, when I was finally old enough to understand the significance of its history and grandeur and my connection to it.

"I think you're teasing me," she said, kissing me again and then taking my hand in hers. We walked around the cloister, admiring the colorful tile-work. I led her into the main chapel where a few tourists were gazing up at the altarpiece. We studied it for a while and then moved on to the far side of the palace where the main living quarters were located. We mingled with tourists as we passed through the ballroom and on into the kitchen and Manuel the Second's bedroom. Laura asked a lot of questions and every once in a while a staff member would notice the card around my neck and acknowledge me with respect. I felt the weight of my legacy in those moments and it made me feel an intense pride. I could tell Laura was impressed but was trying to be cool about it.

Eventually Laura mentioned that her back was hurting so we headed to the car. We'd spent almost two hours inside the palace and had only seen a small part of it, but we'd hit the highlights. We turned in our badges at the gate and had the electronic parking pass removed from the windshield, then I drove us down the twisty road to the bottom of the mountain.

"Thank you, Miguel. That was amazing." Laura placed her hand on top of mine on the gear shift. "Forgive me for asking this question—I know it really doesn't matter—but is all of that," she pointed back over her shoulder toward the palace, "yours?"

"It's a museum now so technically it belongs to Portgual... to the people. If my family were ever to live there again, it would only be in the residential part—the rest would remain open to the public. But that palace was more of a summer palace. My family's ancestors lived most of the time in the Sintra National Palace which is in Sintra Vila--old town Sintra. We're going to pass it on the way to the restaurant. You'll see it. We'll come back one day and tour it. It's very different from the Pena Palace but also beautiful in its own way. You'll like the kitchen—everyone always loves the kitchen there. From the outside the chimneys looks like giant milk bottles. It's kind of funny."

Laura was quiet as we drove. It was a lot to take in. I guess if I wanted to be honest with myself, I was a lot to take in. As we passed the National Palace I pointed it out, although it wasn't really necessary considering it encompassed most of the old town and you couldn't really miss it. We drove to the restaurant and I left my Fiat with the valet. Inside we were seated at a table with a great view of the main street where there were many shops and bars. Laura spotted a bakery across the street and commented on it.

"Ooh, can we go there after we eat? I have a craving I need to satisfy," she grinned at me. As soon as the waiter took our drink orders I reached across the table for her hands. Suddenly she seemed too far away. I liked the way it made me feel to have her close.

"You mean a craving I can't satisfy?" I asked. She blushed

and I loved the way it made her look. *Damn*, I thought. *Get your head out of the gutter, Dos Santos.*

"You can satisfy a lot of cravings, Miguel, but when a girl needs chocolate, nothing else will do." She patted her stomach and laughed. "Especially a pregnant girl."

I shook my head in wonder at her. She captivated me. I didn't remember ever being captivated by Carmen. Thinking of her now made me annoyed with myself. I pushed the thought away and we placed our orders—veal and potatoes for me and a steak and rice pilaf for Laura. She asked me questions about my family and I asked about hers. I still felt badly that I had never met her parents and brother during the time I'd lived in Rhode Island, but it wasn't really my fault considering I was more of a secret she'd had to keep at the time. But I was happy the secret was out and I didn't care who knew we were together. I loved this girl and sometimes I was surprised at just how deep my feelings went.

After dinner we walked across the street to the bakery and I watched as Laura picked out éclairs, donuts, fudge and cookies—all of it chocolate. As the clerked boxed up the items, I walked down to the other end of the counter and ordered my own favorite baked good.

"I know you're all about the chocolate, Laura, but you have to have Portugal's national baked treasure. I'm getting a half dozen—maybe I should get more. They're called *queijadas* and they are amazing. I promise you'll love them." The clerk packaged up the little cream tarts in a separate box and I paid for everything and we headed back to the car. Once inside, Laura went for the chocolate and I took a *queijada*. I watched her eat the éclair and again I felt myself getting worked up just watching her lick the chocolate from her lips.

"I'll try that treasure now," she said. Her voice was quiet and I wondered if she was talking about the tart. I took a bite of it and chewed slowly, saving a piece for her. I leaned toward her. She met me half way over the gear shift and kissed me. The taste of chocolate and some other kind of sweetness made me melt. I heard myself groan against her and I was suddenly in a hurry to get home. I put the last bite of the tart in her mouth and she moaned as she chewed.

"Wow. That is good," she said. "But you taste better." She kissed me again. I tasted the sweetness on her tongue and I decided I'd been tortured enough.

"Let's go home," I said. I started the car and shifted into gear. We listened to fado music as we drove through the streets of Sintra and on into the countryside. I had so much more to show her but right now the only thing I wanted her to see was how much I loved her.

Chapter Six

JEALOUSY

LAURA

I held Felipe and Gabriela in my arms and stared at them in wonder. I had never seen anything more beautiful or more fragile in my life. I was overwhelmed by them. I didn't know how to be a mother—it seemed daunting. Could I do this? I felt tears pooling in my eyes and I fought to control them as I stared down at my children. Suddenly I felt a pain shoot through my heart...a massive, searing, life-ending pain that caused my arms to go limp. I watched helplessly as Felipe and Gabriela disappeared before my eyes. I wanted to scream, but the sound was stuck—my vocal chords twisted and useless. My lungs worked overtime to keep me alive but my mind was keenly aware that I only had seconds to live. My eyes tried to close but I wasn't ready to go yet. I wasn't ready to leave my children and Miguel and my parents and my brother. I heard noises around me and I thought I heard my babies cry. I wanted so badly to call for help but no matter how hard I tried to scream, only a last, few, labored breaths escaped my mouth. I was frozen in place, a statue, with only my brain functioning, but even it was threatening to close down. Why didn't someone sense my distress and come to my rescue? Miguel was here in the room. I could make out his voice nearby. I heard a female voice, too, singing a lullaby in Portuguese. She sounded young and then I heard her tell Miguel how much she loved him and their children. Who was she? I wanted to tell her they were mine, but surely she knew that. Why wasn't anyone helping me? My eyes were open but I couldn't see anything. Or maybe they were closed. I couldn't be sure. The stabbing pain rocked me again and this time, I gave in to it. I gasped and jerked violently, thankful my suffering was finally coming to an end.

"Laura…it's OK…you're OK. You're dreaming," whispered Miguel. I felt his arms pulling me out of the darkness and into the light of early morning. How long had I been asleep? My throat was dry and I felt nauseous. I opened my eyes and looked around the room.

"What happened?" I asked. I tried to sit up but Miguel was holding me so tightly that I couldn't even move my head. "Was I asleep? What time is it?" I hated this feeling of disorientation.

"You were having a nightmare. I heard you moaning and mumbling. I tried to wake you but you were deep into something. Do you remember it?" He kissed the top of my head.

"Someone took the babies." As soon as I said the words, I felt the tears begin their descent. I pushed Miguel's arms away and sat up in the bed, leaning back against the headboard. I looked around the room and felt relief when I recognized where I was. I pushed back the blankets and looked down at my stomach. It was still big. I was still pregnant. I wrapped my arms around myself and choked back a sob. "Someone took Felipe and Gabriela. They're not safe, Miguel."

"Sh…sh…," Miguel shifted his body so that he was next to me. He took my hands and kissed each palm then wiped away my tears with his thumbs. "No one is going to take them, Laura. No one. You know I would never let that happen."

I shook my head. "No…you don't understand…if someone is determined to get them, there won't be anything you can do to stop them." I pushed away from him and stood up from the bed, walking over to the window. I pulled back the curtain and saw daylight. I felt like I had been asleep for days.

Miguel joined me at the window and put his hands on my shoulders, turning me to face him. "You and the babies are safe. No one is going to take them. You were just having a nightmare. Why don't we go down to breakfast? Mama wants to talk to you about getting stuff ready for a nursery. All that baby shopping talk will make you feel better." He nuzzled his lips against my cheek and I felt myself begin to relax. He threaded his fingers through my hair and cupped my face in his hand. "Everything will be fine, I promise." He kissed me and I snuggled into his arms. I did feel safe when I was with him--there was no doubt about that.

"Can I take a shower first?"

"Of course. Come down when you're finished. I love you," Miguel kissed me again and left me to get ready.

As I showered I thought back to yesterday, after we'd returned from visiting the palace and our lunch at the Post Office. Catarina had been excited because Tristan had called to tell her he would be arriving this weekend. He would be accompanied by his attendant, Ronald. Mateo and Tomas had already begun building a ramp for the front porch to make for easy access to and from the house, and Catarina and Juana had set about preparing the downstairs bedrooms for them. It had made me happy to see her so excited. I knew the feeling. I couldn't wait to see Tristan again, but I was also a little apprehensive. I intended to ask him about Andrew and I knew Miguel would not be pleased. But I needed to know if he was OK. Miguel would just have to deal with it. We'd had a huge meal prepared by Juana and Sofia and I'd finally gotten to meet more of the men who were involved in my rescue and the procurement of the items from the duke's safe. I still didn't know exactly what had been in the safe and I decided I would ask Miguel about it soon. After dinner Miguel and I had walked in the vineyard in the moonlight. It was so peaceful there—there was an air of magic about the place that made me feel as if I were in some enchanted kingdom. While we'd walked Miguel had told me that a few of the guys—friends and cousins—would be staying close by to keep an eye on the house for extra security. I'd been alarmed at that but he had assured me it was only for peace of mind and that there was no threat to fear. *Maybe that's why I had the nightmare*, I thought, as I turned off the shower and toweled myself dry.

In the bedroom I stood before the full length mirror behind the door and stared at my naked body. I didn't recognize myself anymore. I turned to study my profile and passed my hands over my stomach. "Damn," I muttered. "I look like a cow." Seeing my distorted body made me wonder how it was possible for Miguel to find me attractive. I thought of Carmen then and felt a sharp stab of jealousy. She was petite with long, dark hair that fell to her waist and perfect, flawless skin. I paled in comparison to her—literally. I'd only spent a few seconds in her presence, but it was enough to know that she was still in love with him. I also knew that I couldn't let that knowledge eat away at me though it would be awfully easy to do so. I tried to imagine being in Carmen's shoes and the thought made me shudder. I couldn't fathom Miguel with anyone else but me. I couldn't stand that. I pressed my hand to my abdomen and felt the movement of the babies—my constant reminder of how much I loved Miguel and how much he loved me. I got dressed, put on some make-up, fixed my hair and went down to the kitchen, expecting to find Miguel and his family there, but there was only one person in the room—the last person I expected to see again.

"Hello," I said, my voice sounding weak to my own ears. "Where is everyone?"

"Good morning," said Carmen. "They're out front looking at some ramp thing the twins built." She was standing by the sink, leaning up against it, observing me intently. Her English was excellent but her accent was thick—much thicker than Miguel's and Catarina's. She was holding a cup of coffee.

I wanted something to drink but helping myself suddenly seemed presumptuous. I smelled coffee brewing and I could see something baking in the oven. There were plates of bacon and scrambled eggs warming on top of the stove. I decided I would ignore the awkwardness and fix myself a glass of juice. I couldn't remember which cupboard held the juice glasses and

I opened and closed several before I found the right one. The whole time I searched for a glass and poured my juice I could feel Carmen's eyes watching my every move. The awkwardness was making me nervous and I felt my stomach begin to react. I started to walk out of the kitchen to go find Miguel when her voice stopped me.

"I want to apologize for yesterday," she said quietly.

I turned around and mustered a smile. "It's OK, no worries," I said.

"You caught me by surprise," she said. "Actually, so did Miguel. I did not know he was back from his travels and, of course, I didn't know about you."

"It's really OK. Miguel told me that you two used to…date." I heard nervousness in my voice. Why was she getting to me? I took a sip of orange juice and it felt good on my parched throat.

She finished her coffee and set the cup down on the counter. She walked a little closer to me and I suddenly felt like a giant compared to her. I was at least half a foot taller than she was— and my body, in its present condition, totally dwarfed hers. She had delicate facial features and her eyes were dark as night. She unnerved me to no end.

"He told you we…*dated*?" she said, stopping by the counter island and leaning up against it.

I nodded and clutched my glass to my chest. My instincts were wide awake and on alert. I sensed she had something to say to me, whether I wanted to hear it or not.

"Then he didn't tell you everything. We were more than two people dating—much more," she said. Her eyes were suddenly shiny with tears and I heard her breathing change. It looked like she was trying to keep herself in check and having a hard time in the process.

"I'm sorry," I croaked out the words. "I don't know what to say."

"Miguel promised me he would come back to me. He promised we would…"

"Carmen. What are you doing here?" Miguel asked as he entered the kitchen. I hadn't heard him at the door and I doubted Carmen had either. His voice was sharp and his face stony.

Without warning, she rushed up to Miguel, her hands forming into tiny fists at her sides. "What? I'm not allowed to be here now? Now that…" she glared at me, "*she's* here?" She charged at Miguel but he grabbed her arms and stopped her. She was no match for him. She burst into tears and let loose with a stream of words in Portuguese. Miguel tried to calm her but she was too upset to listen to reason. I wanted to get out of the kitchen and not be a witness to this. I turned to leave just as Juana came through the door. She must have heard Carmen's raised voice because she immediately chastised her and helped Miguel calm her down. Carmen said something else in Portuguese and, in a repeat of yesterday, stormed out the back door.

Juana turned to Miguel, her face red. She looked embarrassed but I sensed an underlying anger, or maybe it was just frustration, though I wasn't sure if it was with Carmen or me. She exchanged words with Miguel in Portuguese and then began to bring the breakfast foods to the dining table. Miguel came over to me and pulled me out of the kitchen into the hall.

"What did she say to you?" he asked, clearly annoyed.

"She was just about to tell me something about your relationship…she said you'd promised to come back to her and that you'd promised something else but she didn't get to finish because you walked in." I didn't want to be jealous. It was an emotion I'd never experienced before and already I felt it sneaking into my mind, threatening to derail me. It was quite clear that Carmen was going to be a problem and I didn't need the aggravation of a jealous ex-girlfriend.

"I'm sorry," Miguel sighed, slipping his arm around my waist. "I guess I should have warned you about Carmen, but, truthfully, it never occurred to me that she would show up. She lives here with her mother and brother when they're not in school, so I guess it will be hard to avoid her."

"What do you mean…they live here… In the house?" I asked. "Your ex-girlfriend lives with you?" This was a little much to take in. Now it was more than jealousy I was feeling—I was ticked off at this piece of information.

"Did you notice the buildings behind the house? Carmen and her family live in one of the cottages back there."

"Don't they have their own kitchen?" I realized how it sounded as soon as the words came out of my mouth. But I was past the point of caring. I didn't relish the thought of daily encounters with Carmen. I didn't need the stress.

"Juana works here, Laura. And Carmen has always had the run of the house. I'm sure you'll get used to seeing her around… until she goes back to school next month."

I stared at Miguel in shock. "Get used to it? No, Miguel, I don't think I'll get used to seeing your ex-girlfriend every day. I don't want to get used to it. It isn't fair to me."

Miguel's face darkened. I could see that he was upset with me though I couldn't imagine why. "It's not exactly fair to me that you have a husband, but I deal with it," he said.

I sucked in a breath and pushed his arm off me. I felt tears burning behind my eyes. "How dare you say that…as if I had a choice." I was hurt and now all I wanted was to be alone. I hurried away from him and out the front door, down the porch steps and off toward the vineyard. The closer I got to the vineyard the more his words hurt. I was shocked at his insensitivity. I swiped at my tears as I continued down the long row of vines. I heard footsteps behind me and I moved faster. I just wanted to be alone. I suddenly missed my home and family with an intensity that took my breath away. I didn't want to be married and I didn't want to be pregnant. I was days away from turning nineteen and I was already tired of my life.

"Laura, wait…stop," Miguel said, as he caught up to me. "I'm sorry." He grabbed my arm and stopped me but I didn't turn around. I didn't want to talk—I wasn't ready to make nice. What I really wanted and had wanted for a very long time was to go home—back to Rhode Island where I belonged.

He pulled me into his arms with a force that shocked me. He grabbed my chin and made me look at him. "Listen to me, *minha querida*. You know I didn't mean to hurt you. But it kills me that you're married to…*him*. I try not to think about it but it's always there, hanging over my head—our heads—getting in the way. I admit I'm jealous—it's in my nature—but I know it isn't your fault. And you're right about Carmen. It isn't fair that you should have to deal with her. I will talk to Juana about it."

I tried to look away, to pull my chin from his fingers but he shook his head and held tighter. My tears continued to fall and finally he relaxed his grip and wiped my cheeks with his thumbs. I swallowed and let out a pent up sigh. "I'd like to go home…to Rhode Island."

Miguel blinked in surprise and raised his eyebrows. "I'm sure you do, Laura. But not now."

"Why not? I need to see my mother—my family. I'm tired of feeling stressed. I just want…" He leaned down and pressed his lips against mine, silencing me, and pulled me into his arms. I felt his tongue touch my lips, searching for mine and as the kiss deepened, I felt my resolve weakening. His lips had magical powers and I felt myself falling under his spell. I put my arms around him and pressed against him as close as my stomach would allow. When he kissed me like this, there was nowhere else I wanted to be. But there was something I needed to know and I couldn't let his intoxicating kisses stop me from asking. I pulled away from him a bit and looked into his dark eyes and I prayed that he wouldn't lie to me about Carmen. "What promises did you make to her?"

Miguel lowered his arms and stepped away. He looked up at the sky and sighed and then turned back to me. "I have never made a promise to Carmen or to you or to anyone that I have not intended to keep. When I ended our relationship, the only thing I promised her was my friendship. But she didn't want that. She wanted more than I was willing to give. I did promise her that she and her family would always have a home with us if they wanted it, but I never promised her *me*."

I considered his words even as I put myself in Carmen's shoes and felt her pain. For me, friendship with Miguel would never be enough. I knew in my heart that if he were not mine, I couldn't stand to be near him—to be reminded of his existence. I would need to be on the other side of the world and even there would be too close to something I wanted but knew I could never have. Carmen was only punishing herself by being here. I wished she would leave, as much for my peace of mind as for her own. But everyone had their own way of dealing with pain so I would just have to adjust to her presence. Maybe it would prove too much to bear and she would leave. Time would tell. I held out my hand to Miguel and he came to me and placed his in mine.

"Miguel…about Andrew…," I started, but he wouldn't allow me to finish my words.

"No, Laura. Let's not talk about him. It isn't your fault you're married to him. I'm sorry for what I said. Right now, our breakfast is getting cold. Let's go eat. Mama is anxious to talk baby talk with you and Catarina."

I forced a smile and nodded and we walked hand in hand back to the house. Juana was gone but Sofia, Catarina, Antonio and Miguel's brothers were already gathered around the table eating. Mateo looked up and grinned at Miguel.

"Sorry, we couldn't wait. We're starving in here," he laughed.

Miguel shook his head, grinning, and passed me a plate of muffins. I sat down next to Catarina and began to eat. The food was delicious and the atmosphere was reminiscent of meals I'd had with my family back home in Rhode Island. I missed them terribly and I had to turn away so no one would see the tears that threatened again. Sofia brought up the babies and that helped steer my mind away from home. We talked about setting up a nursery and Sofia suggested we redecorate the room next to mine and Miguel's. She was excited about shopping for them and I was reminded of the duchess's excitement at planning my wedding to Andrew. I felt goose bumps rise on my arms at the thought and tried to force thoughts of her and my wedding day out of my mind.

After breakfast, Catarina, Miguel and I went out to the front porch to talk about Tristan's impending visit. He would be arriving in two days time on Sunday evening and Catarina was nervous and excited. Miguel, however, was apprehensive about Tristan's pending arrival.

"What has he said lately about the duke's condition?" he asked Catarina.

"His father is supposed to be discharged from hospital this weekend. He is apparently making a miraculous recovery. It's rather ironic, don't you think?" she said derisively.

"It's ironic, alright. *My* father—a kind, gentle man with a *good* heart—has a heart attack and dies because of that son of a bitch who in turn has a heart attack himself but is making a full recovery. Oh, it's ironic alright." Miguel got up from his chair and paced back and forth on the front porch. His face was red and his footsteps were loud on the wooden floor. I wanted to reach out to him but I thought better of it. After a moment he stopped pacing and gazed down at Catarina. "What exactly is the nature of your and Tristan's relationship?"

She looked at him in surprise. "Why do you ask?"

He came back to his seat beside me and sat down, resting his elbows on his thighs. "Just curious, I guess. It might be weird having him here." He glanced at me as he spoke and I wondered what he was getting at.

"I know what you're thinking, Miguel. You're wondering what kind of a future I could possibly have with someone in a wheelchair. But there's more to him than his legs, you know." Catarina was getting worked up--she was on the defensive.

"That isn't what I was thinking at all," said Miguel. "I was wondering where his allegiance lies. I guess we'll find out soon enough."

We sat in silence for a while until Sofia came looking for us and asked me and Catarina how we felt about going on a little shopping expedition in Lisbon. Miguel jumped up then, kissed me quickly on the cheek and went down the porch steps. "This is where I disappear. You girls have fun." He winked at me and waved and the three of us set out on my first real trip to Lisbon. It was fun and we picked out beautiful furniture and clothes for the babies. I was self-conscious about the fact that Sofia was picking up the tab for everything and it was bothering my conscience. At one point I spotted an ATM machine and excused myself to go use it. Just as I was about to withdraw money, Catarina sidled up next to me and informed me that if I was taking out money to give to Sofia that it would hurt her feelings.

"But I can't let your family pay for everything. I still have money in my savings account. I want to contribute." I knew I sounded whiny but I hoped Catarina could also hear my sincerity.

"Money isn't a problem for my family, Laura. You keep yours and let Miguel and Sofia—my mother—take care of you this way. You have no idea how happy Sofia is right now. She has been deep in mourning since Alfonso—my father—died. You're making her feel alive again and that is worth a million times more than however much you have in your account. Trust me. You and the babies are bringing her back to life. I'm sure Miguel told you that my parents died in a plane crash and that I was the only survivor. His parents raised me and I've been the daughter they never had. My birth father died before I was born and my mother married Sofia's brother, Alberto, when I was two years old and he adopted me. The plane crash happened two years after they married. I nearly died that day--I was very badly hurt. I had several surgeries as a young child to correct the injuries I sustained that day. I can never have children of my own so your babies are very important to her. Let her spoil you, OK?"

I put my ATM card back in my wallet and nodded. I swiped at the tears that her words had brought to my eyes and mustered a smile. She gave me a quick hug and we rejoined Sofia and continued our shopping. In the back of my mind I kept going over Catarina's words. She couldn't have children. It made me feel guilty at being blessed with two at once. I knew then that I was lucky and I had much to be thankful for. We ended up having a wonderful time and not only did I fall in love with this beautiful place that was now my home, I also fell more in love with Miguel and his family and the life we were destined to live together.

The Shadow King

Chapter Seven

Doubt

Andrew

"So you're really going down there?" I asked my brother. We were in his apartment and I was watching him pack his suitcase. Ronald, his attendant, had laid out some clothes and Tristan was choosing the shirts and pants he wanted to take with him.

"Yes, Andrew, I'm really going down there. What's it to you anyway?" Tristan was annoyed with me and had been all day. I'd been on his back about not visiting Father and choosing the gypsies over family. Truthfully, I didn't give a damn about what he was doing, but harassing him helped me unload some of my frustration and anxiety.

I wanted Tristan to know that I wasn't a cold-hearted bastard. I'd had time to think about what our father had done to Laura and I knew it was wrong—downright evil, in fact. I even agreed that Father should be punished for his deeds and perhaps his heart attack was the punishment he deserved. But it didn't change the way I felt about Miguel Dos Santos. I wondered what Tristan would think if he knew the truth about Miguel. What would he think if he knew that Dos Santos was our *brother*? I felt my stomach knot up at the thought. It was too preposterous to believe and, at times, I almost convinced myself that it was just a horrible mistake. I wanted to tell Tristan, but Father didn't want him to know, so for now, I honored my father's wishes. Tristan had told our mother about Father's blackmail scheme and she had turned a deaf ear to it, just as I knew she would. I truly believed that deep in her heart, she knew what Father was capable of, but I also knew that my mother would never do anything to risk her security or her marriage. If she wanted to stick her head in the sand and ignore the truth, then who were we, her sons, to try to talk her out of it? And if she knew that Father had another son, she would be devastated. I pushed thoughts of my mother—and *him*--out of my head and asked Tristan a question that had been eating away at me.

"Do you love this girl?" My voice was quieter now. I didn't understand how Tristan could turn his back on his family, but I loved him enough to try. I was being childish and I knew I needed to rein myself in. Running out of beer and whiskey, which had become my new companions, had apparently impacted my sense of reasoning in a more positive way. I was impressed with how calm I was at the moment.

"I don't know, but if I want to find out, I need to be with her. And I want to see Laura. I'm worried about her. What do you intend to do about your marriage? Father's lawyers can have it annulled or you could get a dissolution of marriage. I don't know how those things work but I'm sure it could be handled quickly and discreetly." Tristan arranged several shirts into the suitcase with care. He glanced up at me, waiting for my answer.

"I don't want a divorce. I want my wife back—and my children. I'm going to make it happen, Tristan. You'll see." I walked over to the window and looked out at the bleak, December day. It would be Laura's birthday in a few days. I needed to see her. I felt my phone vibrate in my pocket but I ignored it for the moment. "I'm going to get her back and I'm going to make her see that marrying me wasn't a mistake. I can give her more than that damned gypsy."

"Stop calling him a gypsy. You know he's just as royal as you and I—maybe even more so." Tristan slammed his suitcase closed and pushed himself around the corner of his bed and rolled toward the door. "You're going to have to accept the fact that Laura isn't the one for you. She never was. I know it hurts, Andrew, but you have to deal with it. Now I'm going to check my email. Please see a lawyer and do the right thing—for you and for her." He wheeled himself down the hall as I stood at the window staring out at the grayness. I pulled my phone out of my pocket and called Peter back. He answered on the second ring.

"Peter? Have you made the arrangements?" I waited for his reply. We talked for a few moments and then I closed my phone and placed it back in my pocket. Tristan wasn't the only Easton going to Portugal. I wanted Laura home in time for the holidays. It would be our first Christmas and Boxing Day as husband and wife and I wanted her home with me where she belonged. I knew if I could just spend a few minutes alone with her I could reason with her. She had loved me once and deep down I believed she still did. She just needed a little reminding. I could do that.

Father appeared to be sleeping when I walked into his room. But he turned his head and said hello as I sat down in the chair next to him.

"I'm going home today, son," he said. "I can't wait to get out of here. I feel like I've been given a new lease on life."

"That's because you have," I said. "Look, Father, I can't stay long. I just came by to tell you that I'm going to Portugal to get my wife back. I told Mother, but she…she just got upset."

"Don't worry about your mother, Andrew. I'll take care of her. But I need you to take care of the situation we talked about. Do you understand?"

"You are one bloodthirsty bastard, you know that, Father?" My father's weakened state and his obvious character flaws were making it easier for me to stand up to him. Sometimes I hated him. But I knew where he was coming from. I just wished I were coming from someplace different. I didn't want the misdeeds of the past to keep repeating any more than he did. I didn't want to be a victim of Princess Gabriela or him or whoever was responsible for the mess my life was now. Oh, I would be fine if Miguel Dos Santos ceased to exist. Nothing would make me happier, but killing him was not something I looked forward to. I would have to play it by ear. I could do it in self-defense, but I didn't want to become my father with the revenge and the drinking, although I had to admit, I was beginning to understand why they called alcohol liquid courage. Suddenly I had the sense that a tennis match was being played inside my head and it was giving me a headache.

"That may be so, son, but this curse has to be put to rest. And you have to handle it. But please be smart and be safe."

"You know, Father…I thought this heart attack would change you. I thought it would somehow…soften you…but I was wrong. You're even worse than before." I glanced at my watch and stood up. "I have to get home. I have an early flight tomorrow."

"Andrew, wait. My heart attack was a wake-up call. It made me realize how important family is—*my family*. When I die, I want to go to my grave knowing that I did my part to fulfill King George's wishes. I want my grandchildren raised in the House of Hanover in England where they belong. King George may have lost his son to the gypsies but I won't lose my grandchildren to them."

"Well, you're losing Tristan to them. Doesn't that bother you?"

"It would if I let it, but Tristan has always marched to the beat of his own drum. He'll come around one day. But you, Andrew, you are more like me. Your sense of tradition and legacy is stronger than his. That's why I'm counting on you to take care of…the situation."

"I don't know what will happen down there. My goal is to bring my family home. Beyond that…it remains to be seen, but you should consider coming clean with Mother about your past. Now I have to go. I'll be in touch." I turned and left the room abruptly before he could say anything else. Peter was in the car waiting for me in the hospital's circular front entrance. I climbed into the car and leaned back against the seat. I noticed the grocery bag on the seat next to me and I pulled it closer and opened it.

"What you asked for is in the bag, Andrew, but remember, you want to be level-headed tomorrow," said Peter over his shoulder.

"I'm not worried, so you shouldn't be either. I can handle myself just fine."

"Of course, sir," Peter replied. I saw his grim expression in the rearview mirror and I was tempted to chastise him for his impertinence but I let it go.

We arrived at the apartment and after confirming my departure time for tomorrow I went upstairs to the kitchen and fixed myself a ham and cheese sandwich. I opened the grocery bag and removed a new bottle of whiskey. I'd never realized before that it tasted better than beer and that its effect was different, too. I poured a tumbler full and sat at the dining table with my food, the drink and the silence of the apartment. I took a couple of bites of the sandwich but pushed the plate away in favor of the drink, which I finished a little too quickly. When I finished my drink I filled the glass again. And when I finished that one I put the glass in the sink and went into the living room with the bottle. It was easier to drink this way. There were two more bottles of whiskey still remaining in the grocery sack but I promised myself that I wouldn't touch them. By the time I drained the last of the first bottle I was too tired to care about the other two anyway. I fell asleep on the sofa in the living room and stayed there until the first rays of morning's gray light awakened me.

I showered quickly and threw a few things into a duffel bag and headed down to the front of the building to wait for Peter. I patted my pocket to make sure my passport and wallet were inside as I waited, surprised that I was ready before him. Once inside the car I took a moment to ask myself a very important question. *What the hell are you doing, Easton?* As we drove in silence to the airport I acknowledged that I had no answer. My stomach was on fire and my head was filled with firing cannons and the only thing I knew for sure was that consuming an entire bottle of whiskey on an empty stomach had been a classically, stupid mistake.

We landed in Lisbon and Peter and I went straight to the rental car office. We picked up a dark blue BMW and headed north toward Sintra. Peter knew where we were going but I was driving, even though he hadn't wanted me to--being behind the wheel made me feel as if I had some semblance of control over my situation. He had made reservations for two rooms at a hotel in the old part of Sintra and we checked in and I left him in the hotel while I took a walk around the area. I saw a massive structure and knew immediately that it was one of the royal palaces. Just looking at it made me angry. I felt a craving kick in for a beer but I knew I needed food. I walked along the sidewalk, glancing in shop windows, eventually stopping at a café. I ordered soup and a steak and as soon as the food hit my stomach I felt a little better. I drank two Cokes to quench my powerful thirst and hoped it would be enough to satisfy my craving. I watched people pass by, noticing that the women were beautiful. I thought of Tristan then and his gypsy girl. He would be here sometime this weekend. I stared ahead as if in a trance, thoughts tumbling around in my brain. *What do you expect to happen here, Easton? Do you even have a plan?* I blinked and looked around, almost forgetting where I was. I realized that my food was suddenly not sitting well and I needed to get back to the hotel before I became sick all over the café floor. I hadn't felt this badly since my honeymoon. I felt a wave of sadness hit me at the memory of being in Mallorca with Laura. I remembered the feel of her skin and the taste of her lips—so soft and so sweet. And then I pictured her with him—kissing him—touching him—and the next wave that hit was one of pure anger. I forced down the nausea as I threw some Euros on the table and ran from the café all the way back to the hotel. I made it to the room just in time to vomit my steak and last night's whiskey into the toilet. I took a shower and wrapped myself in a towel, then stretched out on the bed. I was asleep within seconds.

"Andrew…Andrew?" Peter was shaking me. "Are you alright, sir?"

I opened my eyes and immediately closed them again. "Where the hell am I?" I asked in confusion. I put one hand on my forehead and ran the other one through my hair.

"Portugal, sir. You've been sleeping a long time. I tried waking you earlier but you weren't having it," Peter chuckled. "I told you to be careful of the whiskey."

I remembered a saying my father used to spout about familiarity breeding contempt and again I was tempted to call Peter on his cheekiness, but I let it pass, considering that he had, in fact, warned me about overdoing the alcohol. "What time is it? Hell, come to think of it, what day is it?" I asked as I attempted to sit up.

"It's Sunday morning...just coming up on noon."

"Damn!" I staggered to the bathroom and took a look at myself in the mirror. "*Damn*," I said again to my reflection. I'd lost an entire day and I looked like pure hell. I called out to Peter. "When does Tristan arrive?"

"Later this afternoon," Peter replied. "His gets in at four— he changed to an earlier flight."

Up to now, my only objective had been to get to Sintra. Now that I was here, I needed to make a plan. I needed to talk to Laura. I wondered if she had the cell phone my father had given her. After I'd read the text messages between her and Dos Santos, I'd dropped the phone somewhere in the house. For all I knew it could still be there or one of Dos Santos' henchman could have picked it up. If she did have it in her possession, I doubted she was using it. I took another shower and wrapped myself in a clean towel and went in search of my phone. I called Laura's number but as I suspected, it went straight to voicemail. This meant I would have to go to her but I knew I would be a most unwelcome guest at the Dos Santos homestead. I would just have to somehow get her to come to me. It occurred to me that I might have to wait a day or two and get to know the area, particularly the area where the gypsies lived. They probably had about as much, if not more, security at their place as we had at ours back in England. I got dressed and met Peter in the lobby. We sat at a table in the common area where beverages and pastries were set out for hotel guests. I needed coffee and toast. My stomach still felt tender after last night and my head wasn't in the best of shape either —literally and figuratively.

Peter stared at me, an expectant expression on his face. He wanted to know how to proceed and I didn't have an answer. Quite frankly, his presence was getting on my nerves. I really just wanted to be alone. I regretted bringing him here and re-solved that I would ditch him at the first opportunity—I never should have asked for his help in the first place. This was my problem to solve and I didn't need a babysitter to help me. I *could* do this alone. Laura had always called them goons and mostly I had agreed with her. I knew I had been hard on her about her dislike for them and for my father. If I had only known what she had been going through, everything could have been so different. *Why hadn't she trusted me enough to come to me for help? I could have protected her*, I thought. I finished my coffee and slammed the cup down on the table. A woman at a nearby table jumped at the sound of it and frowned at me. I glared at her and stood up. "Let's go for a ride," I said to Peter.

We drove around Sintra and then out into the countryside. I could see another palace high on a hill and that one made me angry, too. I knew it was more than anger I was feeling—it was jealousy and I could feel it eating away at me. I hated that Sintra was a beautiful town and that the air was cleaner here than in England. I hated everything about this place. I'm sure I could think of more obscure things to hate if I thought about it long enough. I hated the doubt I could feel mixing with the jealousy. I could offer Laura more than him. I could be a good father to the babies. The babies…thinking about them stopped me up short. *Son of a bitch…they were* Easton babies. I felt rage beginning to boil inside me and I wished I could shut off my brain. Easton babies…*dammit*…it killed me to admit to myself that no matter who their father was…they were still Eastons. I rammed my fist down onto the top of the dashboard and cursed, making Peter jump and causing the car to swerve into the oncoming lane.

"Andrew! What's wrong, sir?" Peter shifted back into the right lane and looked at me. He was clearly rattled.

"Show me where they live and then let's go back to the ho-tel. I need to be alone for awhile," I said. I stared out the window at the endless trees that lined either side of the road. Peter drove on for a few more kilometers and slowed the car as we passed a long driveway. He pointed down the drive. "You can't see it from here but their house is down that drive."

"How do you know this?" I asked. He knew his way around here quite well.

"I've been here before, sir," he replied.

"Why?"

He looked at me and hesitated. "On business for your father."

"Say no more," I said. "I don't want to know. Let's go back to the hotel now." Peter drove on ahead and found a place to make a u-turn. As we approached the drive, we had to slow down for a car that was just pulling out of it. I slumped down in my seat and tried to make out the passengers inside the large SUV. Was Laura in that car? I couldn't tell. Peter kept a safe distance and we followed the car for a while. Eventually the vehicle turned onto a major highway that had airport signs posted along the berm. *They must be going to get Tristan now*, I thought. Peter drove back into Sintra and we returned to the hotel. I felt anxious and my mood was sour. I had nervous energy that needed to be released and I considered going for a run. I remembered seeing a sign for a work-out room in the lobby and decided I would run on the treadmill for a while. That should help calm me down— that and finding a pub. I could use a drink or two. Back in the room I changed into a pair of sweatpants and told Peter I was going to work out and then go out for a bite of food. He gave me a strange look and it dawned on me that he was suspicious of me—Peter didn't trust me. *He's right to feel that way*, I thought. I wasn't sure I trusted myself either—I wasn't sure what I was capable of if push came to shove. Peter went to his own room and I went to find a treadmill. As I ran in place, I couldn't help but see the irony in the fact that my life was just like this damned treadmill—that I was going nowhere fast.

Chapter Eight

STAKING CLAIMS

MIGUEL

I had not spent a lot of time with Tristan Easton in the past, although back in Rhode Island we'd had occasion to talk a few times to discuss Princess Gabriela's curse and the king's decree. We had been in agreement then and still were, in the most obvious of ways, that killing me was not an option. If Tristan had been so inclined at the time, there was a fifty-fifty chance that he would have ended up dead because I wouldn't have gone down without a fight. As it turned out, Tristan was an honorable man, and lucky for me, the complete opposite of his father. But Andrew…well…the jury was still out on him and that was something I needed to discuss privately with Tristan when the opportunity presented itself. Antonio and Catarina were just pulling into the driveway with Tristan now and Laura was beside herself with excitement. I pushed away the jealousy that Tristan's arrival was stirring up inside of me and walked with her outside onto the front porch as the car slowed to a stop.

Tristan's attendant, Ronald, exited the car first and went around to the trunk to get the wheelchair. He helped Tristan into it and he and Catarina came around the car to the ramp my brothers had built. Before he had a chance to move up the ramp, Laura was down the steps and in his arms, shrieking and crying.

"I can't believe you're here. I was afraid you would never want to see me again," she cried into his shoulder.

"Hey, hey…," Tristan said, brushing her hair out of her face and smiling at her. "Why wouldn't I want to see you again? You're one of my favorite people in the world. I've missed you—I've missed beating your sorry ass at chess." He smiled at her and she calmed down and moved behind his chair. She leaned down and kissed his cheek and began to push him up onto the porch. Catarina and Ronald followed and Antonio drove the car back to the garage. Laura stopped Tristan's chair in front of me and I looked down at him and smiled. I held out my hand and he took mine, gripping it hard.

"Welcome, Tristan," I said. "These two," I pointed at Laura and Catarina," "have been very anxious for you to get here."

Tristan laughed. "I get that a lot with women."

Catarina moved next to Laura and gently pushed her aside. "I'll take it from here," she said, taking possession and pushing the chair to the front door. I saw a flash of hurt pass over Laura's face as she moved out of the way. I swallowed my own jealousy and took her hand as we all went inside the house. My mother and Juana came out of the kitchen to meet Tristan and Ronald and we convened in the living room. Juana brought out coffee and tea and an assortment of small cakes and cookies and we ate and talked—sticking to safe subjects like sports and weather. I noticed Tristan looking at me and Laura, as if he were sizing us up as a couple, and I wondered what he was thinking. I was anxious to get him alone so I could ask more important questions. I didn't want to talk in front of Laura—I didn't want her to be stressed or worried about unknown factors. And then Catarina asked a question that adversely affected the tenor of the conversation.

"How is your father, Tristan?"

I felt Laura tense up next to me on the couch. Tristan glanced at her before answering, probably sensing that this wasn't the best time to discuss the Duke of Easton.

"He was supposed to go home from hospital today. But I

don't want to talk about him, if it's OK. I'm sure no one here wants to know anything about him and I understand that completely. I've cut ties with him anyway."

I nodded at him and looked at Laura. Her eyes were teary and I put my arm around her. Tristan wheeled his chair closer to her and reached for her hand.

"I'm so sorry, Laura...for everything. I'm ashamed to be his son," Tristan spoke quietly.

And then my mother burst into tears and ran from the room. It happened so fast that her reaction didn't register with me immediately. Catarina jumped up and ran after her, shrugging her shoulders at me as she passed.

"I'm sorry. I've upset your mother, Miguel. Seeing me is a reminder of what my father did to Laura and your children. I should have thought of that before coming down here—about how my presence would affect her...and you, Laura."

"No, Tristan. I'm glad you're here. I needed to see you. I've missed you so much." Laura wiped her tears and turned to me. "Maybe you should make sure your mother's OK, Miguel. I'm worried about her."

"Alright. I'll be back." I squeezed her hand and left them alone. I had no idea why my mother had reacted so passionately to Tristan's words, but I knew Catarina would take care of her for the moment. Right now I wanted to hear Laura's and Tristan's conversation. I was fairly certain I knew what they would talk about and already I could feel my blood pressure rising along with my annoyance. I stood in the hallway just outside the living room and listened.

"Tristan...how he is...how is Andrew?" Laura's voice was soft and filled with emotion.

"Oh, Laura." I heard Tristan sigh. "He's messed up right now. He's not really thinking straight, as you can imagine."

I heard her sharp intake of breath. "I want you to know that I've never blamed him for any of this. I'm sure he thinks I hate him and that I never want to see him again, but, Tristan, that's not the case. I care very much about him and I still feel love for him...but only in a friendship kind of way. From the very beginning of this nightmare I have always felt that Andrew was probably the biggest victim of your father's actions because he was so clueless and innocent and trusting. My heart aches for him."

"I know you care about him. And he has been a victim, no doubt about that, but right now he has one thought in mind… and that's getting you back. He believes the babies are his and he wants his family together and back home. He'll do anything…"

"Tristan…," I said, reentering the room and cutting him off. "I don't want Laura getting stressed out about this. Andrew can't win here. Surely he knows that."

"Were you eavesdropping just now?" Laura asked me, frowning.

"Yes, I was." I sat down in front of Tristan's chair and pulled Laura into my arms, holding her tightly to me. "I was planning to talk to you about…Andrew…privately…when we're alone," I said to him.

Laura tried to move away from me but I held her tighter. I could see that she was upset with me and I could hear it in her tone when she spoke.

"I don't want any more secrets. If you have something to say about Andrew, you can say it in front of me. I have a right to know." She was angry now and I needed to calm her down.

I removed my arm from around her and grabbed her hands to prevent her from getting up. "I can't have you wondering what he's going to do and stressing about your safety." I looked into her eyes—they were a darker blue than I had ever seen them and I could see that she was ready to battle me over this.

"Andrew would never hurt me, Miguel. I bet if I just had a chance to sit down and talk to him, I could make him see…"

"No!" Both Tristan and I said the word at the same time. Tristan continued.

"Laura…I told you, Andrew's not exactly in his right mind at the moment. He's been drinking a lot lately and his temper is…well…volatile, to say the least."

"It's out of the question. You and…*Andrew*…will not be having any conversations alone or in a crowd full of people," I said to her. I got up then and paced around the living room. I wanted to ask Tristan if there was any chance that Andrew could show up here but I didn't want to ask in front of Laura.

Catarina came back into the room then. I raised an eyebrow at her.

"Sofia said she was upset thinking about what had happened to Laura and worried about the stress it had on the babies. She's OK now. She's resting and will see us later at dinner."

"Should I go check on her?" I asked.

"No, she wants to be alone. We'll see her at dinner," repeated Catarina. "Why don't I show Tristan where he'll be sleeping and let him freshen up?" She went to stand behind the wheelchair, placing a hand on Tristan's shoulder. He placed his hand on top of hers and squeezed gently.

I could see that Catarina wanted to be alone with him and I wanted to talk to Laura anyway. I nodded and remained silent until they had left the room. Laura went to move past me, heading toward the stairs but I stopped her, taking her hand in mine. "Where are you going?"

"Upstairs." She rubbed a hand over her stomach and then began to massage her lower back.

"What's wrong?" I asked. I took her in my arms and began to rub her back. She sighed and sagged against me.

"My back hurts," she said. "I think I want to lie down for a little while before we eat. You coming?" She stepped away from me and headed up the stairs.

"I'll be up in a minute. I'm just going to get us some lemonade. You go on up."

I went into the kitchen and found Antonio drinking coffee with Ronald. "Just the people I wanted to see," I said as I went to the refrigerator to get our drinks. "I'm worried about Andrew suddenly showing up here. I am not opposed to sitting down and having a conversation with him about everything that's happened, but I do not want him anywhere near Laura." I focused my gaze on Ronald. "How well do you know him?"

He set his coffee cup down and glanced at me and Antonio. "I spend all of my time with Tristan so I don't know Andrew that well, but from what I've seen of him lately, I'd say he's an accident waiting to happen. He's a lot like his father—much as I hate to say it—at least when it comes to his temper and drinking. But unlike his father, I do believe he can be reasoned with. I've been very lucky not to have been involved in all of that mess. As a matter of fact, I was unaware of most of it until Tristan clued me in over the last couple of days. I want you to know that had I known, I would not have been a party to any of the duke's schemes. I am not a part of the security team. I was hired to tend to Tristan's medical and personal needs. I just want you to know that."

"Of course," I said. "Is it possible that Andrew could show up here without warning?"

Ronald hesitated and looked away toward the window. "I overheard Andrew tell Tristan that he intended to come here and get his wife and children back." He turned back to face me. "I wouldn't be surprised if he isn't on his way here now or even already here somewhere. He sounded very determined."

"*Dammit*," I cursed. "Antonio…"

"Say no more, Miguel. I'm on it. I'll go make sure the guys are on alert." He pushed his chair back from the table and put his cup in the sink.

"Antonio…if he shows up…I don't want him harmed if it can be helped. Are we clear?"

"Of course."

Antonio left through the back door and Ronald excused himself to go to his room. I pressed my hands against the countertop and leaned forward, closing my eyes. I tried to put myself in Andrew's shoes…to feel what he must be feeling…and I knew I couldn't blame him for wanting to claim what he believed was rightfully his. If the situation were reversed, I knew I would stop at nothing to get Laura back. I picked up our drinks and headed upstairs. I tried to push thoughts of Andrew out of my mind for the moment. He was a huge liability but there was always a chance that, as Ronald had said, he could be reasoned with. I walked into our room and found Laura sitting on the bed staring at her old cell phone, which someone had apparently returned to her without my knowledge.

"He called. Andrew called." She held up the phone.

I set the drinks down and walked over to her, taking the phone from her hand. "You didn't answer, did you?"

"No, it was a missed call. I never use this phone anymore.

The duke has it monitored."

"I'll get you a new one. We won't be needing this one anymore." I dropped it to the floor and stomped my foot down on it hard, enjoying the sound of the crunching metal underfoot. When I was satisfied that it was nothing more than a pile of wires, plastic and metal shards, I cleaned up the mess and threw it away. Laura didn't say anything nor had she moved a muscle as I'd destroyed the phone. I walked over to her and crawled up next to her on the bed. "How's your back?"

"It aches," she said. "But I can think of something that might make it feel better." She smiled and pulled me down beside her, pressing her lips against my neck. She kissed me along my jaw and then ran her hand down my chest.

"Are you sure this is a good idea? What if I make your back hurt worse?" I whispered against her cheek. I kissed her lips and tasted something sweet like vanilla frosting.

"If it hurts, I'll let you know, but right now, this is what I want." She slipped her hands inside my shirt and I groaned. I was helpless where this girl was concerned. I felt her passion building and I returned it equally. It was in moments like this when I felt truly sorry for Andrew Easton.

I was worried about Mama and decided to check on her before dinner. I found her in her room sitting by the window staring out at the gathering darkness.

"Mama? Can I come in? I knocked but you must not have heard me," I said as I pushed the door open.

"Of course, darling," She stood up and wrapped her sweater around herself. I noticed then how cold it was in the room.

"It's freezing in here. I'll check the heater when I go back downstairs," I said. "I just wanted to see if you're alright."

"I'm fine…I don't know what my problem was. I think I'm just missing your father. Alfonso would have loved the idea of being a grandfather, you know."

"Yes, I'm sure. He always loved kids, didn't he?" I walked over to her and embraced her. "Are you sure there's nothing else bothering you? Are you OK with Tristan's being here?"

"I'm happy for Cat that he's here and I can see how excited Laura is to have him here. I love having a lot of people in the house. Your brothers did a good job with that ramp, didn't they?" Her voice was sounding lighter now and I sensed she was coming out of her dark mood. But I didn't like her being holed up in her room alone and I told her so.

"It's almost time for dinner. Juana has been cooking all evening. Come down and have a drink with us, Mama. No more hiding in here, OK?" I smiled and took her hand. She nodded and followed me out into the hall. "You go on down and I'll see if Laura's ready for dinner."

She pulled me into a fierce hug then and whispered in my ear. "You know I love you no matter what, don't you, son?"

I stepped back to look at her face. She seemed as if I doubted her devotion to me. "Of course, Mama. Where is this coming from? What's bothering you?"

"Nothing, it's like I said…I'm just missing your father." She hugged me again and went downstairs. I walked down the hall, trying to shrug off the negative impulses that were causing me to feel anxious, and went into the bedroom to see if Laura was ready for dinner. I glanced around the room then into the walk-in closet but Laura wasn't there. *She must have gone downstairs*, I thought. As I headed for the door I caught sight of the talisman on the nightstand. I went over and picked it up. It wasn't like Laura to leave it lying around. When she wasn't wearing it, she always kept it in its pouch in her bag. As soon as I placed it in my palm, I felt it begin to heat up against my skin. I looked down at it and saw a reddish glow coming from it. My heart began to pound hard inside my chest. I had a bad feeling. Something was wrong. I dropped it back onto the nightstand and looked around the room.

"Laura?" I walked across the room to the adjoining bathroom and opened the door. Laura was slumped on the floor against the bathtub. I saw a pool of blood between her legs. I rushed to her and knelt down beside her. "Laura? Can you hear me?" She turned her head toward me. She was pale and her breathing was so quiet I could barely hear it. "I'll get help. Just hang on."

I dashed quickly through the bedroom and out into the hall and yelled for Antonio and Catarina.

"Get the car now! We need to get Laura to the hospital. Hurry!" I ran back to Laura and turned her face toward me. Her skin was like ice. "What happened, baby?" I grabbed a towel and put it between her legs.

"My back was hurting...I...felt a pain...and then a gushing sensation. I got dizzy and had to sit down. Did my water break?" She leaned forward and tried to look down.

"I don't think so. But we'll get you to the hospital. I'm going to carry you downstairs. Please tell me if I hurt you." As gently as I could I bent down and lifted her up off the floor. In spite of being pregnant with twins, she felt as light as a feather in my arms. "You're going to be fine, baby. I promise." I carried her through the bedroom and out into the hall. Mama and Catarina met me at the top of the steps.

"What happened?" ask Catarina. She was breathless and her eyes were wide with fright.

"I found her in the bathroom. She's bleeding. We need to hurry."

"I'll get a blanket," said my mother. She grabbed one from the hall linen closet.

I carried Laura downstairs and passed Tristan and my brothers in the hall. Their faces were grim, Tristan's especially. The front door was open and I was glad to see that Antonio already had the SUV out front and ready. I went down the porch steps and over to the car. Mother came behind me with the blanket. "I'll call as soon as I know something," I said over my shoulder. I settled Laura inside the car and wrapped the blanket over her and ran to the other side and got in. I spoke in Portuguese to Antonio and he revved the engine and tore down the driveway.

I held Laura in my arms. She was shivering and I saw tears falling down her cheeks. "Are you in pain, baby?" I asked her. She shook her head no and clung to me. Seeing her like this was more than I could bear. I told Antonio to hurry and he stepped on the gas. The hospital wasn't far—we would be there in just a few minutes but it felt like it was taking too long.

"Am I losing the babies?" she cried against my chest. "Are

they going to be OK?"

"Sh…sh…, *minha querida*. It's going to be fine. Don't talk. You're safe." Antonio pulled into the hospital parking lot and stopped in front of the emergency room doors. I jumped out and came around the car, taking Laura into my arms. We passed through the automatic doors and I didn't bother waiting for someone to tell me where to take her. I charged straight down the corridor and entered the first empty room I came to. A nurse followed after me and said a few choice words about breaching protocol but I stopped her speech and did something I didn't do very often. I used my royal status to get immediate attention. We spoke in Portuguese as I lay Laura on a table and tried to calm her shaking body. "It's OK, baby. The doctor will be here soon. You're going to be fine. I love you."

"Don't leave me, please," she begged. I brushed the hair back out of her eyes and leaned into her. I felt like I couldn't get close enough, but my body was rigid with fear and uncertainty. After all she had been through to lose the twins now would be beyond cruel. I knew in my heart that if something went wrong, I would curse God and the Duke of Easton. I would not let him live if something happened to Laura or my children.

A doctor and a nurse came into the room and began to speak to Laura in Portuguese. I interrupted them, also in my native tongue. "She's American. Do you speak English?" I asked. I stepped back to give them room.

"Not much," the doctor responded. "You can translate?"

I nodded and he began to ask me questions which I translated for Laura. She told me about her backache and feeling dizzy and then a gushing sensation which she thought was her water breaking. I repeated it to the doctor and he nodded and began his exam. I waited impatiently in the corner watching as he poked and prodded her. The nurse took her blood pressure and temperature and started an IV. She took several vials of blood from the other arm. Laura was quiet during the exam, her eyes closed. The doctor spoke to the nurse and she nodded then went to the phone to place a call. I heard her calling for an obstetrician to report to the room. Another nurse brought in a fetal heart monitor and hooked it up. Within seconds we heard the distinct sounds of beating hearts and Laura opened her eyes. She began to cry and the relief I felt was palpable. I moved over to stand beside her as the doctor studied the monitor. He spoke to me and waited for me to translate.

"He said the babies' heartbeats are strong. Your blood pressure is high. He wants a urine sample." My mind raced as I tried to remember everything he had said. "Another doctor is coming in to see you—an obstetrician."

Laura nodded and reached for my hand. I took hers and jumped at its iciness. I asked the nurse for a blanket. She also brought a cup for Laura's urine sample and a gown for her to change into. They left us alone so Laura could change her clothes and I waited outside of the bathroom while she obtained her sample. A few minutes later she was back in the bed and I covered her with the blanket.

I leaned over her and pushed the hair off of her forehead and kissed it, letting my lips linger near her temple. "Are you in pain?" I asked her.

"I have a dull ache in my back but it's tolerable," she whispered. "But do you hear that? Their hearts sound so strong. They're such tough little cookies, aren't they?"

I smiled against her mouth and kissed her. "Yes, they are, and so are you."

The door opened and the obstetrician entered. I translated for her as she performed her exam. She conducted an ultrasound and I saw the twins for the first time on the screen. She pointed them out to me and I was not prepared for the way the sight of them affected me. I gripped Laura's hand tightly and swallowed a lump of emotion. She looked at me and smiled and it took all I had not to shed a tear. I turned back to the doctor as she explained that the bleeding had occurred because one of the placentas was lying lower than normal. As I translated all of this to Laura, I hoped she couldn't hear the emotion in my voice.

"She wants to see your lab results before she comes to any conclusions. She says you're going to need bed-rest—either here or at home."

"Not here!" Laura cried. "I'll go crazy in here."

"Just wait, sweetheart, until she's finished. Maybe it won't come to that."

The doctor excused herself to go check on the lab tests. I stood next to Laura and gently rubbed her belly as we listened to the monitor beep. She fell into a light sleep and as I watched her, I was struck by how delicate she was—her translucent skin, a hint of pink in her cheeks in spite of her general pallor, her hair like golden stalks of wheat and her hands small and dainty. Even in sickness I found her mesmerizing.

The doctor returned with the test results. She explained them to me and I translated for Laura. "She says you're experiencing pre-term labor and also she's concerned about your kidneys because," I asked the doctor to repeat a technical term, "you have high levels of creatinine in your urine. She wants to admit you for a couple of days to monitor you and stop the labor with medication. She'd ordering a kidney function test and, if everything goes well, she will let you go home, provided you take it easy."

Laura nodded. She seemed to take the doctor's diagnosis in stride. The doctor and I had a conversation in Portuguese that I did not translate for Laura. She explained to me that it was imperative to keep Laura's blood pressure under control with rest and proper nutrition so the babies could stay inside of her as long as possible. If they were to be born now, more than likely they would not survive. She asked me to look over some paperwork and sign the admission forms. I did not bother to inform the doctor that I was not authorized, technically, to sign anything—I just did it anyway. And then I played the royalty card again, introducing myself as a member of the House of Braganza. She assured me we would be taken care of quickly. She left the room and an attendant came in almost immediately to take Laura to a private room. Within ten minutes we were settled into a room on the fourth floor.

"I'm going to call home and give everyone an update, *minha querida*. And I will have Catarina come soon with food for you. I think you'll be happier with Juana's food rather than the hospital's." I smiled at her as I dialed Cat's cell phone number. We had a brief conversation in Portuguese and I hung up the phone, turning my attention back to Laura. I let out a deep sigh as I settled myself into the seat next to her bed.

"You OK, Dad?" she asked softly.

I laughed. "Yes…no…I don't know. They're not even here yet and already I feel old and tired. How are you feeling? Are you thirsty?"

"I'm parched. I'd kill for a glass of water. And don't even talk to me about feeling old and tired," she said, grinning.

I chuckled at her comment. "Glass of water coming right up." I left the room and went in search of ice cubes and water. When I returned, Laura was trying to get out of the bed.

"Laura, what the hell are you doing?" I asked harshly.

"I've gotta go again," she said. "They must be pushing on my bladder."

"Well, if you need to get up, you tell me first, OK?"

I helped her to the bathroom and waited outside the door. Once she was back in bed I pulled my chair up close to her and held her hand. Catarina, Tristan and my mother came to visit and brought food for both of us. They stayed for a while and kept us company and not long after they left Laura fell asleep. I felt myself getting sleepy and when a nurse came in to check Laura's IV bag, she showed me how to turn my chair into a bed and brought me a blanket and a pillow. It wasn't the most comfortable bed I'd ever slept in, but it was a small price to pay to be with Laura. As far as I was concerned, there was no price I wouldn't pay for her safety and well-being. I knew there had been a time not so long ago when Andrew Easton had sat on one of these chairs in a hospital room next to her and had felt the same anxiety I now felt. It seemed I had an awful lot in common with Andrew Easton. We weren't so different after all.

The Shadow King

Chapter Nine

ANOTHER BIRTHDAY

LAURA

"Do you want to call your parents?" Miguel asked me.

His attentiveness was so sweet—he seemed to know exactly what I needed without my having to say a word. Earlier I had watched him sleeping in the chair next to me and I was amazed at his beauty. He would probably be horrified to know that I thought he was beautiful—it probably didn't sound very macho—but it was still the truth. He was beautiful. It made me wonder what Felipe and Gabriela would look like. I hoped they had his dark hair and eyes.

"I want to, yes, but I know my mother. It was hard enough to keep her away when I left Andrew. She'll want to come for sure now." I felt guilty saying his name—I never knew how Miguel would react when Andrew came up in conversation. But this time, he didn't even flinch.

"You don't have to keep your family away, sweetheart. They're always welcome. We have plenty of room at the house for them."

"Oh, I know. It isn't that I don't want them to come—I do. I miss my family so much. But…it's just…" I stopped, afraid to bring up the subject again.

"What, baby? Why the hesitation?" Miguel had been stand-ing by the window watching the rain come down in sheets. Now he came over and sat in the chair next to my bed. He took my hand and tenderly kissed a spot beside the IV site.

"I would hate for them to be here if something happens...I mean...with...Andrew."

Miguel looked away and began to work his jaw back and forth. I stayed quiet, not sure how mad I'd just made him. A nurse came in to check my vital signs and Miguel got up and moved out of her way. She said something to me which I didn't understand and he translated. Finally she left and he came back over to me.

"I'd like to say with certainty that nothing is going to hap-pen with Andrew, but I don't know that for sure. I would be willing to talk to him, but I know that isn't what he wants. And what he wants he can never have, so we have to wait this out for a while. But I want you to know that your family is always welcome."

"Thank you. I'll call home and tell Mom I'm just a little under the weather. But I won't tell her I'm in the hospital. That would freak her out. Can I do it now? What time is it in Rhode Island?"

"How much value does your family place on sleep?" Miguel laughed. He looked at his watch. "It's the middle of the night there."

"Later, then," I said, breathing a sigh of relief. I had a feel-ing that just hearing my mother's voice would set me off on a crying jag anyway and I knew I had to stay calm for the babies' sakes, as well as for my own.

An attendant came into the room then and told Miguel it was time for me to go for tests in another department of the hos-pital. She disconnected the monitors and Miguel helped me into a wheelchair. I wanted him to come with me but I suspected he was exhausted and needed more rest.

"Why don't you stay here and nap for a while? Or you could have someone pick you up. I'd bet you'd love a shower and a chance to sleep in a real bed," I said, noticing the dark circles under his eyes.

"No. I'm not leaving you. You need a translator, remember?" He grinned at me and we started down the hallway, following the attendant to the elevator. On the sixth floor we entered an area called *nefrologia* and though I didn't know Portuguese, I knew a reference to kidneys when I saw one. I was nervous and unsure of what to expect but the tests were no more than giving more blood and urine and having a specialized ultrasound. Miguel stayed by my side and translated the doctor's words and it was over quickly. We went back to the room and found Tristan and Catarina waiting for us. They'd brought a picnic basket of food and the sight of it made my mouth water in anticipation.

"Hey, hospital queen. How're you feeling today?" asked Tristan, a big grin on his face. "You know, you spend more time in hospitals than I do and I'm the crippled one."

I couldn't help but laugh. "No kidding. This is getting old." I stared at the picnic basket and my stomach growled loudly enough for everyone to hear.

"Someone's hungry," Catarina said, smiling. She unwrapped some bread and fixed me a plate of food. "What do the doctors have to say?"

Miguel explained what was happening and we spent the next hour talking and eating. I was relieved to notice that the ache in my back had slowly faded and I felt downright buoyant. I wanted out of this place—into the fresh air. I glanced out the window and saw that the rain had stopped and the sun was now shining. I smiled to myself and sighed contentedly. I didn't know why, but I suddenly felt—good. I noticed Miguel watching me, his eyes heavy-lidded, and I raised an eyebrow at him. "What?" I asked, feeling a little embarrassed.

"Nothing…just watching you…wondering what's making you smile like that," he said. He slid closer to me and took my hand. "You're feeling better…?"

Before I could answer, Tristan's phone rang. He reached into his shirt pocket and pulled it out. I saw him frown when he looked at the screen. "Excuse me," he said, and wheeled himself out into the hall.

"You're looking better," Catarina said. "Which reminds me-

-your birthday is this week. I hope you're out of here before then."

"I do feel better. The babies are active today, too. Do you want to feel them?" As soon as I asked, I feared I'd caused her pain, knowing what she'd told me about her inability to have children of her own. But she smiled and came over to the bed and held out her hand to me. I placed it low on the right side of my abdomen and within seconds, Felipe...or Gabriela...nudged against me into Catarina's hand.

"Whoa," she gasped, her eyes big. "What does it feel like inside? It must be weird, like an alien invasion or something."

Miguel leaned down and kissed me and placed his hand on my stomach. He, too, felt the nudge and grinned. "What did you call them? Tough little cookies? I like that expression." He removed his hand and walked to the door. "I'm going to find a cup of coffee. I'll be back in a few minutes."

Catarina and I talked for a while and finally Tristan and Miguel returned together. As soon as they walked in the door I could tell something was up—something had changed in the short amount of time they'd been out of the room. Though they both tried to act nonchalant, I knew something was amiss.

"Everything OK?" I asked, looking from one to the other.

"Fine. But the coffee here is terrible," said Miguel. He had a plastic cup in his hand. He poured it out into the sink in the corner of the room and then rinsed out the sink, tossing the cup in the trash.

A nurse came in a few minutes later and Tristan and Catarina got ready to leave. Tristan had been quiet since his phone call and I'd wanted to ask who it was but I knew it wasn't any of my business. They both kissed me good-bye and left. It was an abrupt departure and it left me feeling anxious. Miguel sat down beside me and leaned his head back against the seat. He closed his eyes but his body was tense and rigid.

"Miguel...?" He opened his eyes and looked at me. "What's going on? Who called Tristan?" He didn't answer right away. I gave him ten seconds and asked again. "Who called Tristan?" He must have sensed the anxiety in my voice because he leaned forward and sighed, his expression dark.

"It's nothing for you to worry about. You're finally feeling better—let's not spoil it."

"Tell me." My heart began to race in my chest and I knew I had to control myself. Getting worked up wasn't good for me or the babies. I took a calming breath. "Please…Miguel."

"It was Andrew. He called…asking about you. Wanting to know if Tristan had talked to you…if you were OK."

I felt a sense of relief. That didn't sound so bad. My heartbeat returned to normal and I allowed myself to relax. It was understandable that he would call to inquire about me. "Is that all he wanted? To ask about me?" I wanted to make sure there was nothing else. I didn't want to be in the dark—I'd spent far too much time there as it was.

"That's all, *minha querida*…nothing for you to worry about." He pulled the picnic basket closer and looked inside. "I'm hungry. Can I get you anything else? This looks good," he said, pulling out a container of chicken and vegetables.

I stayed quiet while he ate. I wanted to believe him when he said there was nothing to worry about but I had my doubts. As he ate I saw him relax and I decided that everything was fine. But I did wonder about something. "Did Tristan tell him that I'm in the hospital?"

Miguel swallowed a bite of chicken and wiped his mouth with a napkin. He shook his head. "No, thank goodness. The last thing we need is for Andrew to show up here causing problems."

I didn't say anything, but I felt a stabbing in my heart for Andrew. I ached for him but I knew Miguel would never understand. He didn't get that I cared about Andrew—that I wanted—needed—to know that Andrew was going to be OK. I remembered the phone that Miguel had destroyed and I felt badly about it now. If I had a phone I would call Andrew myself and tell him that I was fine and that I loved him—as one friend loves and cares about the welfare of another—and that everything was going to be OK. I would tell him how sorry I was about the way things had turned out and that he didn't deserve any of this. I would ask his forgiveness for betraying him with Miguel even though it wasn't really my fault. I would say anything to alleviate his emotional pain so that he could heal. These thoughts raced through my head as I thought about Andrew and the destroyed phone. There was no need to sit around waiting for Andrew to do something irrational when I had the power to prevent it. I could ask him to come to me and we could talk calmly and work through the pain and somehow find a way to maintain our friendship. I resolved in that instant that as soon as I was out of the hospital I would contact him and arrange a meeting. It would be hard since I was never alone but I would find a way.

"What are you thinking about?" asked Miguel. "You suddenly went somewhere far away."

"Nothing. Just…maybe I'll take a nap. I'm a little sleepy."

Miguel finished his food and put the leftovers away. He settled into his chair and within a few moments I heard his even, rhythmic breathing. I watched him sleep and thought about Andrew. Andrew—who was so sweet and also beautiful in his own way—so innocent and trusting. He'd had a great disservice inflicted upon him and I wanted to make it right. I pushed away the guilt that was pecking at my conscience, knowing I had no reason to feel it. I would fix this somehow—for Andrew—I would try to find a way for him to be happy again. No one deserved it more.

I was discharged on my birthday and allowed to go home as long as I promised to take it easy and rest as much as possible. The medications I had been given had stopped the pre-term labor and my kidneys were functioning, but not as optimally as the doctors would have preferred. I would have to go in for weekly check-ups and stay calm and relaxed to help maintain a healthy blood pressure. *I can do this*, I thought as we arrived at the house. But my blood pressure nearly went through the roof when I walked inside to the surprise that awaited me.

"Surprise!" Mateo and Tomas, Antonio and Ronald, Tristan and Catarina, Juana and Sofia and a couple of other cousins I'd met but whose names I'd forgotten greeted me loudly as I crossed the threshold. Someone had hung colorful streamers and balloons all over the front hall and I saw a pile of presents on the coffee table by the sofa in the living room. I smelled cake and coffee and something savory, too.

"Wow!" I looked at Miguel. "Were you in on this? How is this helping to keep my blood pressure normal?" I grinned, as he pulled me into his arms and kissed me.

"Happy nineteen, baby," he said. "But you can't blame me for this. It was all those two." He pointed at Tristan and Catarina. "I hear the cake is pretty spectacular."

We gathered around the coffee table and I settled into the couch. Catarina was anxious for me to open my gifts so I dived into the pile. I was so touched at the gorgeous navy sweater from Catarina, a brand new chess set from Tristan—that one had made me laugh--and a silver bracelet from Sofia. Mateo and Tomas gave me two teddy bears—one white and one brown—for the babies--and that had made me tear up. I was quite overwhelmed by the surprise and the gifts and I burst into tears.

"Thank you all so much," I said, knowing I sounded like a blubbering idiot. Someone handed me a tissue and I blew my nose and composed myself. And then Miguel turned to me and took my hand.

"You haven't opened my gift yet," he said. He pulled a box from his pocket and set it in my hand. "And before I forget, let's get this back where it belongs." He reached his hand toward Catarina and she handed him my talisman. He placed it over my head and I looked down at it, nestled against my chest. I felt better already just having it on. I looked down at the box and untied the white ribbon that held it closed. I removed the lid and inside there was a velvet box. I couldn't imagine what could be inside of it. Miguel had given me so much already—my gorgeous earrings and the sapphire ring that I wore on my left hand. Plus I had my talisman. I opened the box and was perplexed at what I found inside. It was a key—the old-fashioned kind, big in size, and heavy, with a rounded end. I took it from the box and held it up.

"The key to your heart?" I asked, making a joke.

Miguel smiled and shook his head. "No. You don't need a key for that, *minha querida*."

Sofia coughed and Catarina shifted nervously in her seat. I

looked around at the expectant faces and felt butterflies taking flight in my stomach. Clearly everyone else had already been clued in. I looked at the key again—at its grooves and markings. It was gold and somewhat weighty for a key. Then I had a funny thought, which in retrospect I should've kept to myself, but I blurted it out anyway. "Is it the key to the kingdom?" I giggled nervously.

My joke was met with silence and shifting glances. *Uh, oh...that didn't go over well*, I thought. I turned to Miguel, my face reddening. "I was joking—really."

"But you are correct," he said, his voice suddenly serious. "It *is* the key to the kingdom...in a manner of speaking. It's actually the key to the city of Sintra, your home now. I want you to have it. And now I'd like to introduce you to the mayor of Sintra."

I gasped and felt my face go pale. I'd just gotten out of the hospital and I needed a real shower and better clothes before meeting the mayor. This wasn't good. My stomach twisted as I leaned toward Miguel and spoke in a whisper. "I'm not looking my best right now...I can't meet the mayor today, Miguel." I looked around nervously wondering where the mayor was hiding. Mateo and Tomas began to laugh. Sofia got up and came over to sit beside me.

"Laura, meet Sofia Dos Santos de Braganza, the mayor of Sintra," said Miguel.

Sofia took my hand and smiled at me. I was truly confused and she could certainly tell.

"Honorary mayor, I should clarify," she said to me. "My husband, Alfonso, was the honorary mayor of Sintra and at the time of his death his title was passed on to me. We are so thrilled to welcome you into our family, Laura. Alfonso left the key for Miguel in his will and we both thought you would like to have it as a welcome gift, not only into our family, but also into our city as well. This key affords you a lot of privileges. One of these days, Miguel can read you the list. How does free parking sound?"

We all burst into laughter at that and I shook my head in wonder at these people. I had the key to the city. Wow. "This is the most unusual gift I've ever received. I'm not sure what to do with it, but I absolutely love it."

Juana brought the cake in then and I blew out all nineteen candles as they sang the Portuguese version of 'happy birthday' to me. The cake was delicious—vanilla with butter-cream icing-- and I ate two pieces. Tristan held up my new chess set and wiggled his eyebrows at me. "Just say the word, Laura…just say the word."

I laughed and nodded at him. "Later…Easton…you're mine," I threatened. He and Catarina put their heads together and whispered to one another. I saw him take her hands in his and kiss her palms and I looked away. I felt my cheeks redden at the sight of them together this way.

Miguel leaned over and whispered in my ear. "I have another present for you, but you'll have to wait till we're alone for it." He kissed my jaw and I closed my eyes briefly. I had to force myself to suppress the desire his words sparked inside me. This was proving to be the best birthday ever in my life. Or it was until Carmen appeared.

She burst through the door, coming from the kitchen, and stopped, her eyes scanning the room. She saw the cake and the presents and all of us together and I felt the familiar pangs of guilt cut through me. She settled her gaze on me and saw the key I was holding in my hand. She stared at it, then at me and Miguel, who sat tensed at my side. And then she burst into tears and turned around, leaving as fast as she had come in. A second later we heard the kitchen door slam.

Juana jumped up and spoke in Portuguese to Sofia and Miguel and left abruptly. The twins looked at each other, embarrassed. They got up, too, and left with Antonio. Catarina shrugged at Miguel and she and Tristan went out onto the porch. Sofia turned to Ronald.

"Would you like to take a walk in the vineyard?" she asked him. It was obvious that Ronald had no clue what had just happened. As they walked toward the front door, Sofia turned back to Miguel and said something to him in Portuguese. She smiled at me, wished me a happy birthday and left with Ronald. Miguel and I were now alone.

"Wow. What a way to clear a room," I said in a whisper. "What the hell just happened?"

Miguel looked uncomfortable--angry. He got up and paced around the room. "I'm sorry about that, Laura. I hope you won't let...Carmen...ruin your birthday homecoming."

"What did your mother say to you just now before she left?"

Miguel hesitated. His look was guarded. I sensed he didn't want to answer my question. "She just said she would talk to Juana—that we needed to get the situation taken care of."

"Is that all?"

He came over to me then and pulled me to my feet. He cupped my face in his hands and kissed me tenderly. "That's all. What would you like to do now? Would you like to rest, watch a movie, read?"

I forced Carmen from my mind and concentrated on Miguel's hands on my face. I kissed him again and concentrated on his lips, too. "I'd like to take a shower and get this hospital funk off of me and then how about you give me my other birthday present? Although I don't see how it can top getting the key to the city." I turned my face into his hand and kissed his palm.

"We'll see about that," he grinned slyly. He took my hand and we went upstairs. He left me alone to shower and change. It felt so good to be clean. I felt the babies move and I massaged the place where I felt them pushing against me. I noticed that I had stretch-marks now and I frowned. I rubbed some lotion into them but it was useless. I wondered if my body would ever be the same after I gave birth to these babies. I shook my head as I dressed in clean pants and a blouse that I had trouble buttoning over my stomach. *Oh boy*, I thought. *I'm going to have to go shopping again for new clothes.* I combed the tangles out of my wet hair and brushed my teeth and thought again about calling home. And then I remembered that I wanted to call Andrew. Miguel had said he would get me a new phone. Maybe tomorrow we could go shopping for clothes and a cell phone. I would let him pay for the phone but this time I would insist on using my own money to buy clothes. Miguel would just have to set aside his pride and let me contribute. I heard him come back into the room and I stepped out of the bathroom. He was standing inside the door looking incredibly gorgeous. Sometimes he took my breath away.

"Hey," I said. "I'm all clean. But look at this." I pointed to my middle buttons which I couldn't fasten. "I'm going to need more clothes. This blouse won't button over my fat gut."

He laughed and came to me, rubbing his hand over my stomach. "You don't need this blouse anyway," he said, unbuttoning the couple of buttons I had been able to fasten. He slipped it off my shoulders and looked at my body. I felt self-conscience and turned away from him, blushing. "Hey…what is it?" he asked coming up behind me.

"You must think I'm an elephant. I'm huge."

"I think you're beautiful is what I think," he whispered against my cheek. He lifted the wet hair off of my neck and kissed my shoulders. His lips were so soft on my skin like flower petals. I sighed and turned into his arms. I pressed my mouth against his, pushing my tongue against his lips, in search of his. He tasted so amazing. I felt myself swoon, literally, and fell into him as he hugged me as close as my stomach would allow. He said something in Portuguese—someday I would have to ask him what he was saying to me in moments like these, but right now, I just liked the way it sounded. He stopped kissing me suddenly and pulled slightly away. "Laura?"

"Yes?" He'd suddenly gone all serious on me. I noticed that his eyes were troubled. Something was on his mind.

"I was afraid that I had caused what happened to you the other day—your pain and bleeding. I was afraid I'd hurt you…"

"No, it wasn't you. My back was already hurting. You've never hurt me…that way. Quite the opposite actually," I said, pulling him back against me.

"Well, I asked the doctor about it." He sounded shy now and I was touched at his concern.

"And?" I hoped the doctor wasn't about to rain on my birthday parade.

"She said…under normal circumstances it isn't usually a problem, but in your case, pre-term labor and bleeding—it might not be a good idea. I don't want to hurt you."

I tried to maintain a poker face. "So that other birthday present you mentioned…it was just a tease then?" I swallowed my disappointment and tried to act like it didn't matter.

"No. I do have a present for you. I asked Catarina to get it for me. But I guess calling it a present is a bit of a stretch since I already told you I'd get you one." He reached into his pants pocket and pulled out a cell phone—an iPhone5.

"Whoa. For me?" I asked, excited. This phone made my old one look like a dinosaur.

"You needed a new one since I destroyed yours the other day. While you were in the shower I programmed a few numbers into it. And the code to access it is your birthday—1212."

I took the phone from him and looked it over. "Wow. I love it…but…"

"But?"

"I admit I'm a little disappointed that it wasn't something else." I put on the best pout I could muster, hoping it would work its charm.

He chuckled and raised an eyebrow at me. "I'm disappointed, too, but I won't risk your health. You're too precious to me. But just because we can't do that, it doesn't mean we can't do this." And then he swept me into his arms, kissing me hard. I groaned against him and returned his kiss with equal fervor. As I lost myself in his embrace, I knew I would have to savor this kiss. I had a feeling it was all I was going to get for a while.

Chapter Ten

FORMING ALLIANCES

ANDREW

I knew Laura had been in the hospital. I had Peter to thank for letting me know. He'd found out from Ronald who let the information slip accidentally when Peter had called him to check on Tristan per my father's non-existent request. Peter had to physically restrain me to keep me from going to the hospital to see her. I was her husband and I had every right to be there but I reluctantly admitted that Dos Santos would never have let me near her. But I was determined to see her no matter what Peter had to say about my methods for doing so. I had half a mind to fire him, not that it was within my power, but it would have been so nice to think I could. I'd called Tristan but I didn't let on that I knew Laura was sick. I didn't want him to know I was in Sintra—not yet anyway. I'd driven past the Dos Santos compound several times—unsure what I was looking for or what I expected to happen—but knowing she was with him was messing with my head. And today was her birthday. *I should be with her*, I thought. *This isn't right.* And now I drove the BMW past the driveway again and pulled the car over to the side of the road. I was alone, having eluded Peter, and I was contemplating driving up to the house, their security be damned. It was getting dark but the sun had not completely set. The sky was tinged with red to the west and the temperature had dropped considerably. I adjusted the heater and was about to drive off when a dark-haired girl ran out from the trees and stopped at the end of the drive. I could see her in the rearview mirror. She saw my car and hesitated, then looked in both directions. I wanted to get out of the car and talk to her but I didn't want to scare her off, so I waited. I saw her approaching the passenger side from the side-view mirror. She looked like she was crying or had been recently. I rolled the window down and waited. She came closer to the car but kept her distance from the door. She leaned down and looked at me.

"Are you lost?" she asked, her accent thick. She had her hands in her jacket pockets and I hoped she didn't have a weapon hidden in there.

I hesitated. *Was I lost?* That was one hell of a loaded question. "No...yes...I don't know. Do you need a ride somewhere?" If that question didn't send her running back up the driveway, none would.

"You're English," she said, leaning down for a closer look at me. She said it as a statement rather than a question.

"You're Portuguese," I responded. *Brilliant comeback, Easton.* She gave me a look of disdain. I noticed her tear-stained cheeks and red nose. Something—or someone—had clearly ruined this girl's day.

She stepped a little closer to the car. I saw her hands moving around inside her pockets. I swallowed visibly. Dos Santos had a sister but this was not her. I had seen his sister—the object of Tristan's affection—and though this girl resembled Catarina, they were two different people. Maybe she was a member of their security. I was just working up the nerve to ask her name when she beat me to the punch.

"Who are you?" she asked.

I didn't answer immediately. I studied her face, trying to read her expression. She was guarded, obviously, and wary. I decided to go with the truth.

"Andrew Easton. I'm Laura's husband."

She straightened and looked away down the road. I heard her let out a slow, deep breath. She came closer to the door and stared me down. ""What are you doing here?"

Again I decided to go with the truth. "I'm here to get my wife back."

A half-smile formed on her face. I noticed then that she was quite pretty—her facial features tiny and doll-like, her hair long and dark. She placed her hand on top of the door and said something that caught me off guard. "Yes, I need a ride. Unlock the door."

I didn't even hesitate—it seemed as if the door unlocked of its own free will. She opened the door and crawled in beside me and buckled up her seatbelt. She turned to face me and introduced herself. "I'm Carmen Madeira. Maybe I can help you." She pressed the button closing the window. "I'm Miguel's fiancée and I want *him* back."

She directed me to the main highway and we headed south. Off in the distance I saw the Atlantic Ocean. It was quite dark now but the water glistened in the light of a nearly full moon. I had a sense that in another life I could like this place. She didn't talk much at first other than to give me directions. After we'd driven about thirty kilometers I started to get annoyed.

"Where are we going?" I asked, trying to keep my irritation under wraps.

"Take the next exit and follow the signs to Cascais," she said. "We'll be there soon."

I drove on in silence into the town of Cascais. Even in the darkness I could tell this town was picturesque. But as we skirted past Cascais the area changed. Carmen directed me into a run-down neighborhood—if you could call it that—of shacks and old cars. In some places tents were pitched along the side of the road. I saw dogs roaming around and through the car's vents I could smell the acrid scent of smoke.

"What is this place?" I asked her. I slowed the car, not sure where she wanted me to go. She pointed up the street to a parking lot and had me stop next to an abandoned building. Alarm bells began to sound in my head and I questioned my sanity for trusting this stranger.

"This is where I'm from. It's a gypsy community. I come here sometimes so I can remind myself where I came from and to make sure I don't ever end up back here—at least not permanently. I still have friends here and some family, though."

"Why did you bring me here?" I asked. I failed to see the relevance of mingling with gypsies. As far as I was concerned they were nothing but trouble.

"Miguel and his family saved me and my brother and our parents from this life. They took us in and gave us jobs and paid for my brother and me to go to university. They gave us everything we have." She turned to me then and I saw the tears in her eyes, sparkling in the moonlight. "They gave us everything and I know I don't dare ask for anything more...but...I want Miguel. He's mine. He said he went to study abroad—in America--but I've since learned the truth. And now he's home...with a pregnant girlfriend...? It isn't fair. He promised me we would be together—that he would come back to me and we would be married. Did you know he's a member of the Portuguese royal family?"

I laughed derisively. "Oh, yes. I'm well aware of his royal status. I'm more aware of it than he is." I glanced out the window. I could see a glow in the sky from a distant fire. "So... what...you're hoping to be Queen of Portugal someday?"

She made a clucking sound with her tongue. "The royal family of Portugal is in the shadows. They have no power. Miguel's mother would be the queen if they weren't, though. And one day, Miguel will be the shadow king." She shifted in her seat and unzipped her jacket. It was getting warm in the car so I turned the heater down. "But, yes, if the government ever brings the royal family out of the shadows, Miguel will be king and I am supposed to be his queen. But now that girl is here...and she's *pregnant*...I can't believe this."

I felt anger building and I fought to control it. "That *girl* is my wife and those babies are mine. Dos Santos thinks he has the upper hand now but he can't win. I have the law on my side. I came here to take my wife home and that what's I intend to do. How can you help with me that?"

She talked on as if she hadn't heard a word I'd said. "I know Miguel loves me. We were together for too long for him to just throw it all away for some pretty American blonde that he's known for all of five minutes. Look around and see where I come from. Look at this place." She opened her window and my nose was assaulted by the smoky air. She waved her arm at the abandoned building. "If I lose Miguel, I will end up back here. And I know he would never want that for me. But without him, I can't function. I won't be able to go to my home there because she will be there, rubbing it in my face that she has him and I don't. I can't be around him if he isn't mine and, yet…I can't *not* be around him. "

I didn't comment right away as I weighed her words. I understood her pain. I couldn't imagine my life without Laura. These last couple of weeks had confirmed that. But I still failed to see how we could help each other. "So what are you saying?"

She rolled the window up and leaned forward, staring into the darkness. "I can take you to her. And you could talk to her for me. Tell her Miguel is mine. Say whatever it takes to convince her to go back to you." She straightened in the seat and faced me. "She says Miguel is the father of her babies and yet you say you are. What is the truth?"

I sucked in a breath and turned away from her. This was a question that I'd pushed out of my head every time it came into my mind. How could I possibly know the truth until the babies were born? When had Laura been with Miguel? I thought back to the summer, trying to reason it out. We'd always been together. They had to be my children…there was no way they could be his. And then I remembered Laura's long morning walks in London—alone. Had she been meeting him somewhere? How was this possible? Security was supposed to have been watching her at all times. It couldn't be. The babies had to be mine. I got angry and pounded the steering wheel, hurting my hand in the process.

"*Dammit!*" I looked at Carmen. She was studying me with an expression of hopefulness—as if willing me to be sure of myself. It killed me to say the words. "I don't know the truth."

She said something in Portuguese that I didn't understand, but part of it sounded like profanity. And then she started to cry. *Bloody hell*, I thought. I reached out my hand to touch her arm but pulled it back. I didn't know how to help this girl. I couldn't even figure out my own life at the moment. I turned away from her and looked out the window. *Damn, this place is bleak*, I thought. Across the parking lot I watched as a dog tore something to pieces. I glanced around and was surprised at the absence of people. *Where are all the gypsies?* I wondered. I supposed I should be thankful we were alone out here. I glanced at Carmen. She seemed to be getting herself under control. She pushed her long hair out of her face and gave me a sidelong look.

"I'm sorry. I'm a bit of a mess right now. I'm usually stronger than this," she said, her voice quiet.

"It's OK. I know the feeling." I forced a smile. I felt sorry for the girl. My stomach growled and she heard it and let out a soft laugh.

"You need food," she said. "I know a place…if you're brave enough."

I raised an eyebrow at her. That sounded like a challenge. I wasn't entirely convinced I was up for one but what the hell. "How brave do I have to be to eat?" I asked her.

"Well, you're not afraid of a few gypsies are you?" She laughed again and pointed up the street. "There's a little place owned by some friends of mine just up the road. It might not be what you're used to up in England, but the food is good. And don't be afraid. Gypsies are actually good people—they're just misunderstood."

I nodded and pulled the car out onto the road and drove in the direction she indicated. We drove through an area of boarded up houses and tents and finally came to a dilapidated building that was apparently a restaurant. I pulled into the small parking lot that looked more like someone's driveway and parked, wondering if I'd still have a car when we came out. "Are you sure this is safe?" I asked.

She grinned and opened her door. "Don't worry, I'll protect

you." I heard the sarcasm in her voice as she chuckled to herself and got out. I followed her to the door and again questioned my powers of reasoning as we entered the building. It was dark and smoky inside. There were about a half dozen people sitting at tables and a couple of shady characters at the bar. The place smelled of grease and disinfectant. *Well, maybe they actually try to clean from time to time*, I thought as I followed Carmen to a table. We sat down and an elderly woman approached us and began an animated conversation with Carmen. I noticed the woman had wild gray hair, very few teeth and a lot of faded, sagging tattoos on her arms. Carmen apparently knew the woman well. She talked with a familiarity of someone who is a regular here. I studied Carmen as they talked. She was an interesting girl, to say the least. And now I was seeing a part of the world that until recently, I'd never known existed. I looked around the room, keenly aware that I was now the center of attention. My thoughts swirled as I waited for them to finish their conversation. I felt my stomach rumble again and wondered about the smell coming from the back of the place. Finally the woman left and Carmen turned her attention to me.

"Sorry. I haven't seen Marisela for awhile. We were catching up. She'll bring us Cokes and our meals in a few minutes."

"Don't they have menus?" I asked.

"There are no menus here. This is someone's home. You're in the salon now. She'll bring us whatever she made for her family today."

I raised my eyebrows. "They have tables and a bar in their salon?"

"Every gypsy home is different. They make do with what they have." She gave me a look then—as if sizing me up. "What about you? What's your home like in England?"

I leaned back in my chair and worked my jaw, wondering how much to say. I looked around the room, into the faces of the men staring at me and I felt somewhat ashamed of my station in life. Compared to the people in this room, I had the world in the palm of my hand—wealth, privilege, access. I had everything they didn't. But they didn't look unhappy. Of course, it may have been resignation I was seeing on their faces. I wondered how much to tell her. "I live in an apartment in London—it's nothing special. I go to university. That's about it."

She regarded me with curiosity. I waited for more questions as Marisela returned with two Cokes. I drank mine quickly, wondering if beer was an option on the non-existent menu. I suddenly wondered if Carmen knew more about me than she was letting on. If she did, she played her cards close to her chest.

"What are you studying in school?" she asked me.

"Pre-med. What about you? You mentioned earlier that you attended university."

"I'm an education major at the university in Lisbon. My dream is to teach these gypsy kids how to get out of poverty. I got out of here by chance, but most gypsies aren't so lucky."

Marisela arrived with our food. It was hot—I could see the steam rising from the two heaping dishes. She set a plate in front of me and the aroma hit my nose with a wham. It was some kind of seafood—I could smell the ocean pouring off of it. I watched as Carmen began to eat. She seemed to be enjoying it, so I picked up my fork and took a tentative bite. The fish melted on my tongue and I groaned audibly.

Carmen looked up from her plate and smiled. "It's good, yes?"

"Yes...very."

We ate in silence for a while and I was aware of the eyes of the other patrons on us. Every once in a while someone would come over and speak to Carmen. She asked Marisela for two more Cokes and more bread. I ate like a starving man. When we finished Marisela brought out dessert—two little cream tarts and they were equally delicious. The food was making me sleepy and I glanced at my watch. It was getting close to midnight and I was sure Peter would be wondering what I'd got up to. Carmen saw me look at my watch and signaled Marisela. They spoke and Marisela glanced down at me. I reached for my wallet but Carmen put her hand on my arm and stopped me.

"The meal is on the house," she said.

"But I should pay," I pulled out my wallet, reaching inside for some Euros.

"No, please. You're my guest tonight. Let's go." I shrugged

and thanked her and also Marisela who just gave me a semi-toothless grin and disappeared into a back room. Carmen and I walked outside. I was glad to see my rental car was where I'd left it. We drove back toward Sintra mostly in silence. She directed me back to the Dos Santos compound and I stopped the car in the same place I'd picked her up.

"Are you safe to walk the rest of the way?" I asked. "I'd take you all the way up the drive but I suspect there's a 'shoot on sight' order on my head."

"It's fine. I live in a cottage behind the main house. It isn't that far. But we need to exchange phone numbers."

"Oh, right." I opened my phone and typed in her number as she dictated. I texted her so she'd have mine then dropped my phone back into my pocket. "Thank you again for dinner. It was surprisingly excellent."

She laughed. "We gypsies are full of surprises. Good night, Andrew. I'll be in touch."

She disappeared up the dark driveway. I sat for a moment thinking about the strange evening I'd just had. It had been unexpected but not unwelcome. Carmen seemed like a nice enough girl and pretty in an exotic way. I felt sorry for her but I suspected if she knew that, she'd be insulted. She didn't seem like the type of person who tolerated pity. I still had no concrete idea how we could help each other, but I would wait it out a few days. If she could get me to Laura, maybe I could fix things for both of us. Just as I was about to pull onto the road, my cell phone buzzed with an incoming text message. *Wow, that was fast,* I thought, as I pulled it from my pocket and glanced down at the dial. I froze. My heart thudded and my breath caught in my throat. It was from Laura: *I want to see you. Tristan said you might come here. Where are you? I'm worried about you. Please don't hate me.*

My hands shook as I texted my response: *I'm already here, love. I miss you. I could never hate you. I'll find a way to get to you. Are you OK? How are the twins?*

I looked out the window into the darkness and tried to make sense of her text. Was she trying to tell me something? Was she safe? Did she want me back? My mind raced with possibilities as I awaited her response. It came quickly: *I'm OK but I have a problem with my kidneys. The babies are good though. Tomorrow I'm going with Catarina and Miguel's mother to a mall in Cascais for new clothes. Mine don't fit anymore. Miguel won't be with us. Maybe I could meet you there if I can slip away from them for a few minutes?*

My reply was instant: *Yes...text me details when you know them—place and time. I will find you. I love you. Until tomorrow.* I was euphoric. This communication felt like a victory. I would see her tomorrow and we would work things out. She would come home with me and we could get on with our lives. And Carmen could have...him. Everything was going to work out after all.

Chapter Eleven

CONFRONTATION

MIGUEL

Laura was in the bathroom getting ready for her shopping excursion while I waited for her in the bedroom. I was worried about something happening to her at the mall. My instincts were telling me to go with her, Catarina and my mother, but the idea of wandering around a mall for several hours was more than I could bear. I thought about the doctor's warning that Laura should not over-exert herself—that she should rest as much as possible. I knew she was excited about getting out of the house for a while and I hated to disappoint her, but I would have to put a stop to this outing—it just didn't feel right. I heard her phone buzz on the end of the bed where she had laid it with her purse. I wondered who was texting her. Her phone number was brand new—there couldn't be too many people who knew it. Not even her parents knew it yet. I knew I shouldn't invade her privacy but I couldn't resist. I picked up the phone and took a look. The number on the screen was unfamiliar but I could tell by the country code that it wasn't America—or Portugal. It was England. I felt anger beginning to surge in my gut but then I immediately squelched it. *It's just Tristan, idiot…don't be so paranoid.*

I started to put the phone down but my curiosity was too great. I figured I would look at the text and then not invade her privacy again—unless I feared for her safety. I tapped in her code and a red bar appeared: *Wrong Passcode: Try Again.* I must have hit a wrong number. I slowly typed in Laura's birthday—1212—and got the same response—wrong code. Laura had changed her access code. *Why would she do that?* I felt my guard go up as I heard the bathroom door open and I quickly dropped the phone on the bed and stood. She came out of the bathroom and saw me, then glanced at her phone and back to me again. I saw something cross her face, just for a second—guilt or fear—I wasn't sure what, but it was definitely something negative—and then she came toward me. She was wrapped in a towel and I blinked, pushing aside the cell phone mystery for a moment to drink her in. Even at nearly six months pregnant I couldn't imagine another more beautiful girl in the world.

"What are you doing?" she asked as she pressed herself against me, kissing me. She smelled of lemons again and I swallowed a lump of desire. Maybe she *should* go to the mall after all—she might actually be safer there than here with me, considering where my mind was going.

"Just waiting for you," I said. "I've been thinking that this trip to the mall isn't such a good idea. The doctor said you should stay off your feet and rest. It doesn't feel right to me. What if something happens? What if you start bleeding again? Or what if…"

She silenced me with another kiss. I pulled her to me and held her closer. Her wet hair brushed against my cheek and it, too, smelled of citrus fruits. She was intoxicating.

"I'll be fine. We won't be long. I just need some clothes that actually fit. We'll probably have lunch there and we'll be back in a flash. It'll be OK, I promise. And when we get home I'll put my feet up and let you massage them." She was really working it with the batting eyelashes and the pouting mouth.

Damn, I thought. I looked into her eyes and felt myself giving in. The least I could do was offer a compromise. I would just 'take one for the team' as they say. "Alright, fine. I'll come, too, then."

Laura stiffened in my arms. Her expression changed to something I couldn't identify, but by the look on her face, I had the feeling that she didn't want me to come with her. My instincts fired into action as she moved out of my arms and went over to the closet.

"You'll be bored out of your mind. I know how you guys feel about the mall," she said as she pulled a shirt off a hanger and held it up to herself, checking the size against her protruding stomach. She was looking anywhere but at me now.

"It's OK. I can handle one little trip to the mall. It beats sitting here worrying about you. Maybe Tristan will come, too, for moral support," I grinned.

Laura seemed to get flustered. She came away from the closet with her clothes and began to get dressed. "You don't need to come to the mall. I'll be fine. We won't be gone long." She tried to button her shirt but the middle buttons wouldn't reach. I thought it was sweet but she became impatient and pulled the shirt off and dropped it to the floor. "Nothing fits," she hissed harshly under her breath. I was surprised at her annoyance.

"I'll get you one of my t-shirts." I took one from a drawer and held it up to her. She took it and slipped it over her head and I admired her in it. "That looks better on you than me."

She finished dressing and combed her hair in silence. I studied her in the mirror. I watched as various emotions played across her face as if a dark cloud were passing back and forth over her, washing her in darkness and light and back again. And then I noticed her hands were shaking. I walked over to her and turned her around.

"What's wrong? Are you shaking?" I looked down at her hands and took them in mine. "You are. What's going on?"

She didn't answer right away. I had the feeling that even though she was standing right here in front of me, she was somewhere far away. Finally a half-smile formed on her face.

"I'm not shaking…well…if I am it's because I'm excited to be going out. And you can't come to the mall with me. It'll ruin everything." She walked over to the nightstand and picked up the talisman then slipped it around her neck. "Have you forgotten it's almost Christmas?"

I shook my head and rolled my eyes. "Ah…I see. You want to Christmas shop."

"Yes, I do. But how can I get you something if you come along? Stay here with Tristan and let him teach you how to play chess." She picked up her phone and looked at the screen. I saw a momentary flash of recognition cross her face when she saw the number. She looked up at me and then dropped the phone into her purse. "He's an excellent teacher in spite of the fact that I still can't play the damned game for crap."

I wanted to ask her why she'd changed her access code but then she would know I had looked at her phone so I stayed quiet about it. Something was going on with her but it was possible it had to do with her Christmas shopping plans and I didn't want to spoil any surprises so I pushed aside my suspicions for the moment. I took her in my arms and leaned down, my lips grazing her ear. "Just so you know, I happen to be an ace chess player. I seriously doubt Tristan could beat me."

She threw back her head and laughed. "That's brilliant! I feel a chess challenge coming on. Wait till I tell Tristan." She put her arms around my neck and nuzzled her lips against my cheek. She began to trail kisses along my jaw, down into my neck and I closed my eyes. I was amazed at the hold she had over me. I doubted that she even knew her own power. I kissed her lips, enjoying the taste of her sweetness. I knew if this continued I'd become incredibly frustrated but I couldn't help myself. I pressed her closer and heard her groan against my mouth. "I better get downstairs, Miguel. Your mother and Cat are probably wondering what's keeping me."

Reluctantly I released her. "I wish you wouldn't Christmas shop. You shouldn't be on your feet that long. Why don't you just get your clothes there and then come home and shop online for presents? Speaking of which, I don't need anything."

"I've gotta go. But you…," she kissed me several times in rapid succession, "are not allowed to come. End of story. I love you." She grabbed her jacket off the chair by the door and headed downstairs. I followed after her, shaking my head in frustration. My mother and Cat were waiting by the door.

"I was just about to come up there," said Catarina. Tristan

wheeled into the hall from the living room and stopped beside her. She leaned down and kissed him—a lingering kiss that surprised me. I looked away and saw Laura watching them, a satisfied smile on her face.

"Alright all you lovebirds, the mall awaits," said my mother. "Antonio brought the car around for us. You can drive, Cat."

"Wait. Antonio's not going?" I asked, alarmed.

"No," said Catarina. "It's ladies only today." She winked at Laura and my mother.

I wasn't having it. "No…I don't think so. Hang on. I'll get my coat. I don't feel comfortable with Laura going out for too long. I'll drive."

"No!" Laura shrieked the word. "I mean, no, thanks. I promise to shop only for maternity clothes and then we will come straight back. I will be absolutely fine." She walked over to Tristan. "Tris…Miguel says he can beat you at chess. Will you take care of him for me?" She gave him a sly look and he laughed.

"Is that so, Miguel? We'll have to see about that," said Tristan, exchanging a secret look with Laura.

"You're on," I said, accepting his challenge. "But you, Catarina, are in charge of Laura. I don't want her walking around a lot. Find one store and get everything you need there and then come home. Make her sit down every few minutes. And if you aren't home within a reasonable amount of time, I'm coming after you." I was not happy about this arrangement. My instincts were screaming at me to go with them, but against my better judgment, I ignored them and gave in.

"Stop worrying. We'll see you later," said Catarina, shooting me a look of annoyance.

I watched them get in the SUV and drive off. I turned to Tristan. "Are you really as good as Laura says you are?" I asked.

"When you're stuck in a wheelchair you have a lot of time to become quite proficient at board games. I was pretty good before my accident, but now I'm an expert. You'll see."

I shook my head and tried to suppress a smirk. "We'll see about that." I went upstairs and got the chess set and met Tristan in the dining room. While he set up the game I got us a couple of Cokes and something to snack on and then joined him. And within thirty minutes I knew I was in trouble. I put up a good fight but I lost and asked for a rematch. And then I broached the subject of his family.

"Have you heard from your family?"

He looked up at me, an eyebrow raised in question. "I have. My father is home now and apparently on the mend. My mother knows what happened but she refuses to believe it. And I know for a fact that my father has down-played his actions, framing it as just a terrible misunderstanding between him, Andrew and Laura. My father is delusional in case you hadn't figured that out by now. I can never express how sorry I am for what you—and Laura—have been through this past year. I always suspected something wasn't right with Laura but she never confided in me. How I wish she had."

I didn't particularly care to hear about the Duke of Easton. But Andrew was another story altogether. "What about your brother? Have you heard from him since he called you the other day when we were at the hospital?"

"I've talked to him a couple of times. He doesn't say much. I've asked him about his intentions in regard to Laura and he always says the same thing. That he's going to fight you for custody and he won't agree to a divorce. I only wish I knew where he was right now."

I thought of Laura's cell phone then and wondered about the mysterious text message. I noticed that Tristan's phone was in his shirt pocket. "Would you do me a favor? I left my cell phone upstairs. Would you text Laura and asked her to bring us some food back from the mall?"

Tristan reached for his phone, pulling it from his shirt pocket. "I'll call Cat. I don't have Laura's new number yet." He started to dial the number but I sucked in a breath and grabbed the phone from his hand.

"You didn't text her earlier?" I pushed my chair back and stood up from the table. I felt a pounding sensation in my chest and I was finding it hard to breathe.

Tristan looked startled. "No. I don't have her number yet.

Why?"

"*Son of a bitch!*" I yelled. I pushed the chair out of my way, knocking it over. "Andrew! He's here. I have to get to Laura." I dropped his phone into his lap and started for the door.

"What do you mean?" Tristan rolled his chair away from the table and followed me into the hall.

"I saw Laura's phone on the bed. She had a text from a British number but I couldn't read it because...*for some damned reason*...she changed the access code I'd picked out for her. I'd convinced myself the text was from you. I should've trusted my gut. I know better than to ignore my instincts. *Dammit!* I need to get to that mall." I ran to the kitchen and grabbed my car keys from the hook by the back door. Tristan followed close on my heels.

"I have to come with you. I know it's inconvenient but if Andrew's there I need to be there, too. I can talk to him—reason with him—if it becomes necessary. Please, Miguel. I need to come, too."

I looked down at him, hesitating. It was inconvenient, but he made a valid point. "Fine, I'll get the car. You meet me on the front porch."

I ran out the kitchen door to the garage and hopped into the Fiat. I drove around front where Tristan was waiting. He had already wheeled himself down the ramp. I got out and opened the front passenger door, then turned to him. I looked him in the eyes as I lifted him from the chair and set him inside the car. He was troubled, probably just as worried about his damned brother as much as for Laura. He told me how to collapse the chair and for a second I wondered if it would fit in my trunk. It took some doing but I managed to get it in and then I jumped into the driver's seat. I tore off down the drive and headed south to Cascais.

"Do you know where to go?" asked Tristan.

"Yes. I know which mall Catarina likes. I probably should've double-checked with her though. Dial her number and let me talk to her, please."

Tristan dialed the number and waited. "It's going to voicemail," he said.

"*Son of a bitch!*" I cursed. I stepped down hard on the gas.

My nerve endings flamed to life. My mind raced with every possible scenario. *What is Easton going to do? Maybe he won't even be there. Maybe I'm wrong.* One thing I knew for sure—when she was safe, I would demand that Laura tell me her access code, her privacy be damned. If she refused to tell me then I would take the phone away from her. I realized I was driving recklessly and concentrated on the road. Why did they have to go all the way to Cascais to shop? There were shops closer to home that would have sufficed. I slowed for a car and laid on the horn. The oncoming lane was clear so I passed the slow vehicle but we were entering a curve in the road and I had to fight to keep the Fiat under control.

"Slow the hell down, Miguel!" screamed Tristan. "I'm already paralyzed from the waist down…I don't want to be a quadriplegic, too. *Bloody hell!*"

I didn't respond but slowed the car by fifteen kilometers per hour and it immediately felt like we were crawling. I took the Cascais exit and headed to the town center where the mall was located. If Catarina chose today of all days to go anywhere else I would kill her. The traffic was heavy heading into the shopping district. I banged on the steering wheel and hit the horn again causing several drivers to give me the finger. I finally couldn't stand the slow progress anymore and moved onto the shoulder of the road and drove straight to the mall exit. Out of the corner of my eye I saw Tristan gripping the door handle. I pulled into the mall parking lot and searched for an empty spot. If I didn't find one fast I would damned well make one. I saw a green Renault backing out of a spot and took it. Within seconds I had the wheelchair out and Tristan settled in it. I pushed him to the automatic doors and once inside, he reached back and grabbed my hand, knocking it off the wheelchair's handle.

"I can take it from here. Once you find Cat, tell her to turn on her damned phone. Now, go! I'll try to keep up!"

I nodded and dashed off into the crowd of shoppers. I felt a pang of guilt at leaving him behind, but it couldn't be helped. As I moved through the crowd of people I scanned the faces looking for Andrew or one of his goons. I had no idea if he was alone or if he was even here, but my gut said he probably was, so I hurried, glancing left and right as I ran. I heard cursing and felt shoves as I passed people, but I ignored their irritation and kept running. I glanced at shop signs looking for a maternity clothing shop, not sure if there even was one in the mall. I was heading in the direction of the food court where there would be restrooms and a huge seating area. But if Laura was meeting him she would be smart enough to do it out of the way. She would trick Catarina and my mother into leaving her alone long enough to make contact. Why would she do this? Did she have no regard at all for her personal safety? Had she not learned by now to what lengths the Eastons would go to get what they wanted? I saw a shop sign with a drawing of a pregnant woman on it. I ran over and entered the store. There were only a few customers inside. I described Laura to the clerk and asked if someone fitting that description had been in here recently. She said a young, pregnant, American woman, with long, blonde hair had indeed been in here within the last hour. She'd been accompanied by two other women, both of them Portuguese. The clerk had no idea which way they'd gone. I looked at my watch and saw that it was just after noon. I thanked the clerk and headed to the food court. It was crowded and the lines were long at the various eateries. "*Dammit*," I cursed under my breath. I scanned the crowd and saw a figure in a wheelchair on the far side of the food court. I dashed between the crowded tables and made my way to Tristan.

"Anything?" he asked.

I shook my head. My frustration was palpable and I feared I might destroy something. "Have you tried Cat's number again?"

He nodded. "Still goes to voicemail."

"Where in the hell are they?" I asked, more to myself than to Tristan. And then I saw Catarina and my mother walking in our direction coming from the restrooms. They were talking and looking around frantically. They were both carrying shopping bags. "I see them. Stay here so we don't get separated. I'll be back." I darted through the lines of the various eateries and made my way over to them. Catarina saw me first.

"Miguel...I don't...," she began.

"*Where is she?*" I barked, cutting her off.

"We don't know. She said she needed the restroom and Sofia and I got to talking and suddenly we realized she'd been gone an awfully long time so we went to the bathroom to find her but she isn't in there. What are you doing here?"

"Andrew's here somewhere. I think they've been in contact. He must have lured her into a trap here somewhere. She trusts him—she doesn't understand his desperation. Now tell me exactly where you saw her last?"

My mother pointed to the restrooms. "We watched her walk in there about ten minutes ago. I'm so sorry, Miguel. This is my fault. I should have paid attention. I'd just said to Laura that she looked tired and we ought to head home. That's when she said she needed the bathroom."

"And you're absolutely positive she's not in the bathroom now? Did you check every stall?" My stomach churned as she nodded. Laura couldn't have gotten far...but...if Andrew had help, they could be far away by now. "Cat...why does your phone go to voicemail? Give it to me." She handed me her phone and I dialed Laura's number, thankful I'd had the sense to memorize it. It rang several times and went to voicemail as well. "*Son of a bitch!*" I pointed to where Tristan waited. "Go wait with Tristan. I'm taking your phone. If you see her, use his cell and call me immediately. I'm going to search for her." I left them then and ran back to where the bathrooms were located. At the end of the hall I saw water fountains, a door labeled maintenance and an emergency exit door. I ran to the maintenance door and tried the knob but the door was locked. I went to the emergency exit and hoped it wouldn't set off an alarm when I opened it. I pushed the door open and stepped out into a back alley, but I didn't let it go in case I got locked out. And then I saw them, standing a few feet away behind the open exit door.

"Miguel! Oh, my god! How did you...?" Laura cried. Her face was red and streaked with tears. Andrew was holding her arm in his grip.

"You son of a bitch," I growled at Andrew. "What the hell are you doing? Get your hands off of her."

"What the hell do you think I'm doing, Dos Santos?" Andrew responded. "Last time I checked, husbands were allowed to talk to their wives. What are you going to do, kill me?"

I looked at Laura. "Get inside now, Laura. Come on." I held the door open to keep it from locking us out.

"Miguel, it's OK. We were just talking…," she started to speak but I shook my head and cut her off.

"No. Get inside. Easton and I are going to have a chat and you don't need to hear it."

She pulled her arm free of Andrew's grasp and stepped back. "I'm not going inside. I'm staying here. Whatever you two have to say, you can say it in front of me."

Andrew reached his hand out to touch her again and I lost it. I let the door bang closed and I lunged for him, yelling at Laura to move as I pounced, my fist drawn back. I made contact with his stomach and with my momentum, sent us both down onto the pavement. He rolled backward moaning and got to his feet but I lunged again. This time he expected it and hit me in the jaw. I felt my skin split and blood flowed down into my shirt collar. We circled around each other, fists raised, each of us waiting for an in. And then Laura screamed, diverting my attention long enough for Andrew to punch me in the gut sending me against the wall. I struggled to my feet as he came at me again but Laura moved in front of me and Andrew had to check his fist to keep from slamming it into her face.

"Dammit, Laura! I almost hit you!" he screamed.

"Please, stop this! *Please*! Why can't you just try talking, please!" Laura's voice was so shrill her words were barely understandable.

Andrew backed away from her and looked at me. I wanted to hit him again…I could feel the adrenaline fueling my desire to draw blood and inflict pain, but I held myself in check. "What do you want, Easton?"

He looked at Laura then and his face softened. But his voice was menacing when he answered my question. "You know what I want, Dos Santos. Laura is my wife and I want her back. It doesn't get any simpler than that."

I looked at Laura. She was crying hard and holding her stomach and I became afraid for her and the twins. She backed up then toward the brick wall and leaned against it trying to catch her breath. Slowly she slid down the wall to the ground, her purse falling off of her arm and landing beside her.

I inched toward her, keeping one eye on Andrew. "Laura...? Did you call him? How did he know you'd be here?" I stopped next to her, still watching Andrew.

She choked out a response between ragged breaths. "Yes, I called him. I just wanted to make sure he was OK."

"And you just thought he would answer you and then let you walk away...just like that?" I said, baffled by her misplaced sense of trust. Andrew stepped toward me and I prepared to strike.

"You thought I was going to kidnap her? What do you think I am? A criminal, like you?" Andrew spat out the words. He began to pace around and when he got too close to Laura I snapped and went for him again. He wasn't expecting me to strike and I was able to grab his jacket collar and slam him up against the building on the other side of the narrow alley. He tried to fight me off but I managed to grab his arm and twist it around his back. I now had him in a death grip, his arm bending up at an unnatural angle. The more he struggled against me the harder I pulled his arm. He yelled out in pain and stopped struggling, his breath coming in out harsh gasps.

"Miguel...you'll break his arm! Let him go!" I looked over my shoulder and saw Laura trying to get up.

"Stay there, Laura!" I yelled at her. Why would she never listen? I leaned into Andrew's back, my mouth close to his ear. "If I let you go, will you behave?" I yanked on his arm again and made him cry out in agony. I hoped I was making my point.

"Damn you, Dos Santos. Yes! I'll restrain myself." Andrew tried to shake me off but the movement only caused him more discomfort.

I let him go with a shove and he caught himself against the brick wall and slowly turned to face me, his eyes burning with rage. Laura was up now, on her feet, walking toward us. I wanted her to stop moving—to stay put--but she continued toward me and as she stumbled forward I caught her in my arms. Andrew instinctively reacted and moved to her other side. Together we held her up until she was steady on her feet. I glared at Andrew and he removed his hands from her arm and stepped a few feet away.

As I held Laura in my arms, I spoke to him over the top of her head. "She's filed for an annulment. Have some dignity and don't try to fight it, Easton. Go back to England and get yourself together."

Andrew's face reddened. He fumed with anger. "She told me she loves you so if she wants her freedom, she can have it. But the babies are mine and you can't have them. There will be a custody fight so prepare yourself. As soon as they're born, you'll be served with papers."

I shook my head in disgust. "Give it up, Easton. They're not yours." Laura pulled away from me and turned to face Andrew.

"Don't do it, Andrew…please. Let us get on with our lives. These babies are not yours…trust me. You'll never get them. You would have to see me dead before these babies are ever allowed near your despicable father. I told you I'm sorry for everything that's happened to you. I'm sorry you've been hurt. But don't punish me for your father's sins—and don't punish these innocent babies." She wrapped her arms around her stomach as she spoke. Her tears were flowing freely and I knew she was working hard to keep herself together.

Andrew seemed to weigh her words. He stepped backward and ran his hands through his hair. He was breathing hard and pacing. It occurred to me that he might be preparing to strike out again like a lion who'd cornered his prey and was looking for the right angle to go in for the kill. Instinctively I pulled Laura around behind me and placed myself in front of her. The air was heavy with tension as I waited to see Andrew's next move. I balled my hands into fists, waiting for his attack. But he didn't use his fists to hurt me. He used words—words that made no sense to me—words that angered me and made me want to kill him right here and now.

"You told me to have some dignity…?" He came toward me and I put up my hands preparing to defend myself. "Dignity? Really?" He suddenly reached forward and poked me hard in the chest. I drew back my fist, ready to punch his face but his next words caught me off guard. "Why don't you talk to your mother about dignity? And while you're at it, talk to her about truth and honor. Because I have news for you, Dos Santos...your whole pathetic life is a goddamned lie! Ask your mother what I'm talking about. She's been keeping a secret from you your whole sorry-ass life. And I wish to God I'd never found out. It makes me sick."

I ground my teeth together and fumed. My heart pounded, my lungs filled to bursting and I knew I was going to hurt him then. I flew at him, yelling in Portuguese. I punched his face and blood splattered over both of us from his nose. I was ready to strike again when Laura's scream stopped me.

"No more fighting! I'm leaving!" She began an unsteady walk down the alley, her hand on the wall for support.

Andrew spat out blood onto the ground and wiped his hand over his bloody nose. "So am I. I'm going back to England for the time being, Dos Santos. But this is far from over. Talk to your mother. I'd tell you myself but it makes me sick to say the words." He walked away from me and stopped when he came abreast of Laura. When he reached his hand out to touch her I wanted to kill him, but his words were ringing in my ears. I tried to convince myself he was just talking nonsense out of desperation--nothing he'd said had made sense. I held my ground as he embraced her. I was quite certain that the next words out of his mouth cut through her heart, each one a sharp stab of pain further damaging an already broken girl. "I love you, Laura Easton. That's one thing that has not and will not ever change. So if it's him you want, I won't stand in your way. But like it or not, you and I are tied together for life. Life, Laura. Good-bye, love." He walked away down the alley and as Laura and I watched, he didn't once look back.

I went to Laura and took her in my arms and let her cry herself out. I could tell she was exhausted. I reached up and touched my cheek--the blood had already dried on my jaw. My collar was soaked with my blood and sweat and Laura's tears.

"It's going to be OK, sweetheart. Let's get you home." I supported her weight as we walked the opposite way Andrew had gone. As we passed the exit door, I tried the knob, but as I suspected, it was locked. We walked along in silence through the alley which led us to the front parking lot. I found a bench near the mall entrance for Laura to sit on and I called Tristan. His number was already programmed into Cat's phone. I told him where to find us and then I shoved the phone into my pocket and joined Laura on the bench. As soon as I sat down, she turned into my arms and buried her face into my neck. She sighed, her breaths coming out in a shudder. We didn't talk as we waited for Tristan, Cat and my mother to find us.

Chapter Twelve

LOVE AND SECRETS

LAURA

Miguel and I went home in his Fiat while Catarina, Tristan and Sofia rode home in the SUV. While we'd sat on the bench outside the mall waiting for his family to come to us, he'd been tender and sweet with me, but now he stared straight ahead at the road, his eyes never straying left or right as he worked his jaw back and forth in silence. His body was tense and his hands gripped the steering wheel so tightly that I was afraid at any moment he would rip it from its anchor in the dashboard. Words raced through my mind, but I feared anything I said would send Miguel into a rage so I kept my mouth shut as we drove home. His face was swollen, his shirt blood-spattered and dirty. I bit back tears as we drove and I wished I could go back to last night and stop myself from contacting Andrew.

I knew I shouldn't have done it but I'd wanted so badly to try to make things right for him. When I was alone with my new phone, I'd texted him. I was shocked to learn he was in Portugal. I told him I'd be at the Cascais mall in the morning and when I found out from Cat where it was and what time we'd be there, I'd texted Andrew the details. I was worried about Miguel finding out so I'd changed my phone's access code. I'd felt guilty about that, but it seemed like the right thing to do at the time. He had no reason to touch my phone so he wasn't likely to ever know anyway. I'd been anxious all morning, but I wasn't afraid. I knew Miguel didn't trust Andrew but I also knew that Andrew loved me and would never hurt me. Once at the mall I was nervous and on alert, watching for him. I saw a *saida* sign, which I'd learned was the Portuguese word for exit, pointing around the corner toward the back doors past the restrooms. I texted him from a changing booth in the maternity shop that I would meet him there as soon as I was able to get away from Cat and Sofia. We found a table and sat down to rest, but when I'd said I needed to use the bathroom, Cat had volunteered to come with me and I'd nearly panicked. I told her I would be fine and asked her to surprise me with some food while I was in the restroom. Once I was away from our table I went straight to the exit door and saw him. The sight of him overwhelmed me in a way I was not prepared for. He looked tired, pale and thin and there were dark circles under his eyes. My heart went out to him.

"Laura...look at you," he said. "You're beautiful." He came toward me, his arms open and I let him hold me for a moment.

"Let's go out there," I said, pointing to the exit door, "in case Cat comes looking for me."

He opened the door and followed me outside into the alley.

"How are you, love?" He regarded me, head to toe, and smiled. He ran a hand through his hair and I noticed that he needed a haircut.

"I'm OK, but I don't have long. I just wanted to make sure you're OK. Why are you here, Andrew?"

"I'm here for you. I love you and I want you to come home with me where you belong."

He started toward me as if to take me into his arms, but I stepped back. I couldn't let this happen. I could see that he wasn't going to make this easy for either of us. I hated myself for what I was about to do. I put my hand on his chest and stopped his advance.

"Andrew, please. I'm not going back to England with you. My home is here now. Please don't make this harder than it has to be. I don't want to hurt you. I never asked for any of this… you know that."

"*Dammit, Laura!*" His hand formed into a fist and he drew it back and punched at the wall, stopping just short of hitting it which would have resulted in a broken hand for sure. "Why didn't you tell me what my father had done? Why? I could've prevented this insane nightmare. Why didn't you trust me enough?" I saw tears well up in his eyes and I choked back a sob.

"I'm sorry. I was so afraid. He threatened my family—their jobs--and my brother's life. For god's sake, Andrew, he caused my brother's car accident! He tried to have a bomb planted in my mother's car! He's a sick, sick monster! He threatened over and over and over again to kill Mig…"

"Stop! Don't say his name. I can't stand the sound of it." He came to me and gripped my arms. I saw his tears threatening to fall. "Please tell me you don't love him. I can't believe it's true."

My tears fell in streams down my cheeks as I looked into his sad blue eyes and nodded. "I do love him. I know it hurts you and I'm so sorry, but he's the one I want to be with." He tightened his grip on my arms and I cried out in pain. "Stop! You're hurting me."

"So you never loved me at all then? Not even for a second?" He loosened his hands but didn't let go. Then he pulled me closer, up against his chest, and buried his face in my hair. I didn't resist his rough embrace. "The times we made love meant nothing to you?"

I looked down in shame. He took my chin in his hand and tilted my face up to meet his gaze. It was hard to look at him. "I'm sorry. I don't know what to say except…please forgive me."

"Who is the father of these babies?" he asked, his breathing suddenly becoming rapid. He rubbed his hand over my stomach and pressed against the twins, who I could feel moving inside of me. Maybe he felt it, too. And then I felt the talisman warming against my neck but I tried to ignore it for the moment. I felt like I was breaking out in hives all over my neck and chest as it sent its warning or message or whatever it was trying to tell me.

"Miguel."

He let me go then and kicked at the wall. "No! It's not possible." He turned to me, his eyes wild. "I have to be their father, Laura. It has to be me. When they're born, I'll demand a DNA test to prove it. I won't let that damned gypsy curse be true. *I won't.*"

I stayed silent, unsure how to respond. I watched emotions play across his face as he began to pace around me. I knew I needed to calm him down. "Andrew...please...the gypsy curse doesn't mean anything. Don't believe it. You'll have children some day."

He stopped pacing and suddenly swept me into his arms, pressing himself into me so that we were pushed up against the wall. He bent down to kiss me and I turned my head away, his lips grazing my jaw. "I want to have babies with you, Laura--no one else. Don't you get that? I love *you*." He tried to kiss me again but I pushed him away. And it hurt to do it.

"Please don't do this. You have to find a way to make peace with this. I will always care about you...you have to know that... but..." I stopped, sensing my words were falling on deaf ears.

He stepped back and looked at me. His face was tortured and it pained me to look at him. "Then I guess this is good-bye...for now, Laura." He took my arm then and was about to say something more when the exit door suddenly opened.

I blinked back to the present and noticed that we were parking in the garage. Miguel still had not spoken a word to me and I didn't know where I stood with him. Was I even welcome here anymore? I got out of the car and walked away from him toward the house. I would go inside and pack my things and call the airlines. More than anything I wanted to go home to Rhode Island. Maybe this was for the best. I bit back a sob as I walked up the porch steps.

"Laura, wait." Miguel walked up behind me and took my hand. He pulled me over to the wrought iron chairs and pushed me gently into one and sat down beside me. "We need to talk... obviously."

I shook my head back and forth. "I know you're mad at me, but I don't regret it. I needed to see him. I've told you time and time again that Andrew is not a bad person. He is not his father. I needed to know—for myself—that he was OK. So if you're going to yell at me...or...if you want me to leave, then just get it over with. But I am not sorry for what I did." As I spoke I reached inside my shirt and pulled out the talisman. I had not looked at it since it had sent me its last warning. I looked down at it now and saw a new word on the back of it: *Verdade*. "I felt the talisman when I was with Andrew. What does it mean?"

Miguel looked at the new word. He frowned and closed his eyes for a moment. "It means 'truth.'" He made a sound under his breath and opened his eyes. I couldn't read him...he seemed distant and troubled.

"What truth?" I asked.

"I don't know." He muttered something to himself in Portuguese and then focused his attention on me. He took my chin in his hand and forced me to look at him. "I'm not going to yell at you. And, yes, I'm mad. You took a terrible risk. You scared the hell out of me. What if Andrew hadn't been alone? Any one of his goons could have shown up and taken you away. You did a foolish thing, Laura, and it can't ever happen again. Do you understand me?"

I nodded as tears fell down my cheeks. "I'm sorry I scared you. I'll try to understand if you want me to leave."

He cursed in Portuguese and kicked out at the porch railing. "*Dammit*, Laura! Why would you think that? I would never want that. You're not going anywhere." His body was tense as if he had excess energy he needed to expend. I wanted his arms around me now. I wanted to feel his lips on mine so I could be sure he meant it—that he never wanted to lose me.

"Then kiss me," I whispered.

He spoke in Portuguese as he stood up and hauled me to my feet. He took me in his arms and crushed his lips against mine, nearly knocking the wind out of me. I felt the sensation of many hearts beating in both of our bodies...drumbeats pulsating in my blood and I wondered if he felt it, too. I wound my arms around his neck, weaving my fingers into his hair as he threaded his hands through mine. A tornado formed in my stomach as his kissed deepened and his tongue found mine. I wanted him so powerfully that the sensation overwhelmed me as a surge of desire pulsed through me, causing me to convulse. He groaned against my throat, his lips everywhere—on my jaw, my nose, my eyes and back to my mouth. Suddenly he stopped and whispered against my temple. "Come inside, *minha querida*. We need to be alone. And I have not forgotten the doctor's orders, but still, there are other ways. I want you." We walked into the house, which seemed to be deserted, and went upstairs to our room. He closed and locked the door and took me to the bed and gently pushed me back and lay down next to me. I touched the wound on his cheek and he winced. As his warm hands slid under my shirt and caressed my skin, I felt hot tears slip down my cheeks. I didn't see how it was possible to love someone as much as I loved Miguel. I pressed myself into him and sighed.

"Where is everybody?" I asked Miguel. We were in the kitchen and I saw that someone had been here earlier cooking. There were covered pots on the stove and I smelled something delicious in the air. I realized I was starving as Miguel heated up the food. He poured us lemonade and joined me at the table.

"I'm guessing they've made themselves scarce because they're afraid of me." He sipped from his lemonade and regarded me over the rim of the glass.

"What do they have to fear? I'm the one in trouble," I said, trying to suppress a smile as I remembered our recent lovemaking. If that was my punishment, I wanted to be in trouble all the time.

He gave me a sweet grin. "Actually, they went for a ride. They'll be home soon." He went to the stove and turned off the pots and fixed us both plates of food. I dove into the food, realizing I hadn't eaten since early morning when I'd had only a piece of toast. If Miguel knew that, he would really be mad. I noticed he was watching me eat and he seemed to be enjoying the show.

"What?" I asked, my cheeks pinking.

"Nothing. I just like to watch you."

He reached over and took my left hand in his and brought it to his lips, kissing it tenderly. He looked at the sapphire ring and touched it with his fingertips. "I want to marry you."

I heard something in his voice—something wistful...uncertain. I entwined my fingers into his and tugged on his hand. "You will. I said yes, remember?" I spoke softly and studied him. He pulled our hands to his mouth and kissed the back of mine.

"I want to marry you before the babies are born. I'm going to call the lawyer tomorrow and see what's happening with the annulment. I want Felipe and Gabriela to be Dos Santos children when they take their first breaths...not Eastons." He suddenly pulled his hand away and pushed back from the table. He walked to the back door and looked out at the wooded area that covered the property at the back of the house. I'd heard an urgency in his voice as if time were running out.

I got up from the table and joined him at the window. I wrapped my arms around his waist from behind and laid my head on his back as best I could, considering the size of my stomach. I breathed in his scent--earth and mint and dryer sheets—and sighed contentedly. We stood that way for a while as the kitchen began to darken with the setting sun. Finally Miguel insisted we finish our dinner.

I had something on my mind that I'd been meaning to ask him about and I figured now was as good a time as any. "Miguel...?"

He looked up from his plate, wiping his mouth with a napkin. "Yes?"

"You never told me what you found in the duke's safe...that night...?"

Miguel leaned back in his chair and sighed. He considered my question before answering. "A treasure trove of family possessions that have been missing for more than three hundred years. We found Princess Gabriela's sapphire and diamond tiara and other jewels. Silver coins and gold bars, a lot of other currency particular to the time, a pocket watch...and...property deeds. Everything was in pristine condition."

"Wow. Where is it all now?"

"Most of it was taken to the royal palace—the palace I took

you to. It's being appraised and catalogued. The jewels will go on display for the public to view and the money was put in the Royal Bank of Portugal, placed in trust for my family. The deeds are in the government offices to be authenticated—deeds to three properties here in Portugal, one in England and also an island in the Azores that is under British rule but which we have always knows was ours. Finally we can get it back. We only needed the deeds to prove it. Someday I will take you there, Laura, to Ventura Island. Uncle Antonio is taking care of all of this."

"So you were right. The duke had everything just as you suspected." I was stunned.

"The British royal family has had three hundred years to do the right thing though I bet the majority of them had no idea. They have many branches in their family tree, but it was the House of Hanover that called the shots in this deceit. And the Duke of Easton was the worst of the lot of them. He knew what he had in his possession and he knew it wasn't his to keep. It doesn't matter that everything was stolen hundreds of years ago. What matters is today and the fact that he knew he had stolen property and kept it for his own greed and gain. And he advocated killing me using his own son as a weapon. He is the worst that mankind has to offer, Laura. I feel sorry that Tristan…and, yes…even Andrew…had to grow up calling him their father. I wish everyone could have the kind of father I had. He was a great man, loving and quite gentle," Miguel chuckled at some memory. "I was very lucky.

He got quiet and I let him have silence in his introspection. I thought of my own father and how much I missed him and my mother and Nick. Maybe I would ask Miguel if they could come for the holidays. Just as we finished eating, Tomas and Mateo came in from outside. I was always amazed at how the two of them filled a room and brought so much life to it.

"Hey, guys," said Miguel. "How was the ride? Where'd you go?"

"We showed Tristan the polo fields. He liked it there. He sure loves horses, doesn't he?" said Tomas.

Miguel and I locked eyes for a second before he answered. "Yes, he does."

"I hope you two saved us some food. I'm starving," said Mateo.

Cat, Sofia, Ronald and Tristan came in then. When they saw us, their collective faces froze. They were probably unsure of what they would find in our demeanor.

"We're all good here, people," said Miguel, chuckling. Cat went to the cupboard and brought out plates and silverware. She set out bread and glasses for lemonade. Tristan rolled up to the table and watched Cat, a look on his face that could only be love. I noticed Miguel studying his mother. Sofia was at the stove stirring the vegetables in the pot. I wondered what he was thinking. Suddenly I remembered Andrew's words about Sofia—something about a secret she'd been keeping from Miguel his whole life. I could tell by his face that Miguel was thinking about it, too. I couldn't fathom what Andrew had meant but I hoped he was wrong about whatever it was. We didn't need any more secrets here. We'd had more than enough already.

The Shadow King

Chapter Thirteen

MISPLACED LOYALTIES

ANDREW

"What happened to you?" Peter asked me as I walked through the hotel doors. He was seated in the lobby reading a newspaper, apparently waiting for me. He stared at my filthy, bloody clothes and swollen face.

"Sightseeing accident. But I'm bored with this place. Please book our tickets back to England. I'm finished with Portugal… for the time being."

"You should have taken me with you, sir. I could have prevented your…sightseeing accident," he said, putting his paper down and joining me at the elevator. "It's what I'm paid to do."

"It doesn't matter. Try to get us out of here today." I went to my room and shut the door. I found a Coke in the mini fridge but I would have preferred something stronger. I was also hungry but that would have to wait. I inspected the damage to my face and determined that my nose was not broken but I would have a black eye for sure. *Great, just what I need*, I thought as I turned on the shower. Once I was clean I felt a little better but I had to keep my mind occupied or thoughts of Laura would mess me up. I got dressed and sat on the end of the bed with my phone. I decided I would send her a text, though I wasn't sure what good I thought it would do: *I'm going back to England...for now. I love you. I wish there was a way to go back in time and start over. I miss you.* I hit send and shook my head. What a weakling I was. As if she cared.

Peter knocked on my door and told me we were booked on the last flight out of Lisbon at nine o'clock.

"That's seriously good news, Peter. Thanks. Let's leave now so we can get something to eat. I'd rather spend my time waiting at the airport than here." He nodded and went to his room to get his stuff. We met down in the lobby and waited for our car to be brought around. On the way to the airport we stopped at a restaurant and had dinner and I finally got a proper drink. I had another Coke, but this time it had rum in it to enhance the flavor. After a few of these I'd be able to shut my mind off and keep out thoughts of Laura. When we finished we drove to the airport and turned in the rental car. I was anxious to get on the flight and get the hell out of here. I decided to go to the newsstand and find an English language newspaper. I bought a copy of the *International Herald Tribune* and sat down to read. I scanned the pages reading headlines and something caught my eye in the section called 'Continental Round-Up.' My heart began to hammer in my chest as I read the short paragraph:

The Portuguese government is reporting a recent discovery of missing items from the royal House of Braganza, Portugal's shadow dynasty. Jewels of diamonds and sapphires, including Princess Gabriela's crown, monies consisting of gold, silver and paper currency and deeds to multiple properties long held by Great Britain, including the Azore's famous tenth island, Ventura, were recently recovered from a safe in England at the home of the Duke of Easton, also known as Ernst of Hanover. Easton is a descendant of King George the First of the House of Hanover, the monarch responsible for illegally acquiring the Portuguese royal family's possessions during the time of Princess Gabriela in the early 1700's. An investigation is underway to learn why the duke had the items in his home and to determine his complicity in the concealment of these items. Easton is currently recovering from a heart attack he suffered during a recent fire at his

Buckinghamshire estate.

My head felt like it was going to explode. So, this is what they were after…that night…the night of the fire. It wasn't just Laura they wanted…they wanted the contents of the safe. Dos Santos was, in essence, stealing stolen property. I couldn't seem to wrap my brain around this new information. *Does this change anything?* I wondered, as I stared off into space. I read the article two more times to make sure I was understanding it correctly. It inferred that my father was a thief. I already knew about the blackmail and the attempted murder. I was stunned. My father was just as bad as Tristan had said. Not that being a thief was worse than being an attempted murderer…but when you put it all together, it would seem that my father had no redeeming qualities whatsoever. I suddenly had the urge to hit something…I looked at Peter…or someone. I went to the restroom and kicked the hell out of the trashcan and then left before airport security came to investigate the racket I was making. It was time to board the plane and the first thing I did after buckling myself into my first class seat was order myself a whiskey—neat.

When we arrived in London it was after midnight and I was exhausted. As I settled into my bed with a beer, I heard my cell phone ping with an incoming text message. My stomach knotted at the thought that it could be Laura responding to me. I picked up the phone and saw a number with a Portugal country code. I opened it and read: *I heard about what happened with you and Miguel and Laura…overheard actually…I wish I'd had a chance to tell you good-bye. Thanks for listening to me the other night. If you come back to Sintra, come find me. I still think we can find a way to work things out so we can each get what we want. Call me sometime.* I lay back on my pillow and closed my eyes for a minute, thinking about Carmen. We were in the same boat, but unfortunately, it was more like a sinking ship and maybe she needed to accept that. I knew I wasn't going to get Laura back. I was hinging my hopes on my children now. I wouldn't give up on them until I had incontrovertible proof that they weren't mine.

But Laura seemed so sure. I didn't understand how she could possibly know. I looked at my cell phone and thought about how to respond to Carmen. Finally I typed: *Yeah, things didn't go as planned, but I have to move on where Laura is concerned. You should do the same thing regarding Dos Santos. Life is too short to spend it wanting something you can't have. I'm going to concentrate on my education and you should, too. Your plan to become a teacher and help the gypsy community is a noble one. You're a pretty girl, Carmen. You'll find someone else some day. Good night.* I hit send and shut off my phone. I wasn't sure I believed anything I'd just typed except the part about her being pretty and finding someone else. I wouldn't even consider that possibility for myself. I wanted Laura back—I'd always want that. But I would have to find a way to live with the pain of losing her, otherwise I was guaranteed a miserable existence. I thought of my father then and *his* miserable existence. As much as I hated the thought, I would have to pay him a visit tomorrow. I finished my beer and tried to get some sleep.

I had Peter drive me to my parents' house in Buckinghamshire. As we drove up the long driveway, I saw a construction crew at work finishing the repairs from the fire damage to the side of the house. I didn't want to go in, but I knew I needed to talk to my father. I found my mother in the salon having tea and reading a book.

"Andrew! You're home. I've missed you, darling," she said, putting her book down and getting up to hug me. She frowned. "What happened to your face?"

"Hello, Mother. I walked into a door. How are you?" She looked tired, like she'd aged ten or twenty years since Father's heart attack.

"Fine. Have you talked to your brother lately? Do you think he'll ever come home?" She sounded sad and if I stayed too long I knew she'd bring me down.

"I've talked to him, yes, but he doesn't say much. I'm sure he'll come home some day." I paced around the salon, anxious to do what I came to do and get back to London.

"Well, it's the holidays now and I hope you'll at least be around. You will, won't you?" I couldn't take the pitiful tone in her voice.

"I don't know yet what I'm doing. Where's Father?"

"He's in his study. He'll be so happy to see you. He's getting stronger every day."

I felt a surge of annoyance threatening to overwhelm me. My mother's refusal to acknowledge the elephant in the room was pushing me to the limits of my patience. "Mother...I know you're aware of the horrible deeds Father has committed against Laura. I admit that at first I didn't believe it could be true. But I've come to accept him for the son of a bitch he is. You need to do the same." I turned to leave. I felt badly saying it but it needed to be said.

"How dare you talk to me that way, Andrew! And how dare you say anything cruel about your father. He has only ever had your best interest at heart. I know he can be unreasonable at times. And I hated the reason why we went to America. Going to Rhode Island was the biggest mistake of all of our lives, especially Tristan's, but now I just want things to get back to normal so your father can heal and we can have peace in the house again."

"Things will never be normal, Mother...and there will never be peace in this house. You don't even know the man you're married to. You need to pull your head out of the sand and start asking questions. He's not good...not good for you. I'm sorry to be so blunt but someone needs to say these things—not that you'll listen. I love you, Mother, but I don't understand how you can be so blind. I'm going to talk to Father now. I'll see you later." I left quickly before she could say anything to make me regret my harsh words. But I'd only spoken the truth and there was no need to feel guilt or regret for that. I went straight into my father's study without knocking and found him sitting by the window, his ever-present tumbler of brandy in hand.

"Not even a heart attack can keep you from your alcohol, can it, Father? Ever thought about getting help?" I knew I sounded antagonistic, and perhaps a bit hypocritical, but I truly couldn't help myself.

"Hello, son. How are you?" He ignored my rude greeting and set his glass down, shifting his chair to face me. His movements were slow and deliberate and I guessed he was still feeling the aftereffects of his surgery. I saw him studying my black eye but he didn't comment on it.

"I've been better." I reached into my pocket and pulled out the newspaper article I'd clipped out of the *International Herald Tribune*. I walked over and dropped it into his lap. "Have you seen this?" I gave him a second to look it over. I could tell by his reaction that he had, indeed, already seen the article.

"You can't believe everything you read. Those damned gypsies stole from us and we will get everything back. I have the lawyers taking care of it now."

I shook my head. "You know what, Father? You need to find a new hobby. Now that this vendetta thing is over and Laura isn't here to manipulate and blackmail, you should find something else to do—maybe something *good*…and honorable. Ever thought about that?" I stood before him, staring him down.

"Oh, son. The vendetta isn't over. Unless you've come here to tell me you've taken care of that gypsy thief?" He actually had the audacity to look hopeful.

"You mean did I kill my brother? No, I didn't. I wanted to… but…no. And you know why? Two reasons father. I'll give you two reasons. One: I am not a killer. That doesn't mean I don't wish him dead. But no, being a murderer isn't something I aspire to. It wouldn't look good on my *curriculum vitae*. And two: I couldn't do that to Laura. For reasons I will never understand, she loves that son of a bitch and killing him would probably kill her and I sure as hell don't want that on my conscience. I love her. I always will. When the babies are born, I will request a DNA test and if they're mine then we have a game changer. But if they're…not…then I will get on with my life…with college and medical school." I leaned down closer to his face and said one more thing just to stick it to him. "I'm thinking about having a medical practice someday in a poor area where doctors are needed…like maybe in the London slums or…who knows…a gypsy community." I didn't really mean that, but I wanted my father to think I did.

"Are you quite finished with your little self-serving speech?" he asked, his voice laced with barely controlled menace.

I didn't answer. I stepped back from him and moved toward the door. I couldn't wait to get out of here.

"You're forgetting something, Andrew. Laura is carrying my grandchildren. *Mine.* And I want them raised here in England with me. It doesn't matter who their father is. Either way, they are still Eastons. I told you to take care of that situation and you apparently weren't man enough to do it. So it looks like I'm going to have to take care of it myself. By the time Laura gives birth in April, I will be healthy and able to travel. I intend to go to Portugal myself, take care of the *situation* that you were too cowardly to handle and bring my grandchildren home. If you want to help me, it would be appreciated, but, if not, I will handle it myself."

I couldn't help laughing. "I don't believe you, Father. You'll never do it. You're already in hot water over the contents of the safe. Don't be stupid. Leave the damned gypsies in peace—not that they deserve it. Find a better way to spend your time… like…going to rehab."

Father started to get up but changed his mind. He finished his brandy and poured another, as if to flaunt his drinking in my face. "I had high hopes for you, Andrew, but you're a disappointment—a big one. I have a half a mind to cut off your funding for college. If you want to go out into the world and serve the dregs of society then you can do it on someone else's dime."

I laughed again. "Someone else's dime? Really? You mean someone other than the queen's? Have you ever earned an honest living in your life?"

He started to respond but suddenly grabbed his chest and coughed. His face turned red as he took a few ragged breaths. I stood still watching him. If he was having another heart attack, I'd be tempted not to intervene. *Maybe I am a killer, after all*, I thought. I watched as he grabbed his brandy and tossed it back. Some heart attack.

"I'm going back to London, Father. Your heart attack was supposed to be your wake-up call, but it's looking more like a snooze button to buy you more time for your dastardly deeds. You really are despicable. Happy holidays." I left abruptly. I went straight to the front door and called Peter on my phone. He took me back to London to my apartment. I tried not to think about what I'd just done. I'd probably just shot myself in the foot. I felt badly for my mother and a small degree of guilt as to how I'd treated my father. Especially when I considered that I wasn't sure I believed half the things I'd spouted at him. I'd heard words coming from my mouth that I had not expected to say and I wondered where those words had come from--words about leaving gypsies in peace and not being able to kill Dos Santos. Because truthfully, I thought I was capable...I thought I did want to kill him. I hated him. I got a new bottle of whiskey and removed the lid. I held it up to my lips but stopped myself from taking a drink. If I drank it then I would be no better than my father. I was stronger than that. Without hesitating I poured it down the drain along with the other bottle I still had. My mouth watered as I watched it go down the drain. I felt a pang of re-morse but I forced it away. I took a couple of Cokes from the refrigerator and called Peter. I asked him to get me some food from somewhere. As I waited for it to arrive, I held my phone in my hand and thought about calling someone...someone like... Carmen.

Chapter Fourteen

SOFIA'S SECRET

MIGUEL

"I know you're disappointed, sweetheart, but just think, they'll be here for the birth. That's the most important thing." I cupped Laura's face in my hands and kissed her forehead. She'd just talked to her parents about coming to Portugal for the holidays.

"It's weird that my family is having a life and I'm not a part of it. My father is sick with pneumonia, my brother is going skiing in Vermont and my mother is volunteering to serve holiday meals at the soup kitchen in Newport. It just seems strange that I won't be with them for Christmas. I really miss them." She sighed and turned her face into my palm. I pulled her to me and held her close. She'd finally told her parents more about the changes in her life. They knew about me now, although Laura had told them we were just friends, and they knew she was safe and happy here in Portugal. Her brother Nick remembered me and I hoped he wouldn't give her parents the wrong impression about me considering my gypsy reputation back in Portsmouth. She did not tell them Andrew was not the father of the babies, deciding that was more than they could handle right now. They'd wanted her to come home but she'd told them she loved Portugal and didn't want to leave. They were concerned about her financial situation but she assured them money was not a problem. I was amazed at her power to convince them—I wasn't sure I'd believe her so easily if I were them. She'd promised when they came in April for the twins' birth she would tell them the whole story.

"I know you miss your family, baby. But you'll see them soon and we'll have a huge celebration. We can have the twins christened while they're here. And maybe a big wedding reception. Any excuse for a party, right?" I would say just about anything to cheer her up.

She forced a smile. "I suppose. Is it time to go to the clinic yet?"

I nodded and waited for her to get her purse and coat. We went to the clinic for her weekly check-up. Her blood pressure was still higher than the doctor would have liked and she took note of the slight swelling in Laura's hands and ankles. I inwardly kicked myself for not noticing this myself. Her creatinine levels were also high but her weight was steady and her temperature was normal. But she would have to stay off her feet as much as possible. I promised the doctor that Laura would follow her orders.

When we got home we found my mother and Cat decorating the house for the holidays. Laura wanted to help, but I wouldn't let her. I spoke to them about helping me keep Laura off her feet.

"We'll keep her busy from a seated position, don't worry," assured my mother, giving me a smile. I left them alone to decorate with Laura watching from the sofa and went into the kitchen. As I was filling the kettle with water for coffee, I caught sight of Carmen out the back window, coming from the direction of her cottage. I hadn't seen her lately and I wondered how she was doing. I considered going out to say hello but thought better of it. Any move on my part could be considered encouragement and I didn't want Laura upset—or Carmen either for that matter. She caught my eye as she passed by the window and nodded in my direction but kept going. I had to quash the pangs of guilt I felt at seeing her. I thought I had been fair to her when we'd broken up, but apparently she didn't feel the same. I would have to accept that there would always be awkwardness between us.

I called Alberto Ruiz to check on the progress of Laura's annulment. I spoke to him for a few minutes and hung up just as the water boiled. He'd said he'd called in favors to rush the process and that Andrew would be served papers within the next week or two. If he signed the papers and didn't put up a fight, Laura could sign and the paperwork would be filed in the London court and the whole thing could be over by the end of January, if not sooner. *This will make her happy*, I thought, as I fixed coffee for myself and tea for her. I joined her in the living room where she and Tristan had set up the chess game on the coffee table. I told her the news and she was pleased. Tristan didn't react or say anything, and, in retrospect, I probably should have waited until we were alone to tell her. I watched them play for a few minutes and then turned my attention to my mother who I'd caught staring at me. She'd been doing that a lot lately—staring at me as if she didn't recognize me. Laura was engrossed in her game so I left her to it and went outside to walk in the vineyard. The air was cool but the sun was shining—it would have been an otherwise perfect December day except for the words ringing in my head. Words that had been eating away at my brain in spite of my attempts to ignore them: "*Why don't you talk to your mother about dignity? And while you're at it, talk to her about truth and honor. Because I have news for you, Dos Santos. Your whole pathetic life is a goddamned lie! Ask your mother what I'm talking about. She's been keeping a secret from you your whole sorry-ass life. And I wish to God I'd never found out. It makes me sick.*" The rational part of my mind said that Andrew had just been trying to say anything to get a rise out of me—that his words were empty and meaningless. But the irrational part— the part I knew I should ignore—was telling me to ask questions—to take my mother aside and ask her if she had any idea what Andrew was talking about. I thought it over and decided that if there was some deep, dark secret my mother was hiding, I'd rather not know now. I would wait till after the holidays and then, if it still mattered to me, I would take her aside and broach the subject. It would soon be a new year—2013—and I hoped it would be better than the last one.

My brothers were grumbling about having to go back to school. It was mid-January now and the holidays were over. I'd talked Laura out of Christmas shopping in actual stores in favor of online shopping and even though I knew it wasn't quite the same, she hadn't fought me on it too much. I did agree to take her out one day to the local gypsy market where she bought gifts for her family and Lily and Gretchen. We mailed them at the post office and then I'd taken her back to the other Post Office for lunch. It was good for her to get out of the house and I knew the outing was beneficial. But I also began to notice that she tired easily and slept a lot. We kept up with the weekly appointments and everything seemed OK, but sometimes I had a bad feeling that something was going to go wrong. And Catarina was unhappy because Tristan was preparing to go back to London to begin the next school term. She'd begged him to stay and go to school here but he'd made up his mind that he needed to go home for a while. He had his own medical appointments to keep and he also wanted to see his mother. And then Laura made a comment to me that caught me by surprise. We were getting ready to go to sleep when she mentioned my mother.

"I think your mother is going to miss Ronald," she said as she snuggled up against me in the darkness.

"Oh?" *My mother and Ronald?* "What makes you think that?"

"Well, I've noticed that they spend a lot of together...walking in the vineyard...cooking...talking. I'm just saying...maybe a romance is brewing."

Her innocent comment didn't sit well with me. I tensed up and worked to keep my anger in check. "My mother is in mourning. My father's death is still fresh even though it has been almost two years since his passing. She would never act inappropriately like that. I'm actually offended that you would say that." The words had come out more harshly than was my intent, but the thought of my mother with someone other than my father made me somewhat crazed.

Laura moved away from me, clearly hurt. "I didn't mean anything inappropriate. If they like each other…well…there's nothing wrong with that. Your mother is a young and beautiful woman. Would it be so awful?"

"Yes, it would. She would never dishonor my father's memory like that. My mother is a queen, for god's sake, Laura. She has dignity and class. She would never…" I stopped. The word dignity reminded me of Andrew and that pissed me off even more.

"What an old-fashioned notion that is," she said quietly. "I wouldn't have thought that of you."

I sat up on the edge of the bed, now totally unable to think about sleep. "Why not? I would never dishonor *you* that way."

She reached over and touched my back, rubbing her hand up and down my spine. "Well, lucky for us, we won't ever have to worry about that. But even though I can't imagine you with anyone else but me and vice versa, I would want you to be happy again. And if being with someone else made you happy then you would have my blessing. Just make sure I'm good and dead first so I don't know anything about it."

The bad feeling I'd had earlier washed over me again. I felt my anger dissipate as I tried to imagine a life without Laura. It wasn't possible. I turned around to face her. "You're right. We won't ever have to worry about that because you're not going to die. We're going to grow old together. We're going to spend our retirement on Ventura Island, whale watching and babysitting our grandchildren. How does that sound?"

She chuckled and I loved the sound of it. How quickly she'd turned my mood around. I leaned over and kissed her. She put her arms around my neck and pulled me down. I heard myself groan and I wished these babies would hurry up and get here so I could have their mother back. I tucked her into my shoulder and breathed in her hair—the familiar scent of lemons and now grapefruit—intoxicating. She got quiet and I thought she was falling asleep. But then she asked the question that did me in— that guaranteed I would not sleep tonight.

"Miguel…?"

"Yes?"

"When you said the word dignity…it reminded me of all that stuff Andrew said about secrets and your mother. Have you asked her about it? Or do you plan to?"

I closed my eyes and willed myself not to curse and hurt her feelings again. "I don't know. Maybe…but I doubt it means anything. He was angry—people say stupid things when they're mad."

"Well, he sounded like he knew what he was talking about. Maybe you should think about it."

And that's exactly what I did for the rest of the night.

I waited until after my mother's birthday to ask about the secret. It was now the beginning of February and we'd turned the bedroom next to ours into a nursery. I'd painted the walls the color of sand and my brothers had built a changing table, which I'd painted white. I never realized how good they were at building things. I'd always thought Tristan's ramp was just a fluke. Laura had wanted an ocean theme so she and Cat and my mother had decorated accordingly. It was quite nice when it was finished and I stood admiring the room while Laura and Cat were downstairs ordering baby clothes and cribs online. My mother came into the room and looked it over.

"It's beautiful, Miguel. It really is." She sounded sad. I knew she had to be thinking of my father at times like this. "Maybe the annulment paperwork will come this week and Laura can sign it and then we can plan a wedding."

"Yeah…I hope so. The papers should have been here by now. But, hey…Tomas and Mateo are quite talented with wood-working. Where'd they learn that?" I asked.

"They inherited it from your father, I guess. He was excellent at building things." She turned away from me then and stared out the window. It was now or never. And when it was all said and done I wished I had chosen never.

"I wondered when this would come back to haunt me," she said. She sounded resigned as if she'd come to the end of something. Her eyes filled with tears and her breath caught in her throat.

When I'd told her what Andrew had said to me in the alley behind the mall about my life being a lie and my mother having a secret, she had not even flinched. It was if she'd been waiting forever for the subject to be raised. She was surprised that I'd kept the information to myself this long. She'd asked me to meet her in the library at the back of the house after Laura went to sleep and she would explain everything. And then she had left the house and I had not seen her for the rest of the day until now at ten o'clock in the library. I'd been morose all day—not very pleasant company—and now my stomach hurt and my gut was telling me to forget it and just go to bed. Some secrets were better left unspoken and I sensed this would be one of them.

"Why are you crying, Mama? Surely it can't be that bad." I forced a smile, hoping it would calm her but she only cried harder. I went to her and embraced her. She seemed so small and frail in my arms. "Tell me."

She went over and sat down in one of the wing chairs by the desk—my father's desk—and I sat in one across from her. And then she spoke the words that changed everything about my life that I had always believed to be true. In a matter of minutes Miguel Dos Santos ceased to exist.

"Before I married your father I met someone at a formal event. He pursued me relentlessly all day and evening and I agreed to have lunch with him the next day. He came from a prestigious family in England and he spent a lot of time trying to impress me with his family ties. I never told him I was from a royal family—quite frankly, I didn't want him to know and I hoped he would never find out. I spent the night with him and in the morning I was overwhelmed with regret. It was a terrible mistake and I was wrong to be with him that way. I was about to marry Alfonso and he would have been broken-hearted if he had known. I kept it a secret and went through with my wedding to your father. But I knew before the wedding ever happened that I was pregnant—with you. The worst mistake of my life resulted in the greatest gift I ever could have been given."

I felt tiny pin pricks of tears begin to burn behind my eyes. I gripped the arms of the chair and concentrated on keeping my stomach from heaving. I was close to being sick…close to exploding in a violent rage. I knew I needed to hang on…let her have her say…but already I knew how this would end. She continued.

"You were born about eight months after we were married, and your father—Alfonso—worshiped you. I struggled with my secret…struggled with wanting to tell him the truth but not wanting to hurt him or lose him. In the end I held my tongue because your father would not have survived the truth. He was such a kind-hearted, gentle giant of a soul and very sensitive. It would have crushed him. I just couldn't do it. And the longer I kept the secret, the harder it became to even consider telling him the truth."

Mother stopped speaking and looked at me, her eyes pleading for understanding, but I remained silent. I did not trust myself to utter a word. My heart was like a jackhammer, my breathing nearly non-existent. Her tears fell in an unending stream as she spoke again.

"I saw him one more time, a few weeks after you were born. He had since found out I was a royal and he wanted to know why I had not told him who I really was and he wanted to know who your father was. He showed me a baby picture of his oldest son and I was stunned at the similarity. It looked like the same baby." She broke down then and covered her face in her hands.

I finally managed to croak out one word. "Tristan." My voice sounded foreign to my ears as if I'd spoken his name in a vacuum.

She nodded, her shoulders shaking. "I'm so, so sorry, my

darling Miguel. I have wronged you in the worst way…and your father, too…but I thank God he never knew the truth. Can you ever forgive me?"

A massive wave of heat washed over me as if I had been set aflame. I felt a surging of sound rumbling through my chest and I heard it rip through my throat. Tears of anger flooded my face as I came up out of the chair so fast I sent it flipping backward. *"NO! Goddammit! NO! You're a liar! This isn't true!"* I screamed. I lunged at her. I wanted to pick her up and shake her. She cowered away from me, pressing herself into the chair, and I moved past her and leveled my father's desk instead. I didn't know my own strength as I turned it upside down with one swift motion, sending everything on it flying about the room. The drawers fell out, spilling their contents all over the floor. I picked up a paperweight and threw it at the window, the sound of the shattering glass loud enough to wake someone upstairs. I heard footsteps running overhead. I yelled profanities in Portuguese, then English and then back to my native tongue. I ran out of the room, down the hall, my mother screaming my name all the way to the front door. I had to get out of here. I couldn't look at her. I felt vomit rising but I tamped it down. I grabbed the doorknob, ready to disappear, when I was stopped in my tracks by the one voice that still had any power over me.

"Miguel? What happened? What's wrong?"

Laura stood at the top of the stairs looking down at me. She was in her nightgown and bare feet, her hair mussed and her face flushed from sleep. I looked up at her and felt my heart threatening to explode. I became aware of Catarina and my brothers appearing as if out of nowhere. I thought I heard my uncle's voice. I stared at Laura as she slowly made her way down the stairs. Her face paled when she saw me up close. The nearer she got to me the harder it was to see her…my eyes were flooded and I was too nauseated to speak. I could barely breathe as she came to me and reached for my hands. I think it was the first time ever that my hands were cold and hers were warm. I wanted to say something, but I momentarily forgot the English language. A few words came out of my mouth but they were lost on her. I turned away from her.

"I don't understand...speak English...what happened?" She grabbed hold of my arms and shook me, trying to make me look at her. She turned to my mother and saw her stricken face. "Sofia? What's wrong with Miguel? Why are you crying?" I heard the panic in her voice as hysteria threatened.

My mother began to sob hysterically and ran from the room with Catarina close on her heels. My brothers stared at me in shock and Antonio asked me for an explanation. I finally found my voice. In Portuguese I told him to ask Sofia. I told him I was leaving. All three of them looked at Laura when I said those words. And then I yelled at them to go so I could have a moment alone with her. They disappeared as Laura stood, watching, waiting and not understanding.

When we were alone I shook her hands off my arms and told her to sit down on the steps. She obeyed me without question. I saw her nightgown catch under her stomach, emphasizing her fullness. The sight of it nearly killed me. She began to cry.

"You're scaring me! What the hell is happening?" She started to shake and more than anything I wanted to go to her and take her in my arms and hold her. I wanted to tell her to go get dressed and run away with me but she was frail and too pregnant to travel. And I knew in my heart that I wasn't good enough for her. I never would be. I was disgusting and I hated myself. I was tainted for life.

"I'm leaving, Laura. I'm sorry to hurt you like this, but you deserve better than me. I'm not who you think I am. Hell...I'm not who *I* thought I was. I can't be here—in the same house with my mo...her." I dropped to my knees and pressed my face against her stomach. I felt one of the babies push against my cheek—pushing me away. I felt Laura's hands in my hair. She grabbed handfuls of it in her fists and pulled my face up to meet her gaze. Her cheeks were streaked with tears and her eyes were big and dark blue and frightened. I tried to look away but she pulled my hair, forcing me to look at her.

"Please tell me...don't leave me in the dark...don't leave me...whatever it is, we can work it out together," she cried. I took her hands and stood up, pulling her up with me. She sobbed and the sound of it nearly broke me. "Is this about the secret?"

she whispered, her eyes wide, her breathing shallow.

I turned away and nodded. "Andrew was right. My whole life is a lie. Take care of yourself and the babies...all three of you deserve so much better than...me." Before she had a chance to speak, I kissed her lips, tasting their sugary sweetness blending with the salt from her tears. I fought hard not to choke on my own tears as I ran out the door into the darkness. I heard her calling my name as I ran, but I didn't stop and I didn't look back. I didn't have my car keys so driving anywhere was not an option. I ran down the long driveway, not stopping until I reached the road. I stopped to catch my breath, not sure where to go. A pair of headlights lit up the trees across the road, coming from behind me. A car pulled up, the window down.

"Need a ride?" Carmen asked, unlocking the doors.

I nodded and climbed in.

"Where to?" she asked, sizing me up.

"Anywhere but here."

The Shadow King

Chapter Fifteen

ADRIFT IN THE DARKNESS

LAURA

I had been in darkness before, but it was never this black. It was never this endless and all-consuming. I sat, frozen, on the staircase, the sound of the front door slamming shut still ringing in my ears. I didn't know what had happened or why Miguel was gone, but I knew that everything had changed. I wrapped my arms around myself and shook with a cold that went deeper than my bones. I didn't know how long I sat there rocking and shaking nor did I notice when Catarina came to me and pulled me to my feet. She was speaking Portuguese and I became frustrated. Didn't anyone remember that I couldn't speak this language? She walked me into the living room and settled me onto the sofa. She wrapped me in a heavy blanket and pushed the hair out of my face with her cold hands. I noticed that she had been crying—her eyes were bright and her cheeks tear-stained. It seemed as if crying had become an international pastime—everyone was doing it these days.

"I'm going to make you some tea and then we'll talk." She went to the kitchen and I heard the sound of running water and the click-click-clicking of the burner flaming to life. I heard the sound of spoons clinking into cups and steam rising. I realized that in moments of extreme stress I felt and saw and heard everything with a clarity that I didn't experience in happier times and I wondered why that was. Every sense was heightened, rather than dulled, by pain. It was a conundrum, but an easier concept to consider than the reality I found myself in which made no sense at all.

"Here you go," she said, pushing the hot mug into my hands. I held it for a second, but my hands were shaking too badly and the tea threatened to spill over the side. I was tempted to pour it over my lap just to see if I could feel the pain of it. I set it down on the coffee table and turned toward Cat, waiting for something to make sense.

Tears fell onto her cheeks as she seemed to struggle to find words. "Sofia wants to see you but she's a mess right now. Antonio is with her. She told me something devastating and though I don't know all the details…yet…I know enough to understand why Miguel left. But, Laura…you need to know that Miguel didn't leave *you*…he didn't leave *us*. He's trying to leave *himself* and I'm confident that in time he will realize the impossibility of that. He *will* come back…I know it. We just have to give him time."

"You're wrong. He did leave me—with no explanation other than something about a damned secret. Nothing's making sense, Cat. Everything was fine when I went to bed and now…he's… just…*gone*…?" I pulled the blanket tighter across my body and slumped into the cushions. I didn't even bother to stop the tears that poured like fountains--it would have been useless to even try.

"Laura…*ooh*…I don't know how to explain this…," she muttered. She said something in Portuguese that sounded profane. Her eyes glittered with tears. "Miguel…"

"No, Catarina. Please stop. I will tell her," said Sofia, coming into the room. "I didn't mean to put this burden on you." She was dressed in her usual black attire and I noticed she was wearing a necklace—a silver cross on a long, heavy chain. The sight of it made me gasp. I reached my hand to my neck, wishing I had on my talisman, but it was upstairs on the nightstand. I stared at the cross, transfixed. It was a bad sign—it made me think of death—and I turned my head away, trying to press myself into the sofa as far as my cumbersome body would go. Someone was either dead or dying and I didn't have the courage to find out whom.

"No…I don't think I can take it…whatever it is…please… can't someone just go find him…?" I sobbed, my breaths coming in jagged bursts. Catarina pulled me into her arms and tried to calm me down.

"Pull yourself together for the babies, Laura. You have to be strong for them. They need you and Miguel will need you, too, when he comes home…and he *will* come home. He loves you too much to stay away from you for too long. Remember I told you once that he would die for you? Well, it's the truth."

I pressed my face into her shoulder and concentrated on regulating my breathing. I could do this. I could listen to Sofia… hear her out…and then we could make a plan to find Miguel and bring him home. I sighed, a staccato sound that helped clear my lungs and I forced myself to relax in Catarina's arms. She held me tightly as Sofia began to speak.

When Sofia finished her story, I became aware of the loudest silence I'd ever heard. It was beyond deafening. I realized that what I was hearing was a rushing in my ears, the way Niagara Falls would sound if you were in a barrel going over it. I felt a massive heat wave wash over me and then a strange darkness enveloped me. I was doing what I always did when the going got too tough—I was giving in to unconsciousness. I was always safe there and that is where I wanted to stay.

"Oh, my god, Laura…" I heard Cat's voice. I heard Portuguese again…and Antonio and the twins—so many voices and I couldn't understand a thing they were saying. I drifted off to somewhere and I didn't know how long I was there but when I returned, I saw my doctor, standing beside me in a very bright room—the fluorescent lights were blinding. And then realization hit.

"No…no…I can't be here again. I want to go home." I tried to sit up but a nurse pushed me back and said something in that confounding language that I was beginning to hate. "I need to get out of here." I looked around the room in confusion. "Where is Miguel?" And then I felt panic as memory washed over me. I grabbed my stomach…by some miracle the babies were still with me, but Miguel…where was he?

"Laura. Your blood pressure if off the charts. You need continual bed rest until time to deliver. Your kidneys are not functioning at their best." It was the doctor speaking through Catarina.

"I promise I'll behave if I can go home. I'll stay in bed. But I can't be here. I won't stay here. I need to go home—back to Rhode Island. I have to…"

The doctor must have understood what I said. She began to shake her head vehemently back and forth. She spoke to Catarina and then Cat translated.

"You can't travel. No flying. She wants to see your test results and then we can discuss letting you come home with us but with a twenty-four hour nurse on duty. You need medication and rest."

I turned away from her. I noticed Sofia then and Antonio. Had I known they were even here? The doctor said something else and left the room. I was frustrated and angry at myself for being so damned weak. I grabbed Cat's hand and pleaded with her. "I have to get out of here. We have to find Miguel. Please, Cat. I cannot be stuck in this place again. I swear the minute I get the chance I will yank these tubes out of my body and I will walk out. I promise I'll do it."

Sofia came over to me then. "Laura, darling, I know you're worried about Miguel. But he is a big boy and he will be fine. He has to work out his demons on his own right now. I have hurt him…and you…terribly, but I will find a way to make this right. And one way of doing that is by keeping you safe and healthy. If the doctor allows it, we will bring you home—with a nurse—

and take care of you until the doctor says it's safe for you to deliver the babies. But the longer they stay inside of you, the better it is for them."

I shook my head. "I don't see how. I'm a wreck. I can't believe I haven't killed them yet." I sobbed into my pillow and suddenly wished to be alone in the dark where I belonged. What a mess I'd made of my life.

"They have a strong will to live," said Sofia softly. She tentatively reached for my hand—hers was soft and warm. I tried to imagine what she was feeling right now. It must have been hard keeping that awful secret for twenty years. I wondered if her burden felt any lighter now that the truth was out or if the burden was even heavier now, in light of the destruction its revealing had caused. She smoothed back my hair and stroked my cheek. She spoke softly to me in Portuguese and this time, I didn't mind not understanding. Her voice and words were soothing and I felt myself begin to relax. Eventually I grew sleepy and closed my eyes. I drifted away to a surprisingly peaceful place…surrounded by water and children…and…strangely…whales.

"I have a surprise for you, Laura," said Catarina, looking happier than I'd seen her in a while. "Actually, it's a surprise you'll have to share with me."

"Oh?" I mumbled. I pushed myself up higher on the couch and reached for my glass of water. "What kind of surprise? Is it popcorn? I'm craving popcorn badly right now—with lots of butter and salt."

She laughed. "No, it isn't popcorn but I'll make you some. But no butter or salt, sorry. I don't think the doctor would approve." We were interrupted then by the nurse who came in to give me my medication—something to help with my blood pressure. Her name was Susana and she didn't speak English but we got along well enough, as long as I did what I thought she was telling me to do. My doctor had allowed me to come home— with Susana and Felicia, the other nurse who stayed with me at night—but I had to stay off my feet except to use the bathroom and to take a shower every couple of days. It was the end of February now and I'd spent most of the month in the hospital. My mother had wanted to come, but I'd downplayed my health issues, convincing her that I was OK as long as I rested. She had spoken to both Cat and Sofia and they had assured her I would be fine and that I was in good hands. If my mother had known about my kidney situation she would've made herself sick with worry and I didn't want that. As much as I wanted her here with me more than anyone except Miguel, I didn't want to frighten her or bring her into the situation here in Portugal—into the abyss of waiting and wondering about Miguel and the not knowing when or if he would return. It had been weeks and we'd not had one word from him. I'd wanted to give in to my pain and heartbreak every day but I was never alone long enough to wallow—Miguel's family wouldn't let me. I was ready for something good to happen.

"So what's the surprise?" I asked.

"We have a visitor," she said, grinning widely. She stepped out into the hall and motioned to someone. I leaned forward to get a better look. And I nearly burst out of my skin at the sight of Tristan wheeling into the room and over to me. I sobbed like a baby and started to push myself up off the sofa, which caused Susana to spring to life from her chair in the corner and begin a Portuguese tirade in my direction. I frowned at her and sat back down as Tristan stopped in front of me and opened his arms. We laughed when we realized that neither of us could move enough to properly embrace and so we grasped hands instead.

"I go away for a few weeks and this is what happens?" he said, giving me the smile that always made me feel safe.

"I've missed you...terribly." I felt my ever ready tears begin their descent down my cheeks. "How are you, Tris? How long can you stay?"

"I'm here as long as you want me to be," he replied, his eyes dark.

"How about forever?" I asked on a sob. He reached over and stroked my face and I turned into his hand, closing my eyes. He brushed away my tears with his thumb and made a sound in his throat.

"If that's what it takes to make you happy again, then forever it is," he whispered.

"OK, I think I better cut in here," said Catarina, causing us both to laugh. She came over and kissed him--a long, sweet kiss that started a stabbing sensation in my heart. I turned my head... tried to ignore the hurt their kiss was causing me—and closed my eyes. I felt her sit down beside me on the arm of the couch near my head.

"I thought you were back in school," I said, opening my eyes. My voice sounded breathless. I felt winded. "Did Ronald come with you?"

"I am...or was, but I've decided to make a change. I realized how much I missed Cat..." he squeezed her hand, "and you... and so...I'm thinking of going to school here next quarter. And yes, Ronald is here. He's with Sofia in the vineyard. It looks like you're stuck with me. You're just going to have to play chess with me and when those babies come, let Uncle Tristan spoil the daylights out of them."

I froze at the word 'uncle.' I realized it had a whole different meaning now...in light of the circumstances. I glanced from him to Cat and back again. I sucked in a breath and tried to speak but I didn't know what to say—what I was allowed to say. Tristan saw my distress and squeezed my hand.

"It's OK, Laura. I know the truth. I know that Miguel is my brother. And I know this may sound strange and maybe it won't make sense and maybe it isn't even appropriate...but I'm proud to have him as my brother." He looked at Catarina then. "I hope I haven't overstepped any bounds in saying that, but it's the truth—it's the way I feel."

I buried my face in my hands and cried. I felt Tristan's hands rubbing my legs and Cat's arms around me. I heard them cry, too, and I thought what a mess of humanity we must appear to Susana from her perch in the corner, until I heard a noise and realized she was crying, too. And since our conversation was in English, she probably had no idea why she was even crying. We all must have thought the same thing because our tears turned to laughter then.

"I'm going to check with Juana about some food. I don't

know about you guys, but I'm starving," said Cat, pushing herself up off the sofa. "I'll be back shortly." She headed to the kitchen and I shifted in my seat to get closer to Tristan.

"Tris…how is he…Andrew…is he OK?" I asked softly. Andrew was such a delicate subject. My last communication from him had been a sweet text message about wishing to go back in time and start over—a text I'd never responded to. I pushed away my guilt and waited for his answer.

Tristan looked away, seemingly lost in thought. My heart pounded as I waited for his response. Finally he turned to me, his eyes troubled.

"Andrew is…going to be fine…one day. He…" Tristan stopped for a moment and let out a pent-up breath. "He received the annulment papers. He read them and tried to sign them…several times…but couldn't bring himself. He loves you, you know. It seems like one minute, he's ready to move on…and then…the next…he's adamant about getting you back. But when I left this morning, I advised him to sign the papers so everyone could be free. I tried to make him realize that he's doing more harm than good by hanging on to a slippery rope. I hope he was listening to me."

I didn't say anything. I had no response. Catarina brought us some lunch then, including a bowl of popcorn for me. I ate in silence, listening to them talk. I was struck by the thought that I had lost both Andrew and Miguel. And when I considered the unfairness of that, I remembered my two children. I felt them pressing against me—they had so little room to move around now. I pressed back so they would know I was still here…still waiting for them and I was thankful that at least I wouldn't be alone.

Chapter Sixteen

URGENCY

ANDREW

No matter where I went in the apartment, I couldn't get away from them. Several times I'd held them over the burner of the stove, my hand on the knob, wanting to destroy them, but fear of burning down the damned building stopped me every time. I knew once I signed my name to the annulment papers, my claim on Laura would be relinquished. It would be as if we had never married—as if Laura Easton had been a made up entity that had invaded my life and my dreams but had never existed. She would be free to marry...*my brother*. I swallowed the bile that threatened to erupt from my throat just thinking of him that way. And Tristan's words kept bouncing around in my head. He had urged me to sign the papers and give Laura what she wanted—her freedom. Just so she could give it away to a...gypsy? I knew I should stop calling him that but the word suited him. I looked at the papers again. I tried to read them even though I'd already read them over and over again, but my eyes wouldn't focus. I'd had them for weeks now and I figured Laura was wondering what was taking me so long to sign her away because that's what I would be doing when I put my name on the document. This wasn't what I wanted. *It's too risky*, I thought. *I want my children to be legitimate.* If I signed these papers it would be so much harder to get them back—if they were even mine. *Dammit!* I thought. *I don't know what to do—I could be making the biggest mistake of my life.*

I went to the refrigerator and took out a beer. I held it in my hand and studied the label as if it could tell me what to do. I'd promised myself I wouldn't do this anymore—that I wouldn't drink anything stronger than a cup of coffee or a bottle of Coke. I put it down and walked back over to the table and picked up a pen and without giving it another thought, I signed my name, *Andrew William Edward Easton*, on the papers. I signed all four of my names on every line marked with an x. And then I called Peter. He arrived within seconds.

"I was supposed to sign these in front of someone. Will you sign as my witness?" I asked him.

"You're sure, sir?" he asked, picking up the pen and looking at me, his eyebrows raised. I nodded and watched as he signed his name underneath mine on each page. I took the papers and put them in a manila envelope and handed it to him. "Don't bother with the courier. Just take them to the court yourself. There'll be someone there waiting for them. Thank you." He nodded and left me alone to wonder if I had lost my mind.

I was completely unable to concentrate on my studies. At the rate I was going I would flunk out. W*ouldn't that make Father proud?* I thought. It had been several days since I'd given Laura what she wanted and I refused to allow myself to regret it. I stared at my computer screen seeing only black, blurry lines where I'd just written the introduction to a research paper about the damned Battle of Hastings. I slammed my laptop closed and began to pace. I was considering breaking something when I got the idea to text Carmen. I hadn't heard from her in a while and I wondered if she was OK. I should probably let her know I'd ended my marriage. It made things more urgent for her—it might even ruin her day—but I decided to let her know anyway.

I sent her a text, dropped my phone on the bed and went to the kitchen to find something to eat, but I'd no more opened the refrigerator than I heard the ping of an incoming text. I went back and grabbed the phone and saw that it was from Carmen. She hadn't wasted any time responding: *Thanks for letting me know. But everything will be OK. Miguel is mine again. Maybe it's not too late for you to get the papers back and tear them up. Laura is all yours now.*

I dropped the phone like it was a bomb. *Miguel was hers? What the hell did that mean? What the hell was going on down there in Portugal?* I began to pace again—my favorite activity of late. I had a bad feeling. I texted her immediately: *What do you mean, Miguel is yours again? Explain.* I held the phone in my hand and stared at the screen willing it to light up…to make a sound…to give me an answer. My heart threatened to burst through my chest wall as I waited. Finally she responded: *Miguel left Laura and his family. He's been gone for weeks. He got some kind of bad news…he wouldn't tell me what…but it made him leave and come away with me. Laura's sick anyway… she's too much of a burden for him—he deserves better. No offense…I know you love her. Sorry…phone's dying.*

So am I, I thought bitterly. I was hit with a sense of urgency so strong that I couldn't move fast enough. I didn't know what the hell was happening down there but I was going to find out. I grabbed my duffle bag and began to fill it with random items— shirts, pants, socks, toiletries, phone charger. I found my passport and shoved it into the bag. Then I remembered that Tristan was down there and had been for a while now. He would know what was happening—he'd probably known all along that something was going on and hadn't bothered to tell me. I dialed his number. I grew more frustrated with every ring. He didn't answer so I texted him: *What's going on down there? Carmen said Miguel left Laura. What's happening? Is Laura sick? I'm on my way.* I hit send and went to the front door. I wouldn't bother with Peter or any of the goons this time. I felt closer to Laura just calling them that. I would hail a cab and go to Heathrow and hope I could get a flight out tonight. I opened the door and was stunned to see one of the goons, Nathan, standing in the hallway, looking nervous.

"Nathan? What is it?" He looked agitated, his eyes darting up and down the hall.

"Can I talk to you, sir? It's urgent."

I noticed a thin line of sweat on his brow and across his upper lip. Something was clearly bothering him but I didn't have time for problems. I tried to hide my annoyance at the interruption. "OK, but I'm kind of in a hurry. I need to get somewhere." I stood aside and beckoned for him to come inside.

"Andrew...," He seemed to be having trouble forming words as his mouth opened and closed and opened again.

"What is it? Is it my father?"

"No...I mean...yes...it's about him...yes," Nathan passed his hand through his hair and cleared his throat.

I sucked in a breath as realization dawned. I knew what Nathan was having trouble saying. He didn't want to tell me my father was dead. I spared him having to say it.

"He's dead, isn't he?" I kept my emotions in check as I spoke. I wasn't sure how I felt about this news. I wasn't sure if I could show the appropriate level of devastation.

"No...it isn't that, sir...," he hesitated again.

"Then what the hell is it? Spit it out!" I yelled at him. I was angry now and afraid to acknowledge that it might be because my father was, in fact, alive, when sometimes I felt as if he didn't deserve to be.

"I'm turning in my resignation papers tonight. I no longer want to work for your father. I've played along with this nightmare since Rhode Island and I'm finished with it. You should know he's planning to go to Portugal to await the birth of his grandchildren. He intends to 'bring' them home and I think we both know what he means by that. Andrew...I'm a family man...I have newborn twins of my own and if someone were to take them from me and my wife, I would kill. Peter has kept me informed as to your situation and I know you signed the papers to end your marriage. But it's your choice as to how to handle the custody of your children, not your father's. I won't be a party to his ripping them out of their mother's arms. And I sure as hell won't be a party to murder. He intends to kill Dos Santos.

Kevin has been down there 'observing' and he alerted your father that he might want to come early so the duke is en route. I just thought you should know."

I was stunned into silence. My mind raced as I processed Nathan's news. So my father had been serious about taking matters into his own hands and doing what I had not been 'man enough' to do. I could hardly believe it. I paced around the foyer, trying to think. Finally I stopped in front of Nathan and held out my hand. He looked at me, surprised, and shook my hand.

"Thank you for telling me this. I appreciate it. I can take it from here...and Nathan? Congratulations...not just on becoming a father...but for doing the right thing. It's nice to know that at least one goon has a conscience and isn't afraid to use it." I forced a smile as he nodded and disappeared down the hall. I heard my phone ping with a new text. I pulled it from my pocket and saw that it was from...Laura. Oh, my god, Laura. All the breath I had in my lungs disappeared and my hand shook as I opened the text and read: *Thank you, Andrew, for signing the papers. I meant to thank you sooner. My lawyer told me they'd been received by the court. And for what it's worth, you did the right thing. You will always have a piece of my heart.*

I read it again...three more times...and I kept focusing on four words: 'for what it's worth.' What did she mean by that? Was she trying to tell me that my signing the papers was the wrong thing? *Dammit*! I muttered as I locked the door and raced silently down the stairs to the street. No sense alerting Peter that I was leaving. I sure as hell didn't want any company this time.

Chapter Seventeen

GYPSY LIFE

MIGUEL

I awoke with a start, unsure where I was. I glanced around in the semi-darkness, looking for something...or someone...familiar. My heart was pounding and it took a moment for the memories to surface to the part of my brain I couldn't ignore—my conscience. It was awake and bothering me again and I knew I had to acknowledge it. I'd made a mistake—not in coming here...to Odemira...but in leaving in the first place. It was time to go home to Sintra and make peace with my mother, but more than that, it was time to go home to Laura. I had wronged her by leaving. It was selfish and childish of me to hurt her just because I had been hurt. I had left her at her most vulnerable—when she needed me most. I hated myself more for this than for being an Easton. I couldn't help where I came from, but I sure as hell could control where I was going. I lay back down in the rainy darkness, vowing that I would return home at first light. As I drifted to sleep I remembered how I got here and I wished I could go back in time and make a better choice.

We'd driven for a while, heading south, before Carmen finally spoke. "How far are we going to drive before we get 'anywhere but here?' I'm going to need petrol soon." She'd looked over at me. I could feel her eyes trying to see through me—trying to figure me out.

"Sorry...you can stop anytime. Where are we anyway?" I straightened in my seat and looked around. I'd been watching the road signs at first but now I wasn't sure how far we'd gone. I'd spent the last ninety kilometers trying to shut out my thoughts—trying not to hear my mother's voice as she erased my life... trying not to hear Laura's voice, haunting me...begging me not to leave her in the dark.

"We're in Alentejo country now, almost to Odemira," she said, shifting gears and slowing the car as she took the next exit. She coughed and fiddled with buttons on the dash. "So...are you going to tell me what happened?"

"No," I answered without hesitation. "I just needed to get away. I'll pay for your gas and you can go back home. I'll take it from here."

She forced a laugh. "It's after midnight. I'm not just leaving you here. Tell me what's wrong so I can help you...please, Miguel...I want to help you."

"You already have...thank you. I'll be fine."

Carmen drove on down the dark highway. In the moonlight I could see row after row of cork oak trees to the right and olive groves to the left. There were hardly any other cars on the road tonight—we seemed to be alone out here in Alentejo. I needed to get out of this car and stretch my legs. I was filled with nervous energy that needed an outlet. I wanted to walk it off...run it off...it didn't matter, but I needed to be alone.

"Well, I'll take you to the camp. I have cousins there...and friends. They'll take you in for the night and they won't even question it. They're used to people coming and going all the time. Have you ever been to this gypsy camp here in Odemira?"

I closed my eyes. I didn't want to make small talk with Carmen. I just wanted out. "A few times, yes, but not lately. I used to come down here with my fath...Alfonso...when I was little to see the cork production." *Alfonso...my father...was he still my father?*

Carmen turned off the highway onto a paved road that eventually turned to nothing more than a dirt path. It was lucky she drove such a small car—her Mini Cooper had no trouble maneuvering the non-existent roadway. We were in a wooded area, seemingly removed from civilization. I could smell wood smoke now and I knew we were in gypsy country. Up ahead I could see the glow of several small fires and the scent of smoke was getting stronger now. Carmen drove around a bend in the path and stopped the car. In the headlights I could see dirty white tents interspersed with wooden shacks where some gypsies had attempted to upgrade their lifestyle with something more permanent than canvas walls. We got out and I shook my legs, working out the tingling sensation of my blood flowing normally again. A man came out of one the shacks and approached us. Carmen spoke to him and they both looked in my direction. I saw him nod and point to a nearby tent. Carmen beckoned me over.

"This is Beni. He says you're welcome to stay as long as you like but if you stay more than three days, he'll put you to work." She smiled when she said this but I knew she wasn't kidding.

"That's fine. Thanks." I shook Beni's hand as he looked me up and down. I turned to Carmen. "Thanks again for the ride... and Carmen? Please don't tell anyone where I am. I don't want company...OK?"

I saw some kind of emotion pass over her face. She looked down at the ground briefly and then without warning, she wrapped her arms around me, burying her face in my neck. "I won't tell anyone you're here, but I wish you would tell me what's wrong."

I took her arms and removed them from around my waist and pushed her backward—gently--so as not to hurt her feelings. "I just have some things I need to work out. Thanks again for the ride." In the moonlight I could see tears forming, falling down her cheeks. "Go home, Carmen."

She backed away to her car and opened the door. "I'll be in touch," she said. She drove off and I turned around to Beni.

"Welcome, Miguel. You can sleep here for tonight and if you decide to stay awhile, we'll find you slightly better accommodations." He was pointing toward a tent set back near the trees.

I thanked him and went over to the tent. I looked inside. It was empty. I stepped over the metal rod holding it in place, wishing I had a blanket or at least a jacket, but I'd left the house with nothing except my cell phone and wallet. *I deserve to freeze*, I thought, as I sat down in the middle of the tarp-covered floor. I'd no more than sat down than the flap opened and Beni stuck his head in. He tossed me a pillow and two blankets. "See you in a few hours," he said and dropped the flap back into place. I spread one blanket on the ground and covered myself with the other. I stretched out and tried to get comfortable. *What am I doing here?* I wondered. I tried not to think…to keep my mind a blank slate…but it was impossible. My brain would not shut off. Every time I closed my eyes I saw my father's face…Alfonso Dos Santos de Braganza. I could not accept the fact that he was not my birth father—that Dos Santos blood did not flow through my veins like it did in my brothers' veins. *My brothers…no…it wasn't possible. I had four brothers. No…I had two brothers— Tomas and Mateo—not four. Tristan was my brother.* I shook my head in disbelief as one disjointed thought after another flowed back and forth. *Andrew…no…no…not possible.* Tristan I could deal with…I liked him…I respected him and his integrity…his attitude in light of the tragic accident that had taken away his ability to walk. I admired him. *But…his brother…my brother… Andrew…no…not possible.* I wouldn't accept that. *Dammit…* Andrew was married to Laura…my sister-in-law…*son of a bitch…* I sat up, my hands in fists ready to strike out at something, but there was nothing in this tent except two old blankets and a dirty pillow. I wanted to yell and curse and rage and tear down this damned tent but I was too tired. I lay back down and closed my eyes. Eventually, exhaustion won out over anger and I fell into a troubled sleep.

Beni left me alone for three days…left me to sulk and walk in the countryside surrounding the camp. He lived here with his wife and seven sons—no daughters. There were a few other people here—some distantly related to Carmen--and as I walked the land I saw that this gypsy community was bigger than it appeared. It stretched out in all directions. Most of the people I encountered left me alone, some spoke to me in passing, and others, including Beni's youngest son, Emilio, followed me around like a shadow I couldn't escape. Beni invited me to eat with his family and I appreciated the hospitality--mostly I appreciated that they didn't question me. I wasn't sure if they knew who I was—if Carmen had told them that my family owned the cork and olive groves they worked during harvest season—I didn't even know if they were aware of my royal status. They weren't letting on if they did.

On day four, Beni asked my intentions. "Are you sticking around or heading out? Because we have some jobs east of here and we could use the help."

"What kind of jobs?" I asked.

"Construction. A new house going up in Ourique. Are you good with your hands?"

I didn't know the answer to his question. My brothers were…Tomas and Mateo. They'd often helped Uncle Antonio build boats and they'd certainly proved themselves with Tristan's ramp and the furniture in the nursery…the nursery…just thinking that word made my stomach twist. I forced out the thought of what I'd left behind and answered his question.

"I guess we'll find out, won't we?"

Beni smiled and nodded and I followed him to an old truck. I joined four of his sons in the back and watched the road recede as we drove to Ourique.

Maybe I am my father's son after all, I thought, as I surveyed my handiwork. Beni had shown me how to build a chimney. It wasn't wood-working like what my brothers could do, but it was easy and it made me tired. I wanted to be tired…tired enough to sleep without dreaming...tired enough to keep my conscience from tormenting me. I was surprised that I enjoyed it and I finished the chimney in six hours.

"Anybody who builds a chimney that fast their first time probably did it wrong," said Beni, staring at the chimney. He checked my work, looked down the chamber and checked the flue. He inspected the flashing and finally the cap and then turned to me and smiled. "Looks good. I'm going to check inside and if it looks OK, you can have the rest of the day off." He chuckled to himself as he walked away.

I wiped the sweat off my face and tried to work the stiffness out of my arms and legs. It had rained off and on all morning but now the sun was high and I was hot, tired and thirsty. Beni returned and beckoned me over to the truck.

"Excellent work, Miguel. I wouldn't have thought it possible considering...," he stopped, not finishing his thought.

"Considering?" I prompted him.

He walked closer to me and bent his head close to my ear. "I know who you are. I don't know why you're here and I don't particularly care, but you're always welcome in the gypsy community." He stepped back, pushing his shaggy hair out of his face and regarded me closely. "And just so you know, no one else here knows who you are. I'm guessing you'd like to keep it that way."

I nodded and climbed into the back of the truck with his sons. We headed back to Odemira where his wife had food ready. I was starving and filthy. We washed up in the makeshift showers they'd rigged using water from the Mira River and as I attempted to clean myself I couldn't help but be impressed with their ingenuity. It amazed me that by some weird stroke of genetics they were gyspies and I was born royal. *Royal...twice over.* I felt the rage and embarrassment bubbling up inside me again. I didn't want to be a member of that royal family. They were inferior as far as I was concerned. So they were a seated monarchy and we were in the shadows. So what? We were the lucky ones. I shook my head as I put my clothes back on—dirty clothes over a wet body. For some reason I liked it--being a gypsy. It felt right somehow.

I went back to my tent which now had a chair and a radio inside. Beni had offered me one of the wooden shacks but I'd declined in favor of my tent. I heard a car drive up and stuck my head out of the flap. It was Carmen. Her arrival made my stomach clench and my head pound. I stood beside the tent as she parked. She came toward me with a backpack and another smaller bag.

"Hey," she said, stopping in front of me. "How are you?"

"Alright. What are you doing here?" I didn't need this—I didn't want reminders of home—especially in the form of my ex-girlfriend.

"I brought you some stuff. Some clothes and a toothbrush and other things I thought you might need. And this," she smiled and handed me the bags. I tossed the backpack inside the tent and opened the smaller sack. It was filled with queijadas.

"Thanks. You didn't have to do this," I said, my face reddening.

"I wanted to. And I wanted to make sure you were still here."

"Well, here I am," I said, stepping back toward the tent. I wanted her to go. Her presence was unsettling—a reminder of things I was trying to forget.

She moved past me and entered my tent. Her intrusion pissed me off but I followed her inside and sat down beside her on the tarp. "Aren't you supposed to be in school?" I asked.

"I was there earlier. But I wanted to see you. Everyone's a little freaked out that you left."

"I bet."

"You coming home any time soon?" She leaned forward, pressing her knee against mine. In the close confines of the tent I couldn't get away from her so I sat still and didn't move.

"I don't know what I'm doing. But I like it here."

Suddenly she shifted closer to me and took my arm in her hand. "Miguel…"

I wanted to move away from her but there wasn't any place to go so I remained a statue, staring down at her hand on my forearm. I raised an eyebrow at her. "What?"

"I don't know what happened to make you leave. No one's

talking. But I want you to know that I'm here for you. If you're trying to make a new start then I want to be a part of it. I can help you…be there for you…I love you."

I pushed her arm away and shook my head. "Don't do this, Carmen. Just…don't." I started to get up but she grabbed my arm and pulled me back.

"Wait. Don't run off from me, too. Talk to me, Miguel. Try to remember the way it used to be between us…before you went to America. We had a nice life…I mean it was more than nice… it was perfect. I miss you and if you took the time to think about it, you'd realize you miss me, too. You'd realized you missed this…" She shifted into me and pressed her lips against mine. I tried to move my head away but she pulled me closer, both hands around my neck. She pushed her tongue against my lips and I heard her groan as she ran her hand down my back. I reached up and took her hands and roughly pulled them off me.

"It's not going to happen, Carmen. You have to move on." I got up and stepped out of the tent. I heard her crying as I paced around outside. After a few minutes she quieted and came out. I saw pain and humiliation on her face, mixing with her tears.

"I'm not giving up. I'll keep coming back until you come to your senses. We belong together, Miguel, and deep inside, I know you know that." She pushed past me, bumping into me as she ran to her car. She jumped inside and tore off down the path, the tires spinning and spitting dirt as she disappeared around the bend toward the main road. She was gone in seconds.

I saw Beni watching from a chair in front of his shack. Little Emilio saw that I was now alone and came over to ask me a million questions. He loved to follow me around and pester me. But he was a good kid—sweet and innocent—and I liked him.

"Emilio…I have something for you. Stay there." I went back to the tent and reached inside for the bag of queijadas. I handed it to him. "You have to share these, OK?"

He looked inside the bag and his eyes grew huge. "Wow, thanks!" He raced off to find his mother, already stuffing a tart in his mouth. I smiled and went back inside the tent and stretched out. I was exhausted and ready to sleep. I pushed Carmen's visit out of my mind. Tomorrow I would be learning to install windows and I found the concept fascinating.

It was March now and true to her word, Carmen had come to visit regularly. I'd made sure never to be alone with her. I knew she was hurting, but it wasn't my problem to handle. She commented on my state of hygiene, touching my chin which was now covered with a beard. I'd never tried to grow anything beyond a goatee before and I liked how my facial hair looked. I wondered if Laura would like it. As soon as I thought her name I felt the familiar pangs of regret and guilt. I should be with her. I needed to end this gypsy sojourn. As I watched Carmen drive away, I made a half-hearted attempt to chase down the car and tell her I wanted to go back. But she was around the bend in the road and gone before I could get her attention. I went back to my tent and lay down on the scratchy blanket. I looked up at the highest point of the tent, which wasn't very high at all and stared at the pole there until I grew tired and fell asleep. But I had a nightmare…about Laura…she was dying and I was the only who could save her. I awoke with a start to the sound of rain on the tent. It was still dark out. I tried to shake off the dream along with my guilt and regret. I knew what I had to do. As soon as it was morning I would ask Beni to drive me to Sintra. It was time to make things right. I just hoped that I wasn't too late.

Chapter Eighteen

HELLO, GOOD-BYE

LAURA

I felt winded and hot. My back hurt…a dull ache that rolled over me in soft waves, sneaking up on me, shocking me then fading away. I didn't say anything to Cat, Tristan or the nurse because I didn't want to go to the hospital. It was March 12 and I still had another month to go. I knew what would happen if I complained of pain, but I couldn't face those pale green, sterile walls until I absolutely had to. So I bit my lip, endured the ebb and flow of the ache and plastered a fake, half-smile on my face.

I was on the sofa where I camped out during the day before going to my bed at night. I hated being up there alone even though the night nurse was always close. I felt more secure in the living room with people around. Sofia kept me company in the mornings then disappeared to run errands or visit friends, although this particular morning she had both an appointment in town and would be meeting friends for lunch so she would not be home till later in the afternoon. She had struggled so much in the days after Miguel had left…struggled to make it up to me… but I had assured her over and over again that I didn't hold her responsible for his absence. I had encouraged her to get out and try to resume a normal life as we waited—waited for something to change. Cat took me to my weekly appointments and sometimes Tristan and Ronald accompanied us. Mateo and Tomas played board games with me. There was nothing like playing Monopoly on a Portuguese board using Euros for money. Cat had gone into town and purchased a Scrabble game and decks of cards. She'd made me popcorn any time I wanted it and Tristan had made me laugh more than once just by being Tristan. They were all trying so hard to get me through the days…to keep me too busy to think…but at night, I suffered. I had finally learned to cry in silence so Felicia wouldn't hear me, but suppressing my tears gave me headaches. I wore my glasses again, which helped somewhat, but even they couldn't alleviate the pressure behind my eyes caused by unshed tears. I wore my talisman everyday but it kept a steady silence, refusing to talk to me. The crossed swords were there and the coat of arms and the mysterious numbers. I was keenly aware of the first set of numbers—that they coincided with today's date—but I kept it a secret. I didn't want to alarm Cat and besides, the talisman's strange messages were something I shared only with Miguel. I wanted to keep it that way. I remembered back to one year ago, when I was telling Miguel good-bye at Brenton Point. I couldn't believe it had been a whole year. My life had changed a million times since then. And here I was, without Miguel again. I bit back a sob as Cat came in with Tristan.

"I brought you something to eat. I know you're appetite hasn't been the greatest lately, but you can't survive on popcorn alone," said Cat, setting a tray of food on the coffee table beside the sofa. "Juana made some blueberry pancakes and bacon for breakfast. It's really good. I want you to try some, OK?"

I leaned over as best I could to take a look. My stomach was so huge that I no longer recognized myself. If I still had a center of gravity, I couldn't find it, because every time I got up, I'd topple over if someone wasn't nearby to catch me. The pancakes looked good but my stomach reacted negatively at the scent of them. My mouth began to water, my taste buds infiltrating with a strange sweetness, and I felt sweat break out across my forehead, upper lip and neck. And then a cold internal wave caused goose bumps to break out all over my body. I shivered and gasped as my stomach pitched and rolled.

"Cat...I think I'm going to..." I made a retching sound as my stomach heaved, bringing up what little food I'd eaten last night. I vomited all over myself and then continued to emit dry heaves and gasping breaths. Susana sprang into action from her spot in the corner where she had been reading. Cat grabbed my blanket and began to gather it up, trapping the mess I'd made inside of it.

"It's OK, Laura. I've got it," said Cat. I was crying now and embarrassed. I lay back against the cushions and closed my eyes. I did feel somewhat better now though. I breathed slowly, in through my nose and out through my mouth. I began to relax. Cat and the nurse cleaned me up and Cat went upstairs to get me a clean change of clothes. She was back quickly and asked Tristan to leave us while they changed me. I felt like an invalid—useless and pathetic—until I realized that Tristan had had to learn to deal with this indignity and had accepted it as part of his daily life. Compared to him I was lucky. This was temporary and soon I would be back to my old normal self. I let them clean me up and Cat dressed me and settled me into the couch with a clean blanket and a clean, cool cloth for my forehead. She told Tristan it was safe to come in and he wheeled himself back into the room.

Susana fussed over me. She took my blood pressure and temperature and spoke to Cat. They whispered to each other, looked at me then whispered conspiratorially to one another again. I found this absurd, considering they could have yelled to one another with megaphones and I still wouldn't have understood a word they were saying. Tristan had been silent throughout my little show but now he pushed himself closer to me and reached for my hand.

"I wish there was something I could do for you, sweetheart. You're doing really great though...keeping those babies safe. They're lucky to have you for their mother."

I knew he was trying to help me...to soothe me...but his words made me teary. I felt the ache in my back begin to roll around again, making its way from one side to the other and I winced, squeezing his hand hard in a death grip.

"Hey, hey," he said. "What's wrong? Are you in pain?" His voice was quiet, his eyes dark blue and full of concern.

"I just need to stretch my legs. I'm not sure, but I think the couch has now fused into my backside. That's probably why I fall over every time I stand up. It isn't because of my fat gut, it's because of the sofa growing out of my ass."

Tristan threw back his head and laughed raucously. "You devil. You're getting feisty in your confinement, aren't you?"

I tried to smile but my lips curled into a frown instead as the ripple of pain snaked over me again. I bit back the sound bubbling up in my throat and tamped it down as the pain eased away into nothingness.

"Maybe we should tell your prison guard over there about your pain. You can't hide it from me, Laura. Maybe you're in labor." He was speaking quietly, not that it mattered, because Susana knew next to no English. She and Cat were still talking and I noticed Susana had her phone in hand, about to make a call. That didn't bode well. I didn't want to go to the hospital yet and I feared that's what she was planning.

"I'm OK. I just...," I let out a shuddering breath as yet more tears suddenly fell unbidden. "Tristan

"What is it...what's wrong?" His voice was soothing. He rubbed his thumbs across my palms rhythmically. "Tell me..."

I shook my head back and forth. "I don't want to do this without him. He should be here. I don't want to go to the hospital without Miguel. It isn't fair...what he's doing...what he's done. I understand he feels betrayed...by his mother...by life...but I don't understand why I have to be punished for it. He should be here...today of all days, Tris, he should be here." I pulled my hand out of his and wiped my face and shifted uncomfortably.

Tristan was just about to answer when a loud noise suddenly erupted at the front of the house—a banging sound followed by angry voices. Antonio's voice could be heard arguing with someone speaking with an English accent. It sounded like...Andrew?

Tristan glanced over his shoulder and wheeled himself

around."*What the hell?*" he shouted, as he rolled out of the living room and into the hallway.

Catarina ran out after him and I tried to get up but Susana started in on me in Portuguese, waving her finger at me and shaking her head back and forth vigorously. I slumped back against the cushions in frustration, my heart thudding, my pulse racing, as I waited to learn what was happening at the front door.

"Let me see her!" I heard Andrew yell. "Where is she?" I heard scuffling and cursing and it sounded like something toppled to the floor.

"Andrew! What the hell are you doing here?" I could hear Tristan now, alarm in his voice. I wished I could see what was happening. Then I heard Catarina's voice, speaking in Portuguese, and then another female voice. It sounded like...Carmen...?

Andrew burst into the room then and stopped just inside the doorway. He saw me on the sofa and ran toward me, dropping to his knees beside me.

"Laura...? Oh, my god..." He stared at me as if seeing me for the first time. I was flabbergasted...stunned into silence. His gaze took in my face and body, his eyes darkening in wonder. "I've been frantic with worry about you. I've missed you so much."

Susana began a string of Portuguese that Cat cut off quickly. And then Carmen walked into the room behind Tristan. All eyes settled on me and Andrew while I continued to stare at him.

"What are you doing here? How did you get here?" I was shocked at the sight of him. He looked as thin as I was fat--and pale, with dark circles under his eyes. I noticed Carmen then, staring at me, and I wondered why she was here. Had she come with Andrew? That was impossible. They didn't know each other. Andrew took my hands in his and brought them to his face.

"I needed to make sure you were OK. I was...*am* worried about you. Carmen said you were sick and that...he left you. What happened, love?" He continued to hold my hand and I let him...it felt so nice to have him here...natural almost. I wondered if it was wrong to feel this way. I wondered if he was still my husband. He had signed the papers and I had signed them, but they still had to be officially filed in court—I had not yet received my official annulment decree. Until I received notice that the final step had been completed, I had to assume that we were, in fact, still married. For the moment I still belonged to someone and that thought gave me a strange comfort.

I burst into tears then. I couldn't help myself. I had felt so alone these last few weeks, in spite of Tristan's and Cat's and everyone else's best efforts to cheer me, but I couldn't hold back any more. I let it out as Andrew pushed off the floor and squeezed himself into the sofa beside me and took me in his arms. I turned into his chest and poured everything into him, even as my back spasmed and pain tore through me. I shook in his arms and he comforted me, rubbed his hand up and down my arm and whispered to me that it would be OK, that everything would be fine. I became aware of his scent, like fresh laundry and a light, citrusy aftershave. His shirt was soft and now soaked with my tears. He kissed the top of my head then cupped my cheek in his palm. I put my hand over his, thankful to feel its warmth against my skin. And then I gripped his hand hard and heard a deep, guttural moan tear from my throat.

"Ahh...ooh...oh, my god...what was *that*...?" I gasped, trying to breathe, but it was nearly impossible to make my lungs work right. "Ow...oh...geez..." I forced out a breath as I grabbed Andrew's arm and squeezed it hard.

And then everyone seemed to speak at once. I saw Susana with her phone in hand as she came to me with Cat beside her as translator. She asked several questions about my pain and where I was feeling it and how long had I been feeling it. When she had the information she needed, she stepped to the end of the couch and made a phone call, presumably to the hospital.

The pain ebbed away and I felt OK again...almost like it hadn't happened, except for a persistent ache in my lower back. I looked at Carmen then and turned to Andrew. "What is she doing here? Do you know her?" Carmen's face was expressionless and I found her presence unsettling.

He glanced over at her then back to me. "We've met. It's a long story. She picked me up this morning from my hotel and gave me a ride here. I couldn't exactly walk up the driveway."

Tristan came closer then and sized up his brother. "As much as I've missed you, Andrew, I'm not sure you should be here. You should have called first."

Andrew pulled me back into the circle of his arms. "You would have told me not to come." He kissed the top of my head again. "Why did he leave you, Laura? Why did that son of a bitch leave you like this?"

"Andrew!" Tristan was angry now. "Don't! Laura doesn't need any more stress. That topic is off limits."

Cat came over with Susana. "We need to get you to the hospital. The doctor thinks you're probably in labor. And she said not to be worried that it's a month early…that this is often the case with twins. They probably just don't have enough room in there and are ready to stretch their little legs." She grinned as she spoke. I knew her words were meant to inspire confidence but that was something I was in short supply of these days. She turned her gaze on Andrew and frowned. "Do you mind? I need to help her."

"I've got her," said Andrew. Cat started to protest but I shook my head.

"It's OK. But give me a minute…*ahh…oohh…ohmygod… aaahhh*," I struggled to breathe as the pain wrapped around me in a vise-like grip, squeezing me, then seemed to cut through me like a machete slicing through jungle foliage. I turned my head into Andrew's chest and thought about breathing—how to do it…when to do it…if I could do it.

"It's OK, baby. We'll get you to the hospital. You're going to be fine," Andrew whispered against my cheek as he eased himself off the couch. He reached for me, to help me up, but when I tried to stand, my knees buckled and I fell back into the couch cushions.

"Wait!" I cried. "Let me catch my breath. Please…give me…just…a second." Andrew sank to the floor beside me and smoothed the hair from my sweaty face.

And then…out of nowhere…the sound of a new, deep voice could be heard speaking in Portuguese. All heads turned collectively toward the sound. The voice I had longed to hear for so long. Miguel stood in the doorway, staring at us. I blinked…

unsure if he was real. He looked different. His olive skin was darker than I remembered and his hair was long, down to his collar. He had facial hair—more than his usual stubble—enough to classify as a beard. I gasped, my breath catching in my throat causing me to choke. I coughed and tried to speak but my words were garbled. I suddenly felt beyond exhausted. I'd been waiting for this moment for so long and now that it was here, I was too tired to react. I felt Andrew's arms coming around me again as he knelt beside me, turning his back to Miguel. Miguel spoke again, this time in English. His voice was low...a monotone... and menacing.

"Easton...if you step back from her now I will not kill you. Get away from her now."

Andrew and I locked eyes. His face was only a few inches from mine. His eyes were dark blue, stormy, filled with emotion. He worked his jaw slowly and I felt his hands press into my body for just a moment. He mouthed the words 'I love you' before slowly releasing his hold on me and getting to his feet. He turned to face Miguel and the silence that enveloped the room was deafening and thick as cement.

"I should kill *you*, you son of a bitch. You took off? Left her like this?" He pointed down to me. I looked away, fearful of what Miguel would do and fearful, too, of the knife blade beginning its slicing path through my back, entering into my abdomen. It was coming at me slowly but I could see the knife, sharp and glinting...in my imagination...as it hit me with force.

"*I...someone...aah...ow...please...*" I tried to move away from the pain, shifting as hard as my bloated body would allow. And then I felt a massive gushing sensation like a raging river pouring from my body. I felt the scream I emitted more than I heard it. I closed my eyes...thought I was falling as I reached out my hand for someone to catch me. I felt Andrew's hand in mine. The pain faded away and I relaxed.

Susana and Cat sprang into action. I heard their voices as they spoke, Susana giving instructions, making a phone call, coming toward me, assessing my vital signs. Cat was placing towels around me, cleaning something off of me. I saw Andrew look down at his feet and I wondered what he was looking at.

He seemed scared. Was he afraid of Miguel? And then Miguel was there, beside me. I blinked in shock. My eyes were playing tricks on me. Andrew and Miguel standing side by side? No…it couldn't be. Andrew started to recede, slipping away to another part of the room. Where was he going? I looked past Miguel… saw Andrew standing by Tristan. I reached out to him again past Miguel, who I didn't recognize. He didn't look like *my* Miguel. He looked like a rogue…like a…gypsy. Andrew came toward me…reached for me…I saw blood on his pants and the bottom of his shirt. He was injured.

"You're bleeding…" I whispered. I tried to get up and felt another gush. "Oh, my god…my water broke!" Again, I felt the words coming out of my mouth more than I heard them.

Miguel leaned his face next to mine. He spoke in a whisper and his words tumbled out fast as if trying to have his say before the clock ran out. "You're bleeding, Laura. Susana called for an ambulance. I'm here now. I'm so sorry I left you. I was wrong. I'll spend the rest of my life begging for your forgiveness if that's what it takes. I promise I will never leave you again. I love you."

I started to smile but my mouth twisted into a grimace and I screamed again as another massive wave of pain tore into my back. "*Oh…my…god…my…back…is…on…fire…,*" I gasped. My body burned with an intensity unlike any I'd ever felt. And then my neck began to heat up, in a circular motion going down into my chest. My talisman was finally awake and talking to me again—perhaps it had been waiting for Miguel to return. I grabbed at my throat and felt for the chain, pulling it out from underneath my nightshirt. I saw something unusual on it but my eyes were too blurry to see it clearly. Miguel picked it up and glanced down at it. I saw his eyes widen and his face contort into intense anger as if he didn't like what he saw there. In one fluid movement he removed it from my neck and slipped it into his jeans pocket. I grabbed his arm tightly, my nails digging into his flesh as I reached toward Andrew with my other hand. I needed them both. I needed to say good-bye. I had to be dying…this had to be the end…I saw Andrew moving toward me, tears streaming down his face. I saw that Miguel's eyes were bright with unshed tears. He held my left hand as Andrew took my right one. They were side by side again…not fighting this time. The sight of them together like this made me happy—darkness and light in harmony. For a brief moment I wondered where everyone else had gone. In the distance I heard a siren. I convulsed once more from the knife, smiled and slipped away.

Chapter Nineteen

Birth

Andrew

Laura's hand had grown cold in mine. She was white, her lips colorless. I watched as Miguel tried to lift her, but the nurse yelled at him to stop. He cursed at her and his sister intervened. He spoke to her in his damned native tongue, saying god knows what. I was stunned at his appearance. He looked as if he'd spent a long time alone on a deserted island. He was actually more morose than I remembered. I wanted to punch his face, but when I looked into his eyes over Laura's still body, I could see that he'd already been hit hard by pain—pain he deserved, but not delivered this way—not at Laura's expense.

Paramedics arrived and within moments, they had Laura strapped to a gurney, an IV started and an oxygen mask placed over her face. She came to and tried to fight off the mask but one of the paramedics restrained her hand, preventing her from removing it. We all followed them outside to the waiting ambulance. Miguel followed them to the open back door and started to get into the vehicle with Laura. But I was having none of this.

"What the hell do you think you're doing?" I yelled, approaching him.

"What's it look like?" He started to enter the vehicle, but I grabbed his arm and pulled him back. He cursed and turned toward me, hauling his arm back to strike me. I put up my arms in defense mode, ready to take him down if push came to shove. We glared at each other in silence.

One of the paramedics yelled at us. Out of the corner of my eye I saw my brother wheel himself down the ramp at the front of the porch. Miguel's sister came down behind him. She charged toward us. Carmen followed and stood off to the side.

"For god's sake, don't fight. You two need to make peace—this is not good for Laura. You don't think she can hear you in the back of that ambulance?" Miguel's sister was angry, her eyes blazing. Tristan rolled up to me, taking my arm but I shook off his hand.

One of the paramedics asked a question in Portuguese. Miguel answered in English. "I am." He started toward the ambulance but again I intervened.

"You are what?" I hissed at him. "What did he ask you?"

Miguel looked at me with empty eyes. "Get the hell out of here, Easton," he said menacingly. Again he started for the vehicle. The paramedics indicated that they were in a hurry.

I rushed up to him and reached for his arm to prevent him from getting inside the ambulance but he was expecting me. He swung his arm out, catching me in the stomach. I stumbled backward, winded, but I didn't fall. I heard Tristan yell something at me. I moved back toward Miguel. "What the hell did he ask you?" I spat out the words.

Carmen answered. "He asked who is authorized to make decisions about her care if she isn't able to speak for herself."

Miguel turned to Carmen and yelled what sounded like a tirade of profanity. She looked stricken and began to cry.

"I am her husband. I will ride with her." I barked out the words. I strode over to the ambulance and started to get in but Miguel rushed at me, his fist drawn back. Out of nowhere his hulking brothers appeared and intercepted his punch. They held him in their massive arms, saying something to him I didn't understand.

Tristan rolled closer. "Andrew! You're not her husband anymore. You signed the papers. It's over."

"I don't give a damn about the papers. Until I receive my notice of receipt with the judge's signature from the court, we are still married."

One of the paramedics started to close the door. Miguel tried to charge at me again but his brothers held him back. He cursed and fought to free himself from their hold but they wouldn't let go. His uncle came down the porch steps then and appeared to be reasoning with him. I wished I could understand what they were saying but whatever it was, it was enough of a distraction for me to hop into the vehicle and take a seat near Laura's head.

"Shut the damned door," I yelled at the paramedic. He closed the door and within seconds we were heading down the long drive. I watched as the paramedic did something with Laura's IV. He said something to me but I shook my head. I wasn't about to attempt a conversation in this damned, useless language.

I looked down at Laura. Her eyes were closed. I stroked her pale cheek and leaned closer to her. I moved her golden hair off of her forehead, thinking that each strand resembled stalks of wheat. I studied the details of her face. I had missed this face… so delicate and vulnerable. I closed my eyes tightly for a second to ward off the damned tears that threatened to fall. It occurred to me that I had probably never shed a single tear in my life before I met her. I was turning into a right sodden mass of wimpiness when it came to this girl. She turned her head into my hand and opened her eyes. I saw surprise there…she had been expecting to see a different face.

"Hey, baby…everything's going to be fine. You'll be at the hospital soon. I think you're finally going to bring these little guys into the world." I heard my voice crack as I spoke.

She started to speak but her voice faltered. She cleared her throat. "Where is he?" she asked in a whisper.

Three little words and each one a thrust of a knife in my gut. "He'll meet us there, love…sh…sh…you don't have to talk."

"How…how…did you get here?" she whispered. She frowned and moaned, her face pinching as if in distress.

I caressed her cheek. Her eyes were dark and tired. I thought about what she had been through this past year and it made me feel violent. I wanted to hurt my father. I wanted to kill him. I wanted to kill him more than I wanted to kill that damned gypsy. I trembled with rage, but I tried not to show it on my face.

"I had a feeling you needed me so I hopped on a plane and magically appeared," I grinned, hoping I could make her smile. It worked. I saw the corners of her mouth lift just the slightest bit. She was so beautiful. I wanted to kick myself. How had I messed up this exquisite gift so badly? Where had I gone wrong? My eyes shifted to her stomach, so huge and somewhat misshapen. I reached over and stroked it gently on top of the thin white blanket that covered her. *Twins...a boy and a...did she ever find out what the other one was?* I wondered. Whose were they? I looked back at her face and she was staring at me. Could she read my mind? Did she know how badly I wanted to be their father? She brought her hand down and placed it over mine on top of her stomach. I thought she was going to remove my hand but she didn't. She just held it there...in place...as a wave of movement rolled under my palm. My eyes opened wide in surprise at the sensation. I could only imagine what it felt like for her. Her eyes filled with tears and I wiped them as they fell down her temples into her hair. And then she stiffened, her body growing rigid, a guttural sound coming from deep in her throat.

"*Ah...oh...Andrew...ohmygod...,*"she screamed as her back arched off the gurney. She grabbed my hand, twisting my fingers with an unbelievable strength, causing my wedding ring to cut into my finger. I bit back my own burst of pain as I looked at the paramedic who stood over her, speaking his unintelligible language. I wanted to yell at him to do something but it was useless to even try to communicate with these people. Laura began to relax, her body going slack, her hand loosening its grip on mine. She turned to me. "Andrew...?" she whispered.

"Yes, love?" I leaned closer to her face. Her eyes were huge, glassy.

"I'm scared. This hurts. My back feels...like...fire...," her voice tapered off.

"I'm sure it hurts, love. I'm so sorry. We're almost there. You're doing great..." It killed me to see her like this but I didn't know how to help her.

And then, as if in slow motion, everything went to hell. I watched as her eyes rolled back in her head, her arms tensed and she cried out again in an agonizing sound that reverberated off of the ambulance walls. She tried to draw her legs up and turn sideways, her body convulsing. And then a gushing of blood splattered down onto the floorboards. The paramedic jumped and pulled back the blanket. I had never seen so much blood. It was all over the gurney, all over Laura's legs and dripping down onto the floor. I yelled at the paramedic to do something. We looked at Laura. She had relaxed, but her eyes were closed and she wouldn't…or couldn't…respond to the paramedic's ministrations. I noticed that we were slowing down. The vehicle came to a stop and someone opened the doors. I was frantic, feeling panic and shock setting in. Two attendants removed Laura from the ambulance and I jumped out after them.

"Laura!" It was Miguel. He rushed up to Laura's side but the attendant pushed him away. He saw the blood on Laura and on the paramedic's uniform. He cursed and turned to me. "What the hell happened?"

I answered as we ran in after the attendants. "She had a contraction…I guess…and started bleeding out. I don't think these damned paramedics know what the hell they're doing."

There was a flurry of activity as Laura was taken back into a room. Miguel and I followed the nurse. I had briefly noticed that Miguel's family and Tristan were in the waiting area as we ran down the hall. I wondered how they had gotten here so fast. Once inside the exam room, a doctor and several nurses began to administer to Laura. One of the nurses spoke to me in Portuguese but I ignored her. Laura opened her eyes finally and looked around the room. She began to cry out again as another pain wracked her body. She reached her hand out blindly and I moved to take it but Miguel moved faster. I wanted to break every bone in his body but I fought the desire and moved to stand near her head, silently daring him to make me leave.

"Miguel? Where were you?" she asked, her voice barely a whisper.

"Sh…sh…, Laura," he said in a voice softer than I would have thought him capable of. "Don't worry about that or anything else. Don't talk. I'm here now and I always will be."

"Where's Andrew?" she asked. I saw him grimace, his eyes flashing with annoyance.

"I'm here, love." I reached out and stroked her hair.

A female doctor entered the room then and asked us to step back. She glanced at us questioningly but turned her attention to Laura and began her exam. Machines were hooked up, monitors began to beep and someone came in and drew blood from Laura's arm. Every so often she would stiffen and cry out in agony. Both Miguel and I physically reacted to each sound she made but there were too many nurses around her for us to get closer. I purposely kept my eyes averted from Miguel, training them only on Laura. I was afraid if I made eye contact with him that I might lose what self control I had and take him out here and now.

Finally the doctor turned to Miguel. They spoke in Portuguese which caused me to fume with rage. "What the hell is she saying?"

The doctor turned to me and, miraculously, spoke English. "Who are you?"

"I'm her husband." I said nodding toward Laura.

The doctor's face registered shock. She turned to Miguel, her eyebrows raised in question.

Miguel straightened his shoulders and I saw his hands form into fists at his sides. "Not any more, you're not. Tristan told me you signed. She's not yours anymore."

"Oh, yes, she bloody well is." I faced him, my hands clenching and unclenching, ready to do battle.

"No! No! Stop! Ah! Oh!" Laura screamed. We all turned to her. She contorted in agony and cried out for someone to help.

"Do something!" I screamed at the doctor. Miguel yelled something in Portuguese and the doctor responded, turning her attention back to Laura, though clearly annoyed with us.

I shoved a finger hard into Miguel's arm, causing him to draw back in anger. "They're going to make us leave if we don't stop," I whispered, my tone harsh.

"I *want* you to leave, you son of a bitch."

"Miguel! Stop! Both of you...please," Laura's voice faded

into a whisper.

The doctor barked instructions to the nurses, one of whom made a call from the wall phone beside the door. She finished her call and relayed information to the doctor who nodded and then came around to where Miguel and I stood. She spoke in halting English.

"We take Laura to surgery for C-section. Babies in distress. Much blood loss. We will transfuse in OR. I think problem with kidneys. Test shows minimal function. You stay in father's lounge. No fighting permitted in my hospital. Go out in hallway now, please. You both."

Neither of us moved. I would be damned if I would leave the room before him. We stared each other down. One of the nurses opened the door and pointed to the hall. Miguel looked over at Laura. She cried out again as another contraction hit. I wanted to go to her but I knew what would happen if I did. I inclined my head in the direction of the door. He moved to the door and I followed him out. It probably killed him to go first. We stopped outside the door and a few seconds later, two attendants wheeled Laura out. They started toward the elevator.

"Stop, please!" Laura cried out. "Miguel? Andrew?"

I brushed past the attendant on Laura's right side as Miguel did the same on her left. She reached her hands out to both of us. I took her cold hand, noting the IV in the back of it, careful not to bump it. She looked up at Miguel.

"Miguel...please...don't fight with him anymore. Let this end now, please."

"Don't worry about anything , *minha querida*. I love you," He leaned down and kissed her forehead. The sight of him touching her and kissing her caused an adrenaline spike in my system. I fought hard not to give in to my desire to send him flying against the wall. She smiled at him and then turned to me.

"Andrew...make peace with your brother." I felt a sense of déjà vu wash over me at her words. She'd spoken similar words to me before about Tristan. "Find a way to work things out...for me...please."

"No worries, love. You just stay strong. When we see you again, you'll be a mum...a fantastic one. I love you." I'd no more said the last word than she stiffened and screamed out again as another contraction tore through her. The attendants came to life then and headed to the elevators. Miguel and I looked at one another. He had heard Laura refer to me as his brother and I was quite certain those words were affecting him the same way they were affecting me. I was amazed when he spoke directly to me—actual words that didn't involve beating me to death.

"I'm going to talk to my family. I guess I will see you up there," he said, tilting his head upward to wherever the father's lounge was.

I was stunned. I remained silent and nodded. I watched as he walked away. I went in search of the lounge. Eventually I figured out where to go…thanks to my high school Spanish which had a lot of similarities to the nonsensical Portuguese language I'd grown to hate. There were two other men in the lounge—one was texting on a cell phone and the other was slumped in a chair asleep. In the corner were vending machines for snack foods, soda and coffee. I stared at the coffee machine until my eyes glazed over and I could see nothing but blurred shapes and colors. I heard the door open and I blinked out of my trance. I saw Miguel's reflection in the glass front of the soda machine. I slowly turned to face him. He glanced at the two men, then in my direction, and finally moved over to stand by the windows. It was deathly quiet in the room except for the humming of the machines and the sound of the man tapping on his cell phone. I put my hands in my pockets so I wouldn't be tempted to use them if Miguel pissed me off again. As much as I didn't want to talk to him, I knew we needed to speak—about Laura…about the children…I didn't want to think about the other elephant in the room. I studied him for a moment, thinking that he looked like hell. His hair was long and he needed a damned shave. He might not be an actual gypsy but he sure as hell looked like one today. I approached him slowly and stopped a couple of feet away. He was staring out the window, moving his jaw back and forth, grinding the hell out of his teeth.

"She's going to be OK, you know," I said, quietly. My intent was to speak civilly, but his choice of behavior would determine the course of my intentions. He remained silent. I waited. I had nothing else to do but to wait.

Finally he stopped his teeth grinding and looked at me. "She has to be."

I turned my gaze out the window. I noticed the sun shining brightly over the parking lot. The sky was dotted with cumulus clouds. It was a perfect day…out there. "Why did you leave her?"

"It's none of your business. Why do you care anyway?" He spoke in a low, controlled voice. I noticed that his hands were in his pockets, too, probably for the same reason mine were.

"I *care* about anything that affects her…and whether she is still my wife…or not…she is my business. I have just as much invested in her as you, Dos Santos. Ripping a marriage certificate in half doesn't change the way I feel about her. It doesn't end there." I stared at a cloud, noticing that it was shaped like an elephant. I found it ironic considering the circumstances. "She's been through hell."

He was silent but I sensed wheels turning in his head. Finally he spoke. "Yes, she has." He turned to me then, his eyes glaring into me. "And you know why I left her. It doesn't take a genius to figure that out."

I sucked in a breath. So the elephant was going to be acknowledged after all. "It was just as much a shock to me as it was to you, Dos Santos. Trust me. I wanted to kill my father. I still do."

He chuckled bitterly. "You couldn't possible want to kill him as much as I do. I may still."

I wasn't sure how far I could probe into this subject without starting a war, but as long as he kept his hands in his pockets I would continue. "So you talked to your mother then?"

"I did."

"And?"

He turned to look at me. "I left."

"You didn't take it well, I guess?" I knew my question was the understatement of the century.

"Would you have?"

"I didn't." I thought back to the day I'd learned the same news. I had run out of my father's hospital room. I'd tried to find solace in beer…had chosen drunkenness over rational thought.

I heard a buzzing sound coming from a phone. We both re-moved our cell phones from our pockets at the same time. It was his phone. He spoke in Portuguese to the caller and then placed his phone back in his pocket. "It was Catarina…wonder-ing what's happening."

"How long does it take to perform a C-section anyway?" I wondered more to myself than to him. He didn't answer. We both directed our gazes out the window again.

"Easton…I don't…" The sound of a phone buzzing stopped him from finishing whatever he was going to say. This time it was my phone. It was Tristan. His words in my ear sent me reel-ing backward. I sucked in a breath as my heart began to pound erratically in my chest.

"Son of a bitch. Yes, of course, I'll tell him. Dammit." I ended the call and turned to Miguel.

"What was that about?" he asked, his eyebrows rising in curiosity.

"That was Tristan. He went outside with your sister to get some fresh air and he saw…" I hesitated as anger and fear fought each other in my gut.

"What the hell did he see?"

"A car drove past the entrance of the hospital with one of my father's goons at the wheel."

Miguel's face contorted. "*Son of a bitch!* That bastard's here? No!" He turned away and ran to the door. I followed him. He spoke over his shoulder. "I'll kill him, Easton. I won't let him hurt her…or take my children. He will die." We by-passed the elevators and took the stairs down to the emergency entrance where his family and Tristan were waiting. He went straight to his uncle and brothers and spoke quietly. Though I couldn't understand what they were saying, there was no mistaking the urgency in their voices. Catarina was listening and translating for Tristan. I caught most of it. Suddenly his uncle left. Miguel turned to me and Tristan.

"In a few minutes this place will be surrounded with my security. He won't get near her. I've instructed Antonio to allow anyone who feels the need to shoot the bastard. As much as I would love to do it myself, I need to be up there…" he pointed to the ceiling, "with Laura. I don't give a rat's ass if he is your father. I want him dead if it comes to it. I wouldn't trust the court system to do the right thing anyway, if he gets arrested for his crimes."

I resisted the urge to remind Miguel that the Duke of Easton was his father, too. Instead I nodded in agreement. "I'm with you on this. Let's get back up there."

Miguel signaled to his brothers. They spoke in Portuguese and then one of them stayed behind and the other one came with us back to the maternity ward. Miguel explained on the way up.

"Tomas is going to stay downstairs and keep watch with Cat and Tristan. Mateo will stay with us. At some point, we will be… otherwise occupied with Laura…so Mateo will be our guard. He will alert me if anyone gets this far. But I know Tomas. He won't let one of those goons get past him."

We went back to the lounge just in time to witness one of the men who'd been there earlier receiving news that his wife was out of surgery. Apparently C-sections were all the rage in this hospital today. We paced around for a while in silence eventually succumbing to the lure of the coffee machine. My stomach growled. I perused the snack machine but nothing looked appetizing. My stomach was too nervous to handle food anyway. Miguel's brother stayed out in the hall, keeping watch. Miguel sat in the corner near the door, quiet and brooding. I wondered what was going through his head. I also wondered how my father knew Laura was here. He must have goons watching. They'd probably been down here spying all along. It made me furious that I hadn't thought something like this would happen. I'd been so caught up in my own misery that I hadn't paid attention. I felt myself getting angry and I got up from my seat and paced again. I needed more space. I needed different air. I moved past Miguel and opened the door, stepping into the hallway. Mateo glanced at me but said nothing. I scanned the hall, watching nurses at their station, studying monitors, talking quietly, staring at computer screens. Suddenly blue lights began to flash intermittently in the hall up high near the ceiling. I stared at them in fascination. A loudspeaker crackled to life and I heard a calm voice speaking in Portuguese. Whatever the voice said, it repeated it. I turned to Mateo. "What did that voice say?" I asked.

"Something about code blue to OR three and a crash cart...?" His face reflected the fear that had to be registered all over mine. I heard him open the door to the lounge as I ran to the nurse's station. I went straight to the nurses' desk. Miguel stepped out into the hall and came toward me.

"Excuse me...excuse me..." I cried out loudly to the first nurse I saw. "What OR is Laura Easton in?" She stared at me, her expression blank. Of course...she couldn't speak English. That would have been too easy.

Miguel appeared at my side. "What's going on?" he asked, his expression guarded. I saw him scan the area looking for signs of trouble.

"Ask the nurse what OR Laura's in. *Now!*" I was frantic. Something was wrong. I knew it in my gut.

Miguel asked the nurse. She gave him a curious look as she picked up a clipboard that looked like some sort of schedule.

"Três," she replied.

"Three?" I said, turning to Miguel. He nodded. "Something's gone wrong. We have to get there. Where are the damned OR's?" I looked up and down the hall. I heard Mateo speak to Miguel. I saw realization dawn on his face as it drained of all color. He flipped out on the nurse and she left her desk to come around and stand between us and the hall that curved to the left of her station. We both dashed around her as Miguel told Mateo to stay and keep watch. We raced down the corridor until we came to a set of automatic doors that required a security access card for entry.

"*Dammit!*" Miguel cursed. He looked through the window and pounded on it, trying to get someone's attention. I pushed against the door but it wouldn't budge. I wanted to break it down but somehow I knew that would not end well for me, considering the two armed security guards who appeared out of nowhere. The nurse must have called them.

"We need to get in there," I said to Miguel. I looked through the window and saw two doctors approaching the doors. When the doors opened we both had the same idea to run through them but the security officers restrained both of us. The doctors came through the door and stopped in front of us. One of them spoke in Portuguese. I heard him say Laura's name.

"English, please! Do you speak English?" My voice sounded unfamiliar to my ears.

"Yes. You are with Laura Easton?" he asked.

"Yes, I'm her husband." I replied. I saw Miguel's face out of the corner of my eye. My words had angered him but he was smart enough not to start anything now.

"Come with me, please," said the doctor. We followed him into an empty room. It looked like a conference room. He indicated that we should sit down. He went straight to the point.

"I am Dr. Viqueira. I assisted in the delivery of the twins—a boy and a girl. Congratulations."

I nodded but remained silent. Miguel sat statue-like next to me.

"But the situation is critical for your wife. She lost much blood. We have given her multiple liters to replenish what she lost. Her heart stopped during the procedure and we had to use the paddles to get it started again. The biggest concern right now is her kidney function. It is possible that she had an underlying kidney ailment that she was unaware of. I do not know her patient history so I'm speculating here. Her blood pressure is too high and her kidneys are failing. She will need dialysis. She's undergoing treatment now. We've inserted a tube into her abdomen to cleanse away waste and fluid that the kidneys would normally remove. The Caesarean section was difficult. Her body has been through intense trauma. She is not currently conscious. As soon as she stabilizes we will need to decide on a course of treatment for her kidney situation. I can't stress how critical her condition is regarding her kidneys. She may very well need a transplant, but for the time being the dialysis will do the work her kidneys are unable to do. I will have a nephrologist talk more about it with you. Though her heart stopped briefly because of the blood loss, it is otherwise strong and she can hang on for a while if she doesn't contract any infections."

My limbs suddenly felt like blocks of cement. I couldn't breathe. Tears pricked my eyes as I thought of her in this condition. How could this have happened to Laura…sweet…innocent…beautiful Laura? A tornado of emotions swirled inside of me—fear, love, anger at my father, pity for myself and the hollow human who sat next to me, trancelike.

"Can we see her?" I hadn't meant to use the plural pronoun. It had come out accidentally.

"You can," said the doctor. "Immediate family only is allowed in critical care. Your friend," he looked at Miguel, "will have to wait here."

That statement caused an immediate reaction. "Like hell. I am *not* his friend and I will *not* wait here. Take me to her now."

The doctor's eyes widened in surprise. "I don't understand," he said. "Who are you?"

I spoke up before Miguel could answer. "He is…my brother. He is the father of the babies." I said the words quickly before I could change my mind. It hurt like hell to say it but I knew Miguel needed to be there with her. Beyond that, I knew Laura would want to see his face before anyone else's when she awoke. I glared at the doctor silently daring him to judge.

Miguel remained still and silent but he was beginning to shake. I saw it in his hands as he tried to still them. I saw the tenseness in the set of his jaw. He would either hit me or thank me when we got out of here. I didn't particularly care which one right now. The doctor seemed to consider my announcement, his expression one of confusion, but luckily he kept any thoughts to himself.

"Very well. You can both come then. I'm sure you would like to see your…children," he said to Miguel. "They are both healthy and large—the boy was born first and is nearly five pounds, the girl weighs just over four. They are fine and in excellent condition in spite of their mother's ordeal. Congratulations again. If you'll follow me, please."

We got up and followed the doctor down the hall. We came to the nursery first. There was only a handful babies in the room. We were told to wash our hands and put on scrubs in an anteroom and then two nurses came toward us, each carrying a tiny bundle, one wrapped in a pink blanket and one wrapped in blue. My lungs constricted as I realized that these two mysterious little creatures were finally here. I glanced at Miguel, wondering about my place here. The nurses weren't sure what to do or who to give a baby to. They spoke in Portuguese and Miguel answered their questions. The doctor was still with us and he nodded to the nurses to proceed. I looked at Miguel. He stared at me, his eyes dark and unreadable.

"Would you like to hold one?" he asked, his voice low.

I nodded, biting back tears. I reached my hands out and the nurse placed the tiny creature into them. The other nurse placed a baby in Miguel's hands. I looked down at the little face and saw Laura's son. He had a lot of very dark hair. His eyes were closed and he was drawn up in a little ball. I tried hard not to shed a tear but it was out of my control. I blinked hard so I could study his delicate features, his miniature nose and fingers. I was totally and completely wasted at the sight of him. I choked then, trying to prevent a sob from escaping. This was too overwhelming. Out of the corner of my eye I saw Miguel's shoulders shaking as he stared at his daughter. I glanced over and saw that she, too, had a lot of dark hair though not black like the boy's. Miguel glanced at the boy and blinked hard. So I wasn't the only one crying like a little girl then. He looked up at the doctor.

"Has Laura seen them yet? Has she held them?" he asked, his voice thick with tears.

"No. She is unconscious. Would you like to see her now? The nurses will take care of the babies."

He nodded. Miguel handed the baby to one of the nurses but before I could do the same, he reached for the baby boy. I placed the baby in his arms and reached for the other one. I was quite sure the nurses were curious about what was happening here—I could see the questions in their eyes. For once I was glad I couldn't speak Portuguese. I wouldn't have to answer any probing questions they might have asked. I held Laura's daughter in my arms. She was intensely beautiful. She looked exactly like her mother. I couldn't wait any longer. I handed the baby back to the nurse as Miguel did the same. We both looked at the doctor. He nodded and started down the hall. Miguel and I followed him. We went down a long corridor that seemed to go on forever. I heard the hum of the fluorescent lights as we walked.

Finally we turned a corner where we came to another nurses' station. We entered the room where Laura was and stopped. I was not prepared for the sight of her. I could see that Miguel wasn't either. A nurse looked up from the IV where she was administering medication. She and Miguel spoke a moment and then she stepped just outside the door. We walked over to Laura. Miguel took her hand and began to speak to her in his native tongue. I stroked her hair and stared intently at her, willing her to wake up. She looked beautiful…fragile…surreal.

"We have to call her family," I said to Miguel. "I can take care of that, if you want me to. I have their home number in my phone."

He nodded. "She looks…breakable…doesn't she?" he said, quietly. He placed his hand lightly on her stomach, flatter now but still puffed up like a small balloon.

"Yes." I noticed all the tubes and monitors, clicking and humming, measuring and sustaining her life. Seeing her like this was hard to take. I knew I would never get this image of her out of my mind no matter how long I lived.

"She's going to live. I have no doubt," said Miguel. He reached into his pocket and pulled something out. "Do you remember this?" he asked as he held up Laura's necklace—her golden talisman that I had arranged for her to find such a long time ago. He dangled it in the sunlight filtering in through the slats of the blinds on the windows across from Laura's bed. It flashed gold on and off as it turned slowly in a circle in the rays of light. I nodded.

"I have you to thank for bringing her to me. When she put this around her neck, she was irrevocably tied to me for life, just as Princess Gabriela predicted. I know you didn't mean to, but you gave me the greatest gift of my life." He reached out and ran a finger down her cheek, tracing the hollows there. "And she gave me the second and third. Maybe someday I'll explain."

A nurse came in then and spoke in Portuguese. She was telling us we had to leave. I didn't want to go. I squeezed Laura's hand and reached down and kissed her cheek. I stepped away then and gave Miguel a moment alone with her as I processed his words about the talisman. I didn't understand what he meant but I intended to hold him to that explanation someday.

Miguel joined me in the hallway and he spoke to a nurse at the desk. When he finished he translated for me. "I told her we were going downstairs to speak to our family and then we would come back to the waiting room near the nursery. I'm assuming you'll be staying, too?"

"You have to ask?" I said with some indignation.

He dropped his head…looked down at the floor for a second. I saw a hint of a grin which he suppressed quickly. We went to the elevators and headed downstairs.

The Shadow King

Chapter Twenty

DECISIONS

MIGUEL

My mother's was the first face I saw when we entered the waiting room. I wondered who'd called her—probably Cat. I stepped off the elevator behind Andrew and saw her standing between Ronald and Antonio. She looked stricken...pale...tired... frightened. They all did. Andrew walked over to his brother but I just stood there, staring at my mother. I tried, in that moment, to hate her—with every fiber of my being I tried—but I just couldn't do it. I knew in my heart that she was still the same loving mother who had raised me and adored me--the same woman who had protected me, not only from physical harm, but from emotional harm as well. I was sure she had hoped to go to her grave an old woman with her secret hidden away in her heart, and it may very well have ended that way if not for fate stepping in...a toss of a coin...a golden disk. I walked toward her and held out my hand. She must have been holding her breath, because it came whooshing out of her as if someone had flipped the switch on an industrial-sized fan. I took her in my arms and stroked her back as she sobbed. The last time I had held my mother like this, her tears soaking my shirt, was the day my father died. My father, who was, is, and always would be, Alfonso Dos Santos de Braganza.

"When can we see them?" Cat asked. Andrew had gathered everyone together in the waiting room and had told them about Laura's condition. His memory was better with the details than mine. The only thing in my memory was her, in the bed, machines keeping her alive…her face beautiful in sleep. I suddenly felt an urgency to get back to her. If she awoke alone she would be afraid and I couldn't allow that to happen.

Andrew answered Cat's question. "I'm sure they'll let you all see the babies, but not Laura—not for a while anyway. When I go back up I'll ask about visitation and call you on Tristan's cell. "

I stepped aside to talk to my uncle about security. He assured me the hospital was covered—friends, cousins, vineyard employees—no one could get to Laura or the babies. He told me to look around—asked me what I saw. I saw nothing unusual and answered accordingly.

"That's as it should be," he said. I tried to take comfort in that knowledge but I was still apprehensive…guarded. I had a bad feeling that I couldn't shake.

My mother noticed the interaction between me and Andrew. I could read the questions on her face—in her eyes. I knew what she was thinking. At the moment I had nothing to say about that. Andrew was another human being I wanted to hate. I'd spent almost two years hating him—I couldn't flip a switch and make the hate go away. Life didn't work that way. I looked at my mother—sent her a quiet look—*don't ask, Mama*, I said in my mind. Earlier I had held her in my arms, spoken to her in Portuguese, told her I loved her, said nothing had changed as far as I was concerned—that Alfonso was my father and all the dark secrets in the world would never change that. She'd smiled, thanked me and asked about her grandchildren.

Tristan was asking Andrew about Laura's family.

"I'm just going to call them now. It's morning in Rhode

Island—they'll be up by now. I'm going to step outside to make the call."

"I'll go with you," said Tristan. They went outside through the automatic doors and stepped away from view. I turned back to my family.

"I need to get back to Laura. I need to be there when she wakes up. Andrew will call down when you can visit the children," I said. I started to walk away but Cat stopped me.

"Miguel...?" She moved close to me, her back to my mother. She whispered in my ear in a low voice. "Are you OK?"

I shrugged. "I don't know what I am. I just became a father today but I can't enjoy the feeling. I need to get back up there. She could wake up any minute."

"But...what about Andrew...you and he seem to be...I don't know...getting along better...?" It was a question more than a statement.

I frowned. "I don't want to talk about it now. I really have to go. I'll keep you posted." I left abruptly before she could say anything else. I walked to the elevators and pushed the button. When the doors did not open fast enough to suit me, I headed for the stairs. For a few seconds, at least, I could expend some energy running in the stairwell. When I got to the maternity ward I went to the nursery first. I identified myself and was given a wristband to wear that matched the ones around the babies' ankles. The nurse smiled at me and led me to a chair in the same room where I had held them earlier. She wheeled both bassinettes over to me, gave me some instructions and then left me alone. I looked at both of them. Felipe was asleep but Gabriela's eyes were open. I picked her up first. I held her in my arms against my chest and looked down at her. I felt my lungs constrict inside my chest, threatening to cut off my oxygen supply. She was so tiny...fragile...breakable...like her mother. I felt a burning sensation behind my eyes as tears formed. I brought Gabriela closer to my face and brushed my lips against her cheek. She was so soft I could barely feel her skin. I worried that my beard would scratch her delicate skin and I promised myself I would shave as soon as I had an opportunity. She squirmed and emitted a soft cry. I felt panic set in. Why was she crying? The nurse appeared and offered to take her for a feeding. I kissed her miniature hand and passed her to the nurse and turned my attention to Felipe. Carefully I lifted him and held him against my chest. He felt heavy compared to Gabriela. I kissed his forehead, breathing in his baby smell. I wished Laura could experience this. Felipe made a sucking sound and I watched as his mouth puckered as if in search of something. The tiniest of frowns wrinkled his forehead and he, too, began to cry softly. It seemed I was making everyone cry today, including myself. I tried to soothe him but I didn't know what the hell I was doing. Finally another nurse came to see if I needed help and I asked her to look after Felipe so I could be with their mother. She took him and I stepped back out into the hall.

I walked to Laura's room, my nerves on edge, my stomach churning. There was a nurse in her room when I arrived and I asked her about Laura's condition.

"She's a little restless but all of her vital signs are stable. I think she's close to waking up. It's hard sometimes to wake up after anesthesia. It wants to pull you back under and it's easier to give in to it than to fight it. But if you see her moving her mouth or if her eyes flutter, just talk to her. Your voice will help to pull her out of the twilight world she's in."

I nodded and watched as she finished adjusting the IV and checking Laura's vital signs again. As soon as she left the room I moved to stand beside the bed. I held Laura's hand in mine.... noting its warmth when usually her hands were freezing. I studied her face. I saw things there I had never noticed before. I'd never noticed the tiny scar by her right eyebrow or the tiny mole beneath her left jaw. Her lashes were long and curled up at the ends and there was a little dip in the end of her nose. How had I never seen these precious things before? I leaned down and kissed her forehead and told her about Felipe and Gabriela—how they looked more like her than me but that their hair was dark like mine. I said anything and everything I could think of—filled the air with words—just to tease her back into consciousness. Sometimes I spoke in English and sometimes in Portuguese. I looked at her lips and wondered if there was power in a kiss like in those damned fairy tales Cat used to read when she was a little girl. So I kissed her lips, pressing mine against hers just so…holding still…hoping it would work. Finally I stopped and waited…watched her eyes…willed them to open. But she slept on. *What did you think would happen, idiot?* I was frustrated, anxious, and scared that maybe she didn't want to wake up— that maybe she wouldn't forgive me for running out on her— that maybe she'd choose him over me. I swallowed hard and tried to change the direction of my thoughts. Every so often a nurse would come in and check the monitors and speak to me, ask if I needed anything. I finally sat down, my chair pulled up as close to the bedside as I could get it, and I laid my head down on the side of the bed, with Laura's hand under my cheek. After a few minutes I drifted into a light sleep, aware of the kink in my neck from holding it at such an unnatural angle, but unwilling to move to make it more comfortable. I felt something tickle my cheek, soft fingers pressing into me, rubbing the scruff on my jaw. I sat up and saw a hint of a smile at the corners of her mouth. I stood and leaned over her and noticing that her eyes were still closed, I kissed her lips again—I'd be damned if my kiss wouldn't work this time—and she opened her eyes, turning her head slightly toward me.

"Hey," I said. "So sleeping beauty is finally awake, huh?" I smiled.

"Are the babies OK?" she asked, her voice raspy.

"They're fantastic…healthy…beautiful. I'll let the nurse know you're awake so you can see them." I leaned down and kissed her again. "You know, Laura, for someone who just had surgery, you're damned beautiful."

She smiled. A tear rolled slowly down her temple. I dashed it away with my finger. "What's wrong, sweetheart? Are you hurting?"

"I want to see them now…please." She shifted in the bed and tried to sit up but I stopped her.

"No, no. Don't move until they say you can. I'll call someone to bring the babies." I pressed the button on the side of the bed and a nurse arrived almost instantly. She saw that Laura was awake and asked several questions which I translated for Laura. She said she would have someone from the nursery bring the babies immediately. I brushed my hand over Laura's face, noticing how warm she felt to my touch. "How do you feel, baby?"

She grimaced. "Like I've been doing battle and not winning," she replied, clearing her throat. "What day is it?"

"It's March 12," I almost hated saying it. I knew what she would think.

She reached to her neck and grabbed at her gown. "Where is my talisman? It's today...the date on the talisman...where is it?"

I pulled it from my pocket and held it up so she could see it. She reached for it but I pulled it back. "I don't think you can wear jewelry right now, sweetheart, with all these monitors. I'll keep it for you."

"I need to see it...please," she said softly. Her eyes were troubled...frightened. I handed her the talisman and she checked both sides, frowning.

"It looks the same, but I saw your face...when you took it from me...back at the house. You saw something there...what was it...what did you see on it?" She was anxious now. I was holding her hand and I felt her pulse race under my fingers.

"You cannot get worked up, Laura. You have to stay calm. I didn't see anything...it's just the same as it was." I wanted her to believe my lie. I needed her to believe it. When I'd pulled it from my pocket earlier to show Andrew, I'd noticed that its ominous words had disappeared. I wouldn't have let Laura see it if it hadn't. "It says March 12 because it's Felipe's and Gabriela's birthday."

"No, no, no...it said something else...I know it did. What did you see? Tell me or I'll...," she stopped and moaned.

I leaned closer to her, my face inches from hers. "Listen to me. You need to stay calm. You've just been through hell and you need to heal. Why is it so important to know what was on it?"

Tears fell onto her pillow. She tightened her grip on my hand. "You told me the talisman is never wrong. I should have paid more attention to it. Please tell me what it said. You know how I feel about your keeping things from me. If something's coming—bad or good—I deserve to know. Now tell me, please."

I hesitated, shaking my head back and forth. It didn't feel right telling her this when she was so frail and vulnerable. I wasn't even sure I'd believed the talisman this time. I certainly didn't want to believe it. She squeezed my hand again—hard—and I took in a silent breath and said in a rush of words, "It said *Birth, Death.* But listen, Laura...you gave birth to two perfect babies and you're going to be fine, too. So, you see, we don't have to worry about anything. Everything's going to work out." I wondered who I was trying to convince more—her or myself.

She started to respond but we were interrupted by the arrival of the babies. A nurse was pushing one bassinette and Andrew was pushing the other one. I glanced over at Laura and saw her eyes light up at the sight of them. I hoped it was because of the babies and not Andrew.

"Hey, princess. You're awake," Andrew said, grinning. He stopped just inside the door as the nurse continued into the room to the far side of Laura's bed with one of the bassinettes.

"Andrew! You're here," she sighed, as if the sight of him somehow helped her breathe better. That sigh tore a hole in my gut. I frowned at him and his inappropriate greeting. I felt a sudden urge to wipe the grin off of his face with my fist.

"I need to sit up," said Laura, fumbling with the button on the side of the bed. The nurse waved her hand and shook her head. She said something which I translated.

"She will adjust your bed. She doesn't want you to move too much because of the tube in your abdomen. As soon as you've had a chance to meet the children she said the doctor would be in to explain everything."

"What tube? Do they leave tubes in when you have a C-section? I didn't know that." The nurse helped her get adjusted comfortably and then stepped back and indicated that Laura could hold the babies, one at a time. Andrew and I locked eyes for a moment, his grin gone now. I pushed the thought of Laura's failing kidneys from my mind for the moment and lifted Felipe from his bassinette. Andrew lifted Gabriela and held her while I placed Felipe in Laura's arms. I wanted to tell him to put my daughter down and get the hell out of here, but I held my tongue, though I was sure he could feel the irritation rolling off of me.

I was back to hating him intensely again and I wanted him to leave, but Laura seemed happy to have him here so I stayed quiet.

"Oh, my god, Miguel…look at him," she whispered, her voice breaking. Tears streamed down her face as she held him close to her nose and breathed him in. I watched as she studied his features, touching his cheeks, his chin, his hands, kissing the top of his head. "He's…surreal. I can't believe he's really here." Her shoulders shook and she sniffed. I could see that she was trying to hold herself together. I worried that her emotional state would adversely affect her kidneys and I was anxious for her to lay back and rest. Andrew remained quiet as he held Gabriela. I saw him look at the baby, smiling, and softly cooing to her. I felt adrenaline spiking and I gripped the side rail of Laura's bed to keep my hands occupied. But when I saw him lean down and kiss Gabriela's cheek I was livid. He had overstepped his bounds now and I couldn't take it anymore.

"Why don't you hold your daughter now, *minha querida*," I said, noting the edge to my voice and willing myself to tone it down. I took Felipe from her and nodded to Andrew to give her Gabriela. He was aware of my annoyance—I could see it in his face—but he silently handed the baby to Laura and stepped back to lean against the windowsill. Laura looked down at Gabriela and began to cry again.

"I can't believe this…she's amazing…gorgeous," Laura whispered. Again she touched the baby's nose, chin, cheeks and hair and kissed the soft spot on top of her head. I tucked Felipe into my arm as I wiped off her tears with a tissue and leaned down and kissed her lips. I told her I loved her…that she was beautiful and our children were perfect because of her, and when I stood upright and saw Andrew's hurt expression I felt a sharp stab of guilt which made me madder than hell. Because I knew I deserved to feel it. I was flaunting our love—mine and Laura's--in his face, and I knew it wrong.

A couple of nurses arrived and took the babies away for their feeding just as three doctors appeared and came to stand at the end of Laura's bed. One was her obstetrician, one a pediatrician and the other a nephrologist. They each spoke to me and I translated for Laura. Before I translated for the nephrologist I hesitated a moment, gathering my thoughts. More than anything I didn't want to scare her.

I gripped her hand as I explained. "This doctor treats kidney conditions, Laura. He wants to know if you've ever had a problem with your kidneys in the past."

She shook her head. "Not that I'm aware of. Well, nothing chronic anyway. I had a kidney infection once. I was sixteen and was in the hospital for a week because of it but it was only that one time and I've been fine ever since."

I translated her words for the doctor. He nodded and took some notes. Then he spoke to me at length about her current condition. I didn't want to tell her this. I looked at her for a moment then at Andrew who was listening intently though I knew, like Laura, he wasn't understanding. Finally I translated. "The doctor says your kidneys are minimally functioning. There is a tube in your abdomen now filtering waste because your kidneys aren't able to do it themselves. He wants to talk to you about the possibility of…a…transplant. He says more than likely, without a new kidney, you would be facing years of dialysis."

Her face turned paler than it already was. I saw her suck in a breath and put her hand over her mouth. I leaned toward her and put my arms around her. "It's going to be OK, sweetheart. I promise." Even as I said the words I knew it was a shot in the dark. What the hell did I know about transplants?

"Am I going to die?" she asked on a wavy breath.

Andrew and I spoke at the same time. "No!" I glared at him but he ignored me and came over to stand by her. He reached his hand down to hers and she placed hers in it. I stared at their hands intertwined and I had to look away. He was overstepping his bounds again. As soon as we were alone I would put him in his place.

I translated more information for the doctor and Laura about her dialysis and then Andrew and I stepped out into the hall while her surgeon examined her sutures. The nephrologist said something that caught me off guard but I guess I should have expected it. He asked about possible donors.

Andrew spoke up. "I called her family. I wasn't able to reach her parents—they must not be home—but I left a message for them to call as soon as possible. I'm sure they'll come as soon as they can."

I translated for the doctor. His response startled me. I made a sound in my throat and looked away at a spot on the wall.

"What? What did he say?" Andrew asked, barely controlling the alarm in his voice.

I turned to him. "The doctor said there isn't a whole lot of time to wait on her family. He's suggesting finding a local donor."

"Can we do that? How does this work?" he asked, his alarm turning to urgency. I asked the doctor about procedure and he said he would monitor Laura's condition overnight and come back in the morning and talk about the steps involved in a transplant. I was frustrated at the thought of waiting but equally glad for the delay. Laura had already been through one operation. Could she handle another so soon?

We were allowed back in the room. I could see that Laura was exhausted. I touched her forehead and noticed how warm she was. A nurse came in to check her vitals and when she took Laura's temperature, I saw her frown the slightest bit. My stomach twisted in fear. Something was wrong. I shook off the thought as the nurse finished her work and left us alone again. Laura closed her eyes and sighed. "I'm on dialysis," she said. "That sounds very bad."

"No, no…sweetheart," Andrew said, leaning closer to her. "It's a good thing. And don't worry. It's temporary. You'll be up and running in no time." It was all I could do to keep myself from leaping over the bed and throwing him out the window.

Laura whispered, "I'm so tired. You guys must be, too."

"I'm fine," I said. I felt my stomach growl just as I spoke and Laura heard it. She turned her head and tried to smile.

"I heard that. Go eat. Both of you."

"No." We both said it at the same time—again. Andrew raised an eyebrow at me and shook his head.

"I have an idea. How about if I see if Catarina and Tristan can come up to sit with you for a while? They haven't seen the babies yet and I'm sure they're getting anxious. Miguel and I can grab a bite to eat and then we'll be back quickly. Are you OK with that? Or I can stay here with you while he gets some food."

"No. I don't need food." There was no way in hell I was going to leave him alone with Laura unless it froze over first.

Laura shook her head. "I want you both to go eat—together. And I want you both to solemnly swear that you won't fight. I'm not asking for much here."

We both reluctantly agreed. I asked a nurse if Laura could have another visitor while Andrew and I went to the cafeteria. She said it would be fine so Andrew called Tristan on the cell. He, Cat and my mother would come up and alternate between the nursery and Laura's room. When Tristan arrived, Laura's face lit up like a comet and I knew she would be OK while we were gone. My mother was in the nursery with the babies. We stopped there on the way to the cafeteria and Andrew waited in the hall while I spoke to my mother. She was emotional as she held each baby in turn--as I knew she would be. I told her I would return soon but I was fairly certain she didn't hear me. She was too lost in her grandchildren. Andrew and I rode the elevator down in silence to the first floor and headed to the cafeteria. I was actually starving and figured his royal highness probably was, too. I chuckled at the thought, figuring I probably outranked him in the royal department. I thought he would ask me what was so funny but he remained silent as we entered the cafeteria and bought our meals. We sat down at a table across from one another. I considered for a moment how I would tell him to leave without starting a war in the cafeteria and decided, for Laura's sake, on a polite, controlled, *direct* approach.

"Easton…I think it's time for you to go back to wherever now—England, Mars, I don't particularly care where." I sipped from my Coke, waiting for his reaction, expecting a fight, but he didn't respond the way I'd anticipated. He had the audacity to laugh.

"Oh, Dos Santos. I'm sure you'd love nothing more than for me to leave, but as long as Laura is in this hospital, I'm not going anywhere, and there's not a damned thing you can do about it." He leaned back in his chair, a smug grin on his face.

I put my fork down on my tray. I didn't trust myself with it. "Oh, you think? Well, we don't need you here. We don't want you here. You're nothing but a bad memory for Laura. I understand she has a connection to your brother—I don't get it, but I can deal with it—but you...you're nothing but a reminder of what she's been through. I'm asking you—nicely—to leave. But if that's going to be a problem, we can find another way to settle this."

Andrew pushed his tray to the side and leaned across the table toward me. His eyes were angry, his voice barely controlled. "Listen, you son of a bitch...I'm not the enemy here. I love Laura—I always have and I always will. I'm not going anywhere. As a matter of fact, when we go back upstairs, we can ask Laura if she wants me to go or stay. If she tells me to my face that she doesn't want me here then I will leave immediately, but only if I hear it from her." He glanced away and I could see that he was trying to control his temper. Part of me wanted him to unleash it on me right here, right now, so that I could unleash mine. But I wouldn't allow Laura to be dragged into anything.

"No way. You're not putting this on her so you can just...," I stopped short as a strange expression suddenly transformed his face. He looked as if he'd either had a major revelation or just seen a ghost. I started to ask what his problem was but he stopped me with a quiet command.

"Do not move. Do not look anywhere but at me," he said quietly. I froze, resisting the urge to disobey him. I raised an eyebrow in question as every muscle in my body tensed. He spoke in a low voice, barely moving his lips. "I see one of my father's goons in here." Instinctively, I started to turn my head but he stopped me with his voice. "No. Do not look. Just act normally. It's one of the newer goons. He's sitting behind you three tables away, near the back exit door. He's in disguise but it's not a very good one. His earpiece is giving him away."

Quietly I asked, "Are you sure?" I was desperate to turn around and look. It took all of my willpower not to move.

"I know a goon when I see one. I grew up with these idiots. I just wish I knew how many more are in here."

"I'm going to call my uncle. We need to get them out of

here." I pulled my cell phone out of my pocket and started to dial Antonio's number. Andrew reached across the table and grabbed my arm.

"Wait. If your uncle and hulking brothers suddenly show up here, it'll tip him off." He shifted nervously in his seat. "Listen, Miguel. You and I haven't exactly had a chance to…talk…but you need to know that my father wants you dead. He wanted me to kill you…but…as much as I'd like to sometimes…I refused. And he wants his grandchildren returned to England. You're not safe and we need to get you out of here now without alerting that idiot behind you."

I closed my eyes for a second as fear coiled itself around my gut. Not fear for myself, but for Laura and the babies upstairs, vulnerable to danger. "If they're in here, they could be up there. We need to go now. I will at least send a text telling Antonio to get someone in the nursery and someone outside Laura's room. We need to move now." I pushed my chair back and stood. Andrew stayed seated. I heard him hiss under his breath.

"Miguel…wait…he's moving now, too." He said it quietly but I heard the warning. I was torn between getting upstairs to protect my family and taking the goon out the exit doors and beating him senseless.

I leaned down and placed my hands on the table, close enough for Andrew to hear me. "I'm going to text Antonio and then I'm going to take that son of a bitch out." I straightened and pulled out my phone. I typed: *Get someone upstairs to protect Laura and the babies…Easton's security is inside the hospital. Hurry.* I hit send and picked up my tray. "I have to…disable him…before he hurts my family." I heard Andrew curse under his breath as I turned and walked to the trash cans located near the exit doors. I dumped my tray and stepped to the doors. As I pushed the door open, I turned and locked eyes with the goon. He was moving in my direction. I wanted him to follow me. I had no doubt which one of us would win in hand to hand combat. He came closer and brought his hand up to his waist, lifting his shirt. I saw the gun in the waistband of his pants. I froze. I was aware of Andrew slowly advancing behind him. I had a second to make a decision—run or stand my ground. My uncertainty as to whom or what was on the other side of the door dictated my choice. I remained still and waited.

Chapter Twenty One

IN DREAMS

LAURA

They'd been gone a long time and I was worried. I wanted them both here with me and the babies. I felt a deep-seated need to have as much of my family near me as possible. I couldn't shake the feeling that my days were numbered. I knew it was a fatalistic attitude but I couldn't help it. I missed my mother and father so much. I missed Nick and my two best friends. Why did I suddenly have the feeling that I was never going to see them again? Once again I felt the familiar presence of my endless supply of tears pooling in my eyes, obscuring my vision. I turned away hoping Tristan wouldn't notice, but he was too in tune to me.

"What is it, sweetheart?" he asked quietly. He was holding Gabriela in his arms. She was sleeping, all curled up in a tiny ball. Cat was holding Felipe. Sofia was in the hallway speaking to a nurse.

I sniffed and shook my head. I wasn't sure I could talk without falling apart. I was feeling poorly, so warm, and a headache that had been sneaking up on me for the past hour was beginning to unleash its fury across my forehead. My throat hurt and I was so thirsty—I felt like I'd swallowed the Sahara Desert.

"What can I do for you, sweetheart?" he asked. I cleared my throat and tried to utter something that made sense.

"Tris…can I ask you a personal question?" I almost hoped he would say no.

"Of course…always," he said, his smile already making me feel more secure.

"When you had your accident, did you ever think that… you…might…you know…," I couldn't finish the question. I looked at Gabriela, so beautiful and serene in Tristan's arms. It looked so right that she should be snuggled into his chest. Would he ever, in this life, know the joy of fatherhood? My headache intensified.

"Die?"

I nodded. I felt mortified that I'd brought it up. He didn't need to be reminded of his ordeal. "I'm sorry…I never should have asked that."

"No…it's OK. It's a funny thing…well, maybe not so funny…but…no, I never thought I would die…and that was a problem for me at the time. Because, Laura…? I wanted to die… every minute of every day. At first I didn't believe them when they told me I would never walk again. But pretty quickly on I realized it was true and then I prayed for death. I wanted it desperately. I still get depressed at times but…" he glanced over at Catarina. "I have an amazing reason to want to live now…actually, more than one." He looked down at Gabriela and kissed her forehead. Cat looked up from Felipe and smiled at him.

I thought about the talisman. It had said birth and death. I was under no illusion as to who was marked for death. I lost it then. I began to cry, my shoulders shaking, my breath coming out in staccato gasps.

Cat stood up and laid Felipe in his bassinette. She came to me and leaned in, placing her cheek on mine. "You are not going to die. Do not ever think that. Only positive thoughts are allowed."

Tristan leaned over Gabriela's bassinette and settled her inside it. He wheeled himself closer to my bedside and took my hand. "She's right. You're going to be healthy in no time. Please don't cry."

I tried to get a grip on my emotions. I pressed my hand to my forehead and let out a pent-up sigh. "Where are they? They've been gone so long."

Cat and Tristan exchanged a look. And then out of the blue Antonio appeared at the door. He spoke to Cat in Portuguese. She kissed my cheek and excused herself, stepping out into the hallway where she, Antonio and Sofia entered into what appeared to be a very intense conversation. Tristan watched them and frowned.

"I think...as soon as you get out of here...that you and I should begin Portuguese lessons. I'm tired of not understanding a bloody word they say."

I smiled and nodded in agreement. I stared out into the hall, watching them talk. They didn't look right. Cat looked nervously up and down the hall and Antonio kept checking his phone. Sofia looked frightened. "Tristan...something's going on. Someone needs to go find Miguel and Andrew. They said they'd be back soon. Where are they?"

"I'll find out." He wheeled himself around my bed and out into the hall. I glanced at each of my children in turn, considered picking one of them up, but I felt too tired. I lifted my arms up, noting their heaviness. I was so unbelievably tired. I didn't feel right. Everything was wrong...in the hall...with me...everywhere. Nothing felt normal. A pain shot up my back and though I tried not to react, I heard myself cry out. I was so hot and now so dizzy. I needed something to drink...something to eat...I needed Miguel to come back...and Andrew. Where were they? Why did Tristan suddenly seem angry? I heard a baby cry but I couldn't tell which one. I wanted to reach out to him...or her... but my arms were too heavy. I wanted to call someone to help me but I couldn't find the damned button to call for the nurse. I closed my eyes and drifted, praying someone would pick up my crying baby. I heard a voice...finally...someone was coming to help me.

She had turned into a beautiful young lady. Her hair had grown long with glorious natural curls and it was so dark...dark as night. She was tall like me and she'd never outgrown that dimple in her chin. She was smart, too. She wanted to be a doctor like her Uncle Andrew. She was the proverbial apple of his eye. She had no interest in living a royal life, preferring to spend her time with the gypsies. That had been her father's idea. Miguel had taken her to a gypsy camp during the harvest season when she was little and she had fallen in love with the lifestyle: communal, equal, supportive, hard-working, artistic, free-spirited. She had her eye on a gypsy boy, but at the tender age of twelve, she was far too young for that. I hoped Miguel would steer her away from romance until she was older...at least thirty-five. Sometimes I listened in when she read stories to her cousins. She read to them in Portuguese and though I didn't understand the words, I could see the pictures...I understood the cadence of the language. She had taken violin lessons and I was so proud of her ability. I had never learned to play a musical instrument and it had always been a regret of mine. One day I came early...at twilight...and eavesdropped on her conversation. She was with her Uncle Andrew. I smiled when she asked the question...so happy that my memory was still alive inside of her, though I knew they were second-hand memories...stories she'd been told by others and not from her personal experience.

"Uncle Andrew...tell me about my mother again," she'd asked. It was September and they were in the vineyard, eating grapes straight off the vines.

"Ah...your mother," he'd said and smiled. I leaned in to hear better. I knew it was narcissistic, but I loved hearing Andrew's memories of me. "Well, where should I start?" he'd asked.

"Tell me how you met. It was at school in America, right?" She'd shoved a pale, purplish-green grape into her mouth, causing her face to pucker. She must've found a sour one. That happened sometimes.

"I met her at school, yes, but..." he paused, I think more for dramatic effect than anything. "I actually knew who she was before I moved to America. I'd seen her picture on a website and I just...kind of...knew...I knew I was going to meet her. I knew *she would become a part of my life."*

"Uncle Tristan told me before how much you loved my mother...in a romantic way. But she married my father instead of you. Did that hurt your feelings?" Wow. This was a new one. Gabriela had never gone this deep before in her line of questioning. I was eager to hear his answer but a little nervous, too. I wondered why no one had told her that Andrew had once been my husband.

He'd chuckled. "That's quite a question, Gabby. Wow. It kinda takes me back," he'd said. "Were my feelings hurt...?" He thought a minute...ran a hand through his blond hair. I noticed he needed a haircut...again. "Yes...my feelings were hurt..." I saw him glance down at her, taking note of the sadness that tinged her eyes. She did not like it when her Uncle Andrew was messed with...by anybody. "But, I found a way...a very interesting way...to deal with my hurt." He reached over then and moved her hair out of her eyes.

"What did you do? Find somebody new?" She'd given him a devilish grin then.

"No, I didn't find someone new. What I did was...every time I thought about your mother and got sad, I'd remember that all I ever wanted was for her to be happy and I knew she was happiest when she was with your father and so in a roundabout sort of way, that made me happy, too. It used to make me mad sometimes, but that was normal. Eventually I was happier than I was mad."

"My mother was very pretty, wasn't she?" Gabriela tossed a bad grape onto the ground and plucked more off of a vine. "I loved her hair. I wish I had blonde hair like hers...and yours."

"Yes, she was beautiful and, yes, she had gorgeous hair... but your hair is stunning, Gabby. I bet there are a lot of women in the world paying big money to get hair the color of yours." I watched as Andrew tugged on the ends of her hair, grabbing a handful and tickling her cheek with it. She playfully slapped his hand away and tossed her hair back over her shoulder. I wanted to touch her hair...to braid it and brush it and do all the things a mother does with her daughter's hair. I reached down, tempted, but I drew my hand back. I'd better not.

"Why did my mother choose my dad and not you?" she'd asked. "I bet that made you mad at my dad, didn't it?" Ooh, she was really probing now. I wondered how Andrew was going to handle that one.

He moved away from Gabriela then...walked to the end of a row and turned the corner out of her line of sight. I saw his eyes...glistening. Oh, Gabriela. You've made your uncle sad, I thought. But I knew she hadn't meant to. I moved in closer and listened. I would have held my breath if I'd been able.

"What's with all these deep questions today, sweetheart?" he'd asked when she caught up to him. They walked side by side down another long row of vines.

"I don't know. Just curious, I guess. Just wondering about things..." Her voice trailed off. After a couple of minutes, she asked again. "So, are you going to answer my question?"

He looked down at her. She was staring straight ahead in the direction of the house. Twilight had faded into darkness now, the moon brightening with each passing minute. "Well, Gabby... it was just one of those things. It was fate. No other way to explain it, I guess. Your mother really couldn't help it...your dad either. They were just meant to be. Sometimes that happens...you meet someone and, well, that's it—you're connected for life. You don't always make the choice yourself...sometimes it happens all on its own. And was I mad at your dad?" He laughed then, but I heard the sad tone in his laughter. I knew what it meant. "I admit...I was mad at your dad...yes...but it made your mother sad to see us not getting along so we stopped fighting and decided to make the effort to be friends...brothers. After awhile it became easier...considering we were too busy to fight—we had two screaming babies to take care of." He pulled her into his arms then and gave her a squeeze. "You and Felipe sure knew how to make noise." I smiled to myself. I remembered those nights...two crying babies and a houseful of adults with their hands full, trying to calm them. I'd wanted to help...to hold my son and quiet him...to soothe my daughter's bad dreams... but I couldn't. The adults had to figure things out on their own. Grandma Sofia had the touch though. She was always able to soothe them back to sleep.

"Will you ever have kids someday?" She was really going for it now. Poor Andrew. Another painful question. I heard his intake of breath...saw his expression change. He'd have made a great father.

"I don't know, love. Kids are a lot of work." He glanced down at her and grinned. She laughed. "Maybe I'll adopt some-day...who knows? Right now, though, I've got plenty to do...with the hospital and you and Felipe and your cousins. I don't think I could handle another rugrat." I smiled at that. He was busy alright, playing uncle to Tristan's three boys, all adopted from the gypsy orphanage, and long hours in the operating room. But I wished he'd make time...wished there was some way I could intervene on his behalf. I knew there was a pretty nurse named Erin who had her eye on him. I'd have to see what I could do.

They had reached the house now. Gabriela dashed up the porch steps and stopped, turning back to Andrew. "You coming, slowpoke?" she'd asked.

"You go on in. I'll be there in a minute. Save me a seat at the table." He waved her into the house. He turned his back to the porch and walked around the corner of the house, stopping near the row of yew trees that run alongside the back driveway. He looked around, stared at the gardens lit up by the moon, still partially in bloom in spite of the fact that summer was over then continued walking to his favorite place where the woods thickened behind the garage. He was out of sight of the house now, alone in the darkness. I wished he would go inside and have dinner with his family. I didn't like his being alone out here. I knew what happened when he had five minutes to himself. I knew where his mind went. I saw his shoulders begin to shake and I turned my head. I shouldn't watch this. It was hard to be sad up here—almost impossible. I heard his sobs, wished I could stop them...maybe I could...with a touch. I reached down, my hand hovering just above his shoulder. I knew I shouldn't...

He wiped his hands across his face and took some deep breaths. He told me he missed me. It was bittersweet and then I just couldn't help myself...I pressed just a little. I saw him turn his head sharply...looked over his right shoulder, expecting to see someone there. But he was alone. He pressed his hand down

on his shoulder and sighed. I heard his voice, quiet and sure...
"I love you, too." Ah...good...so he knew. After a minute, he
smiled, got up and went back to the house to have dinner with
his family...our family. When he was out of sight, I hovered a
moment more...and then went home.

"She's waking up...finally," I heard Tristan say. I felt hands touching me. My body was stiff, as if I had atrophied. With sheer force of will I made my legs move and then my arms. "Hey, Laura...welcome back."

I opened my eyes but shut them immediately to block out the bright lights. "Where's Miguel?" I asked. "Did he ever come back?" I opened my eyes again, just a little...enough to see without going blind from the awful fluorescence.

No one answered. I opened my eyes wider. He wasn't here. Andrew wasn't either. I began to cry. Cat moved closer. "Sh... sh...he'll be here soon." She stroked my hair, tucking it behind my ear.

"Where is Andrew? They've been gone too long. Where are the babies? Why won't anybody tell me anything?" I let out a shuddering breath and stared at their faces.

"Sofia is with the babies. She and I have been feeding them and changing them. They're doing great. Tristan's been here with you. The doctor is going to come in soon and explain some things to you. But you don't have to worry about anything. You were a little sick there for a while but you're doing great now," said Catarina.

"I was a little sick? You mean sicker than I already am? With what? Malaria? Typhoid? Lyme disease? Dengue fever?" I spat out every illness I could think of, realizing I sounded like a petulant child. "I'm tired of being sick all the time. I want out of here." I threw back my blanket and tried to get up but Cat blocked me with her body.

"No way. I know you're going a little stir crazy but you have to be still." She looked over her shoulder. "Here comes the doctor now."

The doctor entered the room and spoke to Cat first. That annoyed me. She translated. "You have an infection which they're treating with antibiotics. It caused your temperature to elevate but it's under control now and you're doing better. They've been running tests and monitoring your kidneys. You're stable now."

"Ask him if I need a transplant." I wanted to know now so I could plan my mental state accordingly.

Cat asked my question. The doctor responded. It was a fairly short answer. She turned to me, her face pale. "Yes…you need a new kidney soon. Right now the dialysis is working but a transplant is…the answer to getting you on the mend faster. I know you want out of here…to go home…but you have to hang in there…have patience." Somewhere in her translation the doctor's words became Cat's plea. The doctor read my chart and examined me. He said something else to Cat and then he gave me a pitiful smile and left.

I was mad now. I didn't want a transplant. I didn't want some stranger's kidney in my body. The only things I wanted were Miguel and to get out of here. "*Where…is…he…?*" I asked slowly. As soon as I asked the question, it dawned on me. *Of course.* If I hadn't had a headache I would have smacked my forehead in realization. I knew why he wasn't here…why Andrew wasn't here. It made total sense. I lay back against the pillow and sobbed.

Tristan and Cat were there…on either side of me…soothing me. Tristan stroked my hand. "Laura…what's wrong?"

I hiccupped, tried to catch my breath. "I know the truth. I know what you're not telling me…why Miguel isn't here… and Andrew. And I don't blame them." They exchanged glances. "Can you at least get a message to them?"

"They're coming…I promise…they'll be here soon," said Tristan. I saw him give Cat a look—saw something pass between them.

"Don't lie to me, Tristan. Don't lie to spare my feelings. I don't blame him for leaving. I wouldn't want to be saddled with me either. I'm nothing but a burden."

"Stop that. You're talking nonsense now. Miguel and Andrew will be here soon. Would I lie to you?" Again Tristan looked at Cat as he spoke. He tilted his head at me, cocked one eyebrow. "Are you hungry…thirsty?"

"Yes…both." I couldn't remember when I'd last had an appetite but I felt my stomach growl. I would have killed for a glass of my mother's iced tea. *My mother…ohmygod…my parents…they didn't know I was dying…* "Has anyone contacted my parents? Do they know the babies are here?"

"Andrew called them and left a message. We're waiting to hear from them. As soon as we do, we'll get them here. They're going to be so excited to meet Felipe and Gabriela," said Catarina. She was making her voice sound overly cheerful. "I'll get you something to eat, OK? I think your dinner is in the kitchenette by the nurses' desk." She left and I turned to Tristan.

"Where is he?"

"Sweetheart. Listen to me…Miguel and Andrew are taking care of something. They got delayed but I know they want to be here and they will be soon."

"Taking care of what?" I would be relentless with my questioning until I got real answers.

"I don't want you to get upset. Why can't you just trust me?" He sounded desperate now.

"Tell me. I will not shut up until you tell me where he is… where Andrew is. Has something happened to them? Tell me now!" My voice was on the rise with each word.

"Alright. But first, let me say this. The babies are safe. They're with Sofia and Ronald and Mateo in the nursery. You're safe here with me and Cat and Tomas. He's outside in the waiting room. He's been in to see you but you were always asleep when he came in—Mateo, too. Everyone's safe."

"Why wouldn't we be?"

"Antonio came up earlier and told us that he'd received a text from Miguel while he and Andrew were in the cafeteria. They saw some of my father's security and they got a little worried so they decided to take care of it."

My heart began to pound. My stomach heaved. I must have made a sound because Tristan suddenly pressed his chair up against the bed and grabbed my hand and gave it a squeeze. "Sh…sh…Laura…they're fine. Everything's working out."

"No…they're not fine. That madman is here, isn't he? I need to see my children. Please have someone bring them to me now."

Cat came in then with a dinner tray. She saw that I was upset. "What happened? Tristan…did you…?" He nodded. I saw her flash him a look of anger.

"Don't be mad at him. I deserve to know things. I made him tell me. I want the babies in here, please, now…I'll get them myself if I have to." I was angry, frightened and tired. I dashed tears away and pointed at the door. *"Now…please."*

Cat turned and strode off down the hall. Tristan shook his head. "I shouldn't have told you. You can't afford to get upset, Laura. You need to…"

"Don't tell me what I need, Tristan. Doesn't anyone understand that the not knowing is far worse than the knowing? I hate secrets. I always have." I leaned back against the pillow and closed my eyes. Miguel and Andrew were fine. They would be here soon. Now that I knew why they weren't here, it made it easier to believe they'd come back.

Cat and Sofia arrived with the babies. I held each one in turn…kissed their little faces and I even got to feed them for the first time. And then I fed myself. I was starving and so thirsty. Someone brought me some tea. It wasn't my mother's but it was good. A nurse came in and said there were too many people in the room but I threw a bit of a fit until she relented and let my family stay. I grew sleepy and I finally had to concede that I had to put the babies in their bassinettes and rest. It got quiet in the room…someone finally dimmed the damned lights and I drifted off to sleep.

"Are you afraid, Father?" Felipe asked.

"Absolutely not," Miguel replied. "There's no need to fear death, son."

"You never wanted to be king, did you?"

Miguel smiled. "No, I didn't. But it wasn't so bad, I guess. There are worse things in life than being king of a country."

Felipe laughed at that.

"Why did you never remarry...after Mother...?" Felipe's voice trailed off.

"What's with all the questions, son?"

Felipe sat back in his chair. He looked tired. "Sorry. It's just...I mean...I just want to understand you...your mindset...the way you think. I want to believe that you...that you're...that..." *He couldn't bring himself to finish the statement. Tears pricked behind his eyes. He tried to blink them away but that only made them fall.*

"What, son? You want to believe what?" Miguel reached his hand out to Felipe. Felipe pulled his chair closer to Miguel's bedside and grasped it in his.

"That you...were happy. That you got what you wanted out of life, but I don't think you did."

Miguel sighed. "I've had a good life, son. Better than most people's. You and Gabriela have made me happy. My grandchildren make me happy. I got everything I ever wanted. I just didn't get to keep it." He fought hard to keep his voice normal but the thickness in his throat would give him away if Felipe didn't leave soon.

"I wish I'd known her," Felipe said quietly. "I wonder what she would think of my becoming king of Portugal."

Miguel chuckled softly. "Oh, I think I know the answer to that. She would have loved it and hated it at the same time. She believed kings and queens belonged in fairy tales but she would have been proud. Like I said...there are worse things in life. But you know what your mother would have loved the most...besides her grandchildren, of course...?"

"What?" Felipe leaned forward, eager to hear this.

"She would have loved your choice of queen...you really lucked out with Jessica. They would have been best friends, I bet."

"Yeah, I did get lucky, didn't I? Not sure what I did to deserve her, but...I better not question it, huh?"

"Your mother always did prefer gypsies over royals," Miguel whispered, his voice fading. He was getting tired.

"I agree with my mother. I prefer them, too." Felipe re-

moved his hand from his father's and leaned down to him. "I'll let you sleep now, Father. Call if you need anything. I love you." He kissed his father's cheeks, each one in turn. "Good night." Felipe slowly slipped from the room. He didn't hear his father's response.

"Good-bye, son." Miguel slowly turned his body onto his side. He closed his eyes and within moments he saw me.

"Finally," I whispered as I took him in my arms. "You've certainly kept me waiting long enough," I laughed. "I thought you'd never…" He stopped me with a kiss…the sweetest kiss I'd ever tasted. And he still felt the same…smelled the same… looked the same. Not a thing had changed in fifty years.

"Laura Dos Santos…look at you," he grinned. "Still so beautiful." He wrapped his arms around me and pulled me close…so close I almost went right through him. "I brought you something," he whispered.

I ran my fingers along the line of his jaw…studied his face… kissed him again. "What?" I asked. I really didn't want anything—he was all I'd ever dreamed of…hoped for…imagined.

He took my hand and pushed something into it. It was my talisman. "Wow. You still have it…after all these years…" I was amazed.

"Look what it says," he said, turning it so I could read the words: In Darkness…Light. "Turn it over."

I turned it over and brought it closer to my face…making sure I was seeing it correctly. "Oh…Miguel…" If I'd had the ability, I would have sucked in a lungful of air. "You always said the talisman is never wrong. I've waited a long time to see these words: "A New Life Begins…"

"And not just any life, minha querida…a gypsy's life." He kissed me again…endlessly, tenderly…sweetly…a gypsy's life…a gypsy's kiss…my favorite kind.

Chapter Twenty Two

JUST REWARDS

ANDREW

The goon had to know I was behind him. He couldn't be that stupid. Miguel had stopped just inside the stairwell. He'd looked at the goon who advanced toward him. I followed, pushing through the door right behind him. I reached out to grab him but he anticipated my movement and swung his arm out to stop me.

"He has a gun!" Miguel shouted. He ran down the short passageway as far as the door that led outside to the back of the hospital. *How had he gotten there so fast?* I charged toward the goon but again, he anticipated my attack and swung his arm around, catching me in the chin with his fist, sending me back against the wall. I felt my skin split open as I banged into the wall. I quickly regained my balance as he ran toward Miguel, drawing the gun from his waistband.

"Stop, Dos Santos," ordered the goon, advancing on him, moving sideways...one eye on me and the other on Miguel. "Don't take another step or I'll shoot your legs right out from under you."

Miguel stopped, his hand on the long metal bar holding the

door closed. He looked up...saw the gun pointed at him...narrowed his eyes.

"Drop the damned gun, bloody wanker. You're not going to shoot anybody," I hissed. I started advancing on him, wiping the blood from my chin with the back of my hand as I moved.

"Stay out of this Andrew. I'm sorry I had to hit you. It's not you I want." The goon continued to sidestep toward Miguel who stood like a statue at the door.

What are you bloody thinking, Miguel? I wondered. I was afraid he was planning to do something that could end up getting us both killed, because I would probably have to intervene and try to save his sorry ass life if he acted impulsively.

"Go ahead and open the door, Dos Santos. Open the door and see how far you get," said the goon. He raised the gun and pointed it at Miguel's chest. I had to do something.

"What's your name...you're new, aren't you? I asked the goon, trying to buy us time.

"Don't try to distract me, Andrew...it won't work," he said. "Open the door now and step outside, Dos Santos. There's someone coming to talk to you. We don't want to keep him waiting... no sense prolonging the inevitable."

Miguel spoke then. "And what...*exactly*...is the inevitable?" His voice was low and controlled...barely. I could see that he was coiled...ready to strike. I was still hoping for a peaceful ending to this insanity.

"Why don't you step through the door and find out," replied the goon.

"Is my father out there?" I asked. It suddenly occurred to me that the goon wasn't expecting me to help Miguel. He was probably assuming I would be on their side...that I would want Miguel dead just as much as my father did. I swallowed my apprehension as I stared...first at Miguel...then at the gun.

The goon didn't answer. He chose that moment to close the distance to Miguel, shoving the gun into his stomach and gripping Miguel's arm. I was astonished that Miguel didn't put up a fight. He didn't try to subdue the goon or go for the weapon. He pulled Miguel back...away from the door and spoke to me over his left shoulder. "Andrew...step around us and open the door.

And don't try anything stupid…you might cause this gun to accidentally go off into Dos Santos's gut."

I locked eyes with Miguel. He stared at me…nodded almost imperceptibly. I walked to the door and opened it, then stepped outside onto a paved service road behind the hospital bordered by a dense grove of trees. The goon pushed Miguel out and let go of his arm, but kept the gun trained on him. It was getting dark but there was enough light from the auxiliary lamps posted intermittently along the edge of the hospital's rooftop to see that we were not alone out here. Miguel stood in the middle of the roadway, the goon behind him, pointing the gun at his back. A black Mercedes was parked on the side of the road about fifty feet away. The doors opened. Peter emerged from the driver's seat, Kevin from the passenger side and my father from the back driver's side. Father stopped a moment and straightened his clothing. I noticed he was dressed formally…in a black suit, white shirt and tie. I thought it was a strange choice of wardrobe for this back alley rendezvous. He began to slowly walk toward us. My heart pounded as I stared at my father. He didn't look like the man I'd known as a child—the man who'd made a half-assed attempt to raise me. He'd always been cold and distant, but tonight…tonight he'd reinvented cold and distant. Tonight he was not my father. He was an empty shell of humanity hell-bent on getting revenge on his own son who had never done a damned thing to deserve this pre-meditated fate except exist. For one moment I thought about Laura, upstairs in this hospital, fighting for her life, loving this gypsy who, whether I liked it or not, was my brother, and I knew that if he died, she would die, too. And now it became my life's ambition to keep Miguel Dos Santos alive.

"What the hell are you doing, Father? What is this…some crazy re-enactment of a scene from *The Godfather*? Why are you here?" I walked a few steps toward him so that I was equidistant between him and Miguel. I stood sideways so I could see them both. Miguel stood still like a statue. I wasn't sure that he was even breathing. His face was stony...his expression un-readable...his hands in fists...his arms slightly bent, ready for battle.

"Andrew." My father cast a fake smile at me. "You should not be here, son. I certainly hope you haven't joined forces with the gypsies like your brother has. I would hate to lose all of my sons."

"I haven't joined forces with anyone. I'm here to be with my wife and children. Why the hell are you here?" I saw Miguel flinch at my words...saw his expression darken.

"Yes, son. I understand congratulations are in order...a boy and a girl...well done." My father shifted his stance as if standing for too long was problematic. I was counting on that. "And how is your beautiful wife?"

Miguel lurched forward then, taking the goons by surprise. The new one grabbed blindly for Miguel's shirttail, grasping a handful in his fist as Kevin dashed forward, gun drawn, aimed at Miguel. "She's not his wife you son of a bitch!" Miguel yelled at my father. He strained against the goon's hold on him.

"That is a minor technicality, Mr. Dos Santos. The children are still members of the House of Hanover. I'm here to bring them home."

"*Like hell!*" Miguel tried to jerk away from the goon holding him but Kevin brought his hand up in an arc, hitting Miguel in the face with enough force to knock him backward into the goon. They both went down on the ground in a heap, both of them getting in a few punches to the face, but Peter raced forward and hauled Miguel to his feet. Miguel's face was a bloody mess. It was impossible to tell where the blood was coming from—it could have been multiple places.

"Is that really necessary?" I asked the goons. My voice sounded hollow as if I were speaking in a vacuum. It was three of them on Miguel now. *Where were his bloody hulking brothers when you needed them*? My stomach churned at the sight of Miguel's messed up face, though I was sure mine didn't look much better. My pulse raced as I turned to my father. "I will bring the children home as soon as they're discharged from hospital and not before. You...Father...need to take your...*employ-*

ees…home and let me take care of my family myself."

My father laughed…a sinister noise that rumbled from his gut. "Yes, Andrew. We know what a great job you've managed to do in that regard, don't we? I asked you to do one thing, but have you done it? No…otherwise that damned gypsy thief would have been dead a year ago. The decree will be fulfilled tonight. I'm tired of waiting. *Peter*!"

Peter shoved Miguel hard, sending him tumbling to the pavement. Miguel put his arms out to break his fall and landed on his hands and knees. Peter raised his gun…trained it on Miguel.

"*Wait…wait…wait*!!!" I shouted as I ran toward Peter, insinuating myself between Miguel and the gun. "No, you stupid goon…not like this!" I reached my hand out...pushed his arm away. "Peter…stop for a minute. Let me talk to my father first." Peter turned to look at my father for guidance. I glanced down at Miguel. His eyes were on me, his face impassive and bloody. If he felt any fear at all he wasn't going to show it.

"Fine. What is it, Andrew? Are you going to plead for his pathetic life? Have some dignity." My father took a few steps forward. He adjusted his tie…pulled it away from his neck as if it were suddenly too tight around his throat.

"I need to do this myself. But for god's sake, Father. No guns! That's hardly a fair fight." My mind raced. I felt breathless and unsure of myself. I was running low on options. I didn't know badly Miguel was hurt…didn't know how much resistance I'd meet from him or how much more pain he could take. But I had to try something. "Tell your damned security to put their guns down and let me take Dos Santos out my way." I felt my anger rising, mixing with fear and hatred for my father. I wanted revenge now. I began to pace back and forth in front of my father, my breaths coming out in bursts. "Tell them to put their guns down and step back."

My father shook his head. "I would love to accommodate you, son, but I'm afraid I can't trust you. I think you've become soft…turned into a gypsy lover like your turncoat brother." He unbuttoned his jacket and pulled a handkerchief from his shirt pocket, wiping it across his brow and upper lip.

I strode over to my father and took his arm, grasping him hard by the elbow. "Come with me, Father. Come meet your son. Come watch me beat him to death. I'll even let him throw the first punch." I tugged on my father's arm but he resisted, tried to pull away. Adrenaline coursed through my veins. I was on fire inside and I wanted to hurt someone. I was only sorry it had to be Miguel. *"Now, Father!"* I pulled my father along the roadway. He tried to resist but I wouldn't let go.

Peter called out to him. "Sir...should one of us intervene?"

"No. It's alright, Peter. I'll come closer. Why ever not?" He shook off my hand and I let go of him. We walked over to stand by Miguel who slowly got to his feet. His face was a bloody mess and his breaths were shallow. He stared intently at me... his eyes dark...questioning.

I looked at each goon in turn. "I want all guns down and out of the way. This has to be fair. Don't worry...I'll make sure you get a good show." The goons didn't move. I hadn't expected them to. "Father, please tell them to put their weapons down on the side of the road and step away from them. And hurry the hell up because now that the opportunity is presenting itself, I'm anxious to get started."

Miguel looked at me. He cocked his head to the side just the slightest bit. He spat out a mouthful of blood at my feet. *Good*, I thought. *He's got some fight in him. "Guns down now!"* I shouted.

"Andrew, why should I trust you? Why?" My father's voice faltered a little...just enough to know that he could be swayed if I played my cards right--my father--who didn't deserve to be anyone's father...who didn't deserve his freedom. I felt my eyes begin to burn. I felt the tears of frustration begin to roll down my cheeks and I welcomed them. I needed to cry and I didn't care how weak it made me look.

"Because...he...took...everything...from...me," I yelled. "Because I should have done it a year ago. If I had, Laura would still be mine and so would my children. Tell them to put down the guns. I want to do this with my bare hands."

"Peter, Kevin, Patrick...give him some room. But hold your weapons. I don't trust him yet," said my father. They moved away immediately to the side of the road.

I moved into Miguel's personal space, close enough to feel his breath...to see into his eyes. His facial hair was matted with blood, his cheekbone bruised, his left eye swollen shut, his lips cracked and bleeding. This wasn't going the way I wanted it to. I would have to prove to my father that I meant business. Our eyes locked and I mouthed the words *I'm sorry*. "Go ahead, Dos Santos," I hissed at him. "You can go first."

He spat more blood out of his mouth. He glared at me and spoke. "So this is how you want to play it, Easton? Really?" He drew himself up to his full height. We were eye to eye now... nose to nose. I trained my gaze on him and, knowing the goons and my father weren't close enough to hear or see, I mouthed... *try not kill me* as I brought my hands up into defense mode. "Go ahead...take the first punch. You've got about three seconds."

Miguel didn't hesitate. I recoiled inwardly as he slammed his fist into my gut. I groaned, doubled over and staggered backward. He stopped in front of me, ready to strike again. I straightened, moved toward him...mouthed *my turn now* and charged at him, blocking his right hand with my left, my right fist meeting his rib cage. He staggered backward but maintained his balance. We circled in a ring, our breaths coming out in hard puffs. Suddenly I stopped moving. I dropped my hands down to my sides, mouthed *trust me* and turned my back on him. I glanced at the three goons, who appeared to be watching me in fascination. I stared at my father. He looked pleased, but his twisted grin faded fast. I was aware that at any moment Miguel could jump my back. I had to be prepared in case he couldn't resist. I just needed three seconds of my own.

"Andrew! Never turn your back on your enemy, son. You should know better," said my father. I saw that he'd undone his tie completely now...it was hanging loosely around his neck. He was sweating profusely, his face a sparkling mass of wetness.

"You're right, Father--rookie mistake." I turned half-way around. Miguel was studying me. I could see he was on the fence...wanting to strike out at me and wanting to trust me. I took a step toward him. He brought back his fist to hit me, but I whirled around away from him and I attacked my father instead.

I punched his jaw and he fell instantly to the ground. And then I shouted out a tirade of epithets as I reached down to haul him to his feet. *"You're the goddamned enemy, Father."* I punched him again in the same place. I was fairly certain I'd broken his jaw—if the first punch hadn't broken it, the second one surely had. "That was for Laura!" He'd gone limp on the ground but I didn't care. I reached down for him again but the goons were on me, pulling me back. Peter turned his attention to my father while Kevin brought his fist up into the left side of my face. I felt a cracking sensation and tasted blood…saw it splatter onto Kevin's shirt. As I cried out in pain, pressing my hand to my face to see how much of it I still had left, Kevin suddenly went down hard with Miguel on top of him. The new goon raised his weapon but I charged at him like a demon, yelling obscenities as I ran. I tackled him to the pavement and he dropped his gun. I grabbed it and rolled away from him before he could get to me. I ran to my father, pointed the gun at his chest. Miguel had Kevin in a vise grip on the ground. Peter held my father in his arms.

"Andrew! No!" Peter yelled at me. "Don't do it! He's already down. I think he's having a heart attack!"

"I hope he is! The son of a bitch deserves to die!" I backed away and turned the gun on the new goon who was slowly making his way toward me. "Stop, or I'll shoot *your* legs out from under *you!*" I was breathing hard, my head felt like it had been hit by a block of cement. I felt dizzy but I stayed on my feet, the gun once again trained on my father. I wanted to pull the trigger. *I can do it…it's not that hard…it's the right thing to do…he deserves to die…* I placed my finger on the trigger.

"Andrew!" It was Miguel. "Wait. Think about what you're doing. He isn't worth losing your life or you freedom over." Miguel suddenly popped Kevin hard in the face, knocking him unconscious and stood up.

I heard a godawful sobbing sound tear from my throat. "He deserves this," I hissed, blood and spit flying in all directions. I saw that my hand was shaking, my finger so close to acting of its own volition…to putting my father out of all our miseries. The goon named Patrick moved a little closer. I turned the gun on him. "Stop right there! Not one step closer."

Miguel glanced at Patrick. He seemed to be reasoning something out in his mind. Suddenly, without warning, he turned on Patrick and punched him in the stomach so hard, Patrick doubled over and fell, his body bent in two in a v-shape. Now it was just Miguel, my father, Peter, who was tending to my father, and I. Miguel held his hand out to me. "Give me the gun, Andrew. I can't let you do this." He sounded scared…finally…and anxious.

"No way, Dos Santos! And give you all the glory? No way in hell." I saw my father begin to stir. He was clutching his chest, struggling to stand.

"Peter…help…me…up," he gasped. Peter helped him to his feet. He wobbled. His jaw looked unnatural. Yes, I had broken it. He clutched his chest and tried to step toward me. "Andrew… you can't… shoot me. I'm your…father. Peter will kill you…the minute you…pull the trigger." He sagged against Peter's chest but Peter held him steady.

Miguel began to walk toward me. "Andrew…please…don't do this. You'll get us both killed. Please…give me the gun." His voice had softened. I stared at his bloody face, his swollen eyes, his filthy clothes. And then everything around us was illuminated as bright lights from approaching vehicles lit us up from both directions. I blinked against the brightness and saw Miguel ease toward me. I heard him whisper. "Give me the gun, Andrew. I won't let you be a killer, even though he deserves it."

I let him take the gun as people began to run toward us from all directions. I heard Portuguese voices yelling. I grabbed Miguel's shirtsleeve. "You're not going to kill him yourself, are you?" I looked over at my father who was watching us, his expression one of resignation. Peter had been strangely absorbed in my father's pain throughout this ordeal while the other two goons remained unconscious on the pavement.

"No. I'm no killer either. Let's let nature take its course. Trust me…it's the better way." He snapped the safety in place on the gun as his uncle and several hulking Portuguese brutes arrived on the scene. And then I saw something unexpected. A woman walking toward us--toward my father. A beautiful, graceful, aristocratic woman dressed all in black. She saw Miguel's face and started to cry silently. She glanced around, her eyes stopping on my father. I saw his reaction. He shrank back, holding on to Peter who tried to calm his sudden agitation.

She stopped in front of him. "Ernst," said the woman. "What have you done to my son?"

"Sofia. I never expected to...," my father said in a whisper, his face contorting as he tried to talk through his broken jaw. "You're still so beau..."

She slapped my father's face causing an instant reaction in Miguel. He ran to her side and pulled her a couple of feet away from my father who now moaned as his agony had undoubtedly intensified from her slap. Miguel spoke to her in Portuguese. I saw her nod. She continued speaking to my father from a distance. "You're a disgrace to your queen...an abomination...with no conscience."

My father groaned in pain and tried to speak, but his voice was garbled. He cleared his throat, shifting his weight, causing Peter to almost lose his balance. He pressed his hand to his chest. "Sofia...I...this never would have happened if..." He turned his gaze on Miguel. "Son...I...owe...you...an..." He reached his hand out toward Miguel and his mother, as if he wanted them to take it. Sofia turned away, into Miguel's arms. She saw me and gave me a look of sympathy. Seeing her made me miss my own mother.

The other two goons finally began to show some signs of life. They started to stand up and were clearly shocked to see the Portuguese contingent. When they got to their feet they were immediately apprehended.

"Andrew...we need to get your father inside. I think he's going into cardiac rest." Peter was now struggling to keep my father on his feet. My father tried to speak. He reached his arm out again in Sofia's direction. He emitted a strange sound and then turned to dead weight in Peter's arms. Peter slumped to the ground with my father on top of him. He gently pushed my father's body onto the pavement and checked for a pulse. "Andrew! He's dying!" I watched as he began chest compressions.

I stood, frozen, watching as Peter pumped my father's chest. He tried to blow the breath of life into my father's lungs. He looked at me pleadingly.

"Help me, Andrew! Breathe into him! We can save him!" Peter was frantic. I'd never realized how devoted he was to my father. I'd always thought he'd had a soft spot for *me*. I even remembered once after I'd dropped Laura off at her home after a date, that he'd complimented me on her behalf—told me what a nice couple we made. But he had known all along about my father's blackmail scheme and he'd never tried to stop it—had chosen evil over good. And now he was trying valiantly to save his lord and master. It made me sick.

There was suddenly a surreal quality about the night. I glanced around…saw the goons being hauled away by the hulking Portuguese…watched as Sofia cupped Miguel's bloody mess of a face, kissed his forehead, and then watched as Antonio came, taking her arm, steering her away from my father. I looked down in time to see my father take his last breath…Peter finally realizing the futility in trying to conquer death. How had it come to this? That my father would die on a dark service road behind a hospital in bloody Portugal? That I would stand by and let it happen…not even trying to help him? That the last thing I would ever give my father was a broken jaw? I hadn't even given him the grandchildren he'd wanted. As soon as I thought about the babies I felt the irony stab me in my already aching gut. My father didn't die grandchild-less after all. His middle son had given him his heirs to the House of Hanover. But they were also heirs to the House of Braganza…the shadow monarchy. My shoulders began to shake as damned tears fell, mixing with the dried blood on my face. I was suddenly very tired. I felt a hand on my arm then. I let out a pent-up breath and turned my head…saw Miguel's left hand on my sleeve. I looked at his beaten up face. I was quite sure mine didn't look too much better. He didn't say anything but his eyes spoke volumes. Suddenly, without warning, he grasped my left arm and pulled me into his chest in a very tight hold. He whispered something in my ear in Portuguese. Then he dropped his hands and faced me. "We need to get cleaned up. She needs us—both of us." I nodded.

I looked down at my father's lifeless body…saw Peter softly crying—I was amazed by that—the sight of a crying goon.

I hadn't known they were capable. Laura had always thought they were robots…that my father rolled them off of an assembly line. I should be the one crying for my father…shouldn't I? But my tears weren't for him…they were for Laura…upstairs in the damned hospital room waiting for a kidney to save her life. But could I leave my father here like this…just walk away? I saw Miguel waiting for me to make a move. I looked at him…suddenly needing his—or someone's—blessing to walk away.

"I'm not sure I can leave him here like this…I did this to him…I broke his jaw…I caused his heart attack…" My voice broke…I was a murderer after all. I pressed my hands against my eyes, unable to look at my father any longer.

"Andrew…you did not kill your father," said a female voice. I turned, dropped my hands and saw Sofia. Slowly she approached me, held her hand out to me. I stared at it in confusion. I looked from her to Miguel and back to her again. She stepped closer to me and I caved. I reached out to her, felt her slender arms encircle me and I let myself fall apart in her delicate yet strong embrace. She whispered to me in Portuguese, rubbed my back and comforted me. I thought of my mother then…back in England…completely unaware of the fact that she was now a widow and I cried harder. Sofia stood with me like that for a long time…until I became aware of medical personnel placing my father's body on a gurney and taking him away. Sofia reached up and touched my face.

"Why don't you come back to the house with Miguel and get cleaned up and then we will come back here so you can be with Laura. She's been asking for you and Miguel. And I know you will want to be with your brother as well. We don't live far…we can be back here within the hour. Please come with me, darling."

I nodded and walked with her and Miguel over to one of the black SUV's. Sofia sat in front with the man I believe they called Antonio, and Miguel and I sat in the back. I stared out the window as we drove, aware only of the sound of the road under the tires. No one spoke. When we arrived, Antonio parked and we walked up the porch steps. Propped against the front door was an envelope. Miguel picked it up as we all walked inside the house. Sofia turned on the hall lights as Miguel opened the envelope. He read the one-page document. Sofia must have asked him what it was because he handed it to her and looked at me, his eyes shining with unshed tears. I tilted my head in question.

"The lawyer was here. He dropped off the notice of receipt signed by the judge. The annulment has gone through." He spoke the words quietly. I saw him cross one arm over his chest and press his free hand over his forehead as if he were trying to stifle one of Laura's famous headaches. I knew the feeling. My body ached from the punches I'd taken tonight but that pain was nothing compared to the pain of the blade that sliced through me now. I wondered how long a person could survive with a broken heart.

"So that's it then," I said. "Just like that..." My voice trailed off.

"I don't know what to say to you, Andrew," said Miguel quietly.

"It's just not my day, I guess." I would have laughed at the understatement of my words, but I knew I'd only end up crying again. And I was done with the tears. "Let's get cleaned up, shall we?"

Sofia had been standing by quietly watching us. Now she came over and took my hand and led me to a bathroom, gave me towels and told me she would lay some clean clothes just outside the door for me. "You and Miguel are nearly the same size. And when you're finished, we'll go back to Laura and the children. But for now, Andrew, are you going to be OK?"

I tried to answer her. I opened my mouth but thought better of speaking and managed a nod. She left me and I went inside and turned on the shower. I stood under the hot water and realized I was wrong. I wasn't quite finished with the tears just yet.

Chapter Twenty Three

THE GIFT OF LIFE

MIGUEL

I was a mess. I didn't see how I could face Laura looking like this. Andrew was probably thinking the same thing about himself. My body ached intensely but I was fairly certain I had no broken bones. One eye was swollen shut and my cheekbone was bruised. My lip was cut and it hurt like hell to open my mouth. My ribs ached, making it difficult to take too deep a breath. But I would live—unlike Andrew's father. As I finished showering, I thought about what had happened—what I had just been a part of. I couldn't believe the Duke of Easton was dead. So many times I had dreamed of his death…had dreamed of choking the life out of him with my bare hands…and he had died of a heart attack just like my father. I knew Andrew felt that he had caused his father's death but I didn't believe that. I had stood there mostly in silence watching Andrew taking on the goons and standing up to his father alone. I had itched to help him, but he knew the goons better than I did. When he'd told his father he wanted to be the one to kill me, I had not believed him. I knew he loved Laura too much to hurt her that way. I'd banked on that. I had not wanted to hit him, but I sensed he had to prove to his father his seriousness. I think he went easier on me with his punch than I had been on him. I felt badly about that. I had watched his father grow sicker in front of us…sweating, clutching at his chest, weakening. It had only been a matter of time until his heart gave out. I had been shocked at my mother's arrival. I wished she had not been a witness to his death. But she was a strong woman and I appreciated her tenderness toward Andrew. Never in a million years did I ever think I would feel anything for Andrew Easton other than hatred, but tonight I was under no illusions. He had saved my life and I would be forever in his debt. And now I had to find a way to save Laura. I missed her so much. I'd been away far too long and I was afraid I was hurting her with my absence. And I needed to see my children. I dressed and took one more look at my face in the mirror and hoped that Laura could handle the sight of me.

In the car on the way back to the hospital, Andrew was quiet. I noticed his face was nearly as bad as mine—cut chin, swollen jaw, bruised cheekbone. What a fine mess we were. I would have to have my mother go in first and warn Cat and Tristan so they could prepare Laura for the sight of us. I was anxious to get there and I wished Antonio would drive faster. I glanced over at Andrew. He was staring out the window, lost in his thoughts. I felt emotions stirring in my gut. He had witnessed his father's death and no matter how despicable the duke was I knew Andrew had to be hurting. I reached over and touched his arm. He glanced at me. "You going to be OK?"

He looked down. "Eventually…but not today." He turned away again toward the window. We arrived at the hospital and I told Andrew we should give my mother a chance to warn every-one about our appearances. We decided to go to the nursery first, knowing the babies would not be affected by the ghastly sight of us. The nurses on the other hand weren't too impressed. They seemed reluctant to leave us alone with Felipe and Gabriela so they hovered nearby while Andrew held his niece and I held my son. I watched him with Gabriela…saw tears well up as he looked at her with adoration. We traded babies and I saw that he was equally besotted with Felipe. I kissed my son and daughter and told them I loved them and we headed to Laura's room. I was nervous about seeing her and not just because I looked frightening. I was nervous because I loved her more than any human being on the earth, aside from my children, and I could not wait to hold her in my arms…to kiss her lips—if she would let me, looking like this…and tell her how much I loved her. And I wanted her to know that I had made peace—in my own mind--with Andrew, my brother. I knew how happy this would make her and there was nothing else I wanted to do more than to make her happy. I had to consider though, that just because I was ready to make peace with Andrew, it didn't mean he felt the same, the fact that he had saved my life notwithstanding.

My mother joined us in the hall outside of Laura's room. She looked tired…anxious. "We told Laura about what happened." I sucked in a breath, anger rising, but my mother put up her hand. "We decided to tell her the truth now before you got here, to make it easier for you." She turned to Andrew. "We told Tristan about your father. I'm sorry if I overstepped my bounds but I felt it was best if we were up front about it. I'm sorry for your personal loss, Andrew…and for Tristan. It's hard to lose your father under any circumstances. But Tristan is holding up well. Catarina is with him. He wanted to see your father. They're downstairs and will return in a while. He said he would wait to talk to you before your mother is notified. And now the two of you are needed desperately by that young woman in there." She pointed to Laura's room. "I'll leave the three of you alone. Antonio and I will go see the babies because right now I need to hold my grandchildren." She kissed me and hugged Andrew and headed to the nursery. I turned to Andrew.

"Ready for this?" I asked him. He appeared calm but I saw that his hands were shaking. He saw that I had noticed and put his hands in his pockets. He nodded.

"After you," he said quietly.

I pushed the door open and stepped inside. I was shocked to see Laura sitting in a chair by the window and not in her bed. She looked up, saw me and put her hands over her mouth to stifle her cry. I rushed to her and dropped to my knees in front of her.

"It's OK, baby. It's not as bad as it looks, I promise." I cupped her face in my hands and wiped her tears with my thumbs. She leaned into my chest and I wrapped my arms around her. She was slight...frail...and I felt my stomach clench in fear. It seemed as if she were wasting away in front me. I had to find a way to make it stop—to bring her back to good health—to the Laura I had first met in Rhode Island—sun-tanned skin, pink cheeks, shiny hair. I would make it happen or die trying.

"Oh, my god, Miguel. What you've been through. No one knew any details...just that he...the duke is...," she stopped herself at the sight of Andrew standing quietly inside the door. She gasped in shock. "Andrew! Oh, my god...you, too? Please, come here." She held her hand out to him and he walked over and grasped it in his. I stood up...moved over to give him room. She studied both of our faces as her tears continued to flow down her cheeks.

"We're fine, love. He's right—it's not nearly as bad as it looks." He pushed a lock of hair out of her face. I felt my jealousy trying to take hold, but I clamped it down.

"Did you two do this to each other?" she asked quietly.

I gave Andrew a sideways glance and looked down, deciding to let him answer that one.

"Umm...yes...and no," he replied. "The damned goons got in a few punches...but the great part is...the good guys won." He forced a smile that didn't reach his eyes.

Laura pulled him closer. "I know your father is dead, Andrew. I'm sure that's painful for you, but..."

"You don't have to say anything. There aren't going to be too many people sorry to hear of his passing. My mother will be devastated and, Peter, I suppose, but we don't have to talk about that. I don't want to discuss it anyway. The important thing now is to get you healthy and out of here. Right, Miguel?"

I nodded. "Absolutely." Andrew kissed the top of Laura's head and moved away to sit in one of the chairs at her bedside. I pulled a chair close to her and took her hands, kissing her palms each in turn. "So, they're letting you sit up now? Isn't it too soon to be up?"

"I insisted. But I'm only allowed out of the bed for a few minutes. I'm on this damned dialysis." She pointed to the tube in her abdomen. I could see it through her gown. The sight of it and the IV still in her arm brought me up short. I felt a burning sensation behind my eyes and I didn't want her to see me getting emotional. I cleared my throat and turned away for a moment to get myself together. Andrew saw my reaction and spoke up.

"That *damned* dialysis is only temporary until we get you a new kidney. What does the doctor say about it?"

"He'll be here in the morning to discuss the process. I talked to my parents this evening. They're coming to Portugal. They'll be here day after tomorrow. I can't wait to see them. But, Andrew, they have no idea about anything that's happened and I'm not sure I can be the one to tell them. They'll be hurt, especially because I didn't tell them from the beginning. I don't know how to handle it. And they don't know about my…kidney problem either. All they know is the babies are here and I had a rough delivery."

I snapped out of my sadness and responded. "You don't have to handle anything, *minha querida*. I will explain what happened. Andrew can join me if he's up to it. We'll take care of everything. I don't want you stressing over this."

"My parents aren't going to take any of this well. I'm afraid they're going to resent me for not telling them. They'll be angry—especially my father. They might not understand why I did what I did…" She sighed deeply and leaned her head back against the seat.

"We'll work it out. I don't want you to dwell on it. Right now, I want to know how you feel. Are you allowed to walk around? How's your appetite?"

"I'm OK. I'm not supposed to walk just yet. It's too soon. I had to practically throw a tantrum just to be allowed to sit in this chair for five minutes. I feel so damned weak. As for my appetite…ha…I think I need a steak." She grinned at me.

"You know…I could use a steak, too. I'll see what I can do about making that happen," I said. She reached over and trailed her finger along my jaw, touched the corner of my eye, brushed her thumb over the bruise on my cheek.

"Are you in pain?" she asked. "A goon did this to you?"

"I'm fine. And no talking about goons." I studied her face. I wanted to kiss her, in spite of the fact that kissing would probably hurt like hell…but I wanted to hold her, to be alone with her…just the two of us. I wanted this nightmare to be over. I'd always thought that if we could rid our lives of the Duke of Easton then we could live happily ever after, but until Laura had a new kidney, there would be no happily ever after. I wondered if I could give her one of mine. I would ask the doctor first thing when he arrived in the morning.

We talked about the babies for a while and Laura tried several times to draw Andrew into the conversation but he was a million kilometers away. He sat in his chair staring off into space and I felt a pang of intense empathy for him. I wanted to say something to him to try to bring him out of himself but I knew it was probably futile. And then Tristan arrived with Cat and I knew how much more difficult things were about to get for him. They still had the task of notifying their mother. I wasn't sure how much the duchess knew of her husband's activities but no matter, the news was going to hurt.

Tristan asked to speak to Andrew alone in the lounge down the hall. Andrew stood and walked over to Laura. "I'll be back. Tristan and I have to call our mother. We have to tell her about…," he looked down, his voice breaking. He wiped angrily at a tear. Laura reached out to him. He knelt down in front of her. It hurt to watch them together but I swallowed my jealousy and my pride and let her offer him the comfort I knew he needed.

"I'm so sorry, Andrew…about the way this all…you know…I wish…," she whispered, tears falling down her cheeks. She cupped his face in her hands, touched the bluish-purple bruise on his cheek, rested her thumb beside the cut on his chin.

"Sh…sh…," he whispered. "Don't cry. It's over now. I'm going with Tristan to call home. You and Miguel probably want to be alone anyway. I'll be back soon." He kissed her forehead and stood up. He glanced over at me then back to Laura. "I don't know if I'm allowed to say this, but hell…I don't really care. I love you, Laura. I always will. I'll see you in a bit." He pressed his hand to her cheek and then left the room. As soon as we were alone, I moved closer to her. She looked so damned sad. I ached just looking at her.

"Alone at last," I whispered. "And now we have to find a way to turn off the waterworks. I want to see you happy again—see you smile. How can I make that happen?" I smiled as I leaned in to kiss her. She put her arms around my neck and pulled me close and when she deepened the kiss I groaned in pain.

"Ooh, sorry," she said, rubbing my jaw softly. "Better be careful."

"It's worth it, *minha querida*," I said as I kissed her again. Her lips were so soft...her tongue so sweet mingling with mine. I had to stop this before it killed me. I pulled back, gazed into her blue eyes. "You know...I've just had an idea." I sat back in my chair and held her hands in mine.

"What? Does it involve getting discharged from this place and having steak? Because if it does, I'm in," she laughed.

"I'm going to get you that steak—I promise. I'll go out and get you one tomorrow for lunch unless you'd like it for break-fast...?"

"Ooh, steak and eggs...yum...my dad's favorite breakfast," she closed her eyes, her face rapturous.

"Actually...I was thinking about after your transplant, when you're healthy again—about what we'd do."

"You have something specific in mind?" she asked, looking excited now.

"I do. I was thinking about a honeymoon in the Algarve or maybe we could go to Ventura Island. I want to take you to the beach, get some sun on your skin, get you in a bikini, you know..." I felt myself blush...not something I did very often. I almost laughed at myself but Laura didn't look happy about my idea. She frowned. "What? You don't like bikinis?"

She turned her head away from me. "I'm going to have a scar—two of them. I guess the scar from the C-section won't be so bad but the kidney scar...I'll look awful in a bikini."

I sucked in a breath. "No way. That scar will be a beautiful sign—a sign of life. And I don't think you should deprive your husband of the sight of his wife in a bikini. I see you in a white one...or maybe pink..." She pressed her fingers to my lips... stopped my fantasy in its tracks.

"What about the annulment? I haven't received notice that it's official."

"It came, sweetheart. When Andrew and I went home to shower and change it was there. The lawyer had delivered it. It is official. You're a single woman again—but not for long."

She looked sad again. "Did Andrew see it? Does he know it's over?"

"Yes. He was there when I opened it. I guess it was bad timing, but at least now he can get on with his life." I tried to sound sympathetic. I did feel for him, but I'd wanted that tie severed since the day the knot was tied.

Laura leaned her head back against the chair and closed her eyes. She let out a deep sigh followed by a yawn.

"You should get back into bed, sweetheart. Let me help you." She reached up to me and I helped her from the chair and settled her into the bed. She yawned again.

"I'm so tired all of a sudden. But, Miguel...you're not leaving, are you? You'll stay?"

I leaned over her...brushed her hair from her forehead. "I'll never leave you again. I'll sleep right here beside you."

She put her arms around my neck and pulled me close. I kissed her slowly...gently...until I knew I would be in trouble if I didn't stop. I settled myself into the chair beside her.

"Miguel?"

"Yes?"

"Where did you go? When you went away, you were gone for so long. Where?"

I hesitated and looked away toward the window. "I went south and spent some time with gypsies."

"Wow...gypsies?"

I sighed. "Yes. They welcomed me in and made me a part of their family. They're good people. And being with them made me realize how much I missed you and wanted to be with my own family. I was wrong to leave you like that, Laura. I'm so sorry. I'll spend the rest of my life making it up to you, I promise."

"I forgive you. I love you," she said, her voice quiet.

"I love you, too—more than you know." She smiled at me and I felt we would be OK.

"Do you still have my talisman in your pocket?" she asked, her hand touching her bare neck.

I pulled it out of my pocket and held it up.

"Can I wear it…just for tonight…?"

I nodded and placed it over her head. She held the disk in her hand…studied both sides then tucked it down inside her hospital gown. She pressed her hand so the disk was flush against her breastbone, then turned her head and drifted off to sleep. I scooted the chair as close to the bed as it would go and rested my head beside her, using my arms as a pillow. It would be an uncomfortable way to sleep but I couldn't imagine sleeping anywhere else.

I'd called one of my cousins and asked him to bring three steak and egg breakfasts for when Laura, Andrew and I woke up. I didn't even clear it first with a nurse. Tristan, Cat, my mother and brothers had gone home, but Andrew and I had stayed the night. My mother and Tristan had tried to talk him into going back to the house to sleep but he wouldn't hear of it. A nurse had brought him a pillow and a blanket and he'd slept in the lounge. He wanted to be here in the morning when the doctor came to talk about the transplant. During the night he came in and offered to trade places with me so I could get some sleep but I'd politely declined his offer. I needed to be near Laura. Mine needed to be the face she saw when she awoke. She'd talked in her sleep and I'd listened—as she'd said the babies' names, my name and Andrew's. I'd also heard her speak Portuguese and that had fascinated me. She'd said 'I love you' in my native tongue—it must be rubbing off on her.

Two nurses brought the babies to us early and we each fed one while Laura slept. But when Gabriela began to cry, Laura woke up, smiling. She held Gabriela close and talked to her, soothed her, fed her from a bottle. I loved watching her hold the babies. Andrew was quiet, observing her. I wondered what he was thinking. My cousin arrived with the three breakfasts and I held Gabriela while Laura devoured her steak. She moaned with nearly every bite, causing Andrew to chuckle.

"What?" she said to him, smiling. "A girl can't moan while she's inhaling steak?"

"Of course...but you're reminding me of when you moaned while eating chocolate. Do you remember? At dinner one night at my house in Rhode Island? That was pretty funny. Tristan joined you in a moan-fest so you wouldn't feel self-conscious."

She laughed. "I remember. I couldn't help myself. Chocolate's the next thing on my wish list."

I wasn't enjoying this topic of conversation. I didn't want to hear about any moments in Laura's life that excluded me, no matter how selfish that might be. I saw that Laura had cleaned her plate and I moved her dirty dishes away so she could hold Felipe. He was crying, ready for a feeding.

"Felipe says he wants steak and eggs now," I grinned, placing him in her arms. Andrew was holding Gabriela who'd fallen asleep. As I watched Laura bottle-feeding Felipe I wondered about something. "Laura...are you going to...you know..." I waved my hand over her. "Feed him the other way...?

Her face fell. "I wanted to. I even tried but...the doctor said it'll dry up soon anyway because of this damned transplant and I'll be too weak, so it'll have to be formula. See? I'm failing them already." She looked away and sniffed.

I flinched at her words. "You could never fail them, Laura. Don't ever say that. Felipe seems to be enjoying his steak and eggs just fine." I moved to stand closer to her so I could watch Felipe eat. I brushed my hand through her hair, moving it out of her eyes. She was pale and looked tired. A desperate feeling washed over me—an energy running through me that needed an outlet. I wanted her out of here...healthy...energetic. I was relieved when the doctor finally arrived. The nurses came and took the babies and Andrew and I stood next to Laura and listened as the doctor explained about the transplant process. I had to translate much of the conversation, but he did attempt to speak English for Laura's sake. Finally he asked if we had questions.

"I would like to give her one of my kidneys. Is that possible?" I asked the doctor. I asked in Portuguese and translated my question and his answer into English. Laura gasped and clamped a hand over her mouth. I grasped her free hand and squeezed it gently.

"We can test you to see if you are a match. If the blood type is compatible we would do further testing—urinalysis, x-rays, tissue cross-matching, a complete physical and psychological exam—and if everything looks good, you could donate."

"I want to be tested, too," said Andrew. He had been quiet throughout the doctor's explanation, but now he came to life. He seemed determined. "Can we do it today?"

Again I felt the jealousy trying to take hold—twisting inside of me. I wanted to be the one to save her--not him. I swallowed my annoyance, bit back a response and continued translating for the doctor.

"Ideally, a kidney from a family member would be the best option. When is your family due to arrive, Laura?"

"Tomorrow," I answered for her. "They're coming from Rhode Island in the U.S."

"But why wait?" asked Andrew. "Let's start today. I'm ready now." He turned to me. "Tell him I want to be tested now—today." He sounded anxious—desperate--and I wondered what was driving him—besides the obvious…wanting to save Laura from this dialysis nightmare. I forced my face to remain impassive as I translated.

"You can both be tested today. The sooner we get the process started, the better for Laura. I don't think we should wait too much longer. If you're amenable, I will get you both into the lab for testing this morning." I translated his words. Laura began to cry, her shoulders shaking. I gathered her in my arms, tried to soothe her.

"What is it, sweetheart?" I whispered. The doctor looked concerned…compassionate. Laura's reaction was probably no surprise to him but it was to me and to Andrew who rubbed her shoulder, squeezing it gently.

"How can I let you do this? Rip out a kidney? Mutilate your body? Put yourself at risk? No, you can't do this. It's too scary—

for both of you." She sounded exhausted, frightened, resigned.

Andrew leaned down and kissed the top of her head, then walked to the door where he proceeded to pace back and forth in the space in front of the threshold, like a caged animal desperate for escape. "There's nothing to fear. I'm ready now." He looked at me. "How do you say 'hurry the hell up' in Portuguese?"

I closed my eyes for a second. I wanted to punch him again, harder than yesterday. I felt Laura stir beside me, felt her hand brush against mine. I opened my eyes and looked into frightened blue ones. I leaned down and kissed her. "We'll both get tested, sweetheart. If one of us is a match, then your family can concentrate on being with you and the babies. I want you healthy again and out of here. Don't cry. I love you." She pulled me closer to her and hugged me, pressing her lips into my neck.

"I love you, too," she whispered. "But…I'm scared…"

"I know you are. But everything will work out, I know it will."

"If you two will accompany me to the lab then…" said the doctor. He squeezed Laura's foot through the sheet and gave her a reassuring smile.

"Will you be OK while we're gone? Mother, Tristan and Cat will be here soon…," I hated leaving her alone, but I was anxious to get the testing complete—anxious to get her a new kidney so she wouldn't have to suffer another day.

She started to respond but her face changed. She emitted a short gasp and pressed her hand onto her chest. I glanced down and saw the faint glow beneath her gown. My eyes widened. I glanced over my shoulder toward Andrew and the doctor. "Give me a minute, please. I'll be right out." They walked away toward the elevators. I put my hand on her breasts…felt the warmth of the talisman as it heated up…reacting against her skin.

"I'm afraid to look, Miguel. It told me I was going to die before…" she whispered.

"No, it didn't. It said 'Birth' and 'Death.' We've had both of those already. This will be good news, I know it will. Let's look together." I reached to her neck and lifted the chain…pulled the talisman out and held the disk in my hand where we could both read the word engraved upon it: *Rei*. I turned it over. On the other side was engraved the word *Rainha*. I looked into Laura's eyes...smiled. I saw her confusion and fear. "It's OK, sweetheart. It says 'King' and 'Queen.' Maybe it's a prediction of the future. Who knows?"

"So it's nothing bad...?" her voice tapered off. She relaxed against the pillow and sighed.

"No...it's not. Whatever it's supposed to mean, time will tell us eventually. Now you rest...don't worry about anything. I'll be back soon. I love you."

"I love you, too," she whispered. I kissed her and left her to rest.

We were silent in the elevator on the way to the lab. I had things I wanted to say to Andrew but I didn't want to speak in front of the doctor so I stayed quiet. Andrew stood to the far side of the elevator putting distance between us. He seemed aloof now...intense...as if he were present only in a physical sense... not a mental one. He was getting under my skin and I wanted to know what his damned problem was. Once we arrived at the lab I told the doctor we would be right in as soon as I had a word with Andrew. I grabbed his arm before he could follow the doctor inside. A look of irritation passed over his face.

"What?" he asked, his voice sharp. He shook off my arm.

"What the hell is your problem all of a sudden, Easton?"

He walked away from me and stopped by a window that overlooked the parking lot. He didn't answer right away—just stared out the window. I walked over to him, unsure how to handle his change in attitude. Finally he turned to me.

"I'm sorry, Dos Santos. I don't mean to be an ass. But...I want her to live...just as much as you do—a long, happy, healthy life. I feel like my father did this to her and I want to make it right. I want to do whatever it takes to make her whole again. I'm only angry at the circumstances--not you. I'm angry at my father, but he got what he deserved. But Laura doesn't deserve this. I need to make this right. I'm not one much for prayer and religious crap, but I'm praying today. So let's get in there and see if one of us can save her, OK?"

I didn't answer immediately. I processed his words...knowing he was speaking from a pure place and not one of martyrdom or self-fulfillment. I nodded and extended my hand to him—an offer of solidarity. He took my hand, grasped it hard and shook it once, then nodded. We entered the lab together and joined the doctor who was waiting for us, ready to begin.

Chapter Twenty Four

PERFECT MATCH

LAURA

It felt good to move around. My body was stiff from being in a bed for so long and I had to reintroduce myself to my muscles. Miguel and I walked to the nursery and held and fed the babies. The pediatrician came and said the babies could be discharged any time. I felt empty at the thought of them being allowed to leave when I couldn't, but Sofia assured me that she and Cat and Juana would take care of them. I knew my mother would help, too.

My parents' arrival had been traumatic. We had agreed that Miguel and Andrew would take them into a conference room where Andrew would properly introduce Miguel to my family and then, together, they would explain the events that had led up to this moment. I was so glad not to have to be a part of that, but my heart went out to my parents and Nick. I knew this would not be easy to hear. I also felt for Andrew, knowing he would have to re-live the nightmare, so much of which he had been unaware at the time.

I'd noticed a change in the air, now that I was healing from the C-section and had gotten used to the dialysis treatment. My appetite was picking up and I felt my spirits lifting. My talisman's mysterious message made me feel optimistic even though I had no idea what 'king' and 'queen' referred to. I was just happy it hadn't marked me for death. I'd noticed a slight change in the staff, too—in the nurses and doctors. It's possible I'd been too out of it to notice it before, but when Sofia was around, people acted differently. They seemed to hold her up on a pedestal...with reverence. I began to notice they treated Miguel the same way. They obviously knew that they were in the presence of royalty and this concept intrigued me. I wasn't sure I liked it completely, but I didn't comment on it, choosing instead to quietly observe the interaction of the staff and Miguel's family and keep any thoughts to myself.

My parents adjusted to the news of the past year and a half...slowly. My mother cried a lot and my father was angry. He and Nicholas had to leave the hospital briefly to blow off steam. They seemed to take to Miguel well enough, but I knew my mother loved Andrew and the news that our marriage had been annulled had hurt her deeply. They had many questions, but I wasn't up to answering them, choosing to leave that to Andrew and Miguel. Nicholas was happy to see Tristan again and the two of them spent time in the lounge discussing all that had happened or so I presumed. Tristan had mentioned that he and Andrew would need to return to England soon to see their mother. She was quite distraught over her husband's death and they both felt badly that she was home alone with her grief in England and no family there to comfort her.

The first time I saw my father hold one of the babies I fell apart. He was completely in love with his grandchildren, as was my mother. Nick admired the babies from afar—he found them to be slightly intimidating. When the topic of my kidney problem was raised my mother was the one falling apart. She, my father and brother were anxious to be tested to see if they could be my donor. My father also had my medical records sent via the Internet to the wife of his boss, Marc Hansen. Dr. Anna Hansen was a transplant surgeon at Providence General Hospital and she had agreed to go over the findings and offer a second opinion, including coming to Portugal to examine me personally if she found anything questionable in my file. Due to the large population of Portuguese residents in Rhode Island, the hospital employed translators so she would have no trouble understanding my medical records. And now we were waiting for the results to come back on Andrew and Miguel. We expected the doctor to arrive momentarily. Tristan, Cat and Nick had gone to the cafeteria for a bite to eat and my parents were with me in my room, each holding a baby. Sofia and Antonio were attending to some family business regarding the items found in the duke's safe and Miguel's brothers were back in school. Antonio had told us earlier that the goons had been arrested and were facing several criminal charges back in England. It seemed that life was trying to right itself, little by little. Andrew and Miguel were on either side of my bed when the doctor arrived. He got straight to the point.

We waited for him to finish so Miguel could translate. I tried to figure out his words on my own, but it all sounded garbled. I saw Miguel's expression darken, as if he'd received bad news. *They aren't matches*, I thought. I convinced myself that this was OK. I didn't want either of them to face major surgery anyway. I looked at my parents...thought of Nick...I didn't want them to face that trauma either. Andrew was getting anxious. He kept shifting his weight back and forth from one foot to the other, as if willing the doctor to talk faster and Miguel to translate faster still. Finally Miguel turned to us. His voice was shaky, as if he were having a hard time forming the words. I saw him lock eyes with Andrew. I reached for his hand as he spoke.

"My blood type is not compatible with yours...but Andrew...is a perfect match. The doctor wants to do a psychological evaluation on you, Andrew, to make sure you understand the risks involved. He wants to make sure you're emotionally..."

Andrew put up his hand. "I don't need a damned psych evaluation. I'm fine. Ask him when we can do this. I'm ready now...today. Tell him I'm good to go."

Miguel was silent for a moment. He stared at Andrew but

it seemed as if he were looking right through him. Finally he translated Andrew's words. The doctor nodded. He said something to Miguel and made some notations on my chart. Miguel looked down at me, his voice sounding flat as he translated. "He said as soon as your incision from the birth is healed—at least a month—he will schedule the transplant, if Andrew's other lab tests are OK. He says you will have to be transferred to the hospital in Lisbon. He seems to think it's going to be smooth sailing. This is good news."

I was stunned into silence. I tried to look at Andrew but I felt shame. I had not expected him to be the one. I thought it would be Miguel or my father or even a stranger…anyone but Andrew. He'd already suffered so much and this just didn't seem fair. I buried my face in my hands and sobbed. I felt Miguel's arms come around me. He whispered comforting words to me and I pulled myself together. Andrew was standing quietly beside me, his hand on the bedrail. I had so much I needed to say to him but I didn't know how to begin. I was afraid to look at him. Finally I saw his hand sliding along the rail closer to me. He grasped my fingers…tugged on them a little to get me to look at him.

"Laura…?" He bent down, putting his face close to mine… making eye contact. "What are you thinking right now? I hope these are tears of joy…because I couldn't be happier about this news."

"But…it isn't fair…to you," I sobbed. "You've lost so much…how can I take your kidney, too? It doesn't seem right…" My voice trailed off. I heard my mother crying softly. My father cleared his throat…trying to keep his emotions in check. Miguel remained silent at my side. I didn't even want to consider what was going through *his* head right now.

"Don't you see? Fate is allowing me to make up for the sins of my father. I know I can't erase every bad thing that happened to you…but this? This I can do. I'm ready now…whenever they say it's safe for you…I'll be in the next bed over." He smiled… his sweet crooked Andrew smile. "You'll never be able to get rid of me now."

I pulled him into my arms then and held onto him as if my life depended on it—which ironically, it did. "I would never want that. I don't know how I will ever be able to thank you. This goes above and beyond anything anyone will ever do for me in this lifetime. You truly are a prince among men."

He laughed at my joke and the sound of his laughter trickled over to my parents who chuckled, too. Only Miguel remained silent...unsmiling at my side. I looked up at him but he turned away from me. I wanted to say something to him but I was afraid to speak. The expression on his face was...cold. I felt my heart crack the tiniest bit...threatening to cave in completely.

"I'll be back," he said and left the room abruptly. I stared at Andrew, my mouth open in shock. Miguel was hurt...that much was obvious...but surely he was happy for me, too?

"It'll be OK," whispered Andrew, leaning down, his face close to my ear. "He just needs some time to get used to the idea. He's disappointed that he's not your perfect match, but don't worry, he'll come around. He wants you healthy and home with Felipe and Gabriela. We all do. Just give him some time and be patient, OK?"

I nodded. He kissed my forehead and told me he was going down to the cafeteria for something to eat. He asked if he could bring me back something.

"I'd kill for any kind of chocolate if they have it," I smiled. He nodded and left me alone with my parents and the babies. We talked awhile about things that were happening back home. I asked about Lily and Gretchen. We kept to safe subjects and I noticed my parents finally beginning to relax. Tristan, Nick and Cat came to visit me for a while and held the babies and fed them again then I held each baby in turn until I felt myself growing tired. I could see that my parents also were exhausted. Their jetlag was kicking in.

Eventually Antonio returned to take my parents back to the house to sleep. My father could no longer keep his eyes open and my mother was fading fast as well. Nick said he was starving again so they went to the cafeteria for more food. I'd hoped Miguel would have returned by now--he'd been gone for more than two hours. A nurse came in with some paperwork but it was in Portuguese and I didn't understand any of it. Her English wasn't good enough to explain it to me, but I understood that it had something to do with the babies. I guessed it might be discharge papers but I couldn't be sure until Miguel came to read them to me. She took the babies back to the nursery with her and left the papers with me. Andrew returned with a bag of candy, including Cadbury cream eggs much to my delight. I hoped I was allowed to eat it. I didn't dare ask in case someone told me no. We were alone now…just Andrew and I…and I felt a sudden, unexpected shyness with him.

"Where's Miguel? Did he ever come back?" he asked. He was sitting beside my bed, eating a Kit Kat candy bar and looking peaceful for a change.

My face fell. "No. I don't know where he is. He's been gone a long time. Do you think he'll come back?" I thought back to the last time he'd left me—he'd been gone for weeks then and I'd barely survived it. How could he do this to me again? I saw a pattern forming and it scared me. I willed myself not to cry.

"Of course he will. He just needs time to deal with his inner demons. That's a feeling I know all too well."

His comment made me sad. I sighed and looked out the window. I was having trouble remembering what day it was. It seemed like I'd been here forever but I knew it had only been a few days. It was dark outside and I wanted to go out there and breathe in the night air. I was restless and suddenly fearful of the future.

"Andrew?"

He glanced up from his chocolate bar. "Yes?"

"Are you afraid?"

He didn't hesitate. "Absolutely not. I can't wait to do this for you."

I smiled but didn't respond. I closed my eyes…tried to relax. I heard Andrew shift in his seat.

"He's coming back," I heard him whisper as I opened my eyes. "I'll see you later." He stood and walked to the door. I saw him give Miguel a look—of warning or encouragement--it was hard to tell which—and he left us alone to talk.

Miguel approached my bed as if he were a small child about to be chastised for a messy room. I decided to let him speak first.

"I didn't mean to be gone so long," he said, his voice quiet. A mix of anger and relief swirled inside of me. "Is this the way it's always going to be? The going gets a little rough and you run out?"

His eyes welled with tears. Miguel crying was such a rare sight that it caught me off guard. I couldn't stand it. I sat up and threw back the blanket, swinging my legs out to stand beside him. He took me in his arms and buried his face in my shoulder, sobbing against me. I stayed resolute... trying to be the strong one for a change. I whispered against his cheek. "I love you. It's OK." We stood together, arms around each other until he felt composed enough to speak. We pulled apart and I looked into his eyes—so dark I couldn't see his pupils. I ran my hand down his cheeks, rubbed his stubble with my thumbs, noticing how soft his facial hair was. I tilted my face up to his and he told me he loved me as he brought his mouth down to mine and kissed me. I bet he could taste my chocolate. The thought made me happy. I reveled in the taste and feel of him. Finally I tilted my head back. "Tell me what you're thinking."

We sat down in chairs side by side. He took my hands in his and kissed the backs of them.

"I wanted it to be me," he said softly. "I feel like I'm constantly failing you and this time I guess I just wanted to be the hero." I opened my mouth to speak, but he pressed a finger to my lips and shook his head. "No...please...listen," he said. "But I thought about it and I realized...it doesn't matter where this kidney comes from. It only matters that you get it...soon...so I can take you home. And...no...I didn't run out, I swear. I only stepped outside to get my head together for a few minutes...but, Laura...there's something you should know..." He stopped to look at me, his face serious.

"What?" I was almost afraid to hear whatever had him looking so troubled.

"The reason I was gone longer than I'd intended is because there is an awful lot of press outside the hospital. Somehow word has gotten out about the duke's passing and that a member of Portuguese royalty was involved and they ambushed me outside. I wasn't prepared for that. I gave a very short statement—

not enough for them to even get a story out of and then I called my mother to tell her. She and my uncle are discussing how to handle the situation. Somehow they know about you, too. I don't know how they would know you, but it must be through the duke somehow or the fact that you were married to Andrew... I'm not sure. I suppose we'll find out if this story gets any bigger. But that's why I was gone so long. I promise I wasn't running anywhere. I promised I would never do that to you again and I meant it."

I was baffled. How could the press even know I existed, apart from a brief mention in the London papers when I married Andrew? "Will you tell me, now, exactly what happened out there—with the duke? I know you and Andrew haven't wanted to talk about it, but I want to know...please."

Miguel sighed. "I hate burdening you with the details. But I understand your need to know—to not be in the dark about things." He leaned forward, resting his elbows on his knees, staring at the floor, his body tense. And then he told me about the goon in the cafeteria and everything that had happened after that. I listened in silence, trying not to react. It was hard to hear it, but I felt relief when he finished. He leaned back in the chair and allowed his body to relax. I didn't ask any questions. A nurse came by to ask about the papers. I gave them to Miguel and he read them and told me they were discharge papers for the babies and the birth certificate applications. As he was reading them over, Andrew returned.

"Cat, Tristan and Nick will be up soon," he said. "Nick looks beat. His jetlag is kicking in." He sat down in a chair by the window and stretched out his long legs, leaning his head back against the seat. "What are those papers you're reading?"

"Papers for the babies—discharge instructions and the birth certificate applications," I answered.

Andrew stood up abruptly and turned his back on us to look out the window. He put his hands in his pockets and I saw him drop his head down. I looked at Miguel and he raised an eyebrow and shrugged. He went back to filling out the paperwork. I stared at Andrew's back, knowing something was suddenly wrong.

"Andrew...? You OK?" I asked.

He turned around and faced us. He looked stricken. "I'm sorry...but I..." He stopped...appeared to be formulating his thoughts...considering his words. My stomach twisted. He looked scared. Miguel stopped writing and looked up. I held my breath as I waited for him to continue.

"I don't want to start a war here or anything, but I have a request," said Andrew.

"Anything," I said.

"I'd like a DNA test to prove Miguel's paternity. And your answer isn't contingent on this transplant...nothing will change my mind on that—but I need to know the truth. I need irrefutable, scientific proof that Felipe and Gabriela are Miguel's—for my peace of mind."

Miguel stiffened next to me. I reached over and took his arm, squeezing it gently. I felt the shame I'd hidden away resurfacing, but I fought it as I held his arm, hoping he wouldn't fly off the handle. And though I tried to stifle them, my tears fell anyway—tears at the memory of feeling like a cheap slut who didn't even know who had fathered her unborn babies. Miguel had never doubted paternity and the talisman had told us who these babies belonged to, but, deep in my heart, I'd always had a question mark hovering there...wondering. I'd looked into Felipe's and Gabriela's faces, searching for signs of Andrew there, but I'd seen nothing. I hadn't seen Miguel in them either, aside from their dark hair. But my mother had told me I'd been born with dark hair and I had seen the baby pictures to prove it and now I was a natural Nordic blonde so the seeds of doubt were there and always would be. It was a fair request and I knew we needed to honor it. I looked at Miguel and nodded.

Miguel ran his hands through his hair. I could see that he wasn't happy about Andrew's request. But I knew that if he didn't agree to the DNA test it would be for one reason and one reason only—fear of the results. But it had to be done regardless.

"Miguel...will you ask the doctor to do it when he comes back?" I asked quietly, as I dashed away the damned tears.

For a second I thought he would say no. A myriad of emotions passed over his face before he answered. Andrew stood quietly, hands in his pockets, waiting.

"I will. But we know what the answer will be," Miguel said.

"Maybe we do. But I need to know—for sure." Andrew walked over to the door. "I'm going to go out for a while. Thank you for this." He looked down at me. "I'm sorry, Laura…for doubting you, but…this means a lot to me." He stepped out into the hall and disappeared into the elevators.

A wave of exhaustion rolled over me. I stood up and crawled back into the bed and nestled my head into the pillow. Miguel stood up and pulled my blanket over me, tucking me in. "Are you upset?" I asked him.

"I'll get over it," he replied. He kissed my cheek and went to move away but I grabbed him around the neck and pulled him back to me, pressing my lips into his, kissing him feverishly. I wanted to get a message to him—somehow—that I loved him no matter what and I needed him to return the sentiment. I was ninety-nine percent certain he was Felipe's and Gabriela's father but that one percent seemed so much greater than the ninety-nine. I needed his reassurance that he would love me no matter what the outcome.

"If…the test shows…I mean…will you…still want me?" I said the words so quietly that I wasn't sure he'd heard me. I couldn't breathe as I waited for his answer.

He answered me with a kiss. He half lifted me from the bed, pulling me into his chest, holding me tightly, pressing our hearts together and kissing me hard and long and passionately, leaving me with no doubt. "I always want you. Nothing will ever change that. But we know the truth, so this test…? We'll give him what he wants. He'll have peace of mind and all doubts will be erased. I love you unconditionally, Laura. There are no rules or requirements for that. It just is. OK?"

I nodded and nestled into his arms, breathing in his scent, wanting to stay there forever.

Over the next days we settled into a routine. I finished the course of antibiotics for the infection I'd had and my incision healed nicely. The babies were discharged into the care of my mother, Sofia and Cat who took turns caring for them—but not before we honored Andrew's request. A lab technician had been summoned to take swabs from the babies' cheeks and these would be compared to samples taken when Miguel and Andrew had been evaluated for my transplant. The results would be known any day now. I was going to be discharged while I await-ed the doctor's OK for the transplant and continue daily dialysis treatment. When the duchess learned that Andrew was donating a kidney to me she informed Andrew she would fly down to be with him when the transplant was scheduled. The duke's body had been flown back to England and a private memorial was planned for a later date.

I'd finally been allowed to shower and it felt amazing to be clean again. And now Miguel and I were lying side by side in my bed, much to the amusement of the nurses who just shook their heads and smiled every time they walked by. Miguel had just told me about the current situation with the press. We now knew exactly what the press knew and didn't know and Miguel was relieved that they had no idea about his blood tie to the Duke of Easton.

"Their story is focused on two things, apparently," said Miguel. "The recovery of our property from the duke's safe which the royal family is trying to get back because of the ille-gal way we obtained it. But our lawyers are certain that we'll be allowed to keep everything and eventually the British monarchy will give up the fight. Plus the fact that the Duke of Easton came here to kill me for revenge of the 'theft'—which is the story we're telling—is enough to stop the British monarchy in their tracks. They don't need another scandal."

"But you said two things. What's the other story they're after?" I hoped the goons weren't up there in England telling everything they knew about the duke's blackmailing of me. I would think that would make it worse for them in the long run. I couldn't imagine what else the press could find of interest.

Miguel tightened his hold on me and sighed. "They've become quite interested in the love triangle, as they're calling it. They know you were married to the British royal, Andrew Easton, and that you've given birth to twins here in Sintra. They apparently checked public records and learned of the annulment. I filed the birth certificates so they'll soon know the babies' paternity, if they don't already. They know that you and I are together." I thought I detected a slight change in his voice at the mention of our being together. I raised my head to look at him.

"What? Is there something else?"

He kissed me and then pushed away from me to get up from the bed. He walked around the end of the bed and stood by the window, hands in his pockets, just as Andrew had done not so long ago. Finally he turned to face me.

"This is…difficult…and I didn't want to tell you but I know how you feel about being in the dark. But you have to know that we know the truth and that's all that matters. It doesn't matter what other people think…right?" His words came out as a plea and I knew something awful must be coming.

"What the hell are you talking about, Miguel? What other people? And what do they think?" My voice rose higher with each question.

Andrew chose that moment to arrive. He stopped just inside the door and took in the expressions on both of our faces. "What's going on? What's wrong?"

"Miguel is about to tell me something awful in the papers about us. I can't imagine what could be so bad." I saw them exchange a look. Andrew didn't seem surprised. "You know what he's talking about?" I asked him.

"Yes…and just so you both know…I've already taken care of it," he forced a smile.

"*Taken care of what, for god's sake?*" I was really upset now. I got up and walked over to join Miguel by the window. "Tell me," I said more calmly.

Miguel answered, "According to the press, you left your handsome, British prince to run away with me—the future shadow king of Portugal—one of the tabloids actually referred to me as a dark prince, which, technically, is what I am-- after we had a torrid affair and I knocked you up. Basically, I'm a homewrecker, you're a young, hot American adulteress and Andrew is an innocent, broken-hearted…," his voice trailed off.

I gasped and clamped a hand over my mouth. I felt all the color drain from my face. *"Oh, my god."* I felt faint. I sat down in a chair and shook my head back and forth in disbelief. "This is awful. What are we going to do?"

"I told you I took care of it," said Andrew, looking smug.

I saw Miguel's guard go up. "You took care of it how?" he asked.

"A hoard of media accosted me when I walked in here and I gave them a very short statement." He saw Miguel's face darken and he put up his hand. "Now…don't go getting bent out of shape. I told them I'd only married Laura so she could stay in England legally—you know…the old green card story and they bought it." He laughed.

"Oh, my god—no!" I was freaking out now. "Andrew! No! You didn't!" I wanted to laugh but it was too horrible to make fun of.

Andrew shook his head. "No, I didn't. That was a joke—a bad one apparently judging by the look on the dark prince's face over there," he said, cocking his head in Miguel's direction. Miguel looked like he wanted to toss Andrew out the window. He grew serious then. "No, I didn't say that. But I did give a statement that I hope will satisfy their curiosity. I told them you and I had married in haste and that we were already separated when you got together with Miguel. And I told them it was my idea to end the marriage. I told them that I loved you and that I always would but we just didn't belong together…that way. End of story. I did not mention the upcoming transplant or anything about the vendetta or the damned gypsy curse or anything about my father."

I was stunned—speechless. Andrew was taking the heat for me…for all of us. It seemed there was no end to his generosity. I stood up from the chair and walked toward him. He tilted his head at me and grinned in that way he had and I wrapped my arms around him and hugged him. "I can't believe you—that you said that—that you would do this for me—for us. You're… amazing."

"Yep…I'm amazing alright…a prince among men." I felt him smile against my forehead. "Good old Andrew…rising to the occasion." I heard a catch in his voice and looked up at him. He was so beautiful—inside and out. I was lucky to have him in my life—kidney or no kidney.

"OK then…your love-fest can end any time," said Miguel. I suppressed a giggle and walked over to him…wrapping my arms around him and laying my head against his chest. He rubbed his cheek against my head and I tilted my face up to his for a kiss. We were interrupted by the arrival of the doctor who held a folder in his hands. I stepped away from Miguel and sat down in the chair. He stood beside me while Andrew remained standing by the door. The mood in the room took a serious nosedive.

"I have the results of the DNA test." I was surprised to hear him speaking in halting English, but pleased. I felt butterflies begin to take flight in my stomach even though I knew the answer already in my heart, which was now racing like the wind. The doctor pulled out a lab report and read the results.

"Both babies have your blood type, Miguel. They are both AB positive. There is no question as to paternity." He handed the paper to Miguel.

I glanced at Andrew whose face was expressionless. His blue eyes gave nothing away but I saw a hint of redness snaking its way up into his cheeks. He nodded and left the room without a word. I sank back into the seat as Miguel thanked the doctor. They spoke in Portuguese and then the doctor left. I stayed quiet, letting the news sink in. I didn't know why I was so shocked. I'd known this would be the outcome. I didn't understand why I felt negative emotions flowing through me. This is the answer I believed in and had wanted to hear and yet…why did I ache for Andrew now? I tried to shake off these feelings as Miguel studied my face. I hoped he couldn't read in my expression the confusion I was feeling inside.

"You're not disappointed I hope," he said quietly.

I gasped and launched myself out of the seat and into his arms.

"Hey, careful there…," he said, wrapping his arms around me. "You're still healing."

"You and I already knew the answer. The talisman knew. And now Andrew knows the truth. He'll never have to wonder again," I said.

"You didn't answer my question," he said softly, nuzzling my cheek with his nose.

"Don't be ridiculous—you know better. Felipe and Gabriela are ours—and only ours."

"As it should be," he said and kissed me tenderly.

Chapter Twenty Five

READY WHEN YOU ARE

ANDREW

I'd lied to Laura when I'd told her I wasn't afraid. I'd have to be inhuman not to fear having a vital organ removed from my body. But every time I felt the doubt of my decision creeping in, I saw her face in my mind and I knew I was making the right choice. She was my first great love and I had a sneaking suspicion she might be my last—not in a life-ending, death kind of way, but rather, in a 'love that comes along once in a life-time' way. We would be in the 'one-kidney boat' together and I took comfort in that thought--strictly for her sake—not my own. There was no question I was doing the right thing and I would have no regrets.

I'd gone back to England for a while, but was now back in Portugal, preparing for the transplant. My mother arrived and I was surprised to see that she was holding up well, considering the circumstances. She was happy to be with me and Tristan and I'd made a vow to myself that I would be a better son— that I would spend more time with her when the transplant was behind me and I'd returned home to London for good. Tristan also commented to me that maybe he'd return to London as well to continue with school which made me wonder about the state of his and Catarina's relationship. Miguel's mother had invited my mother to stay with them, but she had declined the offer in favor of a hotel. She was accompanied by a new goon who acted as her driver and personal assistant. If it had been one of the regular staff I probably would have killed him, regardless of his involvement with my father's schemes. I didn't particularly care to see another goon again. My mother still was unaware of Miguel's tie to my father, and Tristan and I had decided that he would break the news of Father's infidelity to her while I was in surgery. We were both afraid someone would let something slip accidentally and we didn't want to risk her finding out that way. I felt for Tristan having to tell her, considering she was still reeling from Father's death, but we agreed it was necessary. She probably wouldn't believe it anyway—my mother may be the Duchess of Easton but she was also--most certainly--the reigning queen of denial.

I rode with my mother, Tristan and Catarina to the hospital in Lisbon. Laura was already there, accompanied by her family and Miguel. Miguel's mother would stay behind to care for the babies with the help of various relatives. I wondered about Carmen—if she would be around. I had a sneaking suspicion Laura would not approve of Carmen being anywhere near the babies. I'd undergone another battery of tests—x-rays, sonograms, blood and urine tests, cardiac and neurological exams and I was quite done with the poking and prodding. And now we were here. I was ready to get on with it.

"Laura's asking for you," said Tristan. He wheeled into my room with Cat and my mother close behind. "They're going to take you down together. She's ready when you are."

"Andrew...are you sure about this?" asked my mother. She'd asked me the same question several times already and I couldn't seem to reassure her enough. "You know, darling...you don't have to prove anything to anyone."

"Mother...please. I want to do this. So...let's get on with it, shall we?" Doctors had been in talking to me—English speaking doctors for a change—and now attendants were here to take me to the operating theater. I lay back against the pillows on my mobile bed, forcing myself not to feel anything—no fear, worry, doubt or anxiety. I just wanted to see Laura. I knew once I saw her, I would be fine. I needed to make sure she was OK.

My mother and Cat kissed me and Tristan wished me well. Miguel's hulking brothers were here as well, and they also spoke to me. In the hall I saw Laura's bed. She was hooked up to her IV as was I and I couldn't help chuckling to myself at what a pair we were. I saw Miguel, talking quietly to her. He looked absolutely bloody tortured. I knew I'd feel the same if he'd been the match and I were in his shoes. The attendant stopped my bed beside Laura's. I looked over at her—thought about how small she looked—and beautiful, in spite of the ordeal ahead. My heart quickened. I wondered if I'd always feel this way when I saw her—runaway heartbeat, collapsing lungs, nervous stomach. And then, as if on cue, I felt the telltale burning of bloody tears behind my eyes. Dammit, I thought. It wouldn't do for me to break down in front of her. I reached my hand through the bedrail. "Hey," I said.

She smiled. Her eyes seemed to search mine, as if she thought I might have changed my mind. "Hey yourself," she said, grasping my hand. She held it tightly, enough to make a knuckle pop. "Sorry," she whispered, looking mortified.

"We agreed on a kidney—not knuckles," I said, joking. "How're you feeling?"

"OK...you?" she asked. I saw a tear slide from the corner of her eye and disappear into her beautiful blonde hair. She was scared—I could see it in her eyes. I held my own tears in check and rubbed my thumb along the side of hers.

"I'm great. Ready to go play toss the kidney with you. You up for the challenge?"

She laughed--finally. The sound of it made me feel better. Miguel was listening to our banter, his face a mask. I'd have given a million bloody pounds to know what he was thinking right now.

"Andrew...I...," Laura started, then stopped. She closed

her eyes a moment and more tears slipped from the corners and trickled across her temples. Her breaths were rapid—I knew it was her nerves getting the best of her.

I let go of her hand then and grabbed her bedrail...pulling my bed closer to hers. I leaned up on one elbow. "Hey, now... maybe we should establish some ground rules...for instance... if you don't cry, I won't. It makes me look very un-macho-like." I knew I risked raising Miguel's ire, but I lifted her hand and brought it to my lips, kissing its softness. "No worries, love. Everything will be fine. I'll see you in a few hours, OK?"

She nodded and brushed her hand along my jaw. "Andrew... thank you...for this...I love you...you know that, right?" Out of the corner of my eye I saw Miguel shift his weight from one foot to the other.

"Likewise, sweetheart. Everything's gonna be great."

Miguel cleared his throat. I looked up at him...saw that he was fighting back tears of his own. I guess we'd be un-macho-like together. He stepped toward me then and held out his hand. I grasped it and we shook.

"Thank you...for everything...," he said, his voice cracking the tiniest bit. "What you're doing for Laura...for us...is...," his voice faltered again. He said something in a rush of Portuguese and blinked back tears.

"I didn't understand a word you just said...but...I'm guessing it was something nice...so...you're welcome," I grinned.

"It was. I just don't have the words—in any language--to thank you enough...for this gift."

"Well, I'd say any time, but I'm only gonna have the one kidney left and I'll need it so...," I smiled, hoping my joke would ease his inner turmoil. He gave me a nervous grin and stepped back to Laura. He walked along beside her bed, holding her hand. Her parents and brother were waiting to wish her good luck. Earlier they'd spoken to me, expressing their gratitude for my sacrifice as her father had called it. I didn't see it that way but I didn't correct him.

The attendant wheeled me into an operating theater. As Laura was taken into the next room over, I waved at her and gave her a wink. She lifted her hand in return and smiled. I tried to listen as the nurses and doctors spoke—in both Portuguese and English—but my mind kept drifting. An anesthesiologist said something to me. I nodded and closed my eyes. I felt a weird sensation—not painful, just unusual—wash over me, and for some strange reason, the last conscious thought I had before the anesthesia took me under, was of my wedding day—Laura in that long, white dress, walking down the aisle, holding flowers, looking like a princess—so beautiful…so innocent and pure. And I truly believed, despite everything that happened after—in that one moment—she had been mine.

The Shadow King

Chapter Twenty Six

FUTURES

MIGUEL

We'd spent the night before Laura's operation with the children at the hospital. The surgeon had wanted Laura admitted the day before to run some precautionary tests but Laura hadn't want to be separated from Felipe and Gabriela. We kept them till after midnight when Cat and my mother took them home. Neither of us knew yet what it truly felt like to be a parent—we'd been too caught up in Laura's health crisis to fully appreciate the idea. One of her surgeons expressed his pleasure and agreement in Laura's having a transplant now rather than waiting for months or years. He'd told us that the less time a patient spent on dialysis, the longer the new kidney would function properly, barring no complications. I'd wanted Laura to get some sleep, but she was too nervous about the transplant, so we'd talked most of the night about the future. We'd talked about our upcoming wedding. I had wanted us to be married before the babies' birth and it bothered me that things hadn't happened in a more natural order. But Laura didn't seem to mind.

"I like the idea of something small, low-key, quiet, if it's all the same to you," she'd said.

"Whatever you want is fine with me. It's April now and the doctors say that you should be feeling pretty normal by summer. How about a ceremony on the beach in August? I want to take you to the Algarve. It's beautiful there and my family has a summer home in Cabo de São Vicente. You'll love it there—it's surrounded by a nature preserve—there are herons and storks everywhere…even sea otters. I wish I could take you there now—it's quite beautiful in the spring when the wildflowers are in bloom—juniper, lavender, narcissus—you'd be amazed."

She laughed. "Wow…listen to you, Mr. Romance. I didn't know you were such a nature lover," she sighed. "Still so much about you I have to learn…"

"That's a two-way street, baby. Soon you'll be healthy and we can start living—really living. We can go to school, run the vineyard—whatever we want—or whatever Felipe and Gabriela want--more like." I'd kissed her then until I'd made myself crazy and had to stop.

"I'm loving this side of you," she said. "I can't wait to be normal so I can feel carefree again. I haven't felt that way since…" Her voice had waivered then, bad memories clouding her good mood.

"I know, sweetheart…it won't be long now. We've never known normal, you and I. I can't wait to be normal with you." I'd held her for a long time, breathing in her hair. It smelled like lemons again. I'd missed that. After a while she'd pulled away from me, her eyes sad.

"Don't get mad, but…I'm worried about Andrew. I'm afraid that in a few days or weeks, he might…I don't know…fall apart and he won't tell anyone…just suffer alone. I know you don't like to talk about it, but I wish there was a way for him to get some kind of resolution—some kind of happily ever after. It isn't fair what he's been through. And now…this…transplant. How much more can he take?"

I rubbed her back, her face against my chest and stared out the window in silence. I didn't really have an answer to her question. I'd been thinking about Andrew a lot lately. I was surprised to realize that I liked him, even though I hadn't wanted to. I doubted I'd ever stop being jealous of him, especially now when he was giving Laura a second chance at life when I wasn't able to. And I could never forget that he had kissed her first, held her first, loved her first in the physical sense. My Latin blood couldn't quite get over that, but it was my private battle to fight, not Laura's...or Andrew's. I reminded myself that Laura was mine now and always would be. I remembered the talisman and pulled it from my pocket where I'd been keeping it lately.

"Why don't you wear this until time for surgery...and try to get some rest, OK?" I'd kissed her lips then, a lingering kiss that she was reluctant to end. I slipped it over her head and pressed it against her chest, then sat down in the seat next to her bed. She'd eventually slept but I never did. I knew I'd be exhausted tomorrow but I would survive on adrenaline. I listened to her breaths, in and out, as I held her hand and thought about our future.

Chapter Twenty Seven

AT EASE

LAURA

I awoke to the sensation of the talisman warming against my skin. Miguel was dozing in the chair next to me. I thought how uncomfortable he must be, his head turned like that, using his arms as a pillow. I heard early morning hospital sounds and I knew the nurses would be coming for me soon. I wondered how Andrew had fared over night—if he was scared—if he'd changed his mind during the night and bolted for England or anywhere but here. I pulled the talisman out from underneath my gown and studied both sides. The Portuguese words for king and queen were now together on one side. The date of September 12, 2013, was on the other side. September was five months away. What was significant about that date? I wondered. I hoped it was going to be a happy day, but with the talisman's ever-changing moods, who knew?

Miguel sat up…worked the kinks out of his neck and shoulders. I removed the talisman from my neck and showed it to him. He studied both sides but didn't get a chance to comment because several nurses and doctors arrived. Eventually I was moved out into the hall where I saw Andrew. I spoke to my parents and brother and Cat and Tristan, Mateo and Tomas. Sofia had stayed home with the babies but would change places with Cat later when the operations were over. I saw the duchess from a distance. She had smiled at me but had not approached me. I didn't know what she knew about all that had happened but I assumed she hadn't forgiven me for breaking Andrew's heart. I wondered what she thought of his donating a kidney to me. She must be confused.

It was time to go in. I'd spoken to Andrew. He'd made me laugh with a joke about playing toss the kidneys. I was happy he hadn't changed his mind. Miguel was the last person I spoke to before going into the operating room. I would never forget his words to me.

"I'll be here, waiting for you, when you wake up, sweetheart. In a few hours, you'll be good as new," he'd said. He'd kissed me and I saw tears in his eyes.

"What if it doesn't work?" I'd whispered to him. "What if my body rejects it? What if Andrew gives me his kidney and it's all for nothing? It's not like I can give it back."

"Sh...sh...no negative thoughts. Don't confuse a kidney with a heart, Laura. I think, at this point, Andrew knows you have both anyway. He's making his peace with that. I may not have been able to give you a kidney, but my heart...that's a whole different ballgame. So no worries about rejections, OK? I love you. Felipe and Gabriela love you. I'll be right here waiting."

I'd kissed Miguel one more time, waved at my family and signaled to Andrew that I was ready. Inside the operating room I was prepped for surgery. My entire body shook with fright and my teeth chattered. I had never felt such intense fear, but everyone around me looked so completely at ease that I tried to convince myself I should relax, too. The anesthesiologist administered something in my IV and within seconds the world went dark.

Epilogue:

PART ONE

ANDREW

I couldn't do it. As thrilled as I was for Laura and her good health and happiness, I couldn't go back to Portugal and watch her marry Miguel. Though I'd made peace with their love for each other, and appreciated their asking me to attend, I knew it would be too painful. I would make a point of being busy that day so I wouldn't think about the wedding. I had compromised though. I'd told them I'd be down to visit when I got a break from my studies later in the year. I'd decided to attend college all year round so I could expedite my entry into medical school. I was feeling quite good after the transplant—completely normal, as a matter of fact. I was back in my London apartment, taking summer classes and settling into a normal routine. My only suffering was of the emotional kind. Losing Laura and the twins to Miguel was hard enough, but I also had to deal with the extreme guilt I felt regarding my father's death. For as long as I lived, I would always know that my last act as his son had been to strike him, breaking his jaw and watching him die. I had half-expected to be charged with a crime as a result, but his death was attributed to heart failure and his broken jaw swept under the rug. I'd wondered about that and finally came to the conclusion that royal strings had been pulled to spare me. I still had to deal with the press, though. That was a never-ending battle. In a strange twist of fate, I'd somehow become a tabloid magnet. *The Daily Sun* had gone so far as to 'honor' me with the title of "Great Britain's Most Eligible Bachelor," beating out my own cousin, Prince Harry.

Dealing with the press had been a full-time occupation in the days after donating my kidney to Laura and returning home to England. The entire world now knew about my short-lived marriage to the beautiful American blonde who'd left me for the heir to the throne of Portugal's shadow monarchy. No matter how many times I'd spoken on the record about being the one to end our marriage, they never wanted to believe me, perceptive bastards. But I stuck to my story. The tabloids had quite a way of romanticizing the transplant. One of the most shocking headlines still made me laugh when I thought about it: *American Beauty Takes Prince's Kidney, Rejects His Heart.* If it hadn't been so comical—and sadly accurate--I would have sued them for libel. I was thankful that most of the details concerning my father were still unknown to the press, though I was under no illusion that that would always be the case. Mostly the press were interested in the love triangle aspect of the story—the forbidden love, broken hearts, failing health, life-saving transplant—it was quite insane.

Tristan had returned home for a short while—on a break from his relationship from Catarina. It had lasted a month. She came to London and proposed to him, saying she couldn't live without him. I'd laughed when he'd told me he'd wanted to get down on his knee and accept her proposal but as he hadn't felt his knees in more than eighteen months, he'd settled for holding her on his lap and saying yes. They were planning a Christmas wedding and Catarina had agreed to move to London while Tristan finished school here. In a strange twist, he'd had to hire a new personal attendant to replace Ronald, who'd decided to move to Portugal permanently. I guess he'd fallen in love with the place—or something.

On August 10, Laura's wedding day, I took my mother to

lunch at the Covent Garden Country Club and listened to her talk about gardening. She'd thrown herself into all things horticultural--her hobby filling up the hole left by my father's passing. She knew about Father's infidelity and just as I had suspected she would, she'd chosen not to believe it—preferring to live in her fantasy world of roses and denial. My poor, sweet mother…she would never change. I knew deep down that she knew the truth in her heart, but if denial was her way of coping, then who was I to argue? We never discussed it again, even when I referred to Gabriela and Felipe as my niece and nephew--she just pretended not to notice.

Later that evening after I'd dropped Mother at home on Bayswater Road, I'd gone to my favorite pub, The Baying Pig, for a drink—Coke being the hardest thing I drank anymore. I figured, as I only had one kidney now, I'd better not abuse it. I sat at the bar with my Coke, eating peanuts, watching a football match. The place was crowded with tourists and regulars. The bartender, Jackson, asked me how I was doing.

"Still wearing Britain's Most Eligible Bachelor crown, are you, Andrew?" he asked, as he refilled my Coke glass.

"Ha ha—very funny. Unless you know something I don't, that status isn't likely to change any time soon," I responded. He grinned and poured beers for some Spanish tourists who were sitting near me. Loud cheers rang out as the football match ended. The other bartender, Amy--Jackson's girlfriend--picked up the remote control and ran through the channels looking for something new to entertain the patrons. Someone called out for a refill and she dropped the remote, leaving the television on a news channel. I glanced up at the TV quickly and then away, but did a double take when I saw a familiar face on the screen. I picked up my Coke and moved down closer to the TV for a better look. My heart pounded as I watched the news report. On the screen was a picture of Miguel in black pants and a white shirt, open at the collar, looking into Laura's eyes. She wore a white, lacy, gypsy-style dress. She had flowers in her hair and bare feet. She looked radiant—healthy--beautiful. They were on a beach—it said Cabo de São Vicente, Portugal, on the bottom of the screen. The sun was shining and in the background, the ocean sparkled. My breath caught in my throat as I leaned in closer to hear the newscaster's report over the roar of the voices of the people in the bar:

"Today, Miguel Dos Santos de Braganza, who may very well become the next king of Portugal, if Portuguese supporters have their way in next month's national election, married his love, the American commoner, Laura Michelle Calder Easton, in a seaside ceremony on Portugal's Algarve coast. Earlier this year, the bride underwent a successful kidney transplant, having received the new kidney from her former husband, Andrew Easton, a member of the British royal family. The couple, both aged nineteen, has two children, Felipe and Gabriela, born in March about a month before the new Mrs. Dos Santos underwent her transplant. Mr. Dos Santos' mother, the shadow queen Sofia, and next in line to the throne, is rumored to be abdicating the throne in favor of her son, if the nation passes the law to reinstate the monarchy in the election to be held September 12. The country of Portugal has not had a sitting royal family since 1910 when King Manuel II was deposed in the revolution of October 5 of that year, thereby establishing the Portuguese First Republic. The bride and groom will honeymoon on the island of Ventura, the Azores' famous tenth island, once under British rule, but recently returned to Portugal's governance and owned by the Portuguese royal family. We will keep you posted on the outcome of the Portuguese election when it is held next month."

I couldn't breathe. I tried to swallow but my throat seemed to be closing off. I shouldn't be so shocked to see this on the news. When the public had heard the love triangle story, they'd fallen in love with all of us. We'd been on every news station and in every newspaper around the world for most of the summer. It made sense that the Portuguese citizens would want to make a fairy tale out of this romance and reinstate their monarchy, but still…I was shaken to hear it. My eyes began to burn with the image of Laura in a gypsy dress, in bare feet, on the beach. She'd looked stunning—the absolute picture of health. I had a sudden, intense memory of meeting her for the first time back in Rhode Island. It seemed like a lifetime ago, and in many ways it was. I closed my eyes against the burning sensation but it didn't stop the images from coming. I saw her on Gooseberry Beach, when I'd had my first real conversation with her; saw how adorable she looked when she got her new glasses; saw her in the backseat of one of my cars, tucked into my arms; saw her face inches from mine when I knew I had to kiss her or die; saw her silky, blonde hair, delicate cheekbones, full, pouty pink lips as they'd blended with mine; felt her soft body against me when I'd made love to her that first time and every other time thereafter; I heard her laughter and saw so many tears, more than anyone should have to shed in a lifetime. My stomach ached with an intensity that rocked me. I pushed my Coke away and left some money on the bar. I slipped out the door and walked home.

The Shadow King

Epilogue:

PART TWO

MIGUEL

It seemed like I'd waited a lifetime for this day. I knew nineteen was young to be a husband and a father, but I couldn't imagine my life unfolding any other way. Of course, I wished the path to this day could have been smoother and pain-free, emotionally and physically, especially for Laura. But it was in the past now and Laura didn't like to dwell on it. She'd taken to motherhood like a mermaid to water—she was born to be Felipe's and Gabriela's mother. Now that she'd healed from the transplant, she handled most of the childcare and we finally knew what being parents felt like—it was amazing but damned exhausting, too. Felipe and Gabriela were funny little people—already Felipe seemed so serious and quiet while Gabriela wasn't fond of sleeping, preferring to be held by someone—all the time.

We'd spent the spring at our home in Sintra while Laura recovered. She'd been sad for a while—the doctors had said this could happen, especially coupled with post-partum depression, but we'd all rallied around her and after a couple of months, she seemed content. She grew used to taking her anti-rejection medication and finally gained some weight. Her family had returned to America and that hadn't helped her state of mind at the time, but she knew they would be back for the wedding and the babies' christening, so she'd channeled her energies into the children and wedding planning. She was excited that Lily and Gretchen would be coming. We'd left it up to her family to explain everything to them in the hope that the subject would not be raised when they came for the wedding. It was a forbidden topic in our household.

We had to deal with the press nearly every time we went out in public. Somehow they had decided that we were the next big royal love story and as such, we read some crazy stories about ourselves in the papers and heard wild reports on the TV news. The most interesting story of all was the public's clamoring to include the reinstatement of the monarchy on the September ballot. This subject had come up many times throughout my childhood—either not making it onto the ballot at all or not garnering enough votes the few times it had. But this time felt different. The television and print reporters seemed certain it would be on the ballot and that it could potentially pass this time. My mother and I had a private conversation about it, just in case we found ourselves out of the shadows in September. She told me she had no desire to be queen of anything except her home in Sintra and she would abdicate in favor of my succession with Laura as my queen consort. When I'd told Laura this, she'd laughed. She'd laughed so hard, I'd feared for her kidney. She found the whole notion of kings and queens and castles antiquated—too fairy tale-like to be taken seriously. When she'd pulled herself together, I'd taken her to visit the palaces—the one I'd taken her to before—Pena Palace—and also the National Palace in Sintra Vila. She'd been quiet as we'd toured them, finally realizing the seriousness of a royal life. She'd been fascinated by Princess Garbiela's crown and I could easily imagine it on her head, the diamonds and sapphires sparkling in the sunlight against her pale blonde hair. She'd been eager to begin Portuguese lessons and had taken to the language naturally.

One issue I'd worried about took care of itself—that of Carmen's occasional presence. Juana had decided to retire and return to the region of Alentejo to live near her family. Carmen and her brother, Carlos, moved with her. They were both attending school in Lisbon, both planning to become teachers at the gypsy school when they'd completed their credentials.

School was something Laura and I talked about often. We'd both decided to begin university in the new year. I would study business and Laura wanted to study literature. It seemed as if the world were making sense again, just as I'd hoped for when I'd written those very words in the note I'd slipped to Laura more than a year ago at Brenton Point. We still had those notes—they were sealed in plastic, inside a metal box and buried in the vineyard.

We'd finally agreed to speak to *Hello!* magazine. They'd been hounding us for months for photos and an exclusive interview. I'd had our lawyer present during the meeting and he'd taped it for insurance purposes. We also agreed to allow them to send a photographer to the wedding for before, during and after photos. We'd hoped that the media's and the general public's curiosity would be satisfied and we wouldn't have to deal with their intrusions again but that line of thinking would more than likely turn out to be short-sighted. We would just have to learn to adapt to the world's curiosity about us, including America's interest, which had grown by leaps and bounds when Laura's home country learned that an American girl was marrying into Portuguese royalty. We'd also refused any photos of the children to be printed under threat of a lawsuit.

And now it was August 10 and I was as ready for this moment as I had been since the day Laura had slipped the talisman around her neck a lifetime ago. Thinking about those days inevitably reminded me of Andrew. We kept in touch and he'd promised to come visit during school holidays. We'd invited him to the wedding and though I wasn't surprised that he'd declined the invitation, I knew it had made Laura sad. I'd made peace with the fact that he would always be in her heart—how could he not be after all they'd shared—but still she missed him and worried about his happiness. The bond Laura shared with Tristan strengthened—if that was even possible—and he kept her informed about Andrew's life and state of mind. She was dismayed that Tristan and Catarina would be moving to London while Tristan finished school, but they'd assured her they'd return after he graduated to live in Portugal. We were all thrilled at their engagement—after a short-lived separation—and upcoming Christmas wedding.

Everything about this day was perfect. My mother was in her element with the wedding preparations, taking all of her cues from Laura who wanted simplicity and a gypsy vibe. We'd asked the local gypsy community of Cabo de São Vicente to attend and prepare the food and provide the music. I'd invited Beni and his family to come and they were thrilled that I'd included them. We'd held the ceremony on the beach in the late afternoon— it was sunny but the heat was bearable—and took our vows twice—in both English and Portuguese. Laura was making her public debut as a Portuguese speaker and she was nervous about it, but she sounded like a native, not even showing a hint of an American accent as she'd spoken her vows to me.

We would be honeymooning on Ventura Island just for a few days—Laura didn't want to be away from Felipe and Gabriela for too long—but our wedding night was spent in a *pousada* just outside of Cabo de São Vicente. The country inn was situated near a nature preserve and Laura was amazed at the beauty of the place, not that we saw much of it. I'd carried her up the stairs to our suite, anxious to finally be alone. I'd sat on the edge of the bed watching her move about the room until I finally couldn't take it anymore. I knew she was teasing me and I let her get away with it for a few minutes. She stopped in front of me and turned her back to me so I could unbutton her dress. It took forever to unbutton each of the tiny white pearl buttons that snaked all the way down her back—there must have been fifty of them. I heard her giggle as my hands fumbled along, getting more anxious the further down I went. Finally she stopped me and turned to face me. She slipped the dress off her shoulders, letting it fall softly into a white cloud around her feet. She stepped out of it and I lifted her slip over her head and took her in my arms. I felt her curves where before I'd felt ribs and bony hips. She'd put on weight and it suited her. We lay down on the bed together and I traced her scars with my fingers and kissed them. She had never looked more beautiful as she did now and I was overwhelmed at the sight of her. I kissed her lips and she wrapped her arms around me and, in the most beautiful turning of the tables, she whispered words of love in my ear in my native tongue without so much as a trace of an American accent. I loved the sound of that.

The Shadow King

Epilogue:

PART THREE

LAURA

The connection I felt to Andrew was stronger than it had ever been. Having a part of him inside of my body for life was something I didn't take lightly. I loved him in a way that far surpassed romantic love…it was more akin to the love between twins—the feeling that somewhere in the world someone was moving in tandem with me even though we were a continent apart. I didn't talk about this with Miguel—I wasn't sure he would understand without becoming jealous, but Tristan understood. When I needed to talk about Andrew it was Tristan who listened and kept my confidence. My feelings for Andrew did not impact my love for Miguel—nothing on earth would ever sever the bond I had with him. I was more in love with Miguel now than I had ever been. It was the strangest of conundrums—loving two people so intensely at the same time…bittersweet… and yet so necessary to my existence.

I'd suffered through post partum depression and the blue period that often accompanies a transplant. The doctors had warned me about this and I was prepared. Miguel's family— my family now—stayed close when I needed them and gave me space when I wanted to be alone. I often wondered if Andrew felt this way, too. The babies made me happy even as they exhausted me. I never knew parenthood could be so hard and yet so fulfilling at the same time.

I'd heard the talk—seen the news reports--about the upcoming election and the possibility of the monarchy being reinstated. I didn't let on to Miguel, but the thought of becoming a queen over an entire nation scared me to my core. I'd laughed hysterically when he'd told me his mother's abdication intention if his family reclaimed the throne, and I'd felt badly for not having had a more mature reaction to the possibility. But it just seemed too far outside the realm of my simple life and humble background that my mind couldn't process it. I'd decided to try to push it from my thoughts until or unless it became a reality.

I'd never forgotten that beautiful gypsy wedding dress I'd see at Sources in London so I'd found the phone number on the Internet and called Catherine Neville to order it. I'd sent her my measurements and she'd tailored the dress for me, customizing it with beads and lace and dozens of tiny pearl buttons up the back. It was gorgeous and I was giddy with the thought that maybe one day Gabriela would wear it on her wedding day.

I was excited to see my parents and brother again. I missed my family every day and I'd told Miguel that I wanted to plan a trip home to Rhode Island soon. I missed Gooseberry Beach and my room and somewhere in my closet I had some favorite clothes and books I wanted with me. And then there were Lily and Gretchen. I couldn't wait to see them again. I knew they would be stunned when they learned about the events of the last year and a half but my father assured me he would explain everything to them so they wouldn't question me too much when they arrived. The only aspect of the whole sordid affair we had vowed to keep secret was Miguel's paternal lineage. He did not want to acknowledge that he was not only a member of the House of Braganza but also a member of the House of Hanover. He and Tristan had spoken at length about this. Miguel had feared insulting Tristan with his refusal to embrace that part of his legacy, but Tristan had understood. They considered themselves to be brothers, though, and that was enough. Tristan was now technically the Duke of Easton but he wasn't all that thrilled with Queen Elizabeth's intent to bestow the title upon him. He'd wanted to be skipped over in favor of Andrew taking on the title, but Andrew had vowed to denounce his British citizenship if that happened and move permanently to Iceland. Perhaps the world didn't need another Duke of Easton—one had been more than enough.

And now it was my wedding day and I was excited and nervous. I wore my talisman every day and I would wear it today with my sapphire earrings and the sapphire ring Miguel had given to me when I'd first arrived in Sintra. And also today I would add a simple, silver band to my finger to match the one Miguel would wear. Even though this was my second wedding, it felt like the first one in my heart. I'd picked beautiful wildflowers to carry in my bouquet and had asked Miguel if we could let the local gypsies come and provide the food and entertainment. He'd been thrilled at the idea and had agreed wholeheartedly. We dressed the babies in matching white outfits—a tiny little white suit for Felipe and a lacy, white gypsy dress for Gabriela. We'd had them christened last night after the rehearsal dinner in the little chapel in Cabo de São Vicente. We'd asked Tristan and Catarina to be the godparents and they'd accepted proudly. And now we would have our dream wedding in the afternoon under sunny, blue skies. Everything would be casual and relaxed and perfect.

We married on the beach, in bare feet. Miguel wore black pants and a white shirt, open at the collar. When the time came I spoke my vows—in Portuguese—without messing them up too badly. We conducted the ceremony in both languages for the benefit of my family and the huge Portuguese contingent. When the minister pronounced us man and wife and Miguel leaned in to kiss me, strands of my hair had loosened all on their own and fallen across my face. Miguel had to brush them away to find my lips. He'd always had that effect on me and always would. After the ceremony we'd eaten amazing traditional foods, including those delicious tarts and a massive chocolate cake, and danced to gypsy music. Eventually the night air grew chilly and Sofia and Cat took the babies home. We said good-night to our guests and went to the *pousada* where we would sleep before leaving tomorrow for a few days on Ventura Island.

I was nervous about my wedding night though I had no reason to be. But there was something about being Mrs. Miguel Dos Santos—Laura Dos Santos—that made my stomach churn with anticipation. I moved about the room, looking at the knick-knacks, admiring the night sky out the huge floor-to-ceiling windows, touching the fabric of the drapes.

"You're teasing me, aren't you?" Miguel asked me, grinning. He had undressed and was sitting on the edge of the bed watching me.

"Would I do that?" I responded demurely. I walked over and turned my back to him. "Will you help me with these?"

"My pleasure," he said softly. I felt his fingers at my neck, unbuttoning each tiny pearl button. Every time his fingers grazed my skin I tingled in the spot. I knew I'd be covered with goose bumps when it was all said and done. His fingers fumbled and he sucked in a breath. I smiled. This was taking far too long. I turned and shimmied out of the dress, letting it fall to my feet. He stood up and pulled the slip over my head and took me in his arms. I pressed my face into his neck and breathed in his scent—it was so intensely Miguel—citrus and pine and something else that invaded my senses, rendering me weak in the knees. We lay down on the bed and he touched and kissed my scars. I called them my battle scars and I wore them proudly.

"You are truly exquisite, you know that, Mrs. Dos Santos?" Miguel whispered against my stomach. I ran my hands through his hair. He'd finally cut it but had left a little of the length which I loved. He'd kept his goatee, too, which I loved as well. He moved up my body, trailing kisses all along the way, until his mouth found mine. I felt a tingling sensation in my hand, snaking across my wrist, up my arm and into my neck and chest. I gasped as Miguel trailed his lips down my jaw and neck and into the recesses of my collarbone. He picked up the disk and held it up so we could see it. It emitted a faint golden glow in the dim light of the room. Our names were engraved on one side and our wedding date on the other. Under the date were the words: *A New Life Begins*. We stared in awe as the glow faded but the disk stayed warm when Miguel pressed it against my skin. He pulled me into him and held me as I whispered in Portuguese in his ear. I told him I would always prefer gypsies over royals and that he would always be my gypsy. He smiled, his lips against mine, his hands in my hair, my hands sliding down his back.

"I truly believe the magic in the talisman is a gift from Princess Gabriela. She can rest in peace now. I love you, Laura," he said.

"I love you, too," I replied as he pulled me on top of him and kissed me again.

The Shadow King

Andrew

London, September 12, 2013, midnight

"The Portuguese Republic has spoken. In a unanimous vote, the citizens of Portugal have chosen to reinstate the monarchy, bringing the royal House of Braganza out of the shadows and into the light. It will be the first time in modern history that a royal family has been restored to their throne. Queen Sofia announced she will abdicate in favor of her son, Miguel, who will become one of the world's youngest kings. Miguel was married last month to the commoner Laura Michelle Calder Easton, an American hailing from the state of Rhode Island. The couple has infant twins, Prince Felipe and Princess Gabriela. It is rumored the new royal couple will reside in the National Palace. They will both attend university in Lisbon next year while performing royal duties and raising their young family. The official date for the coronation will be decided upon in the coming days, but will more than likely occur next month in conjunction with the new king's twentieth birthday. Viewers may recall this young couple captured the world's hearts with their love story all summer long

as we learned of the future queen's short-lived marriage to Andrew Easton, a member of the House of Hanover, a branch of Queen Elizabeth's family tree. In a stunning sacrifice, the young Prince Andrew donated a kidney to save the life of Ms. Calder-Easton who'd recently given birth to twins. Ms. Calder-Easton wed the future king of Portugal in a seaside ceremony in the Algarve last month. We will continue to report on this story as it unfolds and ITV 5 will bring you live coverage of the coronation when it happens. Stay tuned."

"Sacrifice?" I mumbled, as I clicked off the television and dropped the remote on the sofa beside me. It was no sacrifice. In order for something to be a sacrifice I would need to feel the pain of it. The physical pain had long since subsided, such as it was. The emotional pain was merely a numbness now that I had learned to live with. But to call saving Laura's life a sacrifice on my part was more sacrilegious than sacrificial. I would do it again in a heartbeat.

I leaned back against the sofa, the image from the TV of Laura's and Miguel's faces still in my mind. They'd looked happy…at peace…perfect together. So my beautiful princess would become a queen. I shook my head in wonder. It made total sense somehow. I reached for my glass of Coke on the coffee table beside me and raised it in the air in a toast.

"To Laura…my beautiful queen. Long may you reign." I tossed back my drink and smiled.

THE END

The Shadow King